Mandy Robotham saw herself as an aspiring author since the age of nine, but was waylaid by journalism and later enticed by birth. She's now a former midwife, who writes about birth, death, love and anything else in between. She graduated with an MA in Creative Writing from Oxford Brookes University. This is her eighth novel – her first seven have been *Globe and Mail*, *USA Today* and Kindle Top 100 bestsellers.

By the same author:

A Woman of War (published as *The German Midwife* in North America, Australia and New Zealand)
The Secret Messenger
The Berlin Girl
The Girl Behind the Wall
The Resistance Girl
The War Pianist
The Hidden Storyteller

A DANGEROUS GAME

MANDY ROBOTHAM

avon.

Published by AVON
A Division of HarperCollins*Publishers* Ltd
1 London Bridge Street
London SE1 9GF

www.harpercollins.co.uk

HarperCollins*Publishers*
Macken House
39/40 Mayor Street Upper
Dublin 1
D01 C9W8

A Paperback Original 2025

1

First published in Great Britain by HarperCollins*Publishers* 2025

A catalogue copy of this book is available from the British Library.

ISBN: 978-0-00-859925-6

Set in Bembo Std by HarperCollinsPublishers India

Printed and bound in the UK using 100% Renewable Electricity at CPI Group (UK) Ltd

This book contains FSC™ certified paper and other controlled sources to ensure responsible forest management.

For more information visit: www.harpercollins.co.uk/green

To all those in the long twilight hours, who pound and toil through the night, who keep us safe, drive us home, bring babies into the world and comfort the sick. Heroes, the lot of you.

Author's Note

A good ol' Victorian pea-souper is often seen as a cinematic backdrop to a Sherlock Holmes adaption, or one of those classic British black and white noir films – atmospheric and sinister, and sometimes a little romantic. But make no mistake, they were part and parcel of British city life in the 1950s, 60s and beyond – nights when you could barely see your hand in front of your face, forcing a busy metropolis to grind to a halt.

My fascination for those fog-bound scenes sprouts from my own childhood memories of growing up in London. As late as the early 1970s, a dense grey blindness descended once or twice every winter, and I distinctly remember Dad and I having to collect my mum from the bus stop after work, the fog so thick she would have had trouble locating her own home in a few hundred yards. It was *that* dense. Through a child's eyes, it seemed almost fun, having to hunker down and sit it out, warm and cosy.

The infamous fog of 1952, though, was far from fun. In a city of eight and a half million people across Greater London, around ninety per cent of homes had coal fires, many of which burned cheaper, substandard coal (the good quality being exported to help the British economy). Over four days in December, that sulphurous white smoke from domestic chimneys was trapped under a freak weather 'lid', mixing with nature's fog to produce the thick, yellowy toxic smog. Smelly, filthy – and deadly. Estimates at the time put the number of lives lost at 4,000 in almost a week of disruption and the seven days following. Latest figures, however, estimate that an incredible 12,000 deaths were directly attributable to the killer fog: bronchial cases, the elderly succumbing, road accidents and crime included. Thieves and robbers were in their element, swallowed by the blanket as the overworked Metropolitan Police tried to cope, alongside a National Health Service still in its infancy.

It's amid this chaos that Harri and Dexie's story develops, combined with a second component of post-war life that is equally and shockingly real. Novels such as Frederick Forsyth's *The Odessa File* and *The Boys from Brazil* by Ira Levin were fictional, but based heavily on fact, detailing the escape routes – or 'ratlines' – for former Nazis through Europe and on to South America. The big names we're familiar with: Josef Mengele, Klaus Barbie and Adolf Eichmann, but there were many more senior ranks ghosted away by those sympathetic to the old Reich. So, too, there is strong evidence of Allied nations willing to employ former Nazis as intelligence sources, as East and West squared up in the new battleground of the Cold War. It's incredible but true – as revealed in Guy Walter's book, *Hunting Evil* - and distilled here as the villainous Helmut Praxer.

For a taste of London life in the early 1950s, I delved deep into Peter Hennessy's *Having it So Good*, and for a female perspective on the Met, Joan Lock's memoir *Lady Policeman* was invaluable. Channel's Five's excellent *The*

Great Killer Smog documented each day of the fog and its fatal consequences. I will also admit to spending many happy hours watching those old black and white classics such as *The Blue Lamp* and *The Pool of London*, plus *Vera Drake*, where Imelda Staunton's brilliantly portrayed housewife helped shape my Mrs P. In all of them, the ubiquitous teapot and cosy played a starring role.

Where better to land Inspektor Harri Schroder for a taste of a post-war life, a fresh adventure and a new adversary? In writing the closing pages of my previous book, *The Hidden Storyteller*, I sensed I wasn't finished with Harri – he needed space to show us more of his unorthodox policing methods, to shed some of his cynicism, and to heal. Who better than Dexie to help him? She's fierce under that heavy cloak of uniformity, ready and willing to bring criminals to heel. And yet vulnerable in her own way. The remaining cast of characters simply bloomed – Mrs P and Scooter among them – despite the strangulating weather conditions.

I hope that, despite the monochrome vista of those four unprecedented and very real days, the story here emerges as just a bit colourful.

PROLOGUE

Beware

Winter 1952, London

I'm coming. Too far away for you to notice just yet, but I am waiting in the wings, gathering strength and intent on doing my worst. When I make myself known, you will recognise me for who I am, and yet be powerless to act over my dominion.

I come with desire, to infect every pore of what you know as normal, contented life, ever present in your sightline, shifting, morphing, unable to be captured or contained, as I wreak havoc in a city that's already home to a population of predators.

Like an undesirable guest, I come on my own terms, unable to be herded or hounded out, bent on outstaying my welcome. Only when I'm done, once I've sucked in my share of life and claimed what is mine, will I slink away into the ether, leaving no trace except the aftermath of my destruction. A shadow that will be all too tangible, and tragic.

I possess no pity, compassion or empathy, and so I will demand my slice of humanity.

Make no mistake: I am coming.

1

A Perfect O

22nd November 1952, Hamburg, northern Germany

Harri

He's struck by how perfectly rounded the barrel of a gun appears when you see it face on. This shouldn't be a surprise, given the amount of weaponry he's seen over recent years, but when it's just centimetres from his nose and pointed directly at him, the symmetry – that perfect O – strikes Harri Schroder as quite beautiful.

The intent less so. Beyond the sleek snout of the pistol is the sweating face of its bearer, a skinny young man, little more than a teenage thief in Harry's eyes. A tremor ripples down his outstretched arm and towards grubby fingers grasping the gun, causing the O to waver. And that's far more worrying.

'Come on, lad,' Harri begins, adopting a placatory voice. 'You don't really want to use that thing, do you?'

The metal barrel trembles, the young man's face contorted with fear, his sooty, dilated pupils flicking left and right in desperation. As far as Harri is concerned, he's the worst kind of criminal – one backed into a corner with few choices. And he is in a corner, quite literally hemmed in by the rough brickwork of a derelict factory. Above, the grey November day pushes through holes gouged in the bombed-out roof.

Hot from the preceding chase through several busy streets, Harri's breath puffs out in tiny clouds as one hand dares to move slowly up, his palm outwards in a gesture of appeasement. 'Listen, if you shoot me, it's just one over-the-hill policeman off the streets,' he reasons, 'but for you, well, you know where it will end.'

'And if I don't,' the gunman spits, 'what are you going to do – let me go? I'll still end up behind bars.'

'But you'll have a life,' Harri reasons. 'With a future.'

'Yeah, and what kind of a future is that?'

One where you might not die in jail.

'You're young,' Harri presses. 'Don't throw it all away for one stupid mistake. Already, there are too many bodies buried beneath this city. You don't want to be one of them.'

The man's hand shakes violently in response, blurring the edges of the metal snout. 'And what's it to you, old man, eh? Why do you even care?' Despite the freezing air around them, lines of sweat trail down his temples, a sheen coating his forehead.

Oh, thousands of lives lost to hatred. Too much death and destruction, too many widows, weeping mothers, husbands left behind. Only that. 'Because I think it would be a bloody waste, that's why,' Harri argues aloud. 'But, hey, if that's how you want it to end, go ahead. I'm right here.' He raises both arms, signalling surrender in a mad, blasé fashion. 'Go on.'

'I will, you know,' the gunman twitches, nostrils flaring. 'I'm not afraid.'

His wide, glassy eyes say otherwise, a tear on the reddened rim of his eyelid. In that second, fear is what Harri Schroder is banking on, coupled with the faint noises from behind and to either side, a creeping stealth of the back-up he's been stalling for. Perhaps a small prayer has crossed his mind, too.

In one fell swoop, he takes his chance, bringing both hands down on the barrel in a lightning sweep, forcing it towards the gravelled floor as the gunman panics and his fingers let fly on the trigger. A single shot ricochets around the empty building and for a few seconds there's utter confusion, as two officers launch at the culprit and Harri scrabbles to wrestle the gun away, his eyes scanning for blood on the filthy floor – his own principally.

But he's intact, his body at least, as are the officers. So too is the gunman, who sits handcuffed in a stony silence on the floor with such a vacant expression that it's hard to tell if he's relieved or sorry to come out of it alive.

'Thanks, boys – perfect timing,' Harri says to the uniformed men, brushing himself down. 'I was running out of things to say.'

'Close call, Inspektor,' the youngest of them nods, looking intensely relieved not to be dealing with a downed officer and a fatal bullet wound.

Harri watches as the captured man is led away, his head dipped with defeat and shame. He's standing, but it's still a waste, since he'll be sentenced to a decent prison term for threatening a police officer, and all for robbing a paltry amount from the till of a grocery store. Harri has to remind himself it is a life saved, not least his own.

He collects himself and steps out of factory, sweat pricking at his skin now, thrusting both hands in his pockets to hide an unmistakable tremor in all ten digits and the memory of that perfect O pointed straight between his eyes.

'Face it, Schroder,' he mumbles to himself, 'you really are too old for this.'

2

The Armour

22nd November 1952, London, England

Dexie

She adjusts the knot in her tie and smooths the thick serge of her sleeve with one hand, then checks the hair pinned into her neck for any stray wisps. As her fingers work, she wonders if any of the girls in the adjoining rooms go through the same ceremony in preparation, applying the armour, piece by piece, under the dim bulb of section house lighting – thick tights, skirt, shirt and tie, and finally, the jacket displaying her distinct number and rank: Constable 722. She leaves those damned awful shoes – the ones that pinch and rub however long you wear them in – until the very last minute, giving her toes as much respite as possible. Only when the ritual is complete does she feel ready to face what's beyond her own door, and the streets that are still dark at the ungodly hour of six thirty a.m. Each morning, she rolls out of bed (a true hardship on these freezing winter mornings) and steps onto the streets of London as WPC Dexter – 'Dexie' to her friends – her array of defences in situ.

'Morning,' she says, entering the small dining room on the ground floor and trying to feign enthusiasm. There's a unified groan from the table in the corner, led by Jenny, who is probably on her third cup of tea and second cigarette by now. Safe to say, Jenny isn't terribly animated before midday, more suited to twilight duty given the hours she keeps.

'And what time did you roll in, night owl?' Dexie lays down her plate of toast and a wilted, greasy piece of bacon, noting that wartime rationing is still in force on the quality as well as quantity.

'It was gone midnight, that's all I know,' Jenny grouses into her tea.

'Or remember?'

'Yes, that too.' She looks up with bloodshot eyes. 'Have you been talking to my mother, Constable Dexter?'

'No, I'm just a good friend who's trying to save you from a rollicking by the shift sergeant. If he's got even half a nose, he'll smell the alcohol on you.'

'Really?' Jenny breathes hastily into her hand and sniffs at her skin. 'Damn it, I didn't have time for a proper wash.'

'The water was freezing, anyway,' Grace cuts in from across the table, reaching for the salt. 'Mind you, that might have woken you up a bit.'

'Sergeant Thomas will have my guts for garters,' Jenny moans. 'He's already given me a warning this week.'

'Then you'd better get out your perfume bottle, and put him off the scent.' Grace smiles at her own joke, and then scowls at the congealed fat on her plate.

* * *

They leave as a trio, the light fighting to muscle in on the dawn hour and the dreary daytime weather, a light drizzle falling amid the freezing temperature.

'Lord, I wish I'd put my overcoat on now,' Jenny moans. 'I hope we get toilet duty checking on the runaways.'

'Ugh! Why would you?' Grace's face twists, as she peels off towards her own station nearby. 'Those toilets around Piccadilly Circus stink.'

'Smelly but warm, and the attendant makes us a cuppa sometimes,' Jenny calls after her, then quietly, 'plus I might get a few minutes shut-eye in one of the cubicles.'

Walking alongside, WPC Dexter just wishes her toes would decide if they are going to be frozen or squashed into submission today, and which of the two is less painful.

3

A Holiday

22nd November 1952, Hamburg

Harri

Harri's surly temperament is reflected back at him the moment he sets foot inside the solid brick edifice of Davidwache police station, still the most imposing of post-war buildings along Hamburg's lengthy Reeperbahn.

'You look terrible, Schroder,' Chief Inspektor Neumann says gruffly as he crosses towards the front desk.

'That's because I feel it,' Harri snaps back. 'Sir.' A simple hello from his boss would have sufficed.

Neumann frowns, perhaps trying to decide if Harri's attitude is amusing, rude or downright seditious. The chief's innate lack of humour has been further stripped back over recent months by a chronic stomach ulcer, serving to burn away his empathy. Crossing him is like stirring a hot poker into the hornet's nest of his belly. This time, though, Neumann appears to let it go.

'My office,' he barks at Harri.

Then again, maybe not.

Harri limps through, tucking in his shirt as he goes and brushing off the worst of the grime.

'Sit down, Schroder.' Neumann gestures to one of two empty chairs in front of his vast, untidy desk, piled high with files and papers, levering himself wearily into his own chair. 'I've heard you're fond of London,' he begins. 'And that you've visited several times since the war's end?'

'Er, yes, sir, I have. I've got friends living there, and I like to keep my English up to scratch.'

'Hmm,' Neumann grunts. 'Better you than me. It's a dirty, filthy bomb site as far I can tell.'

No more than the dirty, filthy, bomb-blasted streets of Hamburg. Sir.

'Well, it's lucky for you there's an opportunity coming up,' he goes on, shuffling several papers in front of him. 'The Metropolitan Police wants an officer for a secondment, some Anglo-German liaison thing, and your name has been put forward. I don't doubt it's because you speak English well. After all, it's one thing to have a Kraut in their midst, but one that *sounds* like the enemy – sorry, "former adversary" – might not go down so well in the Met canteen. We both know the legacy of the war that hangs over us all.'

'I am grateful to be put forward, sir, but' – Harri scratches at his head – 'I have a backlog of unsolved cases, and several going to court soon. I don't think I can—'

Neumann puts up a large, fleshy hand to halt Harri's speech. 'If I intimated that this is a choice, Schroder, then I apologise. It's not. Yours is the only name on my request sheet.'

'Ah. I see.'

'Good, we're of the same mind. It'll be a month at most. I can ill afford to lose you, but neither can I risk having the regional commanders on my back, who – I'm told – are being harangued by nauseating politicians.' Neumann sits back in his chair and rubs at his substantial stomach, wincing. 'You've no family, wife or child to keep you in Hamburg?'

'No, sir.' Inside, Harri's own gut spasms. Almost ten years on, the needle-sharp barbs of grief arise less and less, but they still catch him unawares. Often on a bad day, like today.

'Then it's agreed,' Neumann decides. 'They want you over there within the week and you leave the day after tomorrow. You'll have a few days to settle in.' Neumann doesn't get up but leans forward to signal the meeting is at an end. 'Think of it as a break, Schroder. It's bound to be a publicity exercise, mostly, and highly unlikely you'll have to do any real policing. By the look of it, you need a holiday.'

'Yes, sir, thank you.' *I think.*

With this latest edict, it's almost midnight by the time Harri types up his last report and prepares written handovers on his current cases. He hates leaving unfinished business, but some of the inquiries have been unsolved for so long that they're still likely to be open on his return. Wearily, he climbs the stairs to his apartment and casts fresh eyes over the tiny space; with four intact walls and no holes in the ceiling, it's a vast improvement on the previous hovel he lodged in. Only his houseplants will need tending, and Frau Holsen from downstairs is happy enough to do that.

Packing a small suitcase with his smartest clothes will take all of ten minutes, but even the best look as old and tired as he feels. He reaches down under a loose floorboard and pulls out a wad of notes, his savings from a life that, these days, involves little more than beer and the odd meal out with colleagues. Perhaps a break is what he needs, and a chance to spend some of his hard-earned money on a decent wardrobe, in shops that have choice and quality. He can visit his old friends Georgie and Max, maybe even take a day trip to Oxford, admire the sights and reminisce about those schoolboy holidays back in the twenties, learning English and cricket. And the British winter is never as harsh as the encroaching German freeze. So, yes, it's timely, and when he thinks about it, quite a welcome prospect too.

Looking at his reflection in the cracked mirror on the wardrobe – the sag of his posture and unkempt hair – he is forced to admit that Neumann might be right, and one of those British idioms he so loves pops into his head: 'A change is as good as a rest'.

The change, two days later, is immediate. Arrival by air is both new and slightly disconcerting to Harri, since his previous visits to England have been by train, allowing a steady assimilation across continental Europe and onwards to the island that possesses a distinct quirkiness, one he finds engaging and confusing in equal measure. Travelling overland has always allowed him time to read and ponder, watching the landscape change and the culture shift. But no such luxury on this trip.

Living among Englishmen is nothing new for Inspektor Schroder, given the years of Allied occupation, Hamburg being the pivot of the British occupying forces when Germany was divided up after the war's end. The occupiers tended mostly to be military squaddies and personnel from the government trying to haul Germany back on its feet, along with diplomatic staff. Some pleasant, and others not, with plenty harbouring a disdainful irritation that the war was over, so why did the losing side need babysitting? Whatever their demeanour, they had one feature in common: all were present in Germany as conquerors. And at the Kriminalpolizei – or Kripo – they had been Harri's overseers in those early post-war years. Controllers.

On his earlier excursions across the North Sea, he's been a guest and a tourist. A 'Kraut', when his accent slips. This, however, will be a first visit as a policeman, on equal footing with London's detective forces, if he'll be allowed to do anything at all. And now, Harri feels forced to make that cultural shift rapidly, though the very expense of an aeroplane ticket means this public relations exercise is clearly important to one side or the other. 'Best behaviour, Schroder', as Chief Neumann had been keen to drive home.

Under the aeroplane's wing, the 'green and pleasant land' of William Blake's celebrated poem is laid out with its distinctive chequerboard effect. Even the muted winter colours make him smile, reminding him there's a chance that he'll be able to escape 'the smoke' of London and breathe the clean air, sip strong country ale (which as a German, he very much admires) and sink his teeth into a well-baked scone, with cream and jam, if the rationing allows.

'Inspector . . . um . . . Schroder, is it?' A man in a dark blue police uniform approaches at the terminal building of Croydon aerodrome.

'Yes, that's me.' Harri wonders if the shabbiness of his own clothes marks him out among the other passengers. Perhaps he'd been expected to turn up in full lederhosen regalia.

The constable seems taken aback by Harri's rounded, softer vowels. 'Welcome, sir. I'm to drive you into London.'

'Thank you, Constable. I'm heading for Islington, if that's all right with you.'

Being a veteran of many German winters – thirty-nine if he's counting – it's not like Harri to feel the cold, but he shivers in the passenger seat of the Met's regulation black Wolseley. The drab November day becomes increasingly monochrome as the car cuts through the mist and into central London and, oddly, it actually feels colder than the Hamburg he's left behind. During last summer's visit to these shores and the vibrant Festival of Britain, he remembers banks of the Thames steeped in colour, full of bright sunshine and the laughter of families pulled out of the post-war mire. Now, the river artery runs like a dirty brown seam, slapping and pushing against its brick boundaries. It's both silly and unwarranted, but Harri can't shake off a heavy sense of foreboding as he peers through the car window. *Not quite the perfect start to a holiday*, he muses silently.

4

A Sharp Wit

24th November 1952, London

Dexie

'Fancy going dancing at the Lyceum this Saturday?' Jenny asks as they clip their way towards Soho on another dull morning in the capital, a sheet of fine rain obscuring the equally grey buildings ahead.

'Jen, it's only Monday,' Dexie laughs. 'I haven't a clue what I'll be doing at the weekend.'

'Far be it from me to second-guess your oh-so-glamourous lifestyle, Constable Dexter,' Jenny pouts theatrically, 'but I imagine you'll either be back at the section house washing your underwear, or on a date with Tony Curtis. I wonder which of those it will it be?'

'Fair point,' Dexie concedes, 'but I still don't know. I might go to the pictures.'

'Alone?' Jenny's eyes narrow in accusation.

'Maybe. And there's nothing wrong with that.' While she attempts to brush it off, Dexie knows that if her words sound defensive, it's because they are. She does like dancing, loves nothing more than jiving to some of the new rock'n'roll coming from America. What she doesn't love is the slower tempo that inevitably follows, and the coupling of men and women as they move in close, dancing cheek to cheek. Sometimes, it's casual and pleasant, but often the hands go wandering, and beyond.

She's been variously labelled as 'cold', other men much less complimentary in labelling her 'frigid' or 'a tease', and even spat at on one occasion, just for resisting her dance partner's nomadic fingers and beery breath on her neck. Even now, the thought sends shivers down her spine underneath her heavy uniform. Privately, Dexie questions when, if ever, it might feel right, and whether it's wrong to want something different. For Jenny and some of the other beat girls, the dance hall seems to be a place of joy and hope, where they might meet Mr Right, someone perhaps to take them away from it all, get married and buy a house in one of the upcoming suburbs of London beyond the sooty centre, sprout a baby or two. Strange how the very thought sends more quivers running through her. Sinking into a seat in the darkness of the picture house seems much less complicated, indulging in another life entirely for an hour or so, travelling to the Snows of Kilimanjaro with Gregory Peck, perhaps?

'Dex?' Jenny's voice cuts in. Her tone is all business this time, not the flighty Jen of the Lyceum.

'What?'

'Up ahead.' Jenny gestures. 'Is that just a tiff or something more?'

Within sight, the woman ejected onto the slick wet pavement would seem normal in the darkness of Soho clubland at midnight, but not at ten a.m in full view of the delivery vans and traders going to and fro. On her knees, she lingers for a second or so, as if she's been coughed up like a ball of dirty phlegm, then staggers upright. She's wearing only a skimpy sleeveless dress and no shoes, her hair dishevelled and make-up running with angry tears.

Dexie and Jenny are already striding towards her. 'What's up, love?' Jenny says.

The woman blinks, takes in their uniforms and seems to retract her obvious outrage at being ousted. 'Nothing,' she grunts. 'I was just going out for a pint of milk.'

'With no shoes on?' Dexie queries. 'Bit cold for that, isn't it?'

Looking down at her own feet, the woman – really no older than late teens – seems unperturbed at her state of undress. 'The shop's only on the corner. What's it to you, anyway? There's no law against it.'

But there might be some law preventing the fracas playing out beyond the scruffy door, the noise of which is now spilling onto the street: shouts, and screams and the audible crashing of furniture. 'Shall we?' Jenny appeals to Dexie, her hand on the doorknob.

'I wouldn't if I were you,' the girl says before she hops away. 'He's in a foul mood, and he 'ates coppers poking their nose in.'

But if there are more beyond the door like the skinny woman, then it is their job to poke their Metropolitan noses in. Jenny is at least three inches shorter than Dexie, but she's never been one to pull her punches when it comes to finding another of her own sex in jeopardy, hangover or not.

Following the noise down a gloomy, filthy stairwell, Dexie squints into a hallway that opens out into a club basement. The bright overhead bulbs cast the dismal surroundings in stark relief, peeling paint and a carpet crusty from last night's liquor-soaked entertainment. As the two constables appear, a man swings around, one splintered chair leg held aloft. Against the opposite wall, three young women – girls, really – have flattened themselves, shrinking with obvious fear.

'What the fuck?' the man shouts. His eyes are ablaze, reddened with drink and, from where Dexie stands, she detects a sickly mix of sweat and fury oozing from him.

'I was just about to ask the same question,' she says. Calmly. It's what Sergeant Thomas drums into them: people find it hard to rail against continued politeness. Most of the time. 'Why don't you put the chair leg down, and we'll talk about this?'

'And why don't you just piss off?' he growls, flecks of spittle spraying from his mouth. 'This is my club and I can do what I like.'

'Of course you can, sir,' Dexie says in a carefully measured voice, 'but not when it involves scaring other people and threatening to hurt them. So, I suggest you let everyone leave now, and we can sort this out.'

'These cows are fleecing me,' he slurs. 'Keeping the tips, and sharing them out.'

And they'd be well within their rights, Dexie thinks, given the paltry wages the hostesses earn for being pawed at while serving drinks to lonely, needy and inebriated men. Besides, the tips legally belong to his employees, though this greedy club-owner won't see it like that. 'That's as may be,' she placates him, 'but it is an offence to beat it out of them. So please put your weapon down.'

'This? It's not dangerous,' he argues, then slides his free hand into a trouser pocket and pulls out something that glints under the stark overhead light, flicking out the blade. 'But this one is.'

Amid the screams flooding the basement, Dexie's eyes go to Jenny, who has been slowly and deftly moving to the owner's side as he brandishes the small but perilous pocket knife. Dexie takes a tentative step towards him, well aware they've entered a battle of weapon against wit. Which one will prove the sharpest? 'Let's just calm down, sir, eh?'

He wavers with the hangover of last night's indulgence, but his eyes remain fiery and all too aware. He lurches to the wall and grabs at one of the women, pulling her waifish body into his and pushing the blade against her neck. 'Move any closer and I'll cut her,' he seethes. 'And you.'

Breathe, Dex, breathe. 'I won't move any closer,' she pledges, one mollifying hand held out. She doesn't, however, promise the same of Jenny.

'Dex?' her colleague whispers, too low for her quarry to hear over his own raggedy panting and the terrified whinnying of his hostage.

'Yes, now.' In the same instance that Jenny hurls herself to the floor and aims for his ankles, Dexie flies at his torso, eyes fixed on that blade, targeting his arm with her own. Jenny's angle means he topples backwards, and away from the woman, Dexie catching his knife arm and twisting it with full force. Before he's had time to holler, he's flat on the floor, face down and with Jenny's knee pinning both arms into his back.

'Bitches!' he screams.

Back at street level, the club owner is pushed into the police van, while Jenny surveys an unsavoury stain on her Met-issue mackintosh. 'I should send him the cleaning bill,' she groans. 'That'll need a good scrubbing.'

'I'll stand you a cup of tea first,' Dexie says. 'Not bad for first thing on a Monday morning, was it?'

Stepping towards the tea stall, she can't help but wonder why dealing with a knife-wielding drunkard seems so much easier to cope with than a slow waltz on the dancefloor.

5

A Balancing Act

2nd December 1952, London

Harri

Spending almost a week at the Islington home of Georgie and Max Spender and their two small children, Margot and Elias, is just what Harri needs to settle back into London life. He's soon adjusting to the relatively frantic streets, etiquette on the Underground and the substitution of Hamburg's bars for pub life, which Max is very keen to introduce him to, as always. There's a welcome trigger to his memories, too, the sharp smell of vinegar outside the fish and chip shop and a lingering aroma of Woodbines, reminding Harri that he's reached what is now considered a second home. And yet, as he walks the chill streets, that sensation of his journey into the capital prevails; the general lack of sun notwithstanding, Londoners do seem more withdrawn than on his previous visits. There's a palpable ripple of anxiety as people rush about, mouths set firm, heading home to the warmth of their fireside. It's as if the city is constrained within a tight corset, holding its breath. But for what?

Once again, the Spenders welcome him into their slightly chaotic but comfortable house, where no one stands on ceremony. As husband and wife, they continue to work tirelessly as Fleet Street journalists, she as a reporter and feature writer, and he as a photographer. The pair appear to be constantly juggling the demands of deadlines and small children, the rooms full of shrill laughter and the tapping of Georgie's typewriter late into the evening. Physically, both look weary with the pace of life, though they're never short on enthusiasm.

Harri senses, too, that both are wary of thrusting the children towards him, ever conscious of his grief. It's nearly ten years since the loss of his wife and only child – Hella and Lily. Nowadays, the pain no longer stabs at him, having softened over time, so that he can allow himself to enjoy the time with the Spender offspring, playing rudimentary football in the park or feeding the ducks. The loss may have been smoothed, but the vacuum stings like the fine hairs of a nettle; watching them play, he often ponders on how different life might have been. Lily would be a teenager by now, and he doesn't like to imagine what she would be getting up to, with friends and boys, let alone how much of a soft touch he would be as a father. Would she have had siblings? Sadly, as the years have passed, he's struggled to imagine how he and Hella would have aged together as parents, unable to picture her face maturing with motherhood, while his own sags in craggy decline.

All too soon, Harri moves into digs near Tottenham Court Road provided by the Met, apparently not far from his designated station. It's a top-floor bedsit with a sink and his own toilet, plus one gas ring, small and slightly drab, with that mustiness common to all boarding houses. It's cold, too, the tiny grate giving off a glow at best, and never quite drawing a decent flame. The place is clean, however, and not too dissimilar from his small one-bedroomed flat back in Hamburg. Besides which, he understands the choices were limited, him being 'from the other side'. A petite, extremely talkative widow called Mrs Painter runs the house; her demobbed brother married a Berliner after the war and, once she'd got over the shock and shame of such a match, has come to view Germans as 'not all bad really'.

'His wife can damn well cook, I'll give her that,' Mrs Painter tells him more than once. Would that the German sister-in-law could have extended her culinary knowledge to Mrs P, as the other boarders call her. Each morning, Harri is served up a flaccid fried egg on soft toast, and wonders how prudent it would be to ask for some plain bread and butter without offending the lady of the house. His saving grace is a small, fluffy white terrier called Scooter, who sits like a sentinel under the table at mealtimes and is fed a good deal by all the residents, it seems. It's only his energetic clipping up and down the stairs in Mrs P's wake that saves him from being a very rounded pet.

'Pleased to meet you. How are you?' 'Yes, please, I would love a cup of tea, milk no sugar, thanks.' Harri practises his stock phrases into the small mirror propped over the sink as he shaves. He repeats the same with his eyes closed, listening intently to his own accent. Too stilted? Too *English*? It's been remarked on before that he could easily pass as a native Brit with his accomplished language and a convincing accent. The question is: does he want to? And should he? It might not go down too well in a London police station, where a good many of the officers are sure to be veterans of the war. Discovering a German hiding in their midst is bound to ruffle some feathers. Despite what the politicians say, an undercurrent of mistrust remains seven years on from the peace, almost as if some would find it easier if he were to go goose-stepping into the station and barking his hardened vowels, the lines clearly drawn. The blurring of international relations is somehow more difficult.

Harri is determined never to deny his origins, but he's learnt there are ways of making the journey through life easier, starting with chipping the hard, guttural edges off his accent. Neither should he try too hard to be 'one of the boys'. Mastering English as a teenager – as the guest of a very well-to-do family near Oxford – it was very much the King's pronunciation. Now there's a new Queen, who sounds just as highbrow with her plum vowels, but he thinks it would be better to employ the middle ground and rough it up a little, aim to give the constables and the desk sergeants something of what they expect, but without offence.

Why, he wonders, is it still such a delicate balancing act? More to the point, why have they chosen Harri Schroder, of all people, to smooth over the wrinkles?

The instruction is to report to West End Central station by ten a.m, leaving time for one last errand. In the first week, Georgie had dragged him the length and breadth of Oxford Street in search of a new wardrobe. Decked out head to foot in decent tailoring, he no longer resembles the poor German come to visit. He strides out from Mrs P's and into a crisp chill – the weather having turned from grey gloom in the past few days to a cloudless and cheery sky blue – glad of his new, heavy tweed overcoat and the shoes that are just about worn in. There's just one more item left to purchase, Harri's personal icing on the cake.

* * *

He looks at his reflection and smiles, a decidedly rare reaction in recent years. On this occasion, though, he is pleased at what he sees, his wide lips tipping upwards to one side to indicate an unaccustomed pleasure, his hair newly cut into the nape of his neck. The flesh and features looking back at him are largely unchanged, perhaps a few more lines since he last looked so intently, but they've not turned to fleshy folds, and he doesn't have that permanent crease of old age. Not yet anyway. Lived in, he judges, rather than outlived. Eyes front, Harri Schroder turns his head this way and that, considering.

'Does sir like it?' A man in a smart three-piece comes into sight behind him, the epitome of a well-groomed sales assistant reflected in the shop's mirror.

'Very much,' Harri says. 'In fact, I'll take it.'

'A wise choice, sir, especially in winter, with the weather yet to close in.'

Harri goes to remove the pristine, black felted trilby from his head, takes one last glance and thinks better of it. 'I'll wear it now,' he tells the assistant.

'Very good, sir. Shall I package your existing hat?'

'Yes, please do.'

Watching the man's long, nimble fingers at work, Harri wonders if the packing away of his trusty Homburg is in any way symbolic, more so when the lid of the box is firmly shut and fastened. The old hat screams of his Germanic roots, a constant presence on the streets of his native Hamburg, in the same way British men sport a trilby as part of their post-war uniform.

So, is this another deliberate act to hide his national identity? Merging with the crowd will be an advantage with any work that lies ahead, of that there's no doubt. Much like his accent, wearing a German heart on your sleeve (or your head, in this case) will win him few friends, Hitler's legacy having chipped into the lives and loss of so many British families. Besides, he's long been an admirer of the stylish trilby, and with each trip to London he's promised himself a visit to Simpsons of Piccadilly to procure the very best they have. Somehow, there was never enough time. Now, he's created that space, motivated by a simple, human desire to blend in.

Delighted with his new look, Harri Schroder steps out onto the bustling thoroughfare of Piccadilly, and is instantly surprised at the sensation it affords, of making him actually feel taller than his five foot eleven inches. A woman passes by and smiles at him, her eyes combing his buttoned overcoat and polished shoes, her glance admiring. The magic of millinery.

Only life left to negotiate now, and diplomacy with the London Metropolitan Police. 'If the hat fits . . .' Isn't that another of those quirky Britishisms?

Outside, under a sapphire sky, he tips his trilby at an elderly woman with an exquisitely groomed toy dog, and strides out towards bright winter sunshine hanging over the Strand.

6

A Necessary Purpose

2nd December 1952, London

Harri

As the square, sharp lines of the Met's West End Central station come into view, Harri's slight trepidation is calmed. It has the pale brick colouring of the BBC's flagship headquarters at Portland House – one of his favourite buildings in London – mixed with the comforting cubism of architecture from back home. To his eye, it's every inch the stark face of the law. Approaching, he notes the pale bricks are darkened by a thin layer of soot, giving the exterior the tired, worn look of post-war. Like Davidwache, it's not bomb-damaged, and that makes Harri feel oddly at home, as if the very shell reflects what will greet him inside.

Inside, the officer sitting squarely behind a dark wooden reception desk makes it instantly clear that sergeants the world over are cut from the same cloth – robust, with police-issue jackets straining just a little on their girth, cheery but with an undercurrent of gruffness. *Mess with me, my lad, and you'll soon regret it.* Davidwache has at least two or three in its own stable.

'Yes, sir, what can I do for you?' The sergeant's smile is uniform.

Harri removes his trilby in due deference. 'I've come to see a Chief Inspector . . .' – he pulls out a folded scrap hastily scribbled on by his own Chief Neumann – '. . . Banks.'

'And what will be that for, sir?'

'I'm on secondment here, for the next month or so. Inspektor Schroder.'

The very name, and Harri's purposeful emphasis on 'Sch', causes the sergeant to pause, even if he covers it well.

'Oh well, Inspector, you'd better come on through. Travers!' He calls behind him to a young constable who just stops short of saluting his senior. 'Take Inspector Shrider up to third floor, will you?'

'It's er, Schroder,' Harri repeats, but to no avail, since the sergeant's attention is already elsewhere. He steels himself for having to spell it out in the days and weeks to come.

Like a whippet, Travers leads Harri through a warren of corridors and up two flights of stairs, where it soon becomes plain that the re-building of London has so far taken priority elsewhere: yellowing paint on the walls is peeling, with a weary creak of floorboards beneath their feet, while a muted trill of telephones mingles with the clatter of typewriters from behind frosted, half-glazed doors. It's a noise Harri relishes, reminding him of a time before the war when Hamburg's detective division, the Kripo, possessed more than a handful of telephones. Days when they didn't need to book time on the few working machines to type up their reports, and spent more time fighting serious crime than the petty thieving after a conflict had stripped the country bare. Year on year since the war's end it's improved a little, but this noisy hum of police industry always affords him instant comfort.

The seemingly mute constable ushers Harri through a door labelled CID and he's bathed in both sight and sound, by the hubs of activity at various desks. A few people are in uniform, but most are wearing civilian suits, all behind a sedentary haze of cigarette smoke.

'Ah! Stroder, there you are.' A stocky man steps forward and holds out a hand, pumping Harri's with a firm shake. 'We've been expecting you, welcome to CID.' He turns towards the room like a ringmaster presenting his troupe.

'It's Schroder, sir. Harri Schroder.' Again, Harri stresses the 'Sch'. 'Pleased to be here, sir.' *Though I'm still not sure what for.*

The chief inspector treads towards a small office within the larger room, separated only by flimsy half-paned walls. 'Sit, sit.' He gestures, and plants himself firmly in a sturdy wooden office chair. 'Welcome to West End Central, for all it sins. Tell me, what would you like to see while you're with us?'

'Well, er . . . I thought it might have already been discussed with you . . .' It dawns on Harri that this truly is some public relations exercise, dreamed up by a junior politician in the British Home Office as a way of 'cementing' former enemies as new allies. There'll be some well-posed photographs, a dinner maybe, after which the dignitaries will retreat back to their government offices, while Harri is left to stagnate, his cases back in Hamburg stacking up. Irritation rises suddenly, and he sees that his opposite number sitting across the desk is equally in the dark, and none too pleased about it either.

'Politicians, eh?' Banks sighs. 'Let me see what I can

sort out, though that might take more than five minutes in getting through to someone who knows. In the meantime, why don't I get one of my lot to show you around? See what kind of policing we do here.'

'Thank you, sir.' If nothing else, he's grateful for Banks' honesty, and doing something useful is always better than twiddling his thumbs.

Banks heaves himself out of his chair with surprisingly agility and beckons Harri to follow through the door. 'DEXTER!' he bellows into the fug. The office noise ceases for a mere second, before it cranks up again, above which there's the single scrape of a chair. A tall uniformed woman strides towards them, her solid black lace-up shoes resonant on the wooden floor. Instantly, he notes that her expression – unlike the near-mute Travers – shows no fear in the face of her blunt summons.

'Yes, sir.' A levelling of her lips, faint with lipstick, rather than a smile.

'This is Inspector Stroder, a colleague from across the North Sea in Hamburg, come to spend some time with you unholy rabble.'

'Yes, sir,' she nods.

'So, would you take him out on patrol and show him our patch. Only please bring him back here in one piece by, say, three o'clock?'

'Of course, sir.' There's neither an obsequious deference in her manner, or supreme confidence, and Harri is struck by the iridescent green eyes aimed directly at her superior, yet giving little clue as to what she's thinking. Her gaze has yet to land on him, and he's already surprised. Pleasantly. The mere mention of his German origin often prompts a crawling assessment, top to toe. Of the clothes that, until recently, have been relatively threadbare, but also a careful combing of his features. He often wonders what the onlookers are searching for. Evil? Humanity? A passing resemblance to Hitler? The most he can often muster is a weary glaze.

Banks turns to him. 'I'll leave you in Constable Dexter's capable hands, and I'll try my best to find someone who knows what the devil is going on.'

So says a man who clearly served his time in the military, Harri thinks. He's well used to chaos before clarity.

Still the WPC hasn't looked him in the eye, only brushing over his face. 'This way, Inspector,' she says. 'I'll need to get my coat.'

Approaching the door, they are met by a man in civilian clothes, sweeping inwards as he peels off a beige mackintosh. He's both pre-occupied and in a rush. 'Ah, Dexie,' he barks as he charges past. 'Get me a cuppa, will you? There's a love. I'm gasping.'

Harri is blindsided not only by such rudeness, but the gruff demands – for tea of all things. Curious, his eyes go to the female officer, who doesn't break her stride.

'Yes, sir,' is all she says.

7

The German

2nd December 1952

Dexie

'Sorry, but we'll have to go via the canteen,' she says as they shuffle side by side into the dim corridor, sensing his presence beside her. In truth, she's more resigned than irritated to be taken away from her desk in order to pilot this visiting dignitary around. As a beat WPC, her time in CID depends on the streets being quiet enough for her to be 'allowed in' to do some filing or cross checking, despite her efforts last week in thwarting that nasty incident in a Soho club, which was inevitably logged as 'a domestic' once they arrived at the station. But the detective division is her pathway, she hopes, to climbing out of the daily routine and doing something different. A track that also means being compliant.

'It's fine,' the German says, with no hint of irritation. 'I don't mind.'

Dexie does glance up at him then, taken aback by his accent with only a hint of European. His suit looks British-made, so too his trilby; at first glance, she would struggle to identify him as anything but English.

'Are they all like that?' he says, matching her rapid pace along the corridor. 'Demanding tea?'

No man has ever asked that question before. 'What, like Harmer?' she scoffs without breaking her stride. 'No. At least he doesn't try and get a grope in at the same time as treating me like the maid.'

He stops abruptly at her admission, causing her to halt too, his eyes directly on her. The well-worn cloak of self-control slips and, for a mere second, Dexie's expression betrays a deep-seated irritation escaping her starched collar and tie. In a little over sixty seconds, this man may well have penetrated her thoughts. His brow, already slightly furrowed, creases some more. Perhaps he's perplexed, or else shocked at her lack of respect for rank. 'Sorry, sir,' she says in response. 'I don't mean to speak out of turn.'

As a way of ending this awkward exchange, Dexie forges down a flight of stairs and into a large room with tables and chairs arranged around a lengthy counter. Along with the blue gauze of cigarette smoke, the air is heavy with the intensely British smell of frying sausages and chip fat.

'How do you take yours?' she asks automatically, stopping at a table with an urn and a ridiculously large metal teapot. 'Milk and sugar?'

'No, thank you,' the German inspector says. 'You don't need to fetch me tea.'

'Coffee then? Though I don't recommend it here, it's vile.'

'Nothing. Thank you.'

Her turn, then, to look at him curiously. Is he slighting the tea, or her? Making a point?

'I'm fine,' he says. 'I'm really not thirsty.'

* * *

After dutifully taking the cup back up to the CID room, Schroder trailing in her wake, Dexie collects her navy-blue mackintosh from the women's cloakroom, pulls on her flat Met cap and turns to her shadow, who seems busy taking in the comings and goings of the reception area.

'You might want to leave your trilby behind,' she advises.

He fingers the rim protectively. 'Oh, why? I thought it made me look more like a detective. A bit of a Dick Barton character.' For the first time, he smiles. The German made a joke.

'It does. And that's the problem,' she says bluntly. 'Walking beside me, you are a sitting duck for any member of the public to report a whole swathe of criminal incidents, however trivial or ancient. I can guarantee we won't get more than a few yards without Mrs Bloggs giving us chapter and verse on her neighbour's dodgy activities. And expecting you to take down a full report. Your choice.'

With obvious reluctance, Harri relinquishes his hat to the care of the desk sergeant and they step onto the clean thoroughfare of Savile Row.

'Not bad around here, is it?' he says, casting his eye over Mayfair and the renowned centre of London's highbrow tailoring world. 'It's a far cry from the hotch-potch of bomb damage around my station.'

'Oh, this is the nice end,' she says, 'but you should see the rest of the patch.'

'So, show me,' he bats back.

She doesn't stop, but her pace slackens a little. 'You really want to?'

'Well, I'm not a tourist,' he says. 'I'd rather get my teeth into something while I'm here.'

She scoffs, for the second time in their brief encounter. 'You and me both, Inspector.'

Eyes front, she walks with ease through the street beyond

West End Central. At around five foot eight, Dexie naturally covers the ground swiftly, and while she notes the inspector is taller by a good three inches, his curiosity, plus his head tacking from side to side, means that once or twice he's struggling to keep up.

'What's your name?' he says out of the blue, as they move towards Soho. That's twice now he's aimed a personal question.

'Dexter.'

'No, I mean your name. Like mine is Harri.'

She pauses. She's at work, dressed in blue and pounding the beat, and it takes a second to reconnect with her other self beyond the uniform. 'It's Helen,' she says, though the word feels odd in the circumstances. 'But everyone calls me Dexie.'

'Do you mind that?'

Lordy, he's nosy. 'Erm, no, not really. Besides, you don't have much option really, when it comes from the higher ranks.'

He shoots her that incredulous look again.

'Believe me, it's better than "angel" or "dear",' she says flatly. 'But, please, I'd rather you call me Dexie.'

'If you'll drop the "inspector",' he replies. 'At home, I'm just Harri. Except to my boss, who calls me all sorts of things, depending on his mood and my success rate.'

They've reached the warren of narrow lanes that make up Soho's backstreets, a stone's throw from Leicester Square, both drawn to pick up the pace by a mild altercation up ahead, a young, heavily made-up brunette arguing with a street trader over the price of stockings he's selling out of a suitcase.

'I took one out of the packet once I'd got round the corner, and it's got a dirty great hole in it,' the woman complains bitterly. 'Look at this!' She pokes a brightly painted finger through the nylon. A few women who've gathered purse their lips in tribal condemnation.

The seller keeps silent as the police presence draws up, no

doubt certain that he stands to lose a lot more than his patch on the street if he kicks back. Dexie steps between them, pulls herself up to full height and assumes the role of WPC in charge.

'Haven't I seen you around here before?' she addresses the woman, peering beyond the thick lashes and bright red lips. 'Around Dean Street. In the doorways, after dark.' Her implication is obvious to all, not least the small gathering crowd.

'I don't think so,' the woman replies petulantly. And yet she's neither insulted nor indignant, as a truly wronged woman might be.

The issue is settled with simple but firm negotiation; the seller refunds the money, the buyer waives her right to press charges and the suitcase is quickly snapped shut. The peddler hotfoots it around the corner and out of sight, lucky to escape a booking and fine.

'So, why didn't you take him in?' Schroder asks as they move off, with more of a curious rather than critical air.

'Waste of everyone's time,' she explains. 'It means I'm off the street for several hours with the paperwork, and he'll be back out selling before you know it, though he might be more wary of dealing shoddy goods. And, clearly, she doesn't remember that I booked her for soliciting about six months ago. Today, she's just a shopper, if a slightly gullible one. By this evening, I guarantee she'll have donned a wig and become a bubbly blonde, ready for a night's work. Shall we move on?'

Several streets on without incident and they've slowed to a stroll. It's then that Dexie sneaks more than a sideways glance at Harri Schroder, observing his comfortable walking posture, one hand in his overcoat pocket. As a German, she'd half expected him to act like a fish out of water, the alien come in to land. By contrast, he looks almost at home. Strangely, too, Dexie finds herself quite at ease with him, far more than if Harmer or any of the other CID egos were alongside.

'Does that shock you,' she says finally, 'my not doing it by the book?'

He shakes his head. 'It's a delicate balancing act, isn't it? Street women have eyes and ears – good ones – and they can be a vital source of information if you treat them fairly. We have a German equivalent of your city "spiv" traders, who see everything and want to remain a friend to all, so I would say it's very sensible. I'm sure you have more vital demands on your time.'

'Hmm, perhaps,' she says.

The 'demands' of a Metropolitan WPC show themselves over the next hour or so. Dexie escorts several elderly men and women across the street, returns a briefly lost child to its frantic mother, checks into the toilets at Piccadilly Circus station to identify for the frequent runaways that use it for a wash and brush up, then helps a rookie constable on the beat who's having trouble with a cat-fight among two drunken women. Dexie wades in to calm both parties, elicits a slurred apology and sends them on their way.

'Thanks, love,' says the constable, who's nearing a decade younger, before turning to Harri. 'The girls are especially good at that, don't you think?' he adds unashamedly. Dexie watches for the inspector's reaction, but his face is deadpan. Why does he seem so hard to read? The men at West End Central, and in every other station she's been attached to, are like open books. Some are nicer than others and less overt with the sometimes crass, often stinging comments they disguise as 'banter'. Nice or not, each treats a WPC's time in uniform as temporary, a convenient distraction until she's either married or 'in the family way'.

And there are a good many reasons why neither of those applies to WPC Dexter. Not any more.

8

The Dream Team

2nd December 1952

Harri

They move on through the market on Berwick Street, where WPC Dexter waves and nods at several of the traders. 'Hello Dex, you keeping well?' they toss back. Less friendly, Harri notices, are the old lags and younger men loitering on corners, smoking and gambling in small huddles. 'Wouldn't mind being locked in the cells with her,' they snigger as she walks past; 'Show me your handcuffs, darlin', and I'll show you mine, ha ha'; 'You want to get yourself a nice husband, girl, and stop playing silly police games.'

Harri's fingers twitch and his fists clench, angry not only for a police colleague, but the insult to her as a person. As a woman. He thinks back to the Kripo office at Davidwache, and the women who were the backbone of his team just after the war. Paula and Anna are both mothers and widows, each almost press-ganged into the job when the men left to fight, and then filled the gaps left by the Nazi-sympathising officers who went to ground at the surrender, plus those detectives buried in the earth. Those women didn't have to spend their time escorting people across the road – Paula and Anna solved major crimes and caught killers. Harri isn't blind to the inequalities between the sexes, in the world of work and the Kripo, the macho talk in cafés where the officers congregate. But not on his watch. He was not brought up by either parent to affront a woman's intelligence. And yet he sees this woman beside him stare straight ahead in the face of such insults – like water off a duck's back, to coin another well-worn English phrase. He's perplexed: why isn't she more incensed?

'Listen, can I buy you a cup of tea now?' Harri suggests as they loop back towards Regent Street. 'Is that allowed?'

She checks her watch, rings into the station using one of the police telephone stands placed at intervals along the beat and tells him that yes, she's officially on a break for half an hour. This time, it's Harri who leads the way towards the New Piccadilly café, tucked just behind the bustle of the Circus, one of Max's favoured spots when he craves good eggs and chips and daren't admit to Georgie that hers don't quite match up.

'What will you have?' he asks, over the hiss of the hot water geyser and shouts from the kitchen in a pidgin mix of English and Italian.

'I've heard the coffee's decent in here,' she says, taking off her cap, but keeping her mac on, despite the heat and condensation clinging to the windows.

'How about some lunch?' Harri asks. 'If only for putting up with the new boy hanging around. I'm having some, if you don't mind. My landlady's breakfast was barely edible and this morning's ended up in the bin when she wasn't looking. Even the dog turned his nose up at it.'

She seems amused at his confession. 'Oh, go on, then. I'll have egg and chips, too. The chips can't be any soggier than the station canteen.'

They order, and he sees her eyes combing the interior, at the adverts for tinned Spam and Spry cooking oil, moving seamlessly over the clientele. Assessing. Like any in the force, she's never really off duty.

'Do you come in here often?' Harri wonders. 'It's right on your patch.'

'Er, not really. In some places the uniform makes you stand out like a sore thumb,' she admits. 'If we can't get back to the station, we usually grab a cup from one of the tea stalls. Besides, the working girls use this for a bit of respite in the early evening. They don't solicit in here, and the owner won't put up with any funny business from the men, so it's a safe space. God knows it's dicey enough out there, so we'd rather not scare them away.'

The egg and chips are up to scratch, the yolk just right and chips crispy, helping the conversation along and serving to warm what Harri senses is a frisson of cool between them. WPC Dexter isn't exactly unfriendly, or aloof, and she's clearly on good terms with most of the general public, the law-abiding ones. Some of those who fall into the grey areas too. Perhaps 'numb' is the description he's looking for?

'Um, forgive me if this is personal, and tell me to mind my own business . . .' he begins.

A fleck in her emerald eyes turns steely, flashing up from her plate and fixing on him.

'. . . but why do you put up with it?'

Now her eyebrows rise several millimetres.

'How they treat you, the way they talk to female officers, in the station as well?' he qualifies. *Christ, Harri Schroder! Diplomacy really is not your strong point.*

Mercifully, she puts down her fork. For a minute, he thought she might drive it straight at him. Forcefully.

Instead, she lets out a deep sigh and purses her lips. 'What's the point?' she says. 'It only fuels them, underlines that the WPCs are just a bunch of old harridans. You either put up and shut up, or you get out. It's that simple.'

'I see,' he says, with a combination of shock and disappointment. 'But have you plans, or ambitions in the job?'

Dexie pushes at a leftover chip. 'The detective division, if I survive my time in uniform first,' she says. 'A few women have managed it. I enjoy the job now, but it can be a bit dull, and I don't want to be on the beat forever.'

'I did my minimum two years pounding the streets, before transferring to the Kripo,' Harri says. 'Then Hitler came on the scene, and well . . .'

There's no sympathy in her tart look of response. 'I'm afraid, Inspector, we don't have that luxury of putting in for a transfer. The Met considers their WPCs only good for dealing with runaways, family dramas and prostitutes. Oh, and helping children across the road. I'm already doing extra duties in the CID office – filing, of course – to have any chance of getting noticed.'

'That you're a viable candidate?'

'No, that I actually have a brain.'

A barely contained bitterness pushes past her constraint, and Harri wonders if she feels safe in revealing so much because he's merely a visitor, a transient, benign force who has no influence in her world. Just an annoying German who needs minding.

Then again, perhaps he'd better get used to it.

Still, he can't help but be curious about the woman sitting opposite, sipping at her coffee with her curious gaze. She must be in her thirties, he guesses, perhaps around the same age as Georgie, though he's not well practised at looking closely at women, not since Hella, anyway. Is she married? Or widowed by the war? It might explain her need to work, if not her choice of occupation.

He notes the sandy hair that is kept short, pinned above her collar in a practical fashion so it stays put when the regulation cap comes on and off. Sensible, and yet, under the heavy serge uniform, she thrums with energy. More than anything, Harri is reminded of Paula in her first few months at the Kripo office – a mother's well practised tenacity and intuition tuned to a new hunger for catching criminals. He senses the same raw resolve in Dexie, wondering at the same time if it's destined be beaten back by the stance of the Met. Along with those irritating jibes.

She glances at her watch. 'That's our half hour up,' she says briskly, replacing her cap. 'Better get back to it. I am absolutely certain there's a children's crossing out there that needs our urgent and undying attention. What do you think, Inspector Schroder?'

He thinks a sense of humour is a must in her position. Plus, she got his name right.

They round back into Soho, further into what feels like the centre of illicit of trade, even in daylight. Harri recognises the same undercurrent as back home, despite the friendly, vocal traders – the ironmongers and deli owners that wave and shout as they pass by. Dexie's smile is fixed, but her eyes are everywhere, peering out beneath the rim of her cap and towards the underbelly.

'We'll take a shortcut,' she says, ducking into an alleyway and sliding by a collection of stinking, overflowing bins that mimic Hamburg's seedier districts.

'Where does this le—?' he begins, cut off by her hand shooting up to silence him, a foxhound on the hunt. Harri follows as she nips sideways into a gateless entrance and flattens herself against damp brickwork. Dexie points noiselessly to a young woman yards in front, lingering below the back stairs that serve a collection of flats above a parade of shops at the far end of the alleyway. Harri moves in closer, enough to smell the faint soapiness of Dexie's skin. His eyebrows arch.

'I've seen her before,' she whispers close into his ear. 'She's a runaway. But I think she's loitering for a reason.'

'A lookout?' Harri queries.

'Maybe. There's a jeweller's business above those shops, and she won't be touting for other business at this time of day.' She shakes her head. 'Something's not right.'

The acrid stench of the surrounding bins creeps into his nostrils in the cold, damp air, and while the bustle of Soho is just audible from the street beyond, it's deathly quiet in the alleyway. Harri sneaks a look around the brickwork. Dexie's suspicions are likely right; the woman – little more than a girl – hops from foot to foot as a way of keeping warm, and very possibly from nerves, too. Her focus is on the iron stairway coiling upwards, only breaking away every so often to scan either end of the alley, the nervous tic of a lookout. He reins his head in swiftly as her attention strays his way. Without any means of summoning help aside from a police whistle, all they can do is wait. Harri feels that familiar prickle of anticipation, the steady rise of his heartrate. Is this a homeless girl whiling away the empty, endless hours of the day, or is there a crime in the offing and chance to catch the perpetrators, 'bang to rights', as the British say? Of all the language's strange maxims, he loves that one the most.

That inner feeling – an odd sort of thrill – is, and always

was, his fuel as a police officer. Since the war, it's been diluted with apathy and a weary resistance to change, so Harri is pleased to note its presence right now – relieved that he's able to feel it, the emotion still within him, if deeply embedded these days.

The wait is only minutes. A resounding crack splits the air almost in line with a man's urgent shout from the stairway above: 'JACK! GET OUT! GET OUT!' Harri's eyes slice to the girl and the horror flashed across her face, before only the back of her head is visible as she takes flight down the alleyway at speed. Dexie is already on the move, the tail of her mackintosh flapping as she sprints not towards the girl, but the base of the steps, where two men are now half-jumping, half-flying from the top of the spiral stairwell, each with a small bag in tow. Dexie throws herself against the brickwork at the bottom step and crouches low. Two seconds behind, Harri does the same, both of them listening to the heavy, panicked panting of the escapees above as they get closer, second by second, rung by rung. She shoots him a look, raises one finger and points to herself, then two, aimed at Harri. He nods at the international language of policing.

The first lithe body launches himself towards the ground with a leap two or three feet outwards. One leg buckles with the force of the thief's landing and Dexie is on him instantly, throwing the whole weight of her body onto his back. He's floored. Harri hears the slump and the air forced out of his body in the same second as man two reaches the ground, his face awash with disbelief at the slim chance or bad luck of two passing coppers lying in wait just as their robbery is going down. Still, that half second is enough for the culprit to dart sideways in dodging capture, using his bulk to ram Harri's shoulder and barge past. Almost like a child's spinning top, Harri is sent skittering, but he rights himself quickly and glances at Dexie, who has her man still pinned with one hand and is pulling out her police whistle with the other, sending three long, shrill blasts into the still, chill air.

As the second man flees back down the alleyway, Harri is hampered by his beloved but dense overcoat; without thinking, he releases the buttons and tosses it off like a cloak, instantly freer – and faster. The thief's bulk is matched by his lack of fitness, and even though he dumps the heavy tool bag en route, Harri is on him several hundred yards into the street, pushing him to the ground with one arm wrenched behind his back, to the raider's cry of complaint. 'OW! Watch it, mate! Go easy.' There's even a smattering of applause from some of the crowd that quickly forms around him.

Bang to rights. How very satisfying.

By the time two uniformed officers have arrived and hauled the offender towards a waiting police van, Dexie has emerged into the street, minus felon number one, but carrying Harri's overcoat, soggy and dirty with London's grime. He's only relieved the beloved trilby, safely back at West End Central, escaped being steeped in street detritus.

Unable to hide a smile, she holds out his expensive tweed garment: 'Now you know why I don't wear a regulation overcoat. Far too cumbersome.'

Slightly smug, but well deserved, Harri thinks. 'And here's me worried that you might have been cold, Constable, when, actually, I see now that I don't need to worry at all.'

Her smile lingers: *the cat that got the cream*.

'What about the jewellery store?' he asks. 'Was there anyone up there?'

'The owner. He's nursing a nasty crack to the head, but

it could have been a lot worse. As a team, I don't think our two were the most professional of villains.'

Harri shakes his head. 'It doesn't take away the success,' he says. 'You suspected, detected and foiled it.'

'*We* did,' she qualifies.

'Then perhaps we are the dream team?'

'Don't let my sergeant hear you saying that.'

Harri assesses the sorry state of his coat, soaked in a pungent grime that he does not wish to know the origin of. The trousers of his new suit are smudged with dirt, and he can only imagine what Chief Inspector Neumann would think of Harri's first day as a diplomatic liaison between once-warring nations. His ulcer wouldn't be the only thing on fire.

'So, what now?' Harri asks. 'Aren't we late for that vital crossing duty?'

'Do you know, I might even prefer that to the hours of paperwork that's waiting for me back at the nick. And I'll need a full witness report from you.' Her nostrils flare. 'Though I think you might need to clean up first.'

9

Fond Farewell

2nd December 1952

Dexie

It's after two by the time they walk back to West End Central and check in with the custody desk. Ferried in by van, the two men are on opposite sides of the charge room, their faces a mix of embarrassment and anger. Harri's 'collar' looks up briefly and gives him a sort of grudging nod, as if to say: 'fair enough, no hard feelings', but Dexie's man oozes a seething fury at being taken down by a woman. Or that's how she sees it.

She notes Harri glancing at his watch once or twice. 'I'll be a good while here sorting out the charge sheets,' she tells him. 'You go on up to CID.'

'If you're sure, thanks,' he says. 'And thank you, Dexie – WPC Dexter – for what has proved to be a very varied morning. I feel properly trained in how to escort old ladies across the road, *and* floor a criminal in a fairly spectacular manner. Never a dull moment.'

What he says would be wholly patronising, were it not for the grin he gives on retrieving his hat from the desk sergeant and tipping it towards her. She's always liked a man with a sense of humour.

'Don't forget my statement,' she calls behind him, watching the trilby disappear towards the stairwell, with an odd pinch in her stomach that stops her scribbling for a moment. Helen Dexter likes plenty of her colleagues, the tight band of women at the station and in her section house especially, but she finds it hard to get close to them. Maybe that's a little unfair: she finds it difficult to let others in. As a group, they go out to have fun, often flirting a little with men in a club. Sometimes – with a gin and tonic inside her – she'll even join in. Always on the periphery, though. That's as far as it goes. In contrast to her friends, intimacy for Helen Dexter isn't easy. Well applied make-up conceals a lot, but it doesn't touch the scars on the inside.

When? she wonders. When will that change, if ever? Today, despite his strange and very direct way of probing (is that a German thing?), Inspector Schroder made her feel less stiff inside her heavy-weave uniform. Perhaps even relaxed, for those few hours. Dare she say it, but valued too. True to their respective roles, he will go on to do something important, and she will return to her old folk, nursery-school children and sad runaways. Aside from taking down his statement, their paths will probably never cross again. And she wonders if it's that causing the little bubble in her stomach to bob around repeatedly, though maybe it's chasing villains on a full stomach of café grease.

'It'll be the eggs, Dex,' she mumbles to herself and goes back to scratching with her pen.

10

Mr Johnson

2nd December 1952

Harri

Harri heads upstairs, by way of the men's bathroom, intent on making himself presentable for whatever else the day holds. Water works well enough on the grime peppering his suit, but the coat will need a thorough clean.

'Ah, there you are, Strider.' Chief Inspector Banks catches him outside the toilets.

'It's Schro . . . never mind. Any luck, sir, on finding out where I'm to be posted?'

'Yes, actually. It took a few phone calls, but it seems you're to report to New Scotland Yard this afternoon, though they didn't specify which department, only a name.' His eyes go to the wet patch on Harri's knee, and his nose twitches. 'I hear you and Dexter had an eventful morning?'

'Yes, sir. Two thieves, caught in the act. All thanks to Constable Dexter's keen eye.'

'Ah yes, she's a good girl,' Banks agrees. 'Excellent with

the women and children, too, I'm told. Anyway, you'd better get yourself over to the Yard. They're expecting you at three thirty. Superintendent Graham, no less. Good luck, Strider.'

Killing time before his appointment at Met's headquarters, Harri is in the canteen when Dexie finds him. He looks up from a muddy cup of tea. 'How's the paperwork going?'

'They're both booked in, and they'll be up before the magistrate in the morning,' she says. 'I hear you're off to the Yard? Lucky for some, but I will need that statement from you, as soon as possible.'

Harri checks his watch again. 'I can't be late for the powers that be, but I'll come back afterwards. What time will you leave?'

'My turn finishes at four, but I'll be here until at least five,' she says. 'Lots to catch up on.'

New Scotland Yard looks anything but fresh as the patrol car sweeps through the gates, drawing up outside the type of a faded red-brick monolith that the Victorians specialised in. There's even a turret or two, adding to the aura of Sherlock Holmes, and it needs only a hansom cab and a decent London fog to complete the scene.

'Thank you, Constable,' Harri says, setting his trilby and persona firmly in place as he moves towards the entrance. From his own sparsely furnished Kripo office at Davidwache, he's long imagined what this auspicious building looks like on the inside.

First impressions? Better maintained than his own station, for sure, but equally chaotic. People in an out of uniform criss-cross the reception area at varying speeds and several telephones trill in the background. Behind is that ever-present tickety-tack of typists at work, and yet, despite the electric lighting and obvious progress in technology, it retains echoes of another age, with a faint hue of coal smoke seeping from behind office doors. At any moment, Mr Holmes and Dr Watson could well emerge from any one of the corridors facing him and blend in perfectly.

'Here to see Superintendent Graham,' he reports to the desk clerk, smoothing out the sharp edges of his Teutonic accent. It's perhaps better not to set the rumour mill up and running just yet of a Kraut in the midst. Directed to the fourth floor, he takes the winding stairway on purpose, readying himself for more disappointment: news that he's been attached to a suburban beat or the traffic department, somewhere they can 'park' the visiting German for the requisite month. It's very possible that the morning's excitement will be the pinnacle of this secondment.

Superintendent Graham emerges from his own office and greets him at the secretary's desk, extending a hand. 'Good to meet you, Schroder, come on in.' Turning to the woman acting as sentry to his inner sanctum, he adds: 'No calls, Miss Fallon, please. We are not to be disturbed.'

Harri follows, doubly astonished by the welcome, and that someone else got his name right. Inside, the large office is warm and almost snug, largely down to a crackling fire in the grate. Almost. It's soon evident this won't be a cosy one-on-one meeting, because there is a third figure seated in front of Graham's vast wooden desk, with a demeanour that hits Harri instantly. He's dressed like those in the CID office – dark grey suit, black brogues and a sober tie – but this man's posture signals something else, looking entirely at ease. His clean-shaven face is blank and he doesn't get up, only registers Harri's arrival with a nod and a gesture of the chair opposite, as if assured of his own importance. The superintendent moves his long, lean body behind his tidy desk and sits gingerly.

‘Welcome, Inspector Schroder,’ Graham begins. ‘This is Mr Johnson.’ He says it with a finality, that Johnson is about all the introduction they will get. That Johnson doesn’t wish to, and will not, elaborate.

‘I’m glad to be here,’ Harri says. *Remember the platitudes and the gratitude, Schroder.* ‘Though I’m still not entirely sure what for. I hope you might have news of a placement, or a task while I’m here?’

Graham’s eyes go instantly to Johnson, whose head dips barely a millimetre.

‘Would you like me to leave?’ Graham asks, and it’s plain he’s not the one who holds the cards, right here in his own office. In whatever capacity, the younger man outranks him.

‘No, you’re fine to stay for a minute.’ Johnson waves a hand, his first words denoting a superiority that comes from a public-school education. Harri notes his nails are clean and well-manicured, a man who does not get his hands dirty. So, clearly not CID.

Now Johnson does turn his attention fully to Harri, uncrossing his legs, sitting upright and seeming to open out his body. The veteran Inspektor Schroder has seen this before in superiors, the ‘buddy’ approach. This man wants something.

‘I’m sorry about all the mix up this morning, Schroder, you really should have come here directly, though it appears the message didn’t get through.’ He flicks a disdainful look towards the world outside, perhaps at its inefficiency.

‘It’s all right,’ Harri says. ‘I had a rather eventful morning. Productive, too.’

‘I heard,’ Johnson says. ‘But we need to get to the real reason for your visit. Why we requested you to come here. To London.’

Harri is rarely confused, but now is one such time.

Johnson is not with the Met, that much is obvious. 'I thought I was here to shore up police relations,' he ventures, 'and perhaps help with inquiries.'

Johnson and Graham trade looks again. It fires something in Harri – irritation for the second time in one day. That his time is being wasted, he's being used, *taken for a ride*, as the British love to say, and it translates in the gravity and volume of his voice, aimed at the superintendent. 'Will someone please tell me what is going on? *Sir.*'

Johnson sits back and crosses his legs again, a further signal that he's entrusting Harri with something. 'The Met is merely a cover, and will remain so,' he says languidly. 'To give you a base and a reason to be in London, on the pretext of building German-Anglo relations.'

'And why would I need a cover?' Harri glances over at Graham, hoping he might betray something in his expression, but the superintendent is entirely absorbed by the workings of his fountain pen. 'What would be my real purpose?'

'We have a job for you.' This time, Johnson's words carry plenty of intent.

'I already have a job,' Harri says. Pointedly. In that moment, he doesn't reveal how much it pains him to get up and go to work on some days, at how his heart is torn out of chest at the sights he's forced to witness in Hamburg, the enduring lack of resources in the Kripo, or the leftover injustices of the war, the homeless kids on the street and the families scratching for a pfennig. The fact is, he has a job, a wage, friends, and a life, for what it's worth. It's a lot to be grateful for. 'Why would I need another one?' he presses.

The two men swap furtive glances again.

'Gentlemen, I have at least ten murder cases on my books back home,' Harry bristles. 'Plus, thirty odd robberies with violence, and that's a lot of families needing explanations. I can't afford to waste time playing games.'

'You were in the SS?' Johnson asks, though the question is evidently rhetorical. Men like him don't arrive unprepared and he's sure to have a complete dossier on Harri Ewald Schroder, right down to his inside leg measurement.

The hackles rise fully, heat spiralling up Harri's neck. 'Look, I explained all this to the Allied forces, and I was fully cleared in '45,' he rails, leaping to his feet. '*All* Kripo employees were SS – that bastard Himmler saw to that, tainting us with his vile ideology. I was a police officer through the entire war, nothing more. God knows how, but I managed to stay out of all that shit.'

Johnson puts up a hand to halt Harri's protest. 'Sit down please, Herr Schroder,' he says, in a tone that's low but commanding. 'I am not accusing you of anything. But it is relevant. There's someone we want found – we *need* to find – and we think you are the best person to seek him out.'

'Me? Why me?'

'Because our intelligence says you knew him, before the war. Right now, you might be among a very few individuals who can accurately identify a very important target for us.' Johnson stands up and circles his chair, eyes drilled into Harri's. 'More importantly, the only one we can trust to do so.'

Almost mute throughout this exchange, the superintendent now coughs his presence behind the desk. 'Perhaps now you would like to be left alone?' he asks Johnson.

'Yes, thank you, Graham. The fewer people who know about this the better.'

The senior policeman exits, and Johnson pulls his chair closer to Harri, near enough to give off a faint whiff of his aftershave and the brand of cigarettes he smokes. He pulls a packet from his jacket pocket, and offers it.

'No thanks, I've given up'.

Johnson effects surprise with his eyebrows, but Harri doesn't offer an explanation – of the damage he's seen from a simple carton of Lucky Strikes, the desperation they've caused as the only stable post-war currency, small children drawn into vicious fighting over a single pack, injured and maimed in some cases for a few sticks of tobacco. Or the crippling bronchitis that saw him spend two months in a sanatorium more than three years ago, a byproduct of the fierce German winters, but probably not helped by his habit.

Johnson lights his own, draws deeply and sends a plume of white towards the office ceiling. 'Inspector, are you aware of how many Nazis were captured after the war's end?'

'I'm sure you're going to tell me that it wasn't enough,' Harri says, 'and I would agree. The Nuremberg Trials seemed to focus on the higher ranks, but too few to constitute real justice.'

'Quite right,' Johnson agrees. 'We estimate thousands of former Nazis escaped – fled when they realised Germany was destined to lose the war, through Europe, Scandinavia, then further afield, to South America. And elsewhere.'

'London?' Harri questions. 'I would have thought that's dangerously close to home, and to the Allies.'

'Not if you have a completely new identity, and a real standing in society.'

'But wouldn't you live in fear of someone from the past coming along at any moment? I've read of several cases where Nazis have been recognised by pure chance, some now in jail, or even hanged.'

'It's much less of a risk if you have money to maintain the pretence,' Johnson argues. Again, he makes a point of looking Harri in the eye, his features stern and fixed. 'Especially if you have friends in high places.'

'Oh.' Now Harri sees it – the secrecy and subterfuge of this visit, Graham leaving the room at the appropriate moment to ensure that 'need to know' basis. Johnson is acutely aware and, from his expression, there's a certainty of capturing Harri's interest. In turn, Harri has a sudden uncomfortable feeling, of being snared by his own curiosity.

He's dealt with his fair share of Nazis. A gutful. Hitler's ideology has tainted his life for almost two decades, robbed him of a family and the future he dreamed of. He thought he'd said goodbye to that ugly portion of his life. Perhaps not yet.

'So, tell me then, who is this person I'm supposed to know?'

Johnson reaches into his jacket pocket and pulls out a small black-and-white photograph, of a man in evening dress just about to get into a car, his face pulled towards the camera, by surprise and irritation, judging by his expression. As if he's been caught out. 'Do you recognise this man?'

Harri takes the picture and peers closely. 'No. Should I?'

'Not now, but you might have once. Your records say you were at the police training school in 1932, just outside Hamburg.'

'That's right,' Harri says. Barely nineteen, full of enthusiasm for a career in the force, but equally green around the gills. 'What's that got to do with anything?'

'By all accounts, you were friendly with another recruit called Helmut Praxer.'

Harri rifles back in his memory; there's almost twenty years, one world war and a mountain of grief in between, but yes, it would be hard to forget someone like Praxer. A posturing peacock, very full of himself and, Harri recalls, very popular with women. More than once, he'd to listen to

Helmut 'entertaining' a lady through the wall, when female visitors were strictly forbidden in the men's section house.

'I remember Praxer, but I haven't seen him for years, and that's not him.' Harri gestures towards the photograph. 'His features were much less sharp. I don't think the years would have changed him that much.' While he wasn't what you'd call traditionally handsome, Praxer had the sort of face women seemed drawn to, alongside his innate confidence, a Humphrey Bogart air of attraction. People who knew him dubbed it 'swagger'. In their eyes, it obviously made up for his lack of grace.

'We strongly suspect this is Praxer,' Johnson says. 'What's more, we think he's undergone substantial plastic surgery in order to change his entire appearance, and to present himself as a powerful but innocent British businessman.'

'Surgery? Is that how he's gone undetected, and for so long?' To Harri, this already seems like a tall tale.

'Let's just say he's had help from all quarters.'

Johnson gets up to open the office door and asks politely for the secretary to bring them a tray of tea. All of which gives Harri time to ruminate, and realise. There's just one word to explain this surreal situation he finds himself in, and it's already been uttered.

Nazi.

11

The Money Man

2nd December 1952

Harri

The fact tea has been requested proves to Harri that he and Johnson are settled in for the duration. Accepting a cup, Harri splays out one palm in his own silent signal: *So, tell me.*

Johnson takes a swig of his own tea and fingers his cigarette packet again, but seems to think better of it. 'The man in the picture calls himself James Remington,' he begins. 'He's chairman of a large holding company that in turn controls scores of other companies across Britain and Europe, everything from toilet roll to tanks, we think, though the weapons side of it is harder to pin down. He's very well known in the business world, but keeps himself hidden, and the majority of his wealth under wraps. He's also a genius at numbers and finance.'

The last sentence causes a distinct ripple in the surface of Harri's drink. Praxer was famed at the police training school for his ability to juggle figures and work out odds on the bets he would then offer the more gullible of recruits, everything from racing to who would be detailed to clean the latrines. If there was a probability on anything, he would accept a wager and pocket the profits.

'Remington first popped up in 1947, coming direct from Buenos Aires,' Johnson continues, grabbing Harri's attention fully. At the war's end, Argentina's capital became infamous as a popular destination for all ranks of Nazis, a perfect sanctuary for those who wished to evade justice.

'That's what first alerted us to him,' Johnson goes on. 'But then he disappeared for almost two years, before establishing his empire, from an office in London. We've spent three years tracking his pathway, and the origins of his money. Do you remember what happened to Praxer after you passed out as recruits?'

'We were both dispatched to a station north of Hamburg, along with two others,' Harri says. 'He made quite an impression in those first few months after we qualified, both good and bad, as I remember. He was always quite brash and probably too confident for some of the old-timers.'

'When was the last time you saw him?'

Harri rubs a hand over his chin. 'Oh, it must have been 1935 or '36. I got posted to a suburban station a little way south and he went elsewhere. We didn't keep in touch.'

'Do you recall what his political views were?'

'Not mine,' Harri says abruptly. 'Hitler and his National Socialists were very much in control by then, and Praxer clearly admired the ideology. He certainly spouted quite a lot of the rhetoric, and was very vocal about it.'

Johnson nods, as if Harri is merely adding to a defined picture. 'Helmut Praxer officially joined the Nazi Party in 1936, and rose rapidly in the ranks, though unlike Himmler, Goring and Goebbels, he didn't seek the limelight. He was quite content to stay in the background, but his role was pivotal.' Now Johnson does take out a cigarette and lights it, puffing rapidly. 'He was the Nazis' money man, the key to juggling millions of Reichsmarks and dollars, turning stolen gold and artwork into hard currency. It's not an overstatement to say that, without him, Hitler could never have financed the war.'

While Harri is shocked at Praxer's reach and prominence, his sheer audacity rings true to the man he trained with. Ambition and arrogance had been evident from the start. 'But I don't understand, if you know this James Remington is Praxer, why can't you detain and question him?' he asks. Back in Hamburg, the occupying British forces had carte blanche to interrogate anyone they suspected as a former Nazi, Harri included. He'd had to fill out the ridiculous questions on the thirty-three-page *Fragebogen,* detailing whether he'd played with toy soldiers as a child. When his sarcasm got the better of him, Harri was subjected to an intense grilling by a senior officer, all to maintain his job as a Kripo inspektor.

Johnson gets up and circles the room, frowning at his shoes clipping on the floorboards until his agitation breaks free. 'We're *almost* certain, but not one hundred per cent. And Remington is well respected, despite some of his murky dealings. He has friends in the House of Commons and the Lords. Plus, he brings in a lot of tax revenue, which the British Government is desperate for, and in certain circles he's thought of as a great asset. We have to tread very carefully, which means we need concrete evidence, or heads will roll.' He shoots a look that says his own would be the first on the block.

'So, what can I possibly do?' Harri says. 'I don't recognise the man, even if you say he is Praxer. Plus, he's hardly likely to greet me as a long-lost friend, is he?'

Johnson flashes an irritated look. 'We're all too aware of that. Only when we're certain of his personal provenance will we have the power to question him. And even then we'll have to do it quickly, and under the radar, before he can exert any of his influence.'

'So?' Harri presses. His own impatience is bubbling to the surface. 'You still haven't told me what I can do.'

'Praxer has been able to change his appearance dramatically, but there are some things he cannot alter. His voice, for example, which I'm told has a certain trait, even though his English accent is cut glass. And a certain way he has of holding himself, a quirk that he can't easily shed.'

Instantly, Johnson has jogged a memory, and Harri is able to recall a specific manner of Praxer's, principally when his blood was up. It's difficult to describe in words, other than a sudden high inflection to his voice when he was aroused, either by competition or anger. It was often followed by an odd movement of his square jaw, as if he was grinding his teeth in a rhythm. But would Harri recognise it after all these years, and couldn't Praxer have eradicated it?

'If you know all of this, you must have a witness already?' he queries.

'We did.' Over a prolonged silence, Johnson suddenly finds his nailbed mesmerising. Then he turns his face upwards. Blank.

'And this person is . . .?' Harri asks.

'Dead.'

12

Arrow Through the Heart

2nd December 1952

Harri

It's Harri's turn to stand, leaning on the mantle of the fireplace and feeling the heat on his legs. He's reluctant to press Johnson on the details, but the question needs posing: 'Dead dead, or murdered dead?'

'Unclear,' Johnson admits. 'He washed up in the Thames several weeks ago. Feasted on by fish and so we've no idea how he died.'

Murdered dead then.

'And so, you think I should somehow befriend this former colleague of mine who may or may not recognise me, engineer a drink with him, observe his behaviour and report back to you. All without getting myself killed?'

Johnson swallows, dry dust judging by the prominence of his Adam's apple above his shirt collar. 'Hmm, it's a bit more complicated than that. Remington has disappeared, having possibly suspected there's a plan to expose him as

Praxer. His office is deflecting all enquiries and calls, and surveillance on his London home has thrown up nothing.'

'So, why don't you just sit it out?' Harri asks. 'You've waited this long, and he's bound to surface at some point, when he's confident you've lost interest.'

'Ordinarily we would,' Johnson says. 'But there's some urgency. Remington is due to sign a large contract with the British Government for raw materials which will aid the nuclear programme.' He remembers to swallow some tea this time. 'It's politically very sensitive. If the deal is made and it subsequently emerges that Remington's money is dirty, steeped in the spoils of the Holocaust, it will bring this government down, politically and financially. There's a certain group of people who believe that will happen, meaning we have no choice but to stop the contract being signed. We imagined having a window of time, which is why you had a few days to settle in here, but the date of the signing has been moved forward. It's now a week from today.'

To Harri, the solution remains commonsensical and very obvious. What's more, it doesn't involve him. 'Then stop those ministers from signing,' he reasons. 'Tell them what he's done. Surely their conscience will put a halt to it? At the very least postpone it, until Praxer shows himself and you can identify him for sure.'

Johnson sighs impatiently, perhaps at the level of Harri's naivety. 'They are virtually deaf to anyone who tries to stall this. Some very influential people stand to make a lot of money from the deal, those men in industry who, in turn, prop up the government. For others, it's a political advantage, in keeping up with the Russians and Americans in the nuclear race. We don't have the power to simply stop it. Yet. But if we can present solid evidence that he was a Nazi – and is still aiding and abetting other war criminals –

then we'll have a valid reason to question him, long enough to prevent the signing.'

'Which brings me to my next question,' Harri says. 'Who exactly is "we"? You're not a policeman. So, are you with the security services, or military intelligence? Which one is it?'

Johnson reverts to type, his face betraying nothing. 'I can't honestly tell you, Schroder. Or it will put you in more danger.'

'Let me get this straight,' Harri demands, his irritation mounting again. 'I'm expected to undertake an investigation of a man I barely know, for a country and an agency that's not my own, and for what? What possible motivation could I have?'

'Because he's extremely dangerous. Praxer was deadly then, as he is now. Perhaps not with a gun, but with his mind and his cunning – we have it on good authority that he calculated exactly how much it cost for each Jew to be gassed, down to the last pfennig. If that's not cold-blooded, I don't know what is.' Johnson pulls himself up in his chair ready to deliver his final shot. The accurate bullseye.

'So, you see, Schroder, it's not for one country, or one government. This is for humanity.'

For a minute, Harri wonders if this Johnson has been talking to his good friend Georgie Young, in gaining tips on how to engage and convince the Kripo man, to land that arrow right into his heart's core. As a journalist, she'd wheedled her way into his key murder investigation back in '46, spotting his Achilles' heel almost at their first meeting. 'I saw that you cared,' she'd later told him. 'It mattered to you that women were being murdered, and it meant that you aligned with others who also felt concern. You just couldn't help it, Harri.'

Achilles' heel is one thing, he thinks now. *Gullible is another. Stupid enough to get yourself killed constitutes a huge leap beyond that.*

Annoyingly, though, Georgie had it right. He's here now, if feeling hoodwinked by the British authorities as to the method of bringing him to London. Being present, he might as well prove useful. And it beats the beat, or traffic duty and chasing runaways. What has he got to lose? Bar his colleagues and a stack of cases (which will never go away), there's no one to tether Harri Schroder to Hamburg, nothing to anchor him to a city that remains, in places, like bombed-out shell. He has no wife, and no family close enough. The war saw to all of that.

You may well regret this, Harri Schroder, but life is for living, isn't it? Just don't think about the dying bit.

He pushes himself off the mantlepiece, and moves to sit squarely in front of Johnson. Even as he mouths the words, he wonders if he'll live to regret them. 'Where do we start?'

Johnson says he'll be put in touch with someone who has experience of this underground culture of dodging justice and assimilating back into society, and where to begin his search in the vast and grubby network.

'You mean a Nazi hunter?' Harri queries.

'For want of a better phrase, yes. Although Wolinski won't be like a partner, as such. Merely a contact for intelligence.'

'Why is that?'

'He's no longer mobile,' Johnson explains, with what sounds like a tinge of regret.

'Oh?' If it's not death, Harri wonders if he's equally in line for a maiming.

'A genuine accident, I promise you,' Johnson adds. 'Damn shame. He was one of our best on the ground.'

'Then I'll need someone else,' Harri asserts. 'I don't know the city well enough yet, and it will slow me down if I don't have that knowledge to hand.'

Johnson nods. 'All right, I'm sure we can find you someone. I'll speak to Superintendent Graham.'

'No need,' Harri says firmly. 'I already have someone in mind.'

13

The Exit Door?

2nd December 1952

Dexie

'*Me?* Are you sure?' Dexie's face skews with more than surprise. The sight of Harri's return to West End Central, earlier than expected, prompts an inexplicable lift in her.

'I got the feeling you wanted to get out of uniform, and do something different,' he says, lips twisting in confusion. 'Sorry, but did I read that wrong?'

'No! Not at all. But . . . erm . . . are you certain I'm the right person for the job?' The prosect is inviting, though she harbours a sneaking suspicion about his motives. 'In spite of your views on my not making tea for all and sundry, neither am I a walking *A–Z*,' she tells him. Straight. 'If it's just a guide you want, you'll have to look elsewhere.'

'You drive a hard bargain, WPC Dexter. It's true I do need someone who knows the city, but it's more than that. I want someone I can trust.'

'Then the answer is yes, though it's less of the WPC, and more of the Dexie.'

He laughs. 'But you don't even know what it involves.'

'You seem to be offering me the opportunity to get out of these god-awful shoes, plus an escape from the beat. You're lucky I don't bite your hand off.'

'If you put it like that . . .' He rubs a several fingers over his chin, as if mired in thought. 'Listen, it's obvious you're still tied up here, so let's meet tomorrow morning and I'll explain it all. You may not like what's in store, and I could easily come away with my hand intact.'

'Don't bet on it, but all right, I'll see you first thing.'

Dexie watches him turn and walk out, with not one, but several bubbles now vying for space inside her stomach. Today, much like any other early shift, she had donned her police-issue armour at the crack of dawn, all the while wondering – hoping – that this would be the day to offer up change. Nothing earth shattering, merely something different, to divert just a little and eke out a path forward, instead of the circular warren she trudges through daily, only to arrive back at the beginning. In those dreaded shoes.

She's not a great believer in fate, and yet the fact she'd bargained with the shift sergeant for an extra hour in the CID office this morning makes her more inclined. The question remains: is this slightly grizzled German detective the one to offer up a way out, and a key to the exit door?

14

Deliberation

2nd December 1952

Harri

Hands deep in the pockets of his grubby overcoat, Harri ruminates over the task ahead as he leaves West End Central and steps out into the darkness of late afternoon. Up ahead, the early Christmas lights mix with reds and yellows of rush hour, buses backed up like centipedes, nudging forward with frustration. He's always known that the war's consequences would continue to ripple for years to come, and not just in the gaping craters dotted across London that have yet to be fixed. Trust between nations and its people takes a lot longer to regrow, especially when the roots have been hacked to pieces.

Now, he's been singled out, principally for the memories he holds inside his head. As always, Harri wonders if it's his duty as a German policeman – officially if not ideologically once employed by the infamous SS – to pay reparation to the British. To weed out his former countrymen who can still do damage and give back a little of what Hitler robbed so mercilessly. Previously, he's railed against the argument that ordinary Germans should be made to suffer for the madness of one man, that 'guilt of a nation' thinking so prominent on people's lips. Except that he is in a position to help. Morally, it seems the correct path.

But right isn't always sensible, is it?

Heading towards the warmth and comfort of the Lyons Corner House on The Strand, he's also troubled by something else. To say he accepted the job rashly is not in doubt, swayed in the moment by Johnson's emotive rhetoric to work for humanity. Harri's next impetuous action is what needles him now, the recruitment of a woman he barely knows to a venture that is potentially dangerous. Johnson never denied it could be, and in that vague manner of the security services, he had sidestepped the issue nicely. Does Harri have the right to expose someone else to potential jeopardy?

It's not enough to say Dexie's presence will undoubtedly ease his task, or that he simply likes her company, a realisation that lights up as he's bathed in the dazzling illuminations of Leicester Square. In all faith, he can't deny it. Much like Georgie before her, he senses a difference in Dexie, something not easily distilled into words, either German or English. Like Georgie, she seems professional and capable, but also strong, as Hella had once been, before his wife's confidence was sapped by war and death, and what felt like a million tons of firepower above the collective heads of Hamburgers. Before their world came crashing down, Hella had been his rock, affording him daily strength. He misses that the most, being side by side with one you trust. Sharing. Now, he might well be guilty of trying to replace that connection to the detriment of others. And is that ethical, or fair?

This feeling hovers like a cloud as Harri eats a good meal amid the clientele of Lyons, both the food and the surroundings a darn sight more colourful than Mrs P might produce back at the boarding house. His stomach full, and the odour of his coat beginning to attract attention, Harri makes his way back to Bayley Street, via a quick stop in a phone box to ring Johnson's contact and arrange a meeting for the next morning. Beforehand, however, he will disclose all to Dexie and hold nothing back, leaving her free to decide. Simple as that.

For now, Harri wants only to set a match to the kindle in his tiny attic grate and sink a glass of the good Scotch he's bought, injecting warmth into his veins as he huddles under his blankets. If he's blessed with sleep, it will be a bonus.

Mrs Painter, an archetypal sentinel of landlady legend, emerges from the back kitchen as his key slots in the door. Nothing wrong with her hearing, clearly.

'Evening Mr Schroder, a good day, I hope?'

'Fine, thank you, Mrs P. And how are you?'

'Oh, mustn't grumble.'

But she does – about the weather, the damp, the traffic, neighbours and the price of groceries. Then a swift pause, if only to draw breath. 'Ooh, Mr Schroder, I don't like to be rude, but there's quite a smell as you came in. A little bit pungent, if I may say.'

Nothing awry with her nose, either. 'Sorry, but my coat got dragged through the mud, and possibly something else, and I've only managed to get the worst off,' Harri apologises. 'I'll take it to be cleaned as soon as I can.'

'Give it here.' She reaches out, eyes sparkling and suddenly galvanised, it seems, by the challenge of grime. 'I'll have it cleaned and dry by the morning, hanging next to the fire.' She turns briskly on her heels towards the kitchen, and Harri finds himself somehow compelled to follow her and the coat. There goes his Scotch and solace. But the room is warm, and when she offers tea and a seat by the coal-fired range, he almost melts into the soft, worn upholstery. Her chatter rolls over him, about the police recruits she's had as lodgers in the past ('nice lads, most of them') and the never-ending chores of a house frau. His eyelids feel heavy, and he can feel himself . . .

'Mr Schroder . . . Mr Schroder, wake up. It's time for your bed, I imagine.'

Mrs P's small, perfectly round face looms above his as Harri's eyes struggle to focus. 'Oh, so sorry, I just . . .' A slight weight on his stomach turns out to be Scooter, curled up and snoozing away. The terrier opens one eye on being disturbed.

'You've had a hard day, clearly,' she says. 'I've lit the fire in your room. Up you go.'

The tender echoes of his own, late mother come rushing back, and he could kiss Mrs P, for making him feel at home and cared for. Welcome, too. Maybe even staunch Kripo officers need pampering from time to time. From now on, he won't have a thing said against her overcooked eggs and anaemic toast. Perhaps.

15

Wolli

3rd December 1952

Harri

As directed, Harri heads back to New Scotland Yard before nine a.m., grateful for Mrs P's laundry skills, hunkering in the coat that smells a good deal more fragrant, if suspiciously like the tin of Vim that she seems to spray liberally around the place. The chill wind whips mercilessly along the wide aspect of Tottenham Court Road, but the sky remains an unceasing seam of blue, a gift for early December.

He's shown back into Superintendent Graham's office, where the senior man issues a police identity card in the name of Harry Stoneham, plus an envelope of cash that seems well in excess of a detective's monthly wage back in Hamburg. He hands over keys to a small car, parked in a lock-up garage near to King's Cross station.

'And how do I get in touch with Johnson?' Harri asks.

'You don't.' Graham reaches into a desk drawer and for a minute, Harri thinks he might be about to be offered a firearm, shuddering at the thought. Instead, Graham pulls out a slip of paper, scrawled with a single phone number: *Whitehall 232*.

'That's for emergencies only,' he explains gravely. 'Johnson assures me it's manned round the clock, but only if you need urgent assistance, understood?'

'Yes, sir.' Harri takes that to mean rescue, possibly from the clutches of death.

'You can use any of the Met's information resources,' Graham goes on. 'We have our own, let's say, unique filing systems, but anyone of our officers should know their way around those.' He reaches out to shake Harri's hand. 'Look after our people, won't you? We need them back in one piece.'

Assuming she accepts the job, Harri thinks of Dexie and her skills already demonstrated. 'In all honesty, sir, I don't think you need to worry about that.'

She's waiting for him next to the front desk at West End Central, though he almost walks past, not recognising the hair that's unpinned and settling on her collar, the muted browns of her clothes and what seems like a softer outline, not just to her body but her entire demeanour. When Dexie turns and smiles, it's as if a burden has been lifted from her shoulders, far heavier than the weight of her uniform.

His eyes go immediately to her feet, now sporting a pair of brown leather brogues. 'You got rid of the shoes!' he blurts. 'Oh, sorry, I don't mean to offend, it's just you did say . . .'

'I did say, and no offence taken. My toes are already having a party in there.' She looks down at herself, pushing out her arms. 'Will this do, for whatever it is we're doing? I wasn't quite sure what would be appropriate.' She's paired practical tweed trousers with a thin weave jumper and a tailored brown jacket, while over her arm there's a beige mackintosh. 'If I don't make it into CID, I can at least look like I'm one of them,' she says, pulling on a neat trilby made of brown felt.

Harri dons his own hat. 'You look both practical and perfect,' he says with genuine honesty. 'Come on, we need to talk elsewhere.'

Dexie leads them through several back streets to an Italian café that's only half full and void of uniformed officers. 'One of my little boltholes after a shift,' she explains. 'A place to catch my breath. And I can vouch that the coffee is more than decent.'

'OK,' Harri says weightily, through the steam rising from two cups placed on the table. 'First of all, I'm going to come clean.'

'About what?'

'I might have been a bit hasty in asking for your help on this venture.' He looks into the thick, dark liquid, rather than face the sharp glint of her gaze. 'The job I've been assigned – the task ahead – could be dangerous. It's a complete unknown, and I wouldn't want to . . . well, you have the choice to bow out.'

She merely sits back, her chest rising as she draws in air, those green eyes to the ceiling. In seconds, they are back on him. Unmoving. 'So, what does this task involve exactly?' she says slowly.

So, he tells her, head-to-head in a low whisper, exactly as Johnson spelled it out, along with the fatal end of the poor soul fished out of the Thames. 'This Remington, or Praxer, is apparently very powerful, and has a lot to lose if he's exposed,' Harri adds. 'Which means he will risk plenty to protect himself. If he is the same Praxer of the Reich, as they claim, he's also ruthless.'

She cocks her head. 'When you knew him, did you imagine him capable of murder, of sending millions to their deaths?'

Harri shrugs. 'I'm not sure. Despite his politics, I might have doubted it before the war, but now, who knows what anyone is capable of? Those long years changed everyone. I remember that he wasn't a kind man, someone who it felt good to have around. There was always an edge, and when he was drunk, he could be especially cruel to the new recruits. But murder and genocide? That's a big leap.'

Dexie drains her coffee and looks into the leftover grounds, as if they will provide an answer. 'I'm not afraid,' she says quietly. 'If I was, I wouldn't go out on the beat every day. We might look like the soft touch of the force, but we women still face the drunks and the tougher toms on the streets after dark.'

'Toms?'

'The prostitutes,' she says. 'The older ones have been hardened by years on the game, and I'm certain that some of their pimps would slash us from ear to ear as soon as look at us. To protect their profits rather than the girls. Besides, if you think I'm putting my feet back in those ruddy shoes so soon, you can think again.'

'All right,' he says, 'but if at any point you want to get out . . .'

'Would you say the same to yourself?' she shoots back. 'Or if another man was sitting where I am?'

Harri purses his lips. 'Point taken. But we're agreed – we look out for each other?'

'Agreed,' she says. 'In which case, why don't we get to work?'

* * *

Dexie steers them north towards Camden, seeming to know which trolleybus to board and the criss-crossing of bus routes instinctively. Harri decides to leave it until later to come clean about a car being available, as he gathers courage to drive in traffic far heavier than back home. He stares from their seat on the top deck, at shoppers laden with early Christmas shopping, wondering where he might be on the day itself – here or in Hamburg? And will it be a celebration for him?

'How does this compare with where you live?' Dexie asks, over the throb of the engine.

'Oh, not much of a comparison, really,' Harri says. 'Hamburg is better than it was, certainly, though the re-building seems to be taking an age. The people have heart, but it's like a long, slow recovery after a major coronary. No one's quite sure how much to push it, or test it, in fear that it might give out entirely.'

'Do you miss it when you're away?'

He considers for a second or two, peering at the moving landscape beyond the window. 'Yes and no. I miss friends, but part of me thinks I should have made the break and started somewhere afresh a while ago. At the same time, there's always been a reason not to.' He smiles to himself. 'Apathy mainly.'

The real reason, of course, is Hella and Lily, pulling on Harri's emotions like a ghostly tether, even though he knows his wife would have hated for him to put life on hold in her memory. If only someone could tell him quite how to loosen or lengthen that truss, enough to build a life away. Severing the bond seems so final, leaving him to hang in limbo. Upright, functional and yet stranded.

He takes his focus from the window, seeing Dexie half turned towards him, though he senses her thoughts are most definitely elsewhere.

'Yes, I know exactly what you mean,' she murmurs.

Just off Camden High Street and a stone's throw from the Regent's Canal, they locate the café where Johnson's man has asked to meet, the windows running with condensation and a puff of steam issued each time the door opens and shuts. Easily recognised by the dark maroon cap perched on his head, Piotr Wolinski sits at a table to the side, eyes on the door and scanning customers as they come in and out. His chin lifts as they walk in, but he doesn't get up as they approach, possibly due to his left leg, which is at an angle to his chair, outstretched and unbending, a walking stick propped nearby. Instead, he offers a rough hand and friendly nod, looks briefly at their identity cards, but with no obvious surprise that Dexie is party to their conversation. To Harri, he appears weary and unwell, a grey pallor to match strands of his hair just visible, hands trembling as he lights a cigarette. There's a lingering odour of last night's alcohol coming across the table.

'Pleased to meet you, Piotr.' Despite his prowess with the English language, Harri's tongue struggles to get around the Polish pronunciation.

'Just call me Wolli,' the man says, in an odd combination of Cockney with remnants of an East European twist. 'Everybody does.'

'I'm Dexie.' She extends a hand and when he takes it firmly, Harri thinks it speaks volumes about an operative who has known and trusted plenty of women as equals over the years. The tea ordered, Wolli leans in, keen to get down to business.

'Being from Hamburg, you'll know what chaos it was straight after the war,' he begins. 'At the time, the Allied forces were very active in tracking down every Nazi they could, the bigger fish and the small fry. There were various groups tasked with this, the British War Crimes Commission being the most prominent of them. I was recruited to a Polish unit that operated in northern Germany.' He slurps from his mug. 'Some of the wealthier Nazis with family money had already moved continents, helped to South America through the rat lines via Italy. But there were still plenty of middle-ranking SS to pursue, those who didn't have enough funds to ghost away. In the beginning, we had a decent amount of success, but as the months wore on, the Allies' enthusiasm for the hunt dribbled to almost nothing, the money ran out and all the units were officially disbanded.'

'When was that?' Harri asks.

'End of '46.' Wolli's frown is a reflection of his disdain.

'So, is that when you stopped looking?'

Wolli shakes his head fervently. 'Up until the late forties, there was . . . well, let's say, a small band of hunters who were kept afloat by interested parties somewhere within Whitehall, though we never asked where the money came from. We simply worked to trace Nazis living nearer to home.'

'The likes of Praxer, you mean?' Dexie says.

Wolli nods, turns towards the counter and gestures to the waitress for a re-fill. He waits until she leaves before he picks up the story again. 'As early as 1943, we know there was a group of high-ranking Nazis who predicted the tide of the war and Germany's loss, moving to protect themselves, all behind Hitler's back. They squirrelled away vast sums of money into overseas accounts, mainly in Spain and South America, where the right-wing regimes were sympathetic to Hitler's old crowd.'

'And that's where Praxer comes in?'

'Yes. He's the genius behind the money, a walking calculator it's been said.'

'So why didn't he stay in Argentina?' Harri asks. 'From what I've heard, die-hard Nazis can have a very good life in Buenos Aires with all the Germanic comforts of home.'

'We think there weren't enough big business opportunities for him, and that his British wife was unhappy away from home. Plus, if you can believe this, he's thought to have been quite enticed by the life of the English upper classes. Fancies himself as a member of the Establishment, hunting and la-di-da house parties. Mainly gatherings where the likes of Oswald Mosley and his wife would have been very welcome.'

Dexie's eyebrows rise.

'Yes, I know,' Wolli agrees. 'It's ironic to say the least, since Praxer's financing helped the Nazis and the Luftwaffe to annihilate a good portion of this fair countryside, and now he's enjoying the spoils. From his point of view, London is also centre of banking, and we think he is still the pivot for money that helps shield Nazis from capture. It's an expensive business keeping so many under wraps, wherever they are.'

A sudden realisation jabs at Harri's brain. 'Do you mean he's bankrolling something like Odessa?' No one has been able to prove it, but he's heard rumours back in Hamburg, of an underground network called Odessa, whose purpose is not only to shield war criminals, but to keep the spirit of the Reich alive. The very thought makes him shudder, and at the time he'd hoped it was simply a product of outlandish gossip.

Wolli's expression says not. 'Odessa, Spinne, Edelweiss – they have different names, but all are thought to be ghost organisations supporting old Nazis, and almost impossible to track. They have a real talent for disappearing.'

'Or hiding in plain sight, it seems,' Dexie suggests.

'Absolutely,' Wolli affirms. 'But we're betting that Praxer's overconfidence will prove his downfall. Clearly, he thinks he's untouchable.'

'Where was the last sighting of him?' Harri asks, silently praying it's not in one of England's great country houses. His accent will take him so far, but not into the seat of the upper classes.

'Two weeks ago, at a house party in Kent, though we suspect he is now back in London. The signing of the agreement is six days away, and he might have a few key people to negotiate with before then. He's lying low, and our surveillance hasn't picked him up at the Mayfair house for two weeks. He could be anywhere. It's your job to find him.'

Oh great, Harri thinks, *only one of eight million in Greater London to sift through*. 'Any pointers?' he asks Wolli. 'Any hobbies or pastimes he can't keep away from? Gambling, casinos, drinking, good friends, for instance.'

Wolli shakes his head. 'That's what makes it so hard. This man seems to have acquaintances rather than friends, he's teetotal and doesn't gamble himself, though he does own a small, fairly elite casino.'

'I'm inclined to like him less by the minute,' Harri murmurs. Praxer's aversion to staking his own cash is ironic, given how he made extra money in the police section house.

'Is there anything at all?' Dexie pushes. 'What about his wife?'

'Ah.' Wolli holds up a finger, pulls out a buff envelope and slides it across the table. 'This is everything we have on Alicia Remington. From what we can gather, he adores her, and will do almost anything to keep her happy, including moving continents, which in turn would have prompted all that facial surgery. Devoted to her, you might say. He shuns the limelight in the London social scene, but she's quite happy to emerge from time to time. She is currently at the London house, but she's had no contact with her husband that we can determine.'

Wolli draws back his hands and rubs at his thigh, as if to signal that's his job discharged, there's no more to tell. Harri knows he shouldn't – almost doesn't want to know the answer – but feels compels to ask. 'Recent injury?' he says, gesturing towards Wolli's outstretched leg.

The face that reflects back is almost devoid of expression, save for the tiniest spark of fury. 'Two years,' he says. 'Fell off a scaffold. Broken in six places, and as many months in a cast.'

'In the field?' Harri presses. Again, he doesn't *want* Dexie to hear this, but she should. She deserves to know the arena they are entering, of gladiators and lions. Those who might fight to the death.

Wolli nods. This time his face reflects the entire story. He was pushed. Hard. Which is quite the opposite of how Johnson explained it. 'Goes with the territory,' the old soldier adds wearily, before hauling himself up. 'Be careful out there.' He pushes a torn strip of a cigarette packet towards Harri with a number written on it. 'Contact me if you need something, but only if you have to. I can't skip out of the way at short notice like I used to.'

'Thanks. We'll try not to.'

16

Something in the Air

3rd December 1952

Dexie

'So, what do you think?' Harri asks when Wolli has limped from the café.

Dexie looks towards the ceiling, where the combined fug of cigarette smoke and chip fat is suspended in a greasy grey cloud. She feels stifled. 'I think I need some fresh air.'

They walk along the canal, keeping pace with sluggish traffic of working barges chugging up and down, Harri ambling alongside in silence. *He's giving me room to consider*, she thinks, without barking orders or demanding action instantly. And he isn't wrong – it's a real case, with consequences to success or failure, and not just to their careers. From Wolli's grave warning, it's clear lives could be at stake. How does she feel about that? Strangely all right, she realises. Not scared, not yet anyway. Excited? That might be going too far, but there's something within that's ignited.

WPC Dexter would never choose to run into a burning

building, but neither does this prompt her to flee in the opposite direction. Unlike Harri, she's never knowingly met a Nazi. No, that's a lie. During the Blitz, there was a man brought into the ARP station by the scruff of his neck, apparently found in a bombed basement scrabbling to burn a load of pamphlets, the singed remnants extoling the Nazis' achievements. The police who brought him in branded him a 'fifth columnist', and then 'a filthy spy' but to Dexie he looked like a sad and lonely man, who spoke in a posh British accent. Then she thinks of Harri's accent and laughs, but only to herself.

Over the years, and especially during the war, she's learnt to have faith in her instinct, and the very fact that she's on this canal bank, alive and well, means it's served her ably so far. Clearly, Praxer is a particular brand of Nazi, but none of what she's heard deters her. He's a felon, plain and simple – guilty of heinous crimes against people – and he should be stopped. In or out of uniform, that's her job.

Dexie stops at a bench and sits, pulling out the information from Wolli's envelope. She inspects the black-and-white pictures enclosed, passing them to Harri one by one. Several are of Alicia Remington alone, plus a cutting from a magazine society page. She is beautiful and groomed, a lean build with porcelain skin, dark, smooth hair and painted bow lips. Dexie is not in that world, but she knows it's a look that takes time and money to maintain, like a film star or a model. Or a woman who has a loving husband, generous with his bank balance; she could be a trophy or the love of his life, but either way he will want to show her off.

'It seems to me that our way in has to be via the wife,' she says to Harri. 'From what Wolli says, she is his weak point. And in my experience, if he's that devoted to her, he won't be able to stay away for too long.' Dexie says it with a conviction that surprises even her, though unable to decide if it's down to five years on the beat, or her thirty-three years on this earth with a woman's instinct.

Harri doesn't question her reasoning, only says: 'Do you propose going in by the back door, or the front? Organising an invitation to a high-brow party where Mrs Remington might mingle will take contacts we don't have, and securing a servant's position in the Remington household seems extreme and time consuming.' He pauses, with an anxious look. 'That's time we don't have.'

'Sideways,' Dexie announces.

'What do you mean?'

She holds out a small monochrome photograph of Alicia Remington captured unawares as she exits a shopfront on what looks to be a smart London street. She's wearing no hat, and her hair is neatly styled. 'Look closer,' Dexie suggests, pointing to the name above the shopfront, clearly a hairdressing salon. 'Whether or not she's trying to keep under the radar, a woman like Mrs Remington does not relinquish her hair appointment for any length of time. Not for love nor money.' This time, it *is* her sex which prompts such confidence in this assertion.

'And what would you say about a trip to the hairdresser, Miss Dexter?' he says.

'Oh, I'll suffer if I must, Herr Schroder. For the good of the country.' She gets up, slipping the package into her handbag. 'No time like the present.'

Dexie only knows of the hairdressing salon by sight, she tells Harri, since it's far too upmarket for her custom, and she wouldn't spend her hard-earned wages on such folly.

'Really? Not even as a treat?' he questions, from the top

of the number 29 back into central London. 'When you need to give yourself a lift?'

'There are far better things to spend your money on,' she insists.

'Such as?' His look is of genuine interest, rather than interrogation.

'Well, erm . . .' Quite. What does she spend it on? Practical clothes, trips to the cinema, a couple of café meals each week when the section house food is dire, and the odd night out with the beat crew. Oh yes, a week with her mother in Cornwall for the past two summers. Hardly extravagant, is it? Luckily, Harri's attention has been caught by something beyond the bus window, and she's excused the embarrassment of having to fabricate a life outside of the Met.

From the bus stop, they weave on foot towards the chic streets of St James, lined with well-kept and freshly painted shopfronts that transcend even the gloom of London in winter. Sable Hair and Beauty sits between a jeweller's and a women's boutique, very much at home amid the opulence, its gold lettering intact and well maintained. From across the streets and through the large plate-glass window, it's plainly busy, even on a weekday.

'Shall we go in together?' Harri says.

Dexie wrinkles her nose, trying to think how to let a senior officer down gently. Whether he's on home territory or not, the inspector will be used to marching in with this official warrant card and demanding answers. 'Hmm, not sure a nosy husband, even the pretend variety, will wheedle out the same information as two women talking,' she suggests. 'Shall I see how much I gain playing the customer?'

'All right. I'll tuck myself in the pub doorway opposite and wait.'

As she pulls back her shoulders and steps towards the hairdresser's, a new thought strikes: *He trusts me. Like he said he would.* In the next second, however, she's hit by a wave of anxiety. Dexie is self-assured enough in her uniform, viewing it as a kind of shield, but in her civvies? As herself?

You pitched for this, she tells herself. *Maybe not overtly, but in everything you implied*. Time to put it into practice. The doorbell tinkles as she enters, forcing a confidence in her stride towards a young woman behind the desk.

'Good morning, how can I help?' the receptionist says.

Dexie is conscious of her voice climbing several social strata. 'Good morning, I was wondering if by any chance . . .' she stops mid-sentence, moving her eyes upwards to the woman's newly lacquered hair. 'Ooh, I do love what you've done to it,' she gestures.

'Thank you, it was only styled this morning.' The receptionist touches the stiff strands and smiles, flushed with such flattery.

'Well, it really suits you,' Dexie goes on. In her next breath, she's apologising for her less than elegant outfit, explaining her arrival back in the city from 'the country', and a sudden invite to a large party. Could they possibly fit her in? 'It would *such* be a life-saver if you could.'

'I'm sure that's possible,' the salon girl says, catching onto the fervour of what's bound to be a society occasion, and fingering her hair again.

'Oh, you're a darling!' Dexie brays in her faux country-girl accent, watching the receptionist leaf through the large salon diary next to the till, scanning for appointments. 'And I'm very flexible. Can I see what space you have?' She leans keenly over the pages, pointing at a date and time, as the woman writes down details on a small card. 'Thank you so much, and enjoy your evening,' Dexie twitters on leaving.

In reality, she wouldn't be seen dead at any society party, though she can't deny enjoying the last few moments. It felt better than any forced play-acting at school.

'Bingo,' she beams, reaching Harri at the pub entrance. Her own fake appointment is irrelevant, but a glance at the salon diary has afforded what they most need. 'Alicia Remington has a regular style and set every week.'

'And?'

'We're in luck, it's tomorrow at ten thirty.'

'Perfect,' Harri says, then scratches at his chin. 'We've got precisely six days until this proposed signing. Even so, I do worry the wife won't lead us to the prize quickly enough.'

'Where does that leave us?' she says.

'Perhaps we need to do use our time wisely, and do some background digging on potential hideaways that Praxer might use?'

'Agreed,' Dexie says. 'How's your sway with Scotland Yard?'

'Given the circumstances, I think I probably have an all-hours pass,' he replies.

'That's what I was hoping. Much as I hate to say it, a little bit of paperwork could be our saving grace.'

Harri's identity card works its magic at New Scotland Yard, the desk sergeant directing them up to the Criminal Record Office without question. In a large room, with fires at either end, there are tables and chairs dotted around the floorspace, the perimeter lined entirely with small wooden filing drawers, stacked above head height. As per usual, a blue haze of pipe and cigarette smoke loiters around the light fittings, while underneath men and women are busily typing or scribbling, some flicking through piles of small, rectangular cards.

Dexie recognises the quiet activity of the room and feels instantly at home. Only two weeks before, she'd been the one to make a connection in the CID room between a wanted armed robber and a registered pawn broker. Of course, the man-heavy team who left to apprehend the suspect didn't include her, but their success earned her a 'well done, Dex,' from the inspector after the arrest. How she glowed, and then hated herself for living off the warmth of his praise.

She sees Harri's eyes widen at the sheer number of drawers, each holding hundreds of cards. 'I've got a teetering pile of paper on my desk, and a cupboard we call "the black hole",' he sighs. 'That's bad enough. Where do we even start?'

This, though, is Dexie's world, where she's in her element. She commandeers an empty desk and targets one of two civilian women in the room who have their own work areas. 'You clearly know this place inside out,' she says, approaching one. 'I wonder if you can . . .' Within minutes, they've struck up a rapport, the filing clerk leading her to one corner section and pulling out several drawers.

'Here,' Dexie says, pushing a stack of reference cards towards Harri. 'These are known business contacts of Remington's, some legitimate, some fraudulent.' Dexie rifles through the envelope from Wolli and finds a typewritten list of Remington holding companies and subsidiaries. 'Pull out anything that makes mention of these, and we'll cross reference to see if we've got any locations to investigate.'

Harri's forehead creases. 'Are you always this efficient?'

'Um, not always,' she says. 'Though I suppose I do get a thrill when I find a connection, however small. It's quite pathetic really.'

'Not at all. Connections are everything,' Harri says. 'In life, on paper.' He coughs and looks away. 'There's always a chance our man is hiding in these cards.'

* * *

After almost two hours, during which Harri insists on fetching tea and bacon sandwiches from the canteen, Dexie's fingers are numb, her eyes smarting with the smoke and the words are beginning to flicker at speed. But they've pulled out nine cards between them, matching up to three locations – one casino and two business addresses at either end of the city. She draws a hand over her face and blinks several times.

'Time to call it a day?' Harri says. 'I feel at least one of my eyeballs is about to pop forth and roll around the table in agony.'

'And that would be very messy, don't you think?' She pulls back her shoulders and rubs at her neck. 'I'm wrung out too, but I can't do another canteen or a café, not without a walk first.'

It's just gone three p.m. as they leave the austere New Scotland Yard, the building wrapped in a light mist that's seeming more ghostly by the minute. Sounds of the river and its traffic overshadow the city grinding away in the background. Dexie hovers on the entrance steps, looking upwards at the encroaching clouds and sniffing at the air. Lost for a minute in her own world.

'What is it?' Harri says.

'Oh nothing.' She laughs. 'It's just a silly habit. I find myself doing it each time I leave the station at the start of a shift.'

'What are you trying to detect?'

'I don't know, anything untoward, I suppose. Danger maybe? My mother tells me I have a nose like a badger.'

'And that's a compliment?' A slight waver to his nostrils looks a lot like amusement.

'I like to think so.' She nods to herself. 'Though when I say it out loud, I'm really not so sure.'

'So, what is your badger nose sniffing out today? I mean, it would be a bonus if you could track down Praxer without too much bother.'

'Now you're mistaking me for a hound dog,' Dexie says. She lifts her nose to the air again and skews her face. 'Nothing perilous, today, though there is . . . something in the air. I can't quite put my finger on it.'

'Success, hopefully,' Harri says as they descend the steps. 'Will a drink aid your super sense?'

'It's probably time to head off to my mother's house,' Dexie says, checking her watch as they turn into Fleet Street. 'I was due to be on an early turn today, and she's invited me over to hers for dinner tonight. Her cooking is nothing fancy, but it's far better than the food at my section house.'

'That's nice' Harri says. 'Are you close to your mother?'

She hesitates. 'Off and on. My father died during the war, and what with my . . . well, instead of bringing us together, it's created a sort of barrier. I don't quite know why. Anyway, she works nights as a nurse at Barts, and we have to squeeze in time when we can.'

'Well, have a good evening, and I'll see you tomorrow.' Harri turns to go. 'Meet at Lyons on the Strand, first thing?'

She stops mid-stride and looks at him squarely. 'No, what I meant was, do you want to come with me, to my mother's? For a plate of food that's not swimming in grease.'

Harri's direct stare is far longer than a polite pause – a shocked silence that bleeds into two, then three seconds.

Oh hell, Dexie curses herself. *He thinks I'm making an approach, some desperate and forward spinster trying to nab the first man to show an interest, or treats a woman as if she has more than one brain cell not dedicated to making tea.*

The truth is, she doesn't hate his presence; more than that, she's actually enjoyed today. Given her stage in life and the men she often meets at the station, that's quite something for Helen Dexter. Plus, there's hot food going spare, and from what Harri has said about his landlady's culinary skills, she imagined it might be welcome. But, with a far-away look in his eyes that says he's frantically searching for an excuse, she's clearly got it wrong. Very wrong.

'Look, it's not a problem,' she stutters. 'I just thought . . .'

'And that's very kind of you, but . . .'

'Harri, you don't have to explain,' she adds, trying not to sound offended, even if she is. It was a friendly gesture, simple as that, and she's no idea why it feels like such a slight.

'But I want to explain,' he says, catching her arm. 'Please. I would very much like to come to dinner at your mother's, if you can assure me of one thing.'

'Well, I can tell you now that she will assume we are "stepping out", but I'll quickly put her right on that score.'

'It's not that,' he goes on. 'I want you to promise you're not asking me out of pity.'

'Pity?' She takes a step back, confused.

'Oh, you know, the sad lonely German. As much as I appreciate people's generosity, I'm not good at playing the conquered victim.'

'No! Whatever gave you that idea? There's some food on offer, and a warm fireside. That's all,' she says. 'However, if you up the English accent a tad, you might avoid the maternal inquisition.'

'Then, I gratefully accept your invitation, while minding my Ps and Qs, as you Brits say.'

'The Ps and Qs will do it. Clearing your plate will earn you extra points, too.'

17

Partners Without Pity

3rd December 1952

Harri

Dexie says they could get a bus, but it's only a half-hour walk, and he senses her need for the space and journey, almost to prepare for the encounter, plus it will give him time to Anglicise his accent to the right level. Harri feels sure the invitation to eat is genuine, but he understands Dexie's reticence about parents only too well. Both his mother and father died in the months before the war, caught up in a fracas on a Hamburg street, amid a crowd of anti-Nazi protestors that turned ugly and fatal. He always sensed they were unnerved by Hitler's rhetoric, but neither parent had ever talked of outright opposition to the Fuhrer, given that everyone in Germany knew exactly what loose talk might lead to, not helped by their son's position in the police force. Harri and his father had an uneasy relationship after his recruitment, tending to avoid politics as a topic. Perhaps Schroder Senior thought his son was pleased to be drawn into the SS, when, in fact, Harri kept quiet out of embarrassment, and as a protection for his family. As an observer, Hella sensed the barrier forming between father and son. It was she who engineered those family visits for Sunday lunches before the war, to strengthen the fragile bond.

'They're your parents, Harri,' she urged him, time and again. 'They won't be here forever.' And so, he forced himself to be jovial, handing over a bottle of wine on the threshold of his childhood home, having prepared in his mind the topics of conversation over which they could talk and not create sparks, where his mother could cook and fuss and not have her face turn to grave disappointment at the obvious rift.

Hella was right, of course, as she was about so much. His mother and father were gone too soon, 'innocent bystanders' crushed in the protest. Hitler's brownshirts claimed the mob was infiltrated by traitors of the Reich, and these so-called traitors . . . well, they were too busy being dead or imprisoned to comment. In the end, nothing was proven. The only certainty was in knowing you don't appreciate what you have until it's too late. Another one of those damned idioms.

Sometimes Harri Schroder wonders why he's been allowed to be a detective at all.

As they walk, he wonders if now is the time to mention the car to Dexie, since they'll need it in tracking Alicia Remington. As a woman of means, the socialite wife is bound to step into a waiting car or hail a taxi on leaving the hair salon. Much like Dexie, Harri would rather walk the half hour to her mother's home, but it seems only fair to raise the topic.

'We could always pick up the car now,' he says as they approach the bright lights of the city centre.

'Car?'

'They've issued me with one, for the duration. We could go there now and drive to your mother's. What do you think?'

'Actually, I would rather walk, if you don't mind,' she says. 'It's still early. Perhaps collect it on the way back?'

'Of course,' Harri says, momentarily relieved, though all too aware he's just putting off the inevitable. Experience tells him it's better to come clean. 'I don't suppose you drive?'

She's smiling as her head turns, with an amused look. 'Don't you?'

'Yes, of course. Back home,' he says, guarded. *Spit it out, Schroder.* 'I haven't driven in England before, since there's never been any real need. I think Hamburg probably has more potholes than London, but the traffic here is much heavier. I'm not sure how fast I'd be.' *Or safe.* By his reasoning, too many in Harri Schroder's personal orbit have come to harm over the years. Call it paranoid, but he wants neither Dexie nor some unsuspecting pedestrian to increase those numbers.

'It's fine, I don't mind driving,' she says matter-of-factly. 'I use the police van on occasions.'

'What occasions?' Too late, he realises how dubious that sounds.

She merely scoffs with amusement. 'Like everything else in the Met, Inspector – when they're desperate, and when they let me.'

'Oh.'

'Don't look so worried. I did a bit of moonlighting for the Transport Corps during the war. When you've navigated these streets in the pitch black of the Blitz, everything else is child's play. As long as you don't expect me to don a cap, I'll be your driver.'

'Thanks,' he says, with enduring relief this time. 'More and more, I'm wondering what twist of fate put you in my path.'

'And once again, don't let my sergeant hear you say that.'

The house is tucked behind Camden High Road, one of those terraced streets that seem to go on and on, two-storey dwellings of red brick turned grimy, with small bay windows and a front garden that just about houses a dustbin and a token rosebush. Behind the successive curtains closed to the cold there are chinks of light, punctuated with a glow that oozes comfort to Harri, of life and welcome, a fire and something delicious in the oven. It's been so long that he doesn't often realise how much he misses it, too used to arriving home in Hamburg to a darkened apartment.

'Here we are,' she says, stopping outside a red gate, and front door to match. There's an obvious intake of breath.

'Is this where you grew up?'

'Oh no, Mum moved here after the war. Our house was bombed out, and with Dad gone she needed something smaller. Though even this is too big for her, and she has a lodger now.' She turns to look at him, holding up a front door key and a twist to her mouth. 'In we go. You ready?'

'Absolutely, my good woman,' he says, effecting his best upper-class gent.

'No need to go that far, Lord Schroder,' she says, turning the lock and calling down the dim hallway. 'It's just me, Mum.'

'I hope you don't mind me intruding, Mrs Dexter,' Harri

says as he enters the opposite of the world outside – a neat and cosy back room, warmed by a kitchen range and lit by varying lamps, the dark furniture brightened by crocheted cushions and detailed embroidery.

'Actually, it's Mrs Chadwick . . . Violet, but everyone calls me Vi,' Dexie's mother says, 'and you're not intruding at all, Harry.' She touches his arm rather than extending a formal hand, surveying them both, and the tiny spark in her eye signals she is perhaps thinking what her daughter predicted.

'Harri is on secondment at the station for a week or two,' Dexie explains firmly. 'He's at a boarding house and the food isn't . . . it's not like your home cooking, Mum.'

'Oh, well, I'm no chef, and it's just stew,' she bats off the compliment, 'but there is plenty of it.'

Harri is urged to sit while an extra place is set at the table, and Dexie follows her mother to the range. From the back, he sees where she inherits her height from; side by side, the older woman is broader and thicker set, and he ponders on whether Mr Chadwick was the leaner of the two.

Snippets of their conversation rise above the background hum of the BBC Home Service, and it makes him smile. 'Is he engaged to someone, or courting?' the mother whispers, to swift censure from the daughter: 'Mother! Can't I bring a friend home without you think . . .'

But Violet Chadwick is far from imposing when she comes to the table, reminding Harri of the German nurses at the sanatorium. She has the same soft face and manner that exudes care and concern in the simplest of things, and he can only imagine that she's good at her job. It's really no effort to clear his plate, since the chicken is delicious, and every bit the home cuisine that Harri enjoys, even if he does have guilty thoughts of Mrs P as he's eating. Dexie expertly steers the conversation towards news of the day and what's happening at the hospital.

'Bronchial cases mainly at this time of year,' her mother reports. 'It's only going to get worse as it gets colder. Which reminds me, Helen, do they give you a hot water bottle at the section house?'

'Yes, Mother.'

Harri watches the dutiful daughter only just refrain from rolling her eyes.

'I've told her she needs to come home, Harry. It's cold and dreary at that place, and I don't think they feed her properly either.'

'They do, Mum,' Dexie asserts. 'And I've told you the reason why. It's nearer to the station, and I can walk to work easily.'

Vi Chadwick clucks and Dexie chides, but Harri sees it only as love that's not easily expressed in other ways. Mothers and daughters, fathers and sons the same the world over.

'Hmm, maybe.' Unconvinced, she mutters while clearing the plates. 'I'm sorry, Harry, and I don't mean to be rude, but I'll need to get off to my shift now. I can't be late.'

'Not at all,' Harri says, moving to get up. 'Thank you for the wonderful meal, and the welcome.'

'We can stay for a while,' Dexie says, gesturing for him to sit back down. 'Is that all right, Mum? I'll lock up as we go.'

'Of course, love.' She kisses her daughter's hair firmly, an injection of devotion into the top of her head, touching Harri's arm as she goes. 'So nice to meet you, and do come again soon.'

There's a hopeful glint in her eye before she turns for the door.

⋆ ⋆ ⋆

Dexie's shoulders droop noticeably when the door latch clicks. With relief? he wonders. The tension appears to drain from her face as she rises and goes to the sink, intent on filling the kettle.

'Tea?' she says. 'There might be some cake in the larder if we're lucky.'

He's awash with liquid, but doesn't want to say no to the ritual or goodbye to the warmth. 'Yes, lovely, thanks.'

She sets the pot down and the milk bottle beside it. 'Please don't let on to my mother that I'm not using the milk jug. She'll have my guts for garters.'

'I promise,' he says. 'But you have to answer me one thing.'

For a split second, she looks truly alarmed. It's not the first time, and he wonders why the prospect of a direct question so often sparks anxiety in her, as if she's about to face an interrogation. A personal probing.

'About the tea,' he qualifies.

'Oh. Go on, then.'

'This,' he says, pointing at the knitted woollen jacket over the brown ceramic pot. 'What's it's all about?'

'It's a pot cosy,' she says flatly.

'Well, I know that, and I've seen them before. But Mrs Painter has a whole selection of them, one for each day of the week it seems. And the pot is never, ever empty. Is there some sort of competition among housewives for a well-dressed teapot?'

'You do know it's the law in this country to own at least one?' Dexie's face is a solemn mask. 'I could easily arrest you for such a heinous crime.'

Harri stares, eyes narrowed in his assessment, but long enough that she can't maintain the guise, the ripple of her lips revealing her tease. 'Do you know, I almost believed you then,' he says. 'OK, so tell me this – why do British women keep their hats on in the house? Mrs P wears a sort of half hat, like a flower petal that's wilted and moulded itself to her head. Last night I caught her boiling the kettle in her dressing gown just before bed and she still had it on. I swear I fell asleep wondering if it's grown roots into her scalp.'

Dexie's face cracks, her smile lighting the room; he's struck by how vibrant her eyes are when she does so, and how relaxed she seems with her mother gone.

'Sorry, I'll stop being very German,' he says. 'But, you see, that's why I need a guide like you. I've visited England a few times now, and I thought I'd absorbed quite a bit of the life, but it will take a lot longer before I really understand it.'

'You and half the British population, Mr Schroder.'

They sip in silence for a minute, she picking at the cake crumbs on her plate, the quiet dulled by a song on the radio.

'Your mother's a nice woman,' Harri says at last. 'I'll bet she's a good nurse.'

'She is,' Dexie says. 'The best.'

'So?'

'So, what?' Her hand becomes still. He doesn't need to see her face to sense fresh alarm. He's just far too curious, too much of a policeman, and too many years spent probing to stop now. 'What comes between you?'

Her lack of response is telling, but she doesn't move, or pour more tea. Or tell him to shut up.

'It's complicated,' she says eventually, eyes to the ceiling. 'And quite boring, I suspect, for those that don't know us.'

Harri stirs the inch of tea left in his cup. 'Try me. Perhaps we ought to know each other a little bit, given what we're embarking on.' He looks towards her and shrugs. 'Partners do that, don't they?'

She sighs heavily, a sound that seems tainted with resignation. 'My mother's entire life has been about protection, with her job, and her family. So, when we lost my dad, I think she felt a sense of failure, even though it was entirely down to the war – he died when our house was hit in a raid. She couldn't help but transfer all her anxiety to me, even though I was an adult at the time.'

'She blames you for increasing the risk to yourself, when you're out on the beat?'

Dexie nods. 'Maybe. But it started before that. I'm out there precisely because I lost someone. My husband.'

'Your husband?' He struggles to contain the surprise in his voice.

'Hmm.' She rubs one finger over the same inch of the tablecloth several times. 'Is it so much of a shock that I've been married?'

'No!' He considers. 'All right, a little if I'm honest, though God knows there are plenty of war widows forced to be independent nowadays. I'm sorry, but I assumed – quite wrongly – you were unmarried, even if it does make sense now that you're not a Chadwick.'

'You thought I was spinster material?' Now she laughs, truly diverted. 'Mind you, so does half of West End Central. Be assured, the war has created plenty of us, Inspector: women who are perhaps looking for a different path in life.'

Thomas Dexter had been a policeman in London throughout the war, she tells him with a certain sense of pride. Kept back from overseas fighting by being in a reserved occupation, he'd survived Hitler's bombing Blitzkrieg of London, both in the early and later years of the war. 'In fact, that's where I met him,' she says. 'I was an ARP warden, and I helped dig him out from under a building on the Old Kent Road. Our eyes met across the rubble, which is quite funny in hindsight. His face was plastered in white and he looked like a circus clown. Hardly romantic, I know, but strangely normal for the war years.'

'Did you get married quickly?' Harri asks.

'No, we waited, for all sorts of reasons, until after VE Day.' She looks to the lightshade, as if conjuring a bright image from deep inside. 'I had a dress made out of parachute silk. So clichéd, but I loved it. From a siren suit to feeling like a fairy princess, just for one day.'

'And then?' he presses. Gently, he hopes.

'Ironic, really. Thomas had dodged several bombs, coming out the other side, and then it was an unexploded bugger that got him. He was chasing a burglar into a derelict house and made one wrong step. That was 1946.' Her voice tails off, moving her gaze from the ceiling to somewhere else entirely. 'We'd only been married eight months.'

'I'm so sorry,' Harri says. He thinks of the officer who fell foul of a hidden bomb in Hamburg's ruins in '47. The man survived, but sacrificed both legs, his livelihood, marriage and his reason for existing, while Harri lost one of his best officers. Those ripples of war all over again.

Dexie shrugs. 'It feels like a long time ago, and I don't dwell on it. At least, I try not to.'

'And is that why you joined the police?'

'Yes, much to my mother's irritation. I sometimes wonder if I was also trying to escape the cocoon she was busy spinning for me, wrapping me in swathes of cotton wool. Mainly, it was because I needed to do something useful, like Thomas. I mean, it's not as if I'm trying to fulfil some of sort of widow's legacy, only that when he came home each day and told me about his shift, it seemed as there was some substance to it. A real purpose. I'd known some of that in the ARP and I missed it.' She gets up and begins clearing the cups. 'Little did I know of the Met's definition of "useful" for WPCs.'

'Does that mean you regret it?' Harri asks.

'Oh heavens, no! It beats that graveyard of a typing pool I joined after the war, suffering a slow demise behind a keyboard.' She sits back down and tucks away a stray fibre on the tea cosy, tossing a fleeting glance at Harri. 'That's me laid bare. Despite what the male fraternity at the station might think, I didn't join up to find a nice chief inspector to settle down with. Believe it or not, I'm very content to be on my own.' The wisp of wool comes away again and she stops fiddling. 'Your turn, Mr Schroder. What means you can be hauled over to London for a month or more, chasing spectres of the Reich?'

'Well, all right.' It's not often he opens up, but there's something about Dexie that makes him tell, plus the passage of time that allows him to speak of Hella and three-year-old Lily. How they died together in 1943 amid the Allied bombings, the aerial raids that battered Hamburg for seven days and nights and the subsequent firestorm which raged across an entire city, burning and suffocating everything in its path. Harri relays it without a thick syrup of sadness in his voice, largely down to the hours upon hours of therapy and contemplation he's undergone since the war; his world is better for having been a husband and father, even if they are both gone – that's the conclusion he's come to. Undoubtedly, it would be better if Hella and Lily were still here, but that's life, isn't it? And it's what he has to believe, otherwise it's only madness that ensues.

By the look on Dexie's face, she is horrified as his tale unfolds, a small gasp escaping from her lips. 'I'm very sorry,' she says. 'It's so hard when a child is involved. Thomas and I planned on a family, but we hadn't got around to it by the time he . . . Of course, I feel awful when I tell myself that's actually a good thing now.'

'Ah, what would we do without those layers of guilt as our constant companions?' Harri pulls up his chin and forces a smile. 'But . . .'

'But what?'

'I don't know you well, Dexie, except you don't strike me as a woman who lets anything stop you, or bring you down, least of all pity. Now that we know what might be the worst about each other's past, can we designate our partnership a pity-free zone? What I said, before, about accepting an invitation to dinner – once people know about my lost wife and child, they tend to overcompensate. Their pity comes from not knowing how else to express their sadness or regret. It's all done with the best intentions but it just gets in the way, don't you think?' Driven by instinct, he extends a hand.

Dexie's long fingers stretch across the table towards his, a warm palm on his rough flesh. 'Partners Without Pity,' she says, her lips pushed together in smile. 'Sounds like a silly name for an organisation, but I'll take it.'

When they shake on it, Harri feels as if they've already cut a swathe through some awkward life strata. And all over a pot that sports a funny knitted jacket.

18

Food For Thought

3rd December 1952

Harri

It's still early as they lock up and leave Vi Chadwick's house, stepping out into the freezing air that's clouded by wisps of mist. Harri pulls up the collar of his coat, eternally grateful for Mrs P's Vim and elbow grease making it wearable again. Moisture catches in his throat and he coughs several times into his woollen scarf, a remnant from his scarred bronchials that's both enduring and annoying.

'Very glad I'm not on a night turn,' Dexie says, shivering inside her mac. 'The girls will be walking at a pace on the streets this evening, just trying to keep warm.'

'Then we can only hope our Mrs Remington does all her crucial socialising in the daytime, and somewhere warm,' Harri says.

Given a sudden drop in temperature, they take another bus back towards King's Cross station, where the top deck is warmed with bodies, and the monochrome of the city streets switches to a dim yellow hue of bus lighting. It's where Harri loves to listen to the conversations around him, in all manner of accents, the phrases coming thick and fast from passengers rubbing their hands together and discussing Britain's principal subject of the weather: 'It's nippy, tonight'; 'Brass monkeys out there, isn't it?', or his favourite of the day: 'It's colder out there than my mother-in-law's heart'.

Beyond the rattle of train tracks and the heavy shunt of steam, the mist lingers as they walk to the lock-up garage where Harri has been told the car awaits. Facing the door, he hands over the keys to Dexie. 'All yours,' he says.

She unlocks the door and peers in. 'Oh Christ.'

'Has it got four wheels and an engine?'

'Just about.' She pulls back the door to reveal a small, black four-door saloon, with short snout of a bonnet. 'Austin A30. It's hardly fast.'

'If it's all right with you, I hadn't planned on careering around London at speed, hanging on for dear life,' he says. 'And it doesn't look like a police car, which is to our benefit. Besides which, small cars are much more discreet.'

Dexie gets in and turns the key, the car coughing into life. As she massages the accelerator pedal to breathe warmth under the metal shell, satisfaction creeps across her face. 'On second thoughts, this seems quite new,' she says when Harri slips in beside her. 'It might not be the fastest but it should be reliable.'

'There's a lot to be said for reliable. Come on, it's about time you showed me your chauffeuring skills.'

She turns her face to him fully. 'I told you, I'm not wearing any driver's hat, not for you or anyone else.'

* * *

Dexie motors slowly along what would be a leafy street in Islington, but where the trees are ghostly apparitions dotted at intervals along the pavement, backlit by streetlights and a haze that shrouds the terraced houses.

'Just about here is fine,' Harri says, as they draw up alongside a large birch overhanging the road. 'There's a café at the end of Mrs Painter's street. Shall we meet there at nine thirty tomorrow morning?'

'Fine,' she says. 'It's still early, so I might drive around a little more and get used to the gears. It beats cocoa and chit-chat back at the section house.'

'Then I'll say good night, Dexie.' He still feels odd saying it, that he's somehow complicit in diminishing her as a person and a police officer, in using the name she's been landed with. He finds, though, that it does actually suit her – her demeanour is no less womanly, but increasingly she doesn't strike him as a 'Helen'.

Georgie seems surprised to see him, but pleasantly so, the door to the Spender house thrown open in welcome.

'No Max tonight?' Harri asks as she leads him down several steps into the back kitchen, where an array of papers is strewn across the table, her small portable typewriter to the side.

'No, he's out working, at some meeting or other, and the children are in bed.' She secures her blonde hair into a loose ponytail, then holds up a glass and a china cup, one in each hand. 'Whisky or tea?'

'The former,' he says. 'I think my insides are stained brown already. But I don't want to stop you working.' He knows time is precious in Georgie's world, juggling motherhood with work, a career that Max is undoubtedly proud of. Still, there are plenty who think she shouldn't be combining the two 'in this day and age', and Georgie keeps her guilt lodged deep inside, seeping out only on occasion.

'I'm all but finished,' she says. 'They're just notes that need typing up tomorrow when the little imps are at school and the house is quiet. I think my brain shut down the minute you rang the doorbell.'

'Which means I'm either an irritation or your fairy godmother.' Harri takes a small sip of whisky, reminding himself of the need to get home to Mrs P's in one piece, and in this mist. In Hamburg, he harbours the innate skills of a homing pigeon, whatever his level of inebriation, but that has yet to be tested in London.

'You're never anything less than my fairy godmother, Harri Schroder,' she says, deadpan. 'Anyway, how's life in the Met – have you been given an assignment yet?'

He allows a sly smile to creep across his face, knowing full well it's irresistible to people like Georgie. 'I have.'

'Oh.' She sits upright, her interest piqued. 'Do tell.'

Since he's not been asked to sign anything official from the British side, Harri is untroubled by revealing Johnson's brief in full. Plus, his own faith in Georgie remains unshakable.

'Do you know him, this Remington?'

Her mouth twists in scouring her memory. 'Not really. Business reporting is not my area, but I have seen his wife in the society pages from time to time, plus a few comments banded about, in various newsrooms.'

'What's the word on her, aside from being elegant and beautiful?'

'Clever,' Georgie says. 'Beneath all the expensive grooming, she's apparently very astute with money. Manipulative, according to one or two who've met her, and very protective of her husband's reputation. Jealous, too, by all accounts.'

'Oh?'

'Yes, I raised my eyebrows at that one,' Georgie goes on, 'but they only said: "You wouldn't want to cross her." As a couple, they apparently moved in the same circles as Oswald and Diana Mosley before they went abroad.'

'Hmm, she sounds intriguing.'

'Sounds to me like you need to be careful, Harri.' She drains her whisky and offers a top up. 'Are you tracking Mrs Remington alone?'

'No, I've been assigned a WPC who knows the area well, plus a car.'

Georgie snaps her eyes to his, a brief flash visible under the kitchen lampshade. Is he right in thinking it's the tiniest hint of envy, she being his former unofficial sidekick back in Hamburg, when they and the Kripo team took down a killer stalking women in the post-war chaos?

'What's she like, this WPC?' Georgie ventures.

'Since you ask, she reminds me of you.'

'Difficult, you mean?'

'Determined and different,' he insists. 'Quick thinking too. Plus, she can drive, and I'd say that's a lucky escape for all London pedestrians. And she possesses the most vital of attributes.'

'Which is?' Georgie's eyes glow next to the amber liquid in her glass.

'She's prepared to put up with a grouchy German policeman in close proximity.'

Georgie sees him to the door, Harri having turned down the offer of another nightcap and a bed in the spare room. It's bound to be warmer and cosier than Mrs P's, and yet he feels a sudden draw to getting back to his tiny attic room and its limited comforts, knowing that whatever the hour, his landlady will be clanking away in the kitchen as his key goes through the door. He's also reminded that Georgie's children are generally up and running around the house at some ungodly hour of the morning.

'So, is she single, this new partner of yours?' Georgie fishes as he steps out into the chill white air.

'Georgie . . .'

'*What?* I'm just asking,' she says defensively. 'It's not an unreasonable question. I mean, isn't it about time, Harri? There's no law that says you have to be a widower and a monk forever.'

'She's a colleague,' he insists, taking pains to avoid the question. 'We've got a job to do. Which, Miss Crack Reporter, you understand all too well.'

'Yes, *Inspektor Schroder*, but it doesn't mean you can't like her.'

Damn it, she's blunt. And yet it is what he loves about her. 'I do like Dexie,' he says. 'What I know of her so far.'

'Then . . .'

'Good night, Georgie.' He pecks her on the cheek and turns down the garden path. 'For the good of the British nation, I only hope you never get a job as an agony aunt.'

He had planned to use the lengthy walk to run over the case in his mind, other avenues he and Dexie can pursue if Mrs Remington proves to be very competent at shielding her husband. But Georgie's playful comments have wheedled their way into his mind and, try as he might, he can't push them away.

There's no denying that loneliness has been a factor in Harri Schroder's life since the war. Back in Hamburg, he's blessed with a loyal circle of friends, and plenty of women among them. Yet the spur driving an average man through the days and months – through life – has been missing. It's true that he's been no monk, as Georgie so eloquently terms it, but any relationship since Hella has been brief, the longest only a few months. Why is that? he asks himself constantly, as he does now. The women have been good company, and the intimacy – when it's progressed that far – very welcome. He is only human, after all.

Mostly, Harri has to admit the fault lies with him: despite months of therapy, and his understanding of the grieving process ('life goes on' being the enduring message), no one has been able to compete with the memory of his wife. She was no saint, and they argued in the same way all couples do, especially when Lily came along and the divide between work and a child inevitably created pressures. But through everything – the rise of Nazism, Hitler's domination and the terrifying slide into conflict – they were able to laugh at the same silly things, debated fiercely over articles in the newspaper, shared pillow philosophy and a vision of the future, when they dared to imagine a time beyond the war. He and Hella read each other like a well-thumbed novel.

As Harri moves through London's streets, his soles pushing up a resounding echo in the biting air, Georgie's desire for him to find love again doesn't so much nag, as pose questions: how do you ever find that type of togetherness again? Can you even go searching for it? He has answers for neither.

He stops and bends his neck upwards towards the pinprick stars that punctuate the navy sky high above the ribbons of mist. Food for thought. For now, after several decent measures of whisky, maybe he should concentrate on employing that innate compass which has reliably taken him safely home after many a drunken spree.

19

Against the Tide

3 December 1952

Dexie

She cuts the engine and sits listening to the comforting slap of the water, rhythmic and unending, before getting out and sauntering towards the brick barrier separating the walkway from the Thames' flow. Quite why Dexie is this far south of the city centre, she can't quite fathom, other than that the gears had slipped easily into place under her fingers, and the motor ticked over with a comforting hum as she drove. For all its practicality and neatness, the Austin is a lot easier to drive than the overworked police vans from the Met garage. With no real destination and the roads clear at this time of night, she'd let her mind wander and the steering wheel lead her east over Tower Bridge towards Greenwich, looking out at the water's edge towards the Isle of Dogs. Leaning against the damp river wall, she can just see the lights of the cranes towering over the docks, and the *Cutty Sark*'s highest mast, standing tall as the clipper undergoes repair on the Dogs. Beauty in sight, but untouchable.

It's hard to decide if it's Praxer's case occupying her thoughts, tapping away at her brain like a popular tune on the radio, or the enigmatic Harri Schroder himself. In all the years of war and beyond, Dexie has to admit that she's never met anyone quite like him, including Thomas. Her future husband had been so kind when they met, if very traditional: he didn't approve of a working wife, and were it not for them saving hard for the deposit on a house, she might never have pushed for a job as an office typist, which she hated. At the time, it was her only way of escaping the endless round of daily shopping in ration queues, when Thomas expected a meal on the table after every shift. Looking back, it was probably where her efficiency first blossomed, in using her lunch hour to wander around London's art galleries instead of queueing for meat or fish, and then having to rush home, hare into the local butcher's and beg for leftovers, and then create something edible and interesting in no time at all. The eddy in the waters below suddenly seems too close to her life then – round and round in circles.

Would she have managed to swim against the tide and break free from that monotony, especially if children had come along? What if Thomas hadn't died? And that's where she curtails her thoughts, steering them instead to Harri and the matter at hand.

Could he be considered enigmatic? No, not with the obviously heavy weight upon his shoulders. Now she knows the reason, it's a burden she understands. But he is friendly, good-humoured and morally sound, she thinks (why else would he take on this perilous task against his own countryman?). So far, he treats her like an equal. To Dexie, this is the most puzzling aspect of the Kripo detective. Not that German men may be any worse than their British male counterparts, but the consideration he displays makes him stand out. A mystery, too.

For all its tragedy, the war opened up Dexie's eyes in so many ways. Like the men on her watch, she risked life and limb every shift as an ARP warden, her slim frame crawling into the tiniest of space in bomb ruins, to locate a voice, a glimmer of existence – a life. Sometimes, it was just the building moaning as it prepared to collapse. On occasion, though, a person could be saved. Once, she'd emerged from the wreckage with a mewling kitten tucked into her siren suit. Two days later, a whimpering baby found in the crook of his dead mother's arm in the same building. That night, like plenty of others, she'd cried, in private or with friends, but never on duty.

In Dexie's mind, she'd earned her place in what had always been a man's world, in the same way factory women making armaments through the war were entitled to their share of the job market afterwards. Except the politicians and the returning soldiers didn't see it like that in those early post-war years. 'Get back to where you belong and be grateful,' was their stark message – to the kitchen, the laundry or the nursery. Or that awful typing pool.

Hence the 'Get us a cup of tea, love', and 'Hey, Dex, give us a kiss' (along with a smile as they extend a hand to grope). So, what is it about Detective Schroder that makes him not engage like that? Why is he different? Intuitive?

'Be damned if I know,' she mutters, then wonders quite when she developed this habit of talking to herself aloud.

She's pulled up short by a couple walking by arm in arm behind her, watching their combined shape move into the distance, nuzzled and moulded into each other. In a weak moment, and too late to mount a defence, a sharp pin pricks somewhere within her, just under her ribcage. Time to go.

I am not lonely, she hammers home to herself.

Turning the key in the Austin's steering column produces an instant, comforting thrum beneath her. 'Cocoa, a hot water bottle and chat with the girls. Hmm?' she says into the rear-view mirror, letting out the clutch. 'Not exactly the high life, but better than a kick in the teeth.'

20

The Curtain Comes Down

4th December 1952

Harri

Harri is still pensive the next morning, when he wakes to a dull, weak light poking through the slit in the curtains, musing on where the sun has gone. He lies back and stares at the cracked ceiling rose, half-dreaming and wishing for a folkish maiden to bring him thick, strong coffee and slide in under the covers, to warm both feet that have turned to ice in the night.

In the absence of coffee (or the maiden), he deliberates on two things: firstly, the best way of avoiding Mrs P's particular kind of egg cuisine and not giving offence in doing so. Secondly, the day ahead and the time frame he and Dexie are now locked into. They have to track down and identify Praxer, alerting Johnson instantly – all in the next five days, before the proposed signing on the ninth. He's faced tighter time frames and worse consequences in the Kripo, and yet hour by hour, he feels his own resolve multiplying, in a need to complete, and deliver. It's either the innate drive in Harri – a 'dog with a bone' Georgie has tagged him more than once – or the fact that Praxer is a Nazi, beneath the surgery and gentlemanly façade. He can't decide which, but he knows Praxer the man should answer for his crimes. To Harri, this is not about reparation for being German, not when he saw so many of his countrymen, those like his parents, oppose the very idea of Nazism from the outset and suffer for it at the hands of Hitler's followers. It's the architects and engineers of fascism, plus those camp guards and SS, who should pay a price; those hanged in the wake of the Nuremberg, Ravensbrück and Auschwitz trials are just the tip of a deadly iceberg. As a financier of death, Praxer needs to face a reckoning, instead of reaping the benefits and living his comfortable life. Perhaps that's what is driving Harri now (albeit not quite out of bed yet), to look his former colleague in the eye again.

Or perhaps it's that Praxer was always a cocky little shit, and he should pay for that too.

Up and out before Mrs P has a chance to engage him in a detailed exchange, Harri sees the sun has not yet risen in tandem. Unlike the previous, crisp days, a grey shroud has descended over Bayley Street, leaving the air bone-cold and damp, with a patchy mist yet to clear. Not exactly prime hunting weather. He walks to the end of the street and into the warm humidity of the café, his blushes having been saved at the breakfast table by Scooter, who gladly relieved Harri of his grease-laden offering while their landlady was out filling the coal scuttle.

He's finishing off a well-cooked 'full English' when Dexie walks in. 'Morning,' she says, signalling at the counter for tea and sitting down. 'You must be hungry. Seconds, is it?'

'Firsts actually,' Harri says. 'Remember what I said about

my landlady's cooking? Well, it starts off fairly bad and gets marginally better by the end of the day. But only marginally.'

'Ah.' She sips at her tea automatically, her thoughts clearly elsewhere.

'Everything all right?' he asks. 'Nothing wrong with the car, I hope, only I think we'll need it today.'

'No, it's fine,' she replies. 'I'm tired, that's all. Those section house beds are not very comfortable.' She manages a weak smile behind her cup, the space under her eyes dull and smudged. 'Keen to get on with the job, though.'

Dexie parks up not quite opposite Sable Hair and Beauty at just gone ten, in plenty of time to see Alicia Remington's sleek black Bentley draw up on the dot of ten thirty, her chauffeur scurrying around to open the car door. Mrs Remington mutters something as a form of dismissal and he drives away, leaving a clear view of the salon window.

'How long do these things take?' Harri says from the passenger seat.

She's quick to whip her head around and fix him with an irritated stare. 'Why are you asking me? I go once every six weeks for a trim, but only because I have to. I can't bear all that primping.'

'Sorry,' he says. 'I shouldn't assume.'

Her look agrees. 'I'm guessing a proper cut and set might be an hour,' Dexie concedes, 'but if she's having a colour put on, maybe up to two hours?'

'Good God.' Harri wriggles down into the Austin's leather seating and tries to stretch out his legs in the tiny footwell, resigning himself to an uncomfortable wait.

For a time, they lose of sight of their target, prompting Dexie to fidget and suggest a sortie inside. 'Do you think she's given us the slip out the back?'

'Let's just wait a second,' Harri suggests, knowing that being too keen on a stake-out could easily weaken their cover.

Within minutes, Mrs Remington is visible again, presumably having moved from the hair washing chair to the cutting and styling section just beyond the plate glass window. They watch as she fingers her wet locks in the mirror, turning her head this way and that. There's plenty of discourse with the stylist standing behind.

'What on earth do you think they talk about?' Harri muses after twenty minutes of continual chatter between customer and hairdresser.

'I haven't a clue how those stylists keep it up,' Dexie says. 'I spend all day talking, so when I do go for a trim, I just want to close my eyes and drift.'

'I'm with you,' Harri agrees. 'Luckily, I have an understanding with my barber – he pokes me awake when he's done and I tip him extra for no conversation.'

After more than an hour, the preening finally appears to be over. A neatly coiffured Mrs Remington, looking uncannily like screen star Elizabeth Taylor, is seen signing her name at the front desk and moving onto the pavement. There is, however, no sign of the Bentley returning. Instead, she trips lightly across the road in her heels and begins walking along Duke Street, attracting looks from several men and women passing by.

Knowing they can't trail her in the car at a snail's pace, Harri and Dexie swap looks.

Ideally, it should be a woman to follow on foot as the more innocent-looking tail, but in this case she's the driver. Harri considers for a moment; there's very little traffic, and yet if he were to stall the car's engine it would mean losing their main – and only – lead to date.

Dexie is already a step ahead. 'I'll loop round the block and catch up with you again,' she suggests. 'I won't be far away. It's just gone midday, so she might just be going for coffee or an early lunch.'

'Good plan.' He gets out, feeling a welcome stretch in his legs and soon having to slow his pace as Mrs Remington is kept within sight, taking her small, kitten-heel steps up ahead. The Austin accelerates past with a wisp of exhaust smoke as Dexie disappears at the next corner. It's a while since Harri has been engaged in pure surveillance work, but the basics come back quickly; he logs every doorway on each side of the pavement, and moves his head in a curious, nonchalant manner, glancing at his watch once or twice. He stops at a newsstand to buy a copy of *The Times*, tucking it under his arm and keeping Mrs Remington in his eyeline at all times. In this chill, her pace is purposeful, and – luckily for Harri – she's not keen on window-shopping. After several minutes, he's aware of the familiar soft chug of the Austin's engine at his rear, swaps *The Times* into the hand nearest the kerb and swings his arm, in a signal to wave Dexie on once more. The wheels pause for all of a second, and then drive on past. Mrs Remington, meanwhile, has turned left into a parade of smart shops and cafés, their lights projecting onto the grey concrete in the increasingly dim daylight. She slips into a doorway with a small but chic frontage, possibly a bistro. Dexie is nowhere to be seen, presumably making another loop of the block, forcing Harri to sidle into the porchway of some flats.

He hovers impatiently, seeing no point in following Alicia Remington if Dexie doesn't know where he is. *Come on, come on.* His fingers tap impatiently on the folded newsprint. Within a minute, the Austin rounds the corner, Dexie's eyes above the steering wheel, first searching and then settling on him. With one slight nod of the head towards her, he walks several paces on and into the bistro, greeted by a welcome gust of warm air, and the unfamiliar – but unmistakable – smell of expense.

Inside, brass fittings gleam against clean lines of the furniture and a low hum of privilege rises up while waiters glide the floor as if on ice, customers reaching far back into the restaurant. It's just before the busy lunch crowd, and he's pleased when he spies the smaller tables stationed near the bar counter, those reserved for what lesser establishments advertise as 'light bites'. Here, the well-to-do patrons need no such instruction, and he sees Mrs Remington tucked into a corner at a small table for two. Dexie must be right in guessing she's here for refreshment only, and it's a huge relief when Harri slides himself several tables away and picks up the menu, hoping his face hasn't given away shock at the prices. That much for a mere cup of coffee! Gratitude goes to the wad of cash in his pocket, though it won't go far if this becomes a habit.

'Coffee, please,' he says to the attendant waiter, adopting his best blasé manner. Across the way, Praxer's wife doesn't seem to be expecting anyone, pulling out a thin novella from her handbag, sipping her own coffee as she scans the pages. Harri concentrates on the text of his *Times*, though when he flicks a glance, he observes a woman who would ordinarily attract little attention, other than to say she is classically good looking. It's her styled brunette hair and flawless make-up that gives her that screen star look, plus a tailored couture suit and coat, dainty shoes that would easily cost a month of Harri's Kripo wages.

'Anything else, sir?' the waiter cuts into his assessment. Suspicious rather than polite. Perhaps he has the measure of Harri – an imposter into this particular world?

'No, thank you,' he effects with irritation, as a man of means might in being slightly badgered by 'staff'. The waiter moves over to Mrs Remington and, by contrast, his address is one of deference. How is madam today? And would she like a top up to her coffee?

'Fine' and 'no, thank you', are her responses, Harri straining to hear across the hum of conversation, her tone succinct rather than superior. Finally, she dabs at her perfectly painted lips with the napkin, puts the book away and snaps her handbag shut. Instead of laying down coins or notes, she signs a chit that the waiter provides – as an account holder, clearly.

Then she's up and heading out, Harri casually pulling out some cash and leaving it next to the saucer. *Not too close*, he reminds himself, as he tracks the click of her heels towards the door, and a thought flits across his conscious mind, from somewhere in the shadows: she's too cool by far. Is she onto him?

Several steps from the door, Alicia Remington swivels on the balls of her feet, ninety degrees to her left, and walks towards the back of the restaurant, a discreet whisper in the ear of an oncoming waiter. Harri's mind skates over the possibilities: to the bathroom? But can he afford to take that chance? Or be so obvious in trailing her so closely?

With little calculation, he glances at his watch as if to suggest he's lost track of time and lurches towards the front entrance. The Austin is parked immediately outside, Dexie in the driver's seat. Harri bends as if to tie his shoelace and gestures to signal she should move to the rear of the café. She nods and starts the engine, while he leaps back inside and feigns discovery of the newspaper he's left purposely on the table, asking where the bathroom is, before being directed towards the rear. Approaching the toilet, he sees the flap of Alicia Remington's elegant coat as she disappears through a swing door labelled: *Kitchen. Staff only*. Seems it doesn't apply to a certain breed of customer.

Oh hell! Harri freezes, counts what is a painstaking four or five seconds as he pretends to check his coat pockets, and then breezes through the same door.

'Hey!' a man in chef whites cries, holding up his hands in protest. 'Here is not for customers.'

'Sorry, wrong way,' Harri bluffs, spotting the back door that, due the heat of the ovens, lies fully open. 'I'll go out this way,' and he's striding towards it before the chef can object any further.

He's just in time to see the back door of a non-descript dark blue Ford bang shut, much less notable than the limousine of earlier. But as it pulls away with a growl of the exhaust, he's more than pleased to see the Austin parked a few yards behind.

'I'm assuming that was her?' Dexie questions as Harri sinks heavily into the passenger seat.

'Yes. Either she's spotted me, or her ruse is just part of being extra careful, and I hope for our sakes it's the latter. Something tells me she's not on her way to Harrods for some light shopping.'

Dexie has already drawn away from the kerb, accelerating only to catch up, and then moderating her speed to sit one car behind, with their target just in sight. She won't want to fall back any more, since the air has turned – in the last hour or so – from a light haze to a thicker mist, a familiar but untimely feature of British winter. Although it's only just gone one o'clock, car headlamps are being switched on, soon lost in the milky-white of the afternoon.

Harri glances at Dexie, sitting close against the steering wheel, her face a mask of concentration as she tries to separate one set of red tail-lights from a half dozen others.

'Damned typical,' she grumbles. 'Today of all days.'

While she concentrates on navigating the hazy landscape ahead, Harri's eyes are focused on their target, watching intently for any evasion tactics a driver might employ if they have suspicions of being followed: a swift acceleration away from a junction or a sudden turn. But the car ahead merely bumbles along the northern embankment, hugging the just-visible divide of the river, making it easy for Harri to track their direction west to east. The squat presence of the Tower of London appears even more sinister and deathly as they pass, wrapped in threads of mist. But on they go, further east through Wapping and Limehouse.

'Do you remember any of Praxer's business addresses as being in East London?' Harri asks. 'Or in Essex?' More worrying is the prospect of a lengthy journey beyond London and out into the countryside, where it will be harder to remain elusive as a tail.

'No, but to be honest, I didn't commit all of them to memory,' Dexie says, eyes glued to the windscreen. 'We certainly seem to be heading for the docks.'

The next quarter of an hour proves her right. They leave behind the London of business and government, as Mrs Remington's car veers right towards a horizon of cranes and heavy shipping, along with the odd mast pointing skyward.

The odour of salt and diesel oil that seeps into the car prods at Harri's nostrils as a kind of balm: memories of Hamburg's once industrious docks on the river Elbe, a hive of trade before the war took its heavy toll. After the surrender in '45, thick fuel pooled in oily rainbows on the water's surface, a testament to the hundreds of small fishing trawlers sunk and scuppered by bombs or by the politics of the occupying forces. Nowadays, Hamburg's lifeblood creaks and clanks once again, rising less like a magnificent phoenix from the ashes and more of an aged swan with a fractured wing. As with so much in Germany, it's getting there.

'She's definitely not going for a manicure anywhere around here,' Dexie says, giving voice to Harri's self-same thoughts.

'And if she is meeting her husband, this is a perfect place to keep out of sight.'

They watch the Remington car steer further towards the dockside, until it's stopped at a gate by a man in heavy boots and a thick reefer jacket. Dexie comes to a gentle halt with the vehicle just in sight, she and Harri watching the gatekeeper bend and nod towards the driver, then allow access to through the sturdy iron entrance, closing it behind them.

Harri blows out his anguish. 'OK, so how do we get in there? Any good at climbing, Miss Dexter?'

'Not really. I'm far better at bluffing, Herr Schroder. It's worth a try.'

Before he has time to even think, let alone object, Dexie has plunged a hand into her coat pocket and is piloting the car towards the gate. She brakes in front of the man and winds down the window, at the same time taking in a breath and pulling back her shoulders noticeably, the exact same stance he witnessed several times on the beat with her.

'This is private property, Miss,' the man starts.

Dexie holds out and flashes what Harri supposes is her warrant card, snapping it away smartly, just enough exposure for an observer to catch the word 'police' but little else. 'We're on the lookout for a runaway,' she lies briskly. 'A dangerous one, a young lad. Seen anyone who shouldn't be here?'

The man shakes his head, with a look of apprehension. 'No.'

'We're searching all the wharf warehouses along this stretch,' she goes on officiously. 'My inspector here would be grateful if you'd let us through.'

Harri nods and smiles as the man stoops to look at him through the open window, his eyes narrowed. 'It would be helpful,' he echoes.

'Well, I suppose, though I'll have to ring it through to the foreman.'

'Of course, but if you can do that as we're looking, then we'll be out of your way as soon as possible,' Dexie presses. Even from behind, Harri senses she is aiming one of her practical, no-nonsense WPC smiles, the one that invites no other response but to do as she asks.

The man blows out a cloud of angst into the air that feels chillier by the minute. With reluctance, he unhooks the gate and waves them through.

'Well bluffed,' Harri mutters. 'Now we just have to keep it up.'

Dexie steers the car to a space next to a warehouse, where the wooden slats of the wharf narrow, coils of rope and chandlery littering the dockside. Over the nearby edge, the water looks cold and uninviting, thin curls of white vapour hovering above its surface. Nosed up against the wall of the same warehouse is the dark blue Ford.

'Looks like we've found our runaway,' Dexie says.

'Let's stick together,' Harri suggests. 'No need to go skulking around, since we have a cover' – he fingers his own fake identity card in his pocket – 'but let's do it quickly. If she and her crew get wind and head onto the water, we've no hope of following.' Besides which, he'd rather not; despite growing up in a port city, water is not his forte.

Entering through a small side door, the warehouse is a cold, ghostly space with little to search, the grey light from high windows only just picking out piles of packing cases and boxes stacked in the middle. There's no office tucked into the corner, and when they stand and let the air settle, no noise either.

'Next one,' Harri urges. But it's the same again, and he's beginning to wonder if Mrs Remington has been canny enough to board a small vessel the minute she arrived, and is already speeding along the wide expanse of the Thames, on her way to a rendezvous with her husband. If they've been spotted, she'll be congratulating herself for giving them the slip so easily.

Dexie spins full circle on her heel, peering past the open doorway. 'There's a smaller building over there,' she says. 'I can see a dim light.'

'Worth a try,' he says, though hope is diminishing with each passing minute.

It's a two-storey wooden building, one step up from a shack, the type of place which could house a harbourmaster's office, if the surrounding area weren't so ramshackle and run-down. They might be walking straight into a confrontation with the site foreman, but there's nothing to lose.

The yellowy radiance in the second-storey window draws them like the glow of lighthouse beacon. Suddenly, Harri stops and holds up his hand in military fashion. He turns on one foot, in reaction to a faint wormhole sound in his ear. Amid the familiar clanking of dockside noises, it's difficult to discern, but he'd swear it was a resounding click. Of metal. The unmistakable – and unwelcome – catch of a gun.

'What is it?' Dexie breathes, suddenly motionless.

'Could be nothing. But just watch your back.'

When their focus goes back to the window, the view has changed. Now, in the rectangle of light, the silhouettes of two people are visible: one is slight and sleek in profile, unmistakably female and undoubtedly Alicia Remington, the man opposite and locked in an embrace with her must be . . . Harri's heart quickens. Does he feel any recognition of Praxer's profile, which had always been distinct?

There's nothing. No sense of the past, no flood of memory. But, keeping in mind Johnson's reports of extensive surgery, it could still be his former colleague.

In the same instant, he's hit by something that feels more troubling. Can it be this straightforward? He would dearly love it to be, but something tells Harri that in the grand scheme of things – and in the less than smooth shitshow of his life – it shouldn't be. It's just not right. Slowly, Dexie turns her face towards him, and even her expression indicates this is too good to be true.

'Shall we wait for them to come out?' she says.

Harri's eyes skate over the grey scenery, the light rapidly fading. 'I've got to be able to identify Praxer and get him talking, and there's little hope out here. We've no choice but to go in.'

Dexie seems unfazed, as she reaches into the lining of her jacket and pulls out a wooden truncheon, her hand gripping at the polished shaft. She catches Harri's look of astonishment. 'Courtesy of West End Central,' she explains. 'You said Praxer might go to dangerous lengths. Better to be prepared.'

'I suppose so,' Harri agrees, wishing then that – even with his hatred of weapons – he had pressed Superintendent Graham for a handgun; phone numbers and a wad of cash won't protect either of them out here. Instead, he picks up a length of metal piping lying on the ground and slides it into the sleeve of his overcoat. 'Ready?'

The green in her eyes stands out in the gloam as she blinks her answer.

Dexie takes a stealthy lead towards a set of wooden stairs on the building's exterior. If they can reach the top step without alerting those inside, there's a good chance to both see and hear Praxer once they make it through the door, even if the exchange is short and heated. Just as with their thwarting of the Soho burglary, Dexie halts at the base of the stairs, turns and motions with her hand that all is well, before putting one foot on the stairs.

And then it's not. Not well at all, reflected in the lightning change in her features and a flash of movement, in the exact moment he hears that bloody click of gun metal again. Closer. Very close. He can't see the 'O' shape because it's snug into the back of his neck.

'Stop.' The tone is low and masculine. Obviously, Praxer is surrounded by more of a firewall than either he or Johnson gauged.

Instinctively, Harri raises both hands. Quickly, he judges that if Praxer's minder is intent on shooting him, they'll almost certainly dispatch Dexie too. Meaning there's no physical response left open to him, only fakery. 'We're police,' he says, effecting his best British accent. 'Looking for a runaway. I'm not sure what you're doing here with a gun, and I don't care. But I do not suggest you shoot either of us, because the might of the Met will come raining down on you.' He's under no illusion they'll care much about a German officer, but feels certain the force will muster its strengths for Dexie, as one of its own. Equally, that's no good to either of them if the trigger is pulled.

In the following seconds, the gun doesn't twitch. The hand is steadfast and the bearer is no amateur, Harri decides. Upstairs, a flat tone of muffled voices can be heard in conversation, seemingly undisturbed.

'Turn around, now, and get out,' the voice growls, with an accent that's not unfamiliar. Baltic, perhaps to the untrained ear, but with Harri's experience of post-war refugees in Hamburg, he pinpoints it as Soviet. Russian, more likely.

'We're going,' Harri assures the unseen figure. 'Quietly, and without fuss.'

Dexie clearly has other ideas. The gunman hasn't seen or heard the slip of sleek wood as the truncheon releases from her coat sleeve, caught in her palm. Facing her, Harri glimpses more movement from the corner of his eye. He ducks as she aims low and hard at the gunman's legs. Clonk! He goes down with audible cry of pain as Dexie levels a second at his shoulder, and the resounding crack of wood on bone is swallowed by the wintry air. The Russian is on the ground, dazed but not unconscious, as Harri and Dexie turn and sprint back towards the gate, hearing cries of alarm triggered in the room above. 'Get out! Get out!' a fresh voice shouts furiously, as a warning to Praxer.

The gunman is not immobile for long, dragging himself upwards and signalling to a second body who appears from behind a barrel. '*Idti! Idti!*' he shouts. *Go, go!* Harri hears in his patchy Russian. Without pausing, he glances behind at their pursuers, only to realise neither is now chasing after him and Dexie, but are heading in the opposite direction, towards the dockside. Are they both ensuring Praxer's safe getaway?

And yet, the pieces aren't adding up. The gunman and his comrade join in a pincer movement towards the water's edge, in a desperate pursuit. Harri hears a panicked voice shout: 'Head them off!'

'Dex!' he hisses to the back of her fleeing body. 'Wait!'

She halts and turns on a penny.

'We need to go back,' he says.

'*What?* Why?'

'Those thugs, they're not protecting Praxer.' Harri is still calculating as the words leave his mouth. 'They're *after* him too.'

A thought chases rapidly behind: *what in the hell are Russians doing here?*

Dexie must realise there's no time to argue, because she doesn't question, only follows Harri at a run towards the dockside, where the rev of a motor is audible. As they round the corner of the first warehouse, he sees dirty smoke from an engine merge with mist clouds over the Thames. The two Soviets are gaining on three people clambering at speed into a small riverboat, one scrabbling to untie the rope tether as another, slighter form is helped into the boat – no prizes for guessing who it is. As the two pursuers finally reach the water's edge, the boat fires away with an urgent roar to its throttle, soon swallowed by the grimy river and filthy weather. Harri presses himself against the wall as one thug slams something hard onto the wharf in frustration and shouts Russian obscenities into the air.

In seconds, Dexie is at his side, peering round the side of the building.

'Shit!' she gasps, echoing Harri's own sentiment. 'That must have been Praxer, and we've lost him.'

'So have they, it seems.' Harri is careful not to take his eyes off the two formidable figures dressed identically in black, now in a close huddle. It's obvious by their tense bodies and clipped exchange of half words that they are not planning on licking their wounds over a cup of tea in the nearest café.

'Time we weren't here,' he whispers to Dexie, just as the men peel apart and run in the same forked movement towards the wharf entrance – one headed in their direction.

Praxer may be gone, but it seems they are now intent on tracking down any witnesses, those who have already seen too much.

Harri is certain the Russians will soon spot the Austin parked next to the warehouse, calculating that he and Dexie are still on site. And exposed. Harri grabs her arm as they prepare to move, yanking her further down behind a packing case, as one runs past only feet away, his footfall and breath heavy.

'Go through the warehouse?' Dexie half mouths, half whispers.

He nods. Stooping as low to the ground as possible, they scurry like rats towards a side entrance. Dexie pulls hard on the warehouse door and the catch gives way easily. The interior is still, almost ghostly, as they edge cautiously around a mountain of packing cases, stacked well over head height, wary of their footsteps clipping on the concrete floor. But there is little they can do about the hot breath of the chase creating small clouds that puff upwards in the freezing air. It's like sending up smoke signals to the Russian twins.

In unison, both pull scarves up over their mouths, eyes wide above.

Reaching a gap between the boxes, Harri peers through and signals for Dexie to take a look. Across the room a grey rectangle of light indicates a door stands open. Open because one Russian, followed swiftly by the other, is coming through it. There are hushed but urgent orders in Russian to search the entire space.

Harri cocks his head to gauge the sound of their footsteps and sees Dexie do the same. Silently, she gestures to a shadow creeping under a nearby window to their left. A barely perceptible shuffle places the second inching along the wall to their right. All too soon their pursuers will reunite – exactly where Harri and Dexie stand pressed against the wall.

Instinctively, both melt into the warren of packing cases stacked at well over head height, moving back-to-back as a single unit. In the dense gloom, they blindly track the scuff of Russian shoes as one circles the cases, the other poking into debris left around the perimeter. The footsteps enter the maze of pallets and Harri pilots them through each nook, closer to the door. The temptation to run for it is overwhelming, but Harri pulls up sharply. Judging by the sour taint of sweat, one Russian is little more than a few feet away. The barrel of his gun glints as he peers into the shadows.

Harri can hear his own breath running riot inside his head, calmed by Dexie's shallow, even breathing against his body. The dust and cold, though, is unforgiving, trapped behind the wool of his scarf and backing up into his lungs. If he coughs, these men will spring upon them without mercy.

Abruptly, one voice barks at the other, and it seems the search is called off, the footsteps retreating quickly. Harri yanks down his scarf and exhales heavily into cupped hands, slumped against the packing cases. Dexie says nothing, the bright whites of her eyes telling the whole story.

'Safe enough to go now?' She nudges Harri after a few minutes.

He looks at his watch. Gone three p.m. 'Yes, I think so,' he says. Praxer and his wife are long gone, he's damp and cold and, right now, he really does want to lick his wounds in a warm café with a large pot of tea. And a sticky bun.

They push through the last of the boxes towards the door nearest to the parked Austin, slowing up at the curls of grey smoke pushing their way into the building. A fire? Harri's thoughts go instantly to the Austin, set alight as bait, with the two Russians ready to pounce.

Gingerly, they peer out through the entrance. The view is astonishing because it's . . . well it's barely there. If the Austin is pushing out smoke, then the rest of London must be too, because in place of boats, hoists and water – any landscape, in fact – there's just an opaque, grubby coating, from the ground to wherever it meets the indeterminate sky. A curtain has descended over the capital.

Fog.

Harri has heard about it. Who hasn't? Those famous pea-soupers characterised in Victorian novels and tales of Sherlock Holmes, the 'London particulars' under which fictional criminals run about carrying out their devilish business. But he's never experienced dense fog on any of his trips so far, at least not where tendrils of a misty morning develop to this grey blindness.

'Damned weather,' Dexie utters behind him, as a veteran of many, no doubt. 'This really is all we need.'

River sounds are muffled, though there does appear to be life beyond the shroud. With ears on alert for the Russians, they locate the Austin, fully intact and not ablaze.

'Can you drive in this?' Harri asks.

She only shrugs. 'We have to get out of here, and I've seen worse. If we can make it to somewhere familiar, I can park up and we'll go on foot the rest of the way. This'll be gone by the morning.'

Harri sinks his faith in Dexie's experience of her city, the streets and her driving abilities. He has to, since he can't see a bloody thing and time is running away like desert sand through their fingers. The gatekeeper has ghosted away, leaving a large padlock chaining up the gates. Dexie noses the car up to it while Harri picks the lock with ease, and a good deal of satisfaction. It's been a while since he's needed to flex those skills.

With headlights on full, visibility is down to ten feet at the most. There's little traffic in the dock area, but once Dexie steers the car out on the main road and west towards the city centre, the pace is painfully slow behind other drivers now crawling their way home after the curtain rapidly descended. At intervals, Harri spots cars that have already been abandoned, half-cocked on the pavement. Dexie's eyes flick from the tarmac in front, to the white line in the middle of the road, her knuckles white as they grip on the steering wheel, the car in permanent second gear.

'All right?' Harri queries.

'So far,' she says through a mouth tightly shut with concentration. They're both too focused on reaching home in one piece to discuss what just occurred back at the dock, with guns and Russians. And failure.

Dexie shoots back in her seat as the yellow rectangle windows of a double-decker loom out of nowhere, heading straight towards them. With only yards to spare, it trundles by on the opposite side of the road. They exchange a brief look of alarm, at how the fog has so rapidly robbed them of any orientation.

'This is hopeless,' she says only a minute later. 'I'm going to try and find Bethnal Green station and then we'll go by Tube,' she says.

'Very sensible,' he agrees. 'I need to ring someone urgently, and find out what the hell is going on. Not least why Praxer had a welcoming party of Soviets waiting.'

'That,' she says with conviction, 'is an even better idea.'

The familiar red signage of London's Underground is only evident once they've parked up at Bethnal Green, the route somehow mapped in Dexie's mind. She joins the queue at a tea stall for two much needed cups to stave off the plummeting temperature, while Harri slips into a phone box and picks up the receiver.

'Whitehall 232,' he says to the operator.

'Sorry, sir, that number is not taking calls at present,' she chirps back.

'Well, please inform those unavailable *at present*, that if I'm not put through, I will be marching in there and raising merry hell.' It's another bluff – he's no idea which monolith in Whitehall houses the number he's ringing, but the telephonist doesn't know that.

'One moment, please.'

Harri thrums his fingers impatiently, when at last there is a click.

'Tell him I want to meet,' Harri insists to the voice at the other end. 'Now.'

21

The Russian Problem

4th December 1952

Dexie

As expected, the fog has driven a good deal of Londoners underground and the platforms are packed with despondent commuters bemoaning the weather above their heads. Tired faces project a collective feeling of dread at needing to feel their way to their front doors once they venture onto the streets again. Any other day, Dexie would be up top, as the helping hand for suddenly sightless Londoners, and she's almost grateful for an excuse to stay out of it.

Harri is silent as they stand in the carriage, rattling along under the capital's streets; he looks both thoughtful and angry, though he didn't object when she insisted on going with him to the rendezvous back in the city centre. 'I want an explanation, too,' she'd qualified, with a face that reflected her own fury. The weather is one thing, controlled as it by nature, but being sent in blind by your own side is another.

Back on the street, London's rush hour is a step up from

its usual level of chaos. Police in heavy overcoats are doing their best to direct wayward vehicles as the red, amber and green of traffic lights are swallowed into the grey miasma, while a symphony of car horns buffers against the dense shroud. In the short journey on the Tube, the fog has become noticeably thicker, visibility reducing by the minute.

Dexie knows where the appointed building is, and so their progress along High Holborn is faster than most, only held up by less steady pedestrians pigeon-stepping along the greasy pavement, gripping onto each other. Even so, she has to count the doorways in her head. Finally, she stops and climbs the step to a solid, ornate entrance, squinting at the gold plaque etched with 'Trent Holdings'. 'This is it.'

Harri raps three times as instructed on the heavy wooden door, which is duly opened by a man in a black suit, who nods when they give their names. 'Second floor,' he says, with little movement to his face. 'First on the right.'

The inside is cold and impersonal. There's a sense of abandonment through the entire building, and Dexie muses on whether it's merely a convenient empty space, or something more sinister. When they reach it, the room on the right is equally chilly and barren of furniture, and the man inside adds nothing to its warmth.

'This is Dexie,' Harri introduces, though there is no hand shaking, and Johnson doesn't volunteer a name, fake or otherwise to her. Perhaps he assumes Harri has told her.

'You called.' Johnson's voice is icy, face motionless and lit only by a small floor lamp in the corner. He's patently not happy.

But then neither is Harri, whose feet are planted firmly on the bare boards, the stance that says he's spoiling for a fight. 'Yes, I called you, and no, it was not an emergency as such,' he starts. 'Having said that, when a thug stuck a loaded gun into my neck and demanded that I vacate the area where Praxer so obviously was, I did wonder if I would live to make that call. He was Russian, as was his charming sidekick. Care to explain?'

Still, Johnson's face doesn't falter. Instead, he moves several steps and leans an arm on the mantelpiece of a large, empty grate. 'I had hoped the Soviets weren't party to our intentions,' he says without a shred of emotion. 'That's unfortunate.'

'*Unfortunate?*' Harri's voice is strangulated with obvious disbelief, staring hard at Johnson. He seems literally lost for words.

'So, who were they exactly?' Dexie crowds in. 'Why were Soviets trying to . . . "rain on our parade" I think is the polite saying? Because I clouted one of them quite hard, and I don't think he was too pleased about it.'

Johnson startles at her admission and looks smartly to the floor, but when his face rises there's a different expression. Irritation, with a mere hint of sheepishness, if she's reading it right.

'Praxer isn't valuable to only the British economy in terms of his financial might,' he explains, ignoring her and focusing hard on Harri. 'Have you heard of the Gehlen network?'

Both shake their heads.

'Well, it's a group of former Nazis who, through a process of blackmail and desperation on the part of secret services worldwide, have managed to market themselves as reliable sources of intelligence, saving their necks from the hangman's noose at the same time.'

Dexie slices to Harri and watches his already angry eyes narrow, struggling to grasp Johnson's gist perhaps. She sees it land a second later – smack bang into his understanding, a realisation that seems to send him off balance physically.

Harri shuffles, before finding the words. 'You mean former Nazis – war criminals and murderers – are now employed by various security services? *As agents?* That governments are now rewarding these bastards for doing the Fuhrer's bidding? You can't be serious.'

Johnson merely scuffs an expensive shoe on the hearth. His silence says it all.

'And does this include the British Secret Service?' Dexie cuts in, with equal and blatant disgust.

Like all good spies, Johnson refuses to confirm or deny, merely says: 'We can't afford to lag behind the Russians or the Americans where intelligence is concerned. You have to understand that this is a new war we're fighting, a cold war that will become a lot hotter if other nations are ahead of us in securing the secrets of nuclear engineering. The Russians are no exception, and they want information as badly as we want Praxer. He knows money inside and out, but a lot else besides, from inside Hitler's circle. While he is about to sign a deal with British industrialists for raw materials, he is also devoid of any loyalty, and could easily sell what's locked in his head to the other side. He is a true mercenary.'

Harri's mind, meanwhile is calculating again. 'Am I then to assume our Soviet friends have got wind that MI5 – or whoever you are – is on Praxer's tail, and now want him for themselves? They don't want to kill him, but employ him?

Johnson pulls out a pack of cigarettes from his jacket pocket and makes to light it.

'Don't smoke in here,' Dexie snaps, surprising herself at how much of a school marm she sounds. 'It's bad enough out there. And I'd like to see you clearly as you explain yourself.'

Johnson quickly disguises his look of alarm at her forthright censure. He covers it by replacing the packet, pushing out a long sigh. 'Look, I promise you we didn't know how close the NKVD – the Russian services – were, or that they even knew much about Praxer.'

'Evidently not,' Dexie sneers.

'And had I known, I wouldn't have sent you after Praxer,' he goes on.

By now, Dexie is beginning to doubt that. Beside her, Harri looks as if he does too. Clearly, Johnson has no loyalties to a German detective or a WPC. She heard it described often enough in wartime as 'civilian casualties', those sacrificed for the greater good. It's a poor defence for any act, because it still results in pain, and death. Harri, she now sees, stands as a disposable asset, just one more German. Maybe her life as well. The room is uninhabited and freezing, but she feels the heat soon rise in Harri, a dragon stoking his fire breath.

'You sent us in there as bait,' he unleashes vitriol at Johnson, 'knowing we could run straight into trained killers on a similar pursuit. You merely gambled on the fact we might get there first. And if we didn't, we're easily expendable.'

'No, that's not—' Johnson tries.

'You're a spy, *Mister* Johnson, which makes you a fucking good liar, too, so don't try telling me you had no idea.' He looks at Dexie and she doesn't try to stop him, either with words or a look. 'Well, I am no one's bait, and so you can take your job and go to hell, because I'd rather go back to fighting villains in Hamburg. At least they have the decency to wear their dishonesty openly.'

Johnson is mute, absorbed by the shine on his toecaps. How can he justify it? Harri has caught him out, and the MI5 man dare not chance appealing to Dexie's better nature. There's a yawning three-second silence where they all listen to a crescendo of traffic fury outside.

'I wish you would re-consider,' Johnson says finally. 'For—'

'And don't you dare give me all that *scheisse* about duty to humanity,' Harri cuts him off again. 'You wouldn't recognise ethics if they stamped on your head.'

'Even so, Inspector Schroder,' Johnson tries again, 'you must see that having that identification is ever more crucial now. It's absolutely vital for this nation's security.'

Christ, he's got the skin of a rhino hide, Dexie thinks. But then he is MI5. Goes with the job. Harri only stares, his jaw set rigid.

'We're going,' she announces suddenly. 'The air in here is suddenly very stale.'

Not waiting for Johnson's reaction or his permission, she heads for the door, Harri's footsteps close behind.

Outside, the blackout curtain of fog has drawn a tighter veil over London. Dexie watches Harri launch himself into a grey oblivion, but with visibility little more than a man's length in front, he's instantly sucked into the ghostly void.

His strides are long and determined as she pursues Harri's faint outline, intent on ploughing through the thick cloud like an ocean liner in a high swell and cursing under his breath in German.

'Harri! Stop, Harri! she urges. If he meets with a solid lamppost head on, she's certain which of them will come off worse.

He halts abruptly, spinning a half-circle to face her, looking suddenly disorientated, as if he doesn't know which country he's in, never mind the city or street. Through his nose, he inhales London's seepage and coughs, before seeming to come to.

'Slow up,' she says. 'People have been known to die

falling off the pavement in fogs like these. And you don't want to give Johnson that satisfaction, do you?'

Incredibly, that does makes him smile. 'No, that wouldn't be good, especially now.'

They shuffle to the side of the pavement, backs against a cold, damp wall of a building, and watch people stumble by, couples blind and entwined. On the road, the traffic is almost at a standstill, motorists' frustration reaching a climax.

'What now?' Harri says, casting left to right, even when there's little point.

'We should go home,' she says. 'No point heading back to West End Central now, they'll all be out dealing with this chaos.'

'Escorting people across the road, you mean?'

That's her cue to laugh. 'Yes, probably. And as you know, it is my forte. I should really present myself at the station to help, but I'm too tired and too hungry.'

'Come to think of it, I'm starving too.' Harri pats down the pockets of his overcoat, reaches inside and plucks out the envelope containing notes. 'Damn it! If I'd remembered, I would have pulled this out in front of Johnson, slapped the money down in disgust and turned tail in a dramatic fashion.' He grins, a flicker of humour rising above his bedrock of anger. 'I do think they owe us something for almost getting our heads blown off. What do you say to dinner? Johnson is paying. And we should definitely get drunk on the proceeds.'

'Why not? It's a better offer than leftover soup at the section house.'

'Do you know anywhere around here?'

'Not really. But I can get us to Soho on foot with my eyes closed.'

'And here's me thinking you weren't a walking *A–Z*?' he ventures.

'When it suits,' she comes back. 'Right now, it suits my stomach.'

Once they pick their way through the streets, the sight and sounds of Soho are a familiar comfort. The blurred but vibrant neon announcing clubs and bars is present, albeit unreadable, and it does seem quieter, even for seven o'clock. Whatever the weather, Dexie is certain the determined thrill-seekers won't be dissuaded from the infamous buzz of the clubs and shows later on.

For now, the brightly painted lips and fiery cigarette tips of the street girls emerge from doorways as they round each corner, almost when they're on top of them. 'Business, love?' one punts to Harri, then shrinks back as Dexie appears out of the miasma. 'Ne'er mind, handsome, next time, eh?'

'I've heard this is good,' Dexie says, stopping outside a small restaurant on Dean Street. 'Do you like Spanish food?'

'Can't say I've ever had it. But I know they're very keen on meat, and I'm German, so let's give it a go, shall we?'

The inside of Casa Pepe is another universe, instantly warm and snug, with tables set close together and a rich, enticing smell coming from the kitchens at the rear. In the background, traditional classical guitar is piped on a low volume, against décor that is distinctly Mediterranean. They're ushered in by a short, stout waiter who introduces himself as Pepe, seated in a corner booth and instantly brought a small carafe of Spanish red wine. 'Never mind the food, I like this place already,' Harri says.

Slightly bewildered by the menu, they both order whatever Pepe recommends in his rich and beguiling Catalonian accent – paella, followed by a thick regional stew of meat and beans.

Harri refills their glasses and raises it up to suggest a toast.

'To not getting killed today,' he says, in a tone that's only half-joking. 'And I don't think I've thanked you properly for saving my life with your trusty truncheon.'

Dexie chinks her glass against his. 'I would say anytime, Inspector Schroder, but I'm really banking on that being a one-off. Small-time jewel thieves are bad enough, but Russian agents that have no accountability to man or nation are another kettle of fish entirely.'

'Kettle of fish?' Harri says. 'Oh, I like that. Consider that squirrelled away for my little collection.'

Chewing on some bread that's deposited on the table, she takes a sip of wine. It slips down smoothly, but given what's just happened, this whole scenario feels too much like a farewell supper. Dexie isn't quite sure how that makes her feel. Relief, in a way, but a sadness too. It's a stretch to say the afternoon has been enjoyable, but for a brief second, there is a sense of loss. 'So, what will you do, now you've cast off Johnson?' she says, as a dish of paella is set down.

He shakes his head. 'Go back to Germany, I suppose, face the wrath of my boss in failing as a Kripo diplomat and then pick up my old cases.'

'Oh.' She looks to the ceiling, always her safe space when she can't engineer what feels like the right response.

'And you?' Harri asks.

'Same, I suppose. Pull out those ruddy awful shoes and get back on the beat.'

'Surely, the last few days will have put you in a good position for CID?'

'Maybe.' Her face moves from dread to pleasure as the warm spices hit her tastebuds. 'But I think it will take a lot more banging on their door to get in properly. I'll just keep bashing away, as they say.'

'I'll certainly put in a good word with your boss before I leave London,' he says.

'Thanks, I'm sure it can't hurt.' But neither will it have a magical effect. The only two women Dexie knows in CID across London worked for years to gain their places, forsaking relationships and marriage, and yet remain stuck on the promotion ladder, destined never to make inspector. That's just the way of the Met, and probably forces nationwide.

'When do you think you'll leave London?' she asks, as they begin on the rustic stew, brought to the table by Pepe with a wide smile and more wine.

'I'm in no hurry to come face to face with my own chief inspector,' Harri says. 'Beside which, he's not expecting me back for a while, and I have a lot of leave due. I think I'll take a holiday.'

'Anywhere nice?'

'The coast possibly.'

She stops eating. 'At this time of year?'

Harri looks strangely innocent all of a sudden. 'I like English seaside towns in the winter. Very melancholic, I think is the right description.'

'Wet and grey, I'd say,' she replies.

'Exactly, suits me perfectly. I'll see how this weather goes, and start with a simple day trip to Oxford,' he adds. 'It's on my list of things to do. If I see the superintendent early tomorrow to hand in the car keys, I could be on the train and in Oxford by lunchtime. When are you back on the beat?'

'I've got weekend duties, so it's an early turn on Saturday.' Her mouth twists at the prospect. 'That should be fun, clearing up the debris from drunks and pimps the night before.'

'But does it mean you're free tomorrow?' Opposite,

Harri's eyebrows rise with anticipation. 'Would you like to come with me, to Oxford? It's the least I can do after today.'

He pitches it in a friendly, relaxed manner as he forks up more food, but the question unseats her nonetheless. It's not a proposition, Dexie feels sure of that, or anything like a date. Even so, work is one thing and she's become adept at hiding behind her uniform, using it as chainmail against the banter. These past few days they've been colleagues, with a task and purpose (if a wild goose chase), but she'd donned her light armour of professionalism in place of the heavy metal. An innocent day out means she has to be herself – Helen, and not WPC Dexter, or even Dex. It's been so long, she's not sure which one is the real thing any more.

'I don't know,' she manages. Pathetically. 'I have a pile of dirty clothes to deal with, and some shopping.'

'Which you would rather do than spend the day with a grumpy old German policeman,' he says, a mawkish, mocking face into his stew. 'I understand, WPC Dexter. I understand completely.'

He's letting her off lightly, with humour and courtesy. Which is more than she's affording him by refusing.

'I didn't mean it like that . . .' she begins, then is hit by a sudden flush of reason, that dirty clothes and her life will still be there when she comes back. 'Actually, you're perfectly right. I could do with getting out of London, if only for a day. The blasted washing can wait. So yes, I'd love a day in Oxford.'

'That's settled then. We'll see Superintendent Graham first thing, wrap up at Scotland Yard and go from there.'

* * *

Stepping from the warmth of the restaurant, they are slapped in the face by the chill swathe hovering in the streets, wading through a filthy-looking sediment pooling around their ankles.

'Christ, it's even worse,' Harri says, wrapping his scarf tighter, up and over his mouth.

The particles settle instantly on Dexie's skin, clawing at her skin like a burrowing insect, the sting of something alien felt across her cheeks. As a child, similar fogs had felt somehow protective, forcing the whole family to hole up at home, cosy and warm. This, however, has a sinister edge to it. The smell is foul and sulphurous, far worse than the stinking bins and pools of vomit after a particularly raucous night in Soho. She doesn't like to dampen Harri's expectations, but she might have to revise her earlier predictions. This fog looks like it's here to stay. 'I'll walk you back to your digs,' she says instead.

He doesn't object. Tradition dictates the roles should be reversed, but both know he hasn't a hope in hell getting home under his own steam in this fug. After one or two false turns – possibly due to Pepe's good wine – they arrive at Mrs P's gatepost.

'Meet for breakfast at the café around the corner, say eight thirty?' Dexie suggests.

'Perfect.' Harri looks suddenly concerned. 'Are you sure you're going to be all right, getting home?'

'Fine,' she says. 'If I was on duty, I'd be escorting the world and its wife around the streets, so this counts as a luxury.'

'Good night, then,' he says. 'And thanks again, Dexie.'

This time, he doesn't say exactly what for.

22

Cocooned

4th December 1952

Harri

Mrs P doesn't emerge from the kitchen as Harri takes off his coat in the freezing hallway, nor does she call out her usual greeting. Tentatively – since the kitchen is a landlady's fiefdom – he opens the door to find her huddled in the chair nearest the fire, a blanket over her knees, Scooter tucked in beside her and a large handkerchief to her mouth. The felt hat, of course, is still in situ.

'Mrs P, are you unwell?'

Her small watery eyes peer out, amid a grey face that seems thinner. 'It's this fog,' she rasps. 'It does nothing for my chest, but I'll be all right once it's gone. Don't you worry about me.'

Harri makes some tea – under instruction, of course – and secures the cosy on the pot, banks up the fire and brings in a bucket of coal from the small yard out back. 'Why don't you go to bed?' he suggests.

‘I won’t sleep lying down,’ she says, after a sudden bout of coughing. ‘I’m much better sitting up in the chair here, where it’s warm. You go on up.’

‘Well, if you’re sure. But do wake me if you need anything,’ he says.

‘Thank you, dear, you’re very kind.’ Scooter gives a whine that is either good night or a sudden plea for him not to leave.

Up on the third floor, Harri’s room is just a notch off freezing, despite the fire that Mrs P had laid earlier, now burnt down to almost nothing. He pokes at the embers, lays on several nuggets of coal and undresses in double quick time, noting how the space resembles even more of a cocoon, the previously distinct sounds of the city muffled by the weather outside. Shivering under the blankets, he feels isolated, then he curses himself for not bringing his precious Scotch into bed. Isn’t a tot of good liquor supposed to ‘warm the cockles of your heart’, so the saying goes? Right now, every inch of him needs heat, but the bottle is across the room and he’s too cold to contemplate moving. Besides, whisky on top of Pepe’s red wine might not mix so well. He’ll need a clear head to face Superintendent Graham and make his escape from the Met.

Sleep doesn’t come easily. The day’s events churn over in his head – the near success in spotting Praxer, snatched away by the Russian’s interference. Was he right to be so angry at Johnson? Yes, he assures himself. As an *inspektor*, he would never send any one of his team into a situation, a dangerous one at that, without laying out all the facts. The feeling that he and Dexie are so expendable to Johnson causes his stomach to tighten. Harri nods to himself in the darkness: he was absolutely right in telling the MI5 man to go to hell. Let someone else take the fall.

Still, his thoughts refuse to settle. He can't deny the day had its upsides, in the adrenalin that fuelled every step, flooding his veins with a feeling that has been dormant for far too long. Plus, there was the comfort (if you can call chasing men with guns a comfort) of having someone solid behind you, a second self, like he's had in the past with previous partners, with Paula, and Georgie too. He felt that with Dexie today, affording a positive slant to this whole dirty business. Is that what's causing him to question the decision to quit?

But the facts stand: Johnson was duplicitous. Criminals fulfil that job very well, and you don't need anyone adding to it, least of all a man who's supposed to be on your side. He has tomorrow to look forward to, and who knows how many weeks he'll remain in England, to catch up with Georgie and Max some more, and maybe even stay for Christmas. First, though, he wants to walk the windy, deserted beaches of the English coast, and perhaps think long and hard about a new direction for his life. Hell, he might even enjoy life for a change.

It is the right decision, Harri Schoder. You've faced up to raining hellfire before now, so what's one British superintendent against that?

23

The Lid Over London

5th December 1952

Harri

The minute he wakes, Harri has a strong suspicion that his day is already heading downhill fast. The air in his room is more stagnant than normal, and he wonders if Mrs P's breakfast fare has reached a new peak of dreadful, judging by the smell of bad eggs wafting through the house. Opening the window is pointless, with nothing but grey fug in its view, as if someone has taped a sheet of paper over the expanse. Switching on the overhead lamp, the yellowy glow highlights strands of vapour coiling in the air. An unwelcome trespasser.

A little like a child lamenting the last of the snow, Harri can't help feeling a deep sense of disappointment at the ruin of his promised day. The trains will almost certainly be disrupted, and even he knows it's unwise to venture far in this, meaning the Oxford trip is off. Dressing in layers and descending the stairs, he notes the house seems unusually quiet, as a faint grimy film spirals up to meet him. Harri has seen decent fog in London before, and at home, but never inside the house. Approaching the kitchen, there's none of the tell-tale clanking of pots that signals Mrs P is on the breakfast warpath. Ordinarily, it would mean relief, but after last night, it's a worry.

She's still in the chair, wrapped in a blanket, in yesterday's clothes and hacking away into her handkerchief. 'I'm so sorry, dear,' she croaks. 'But I don't think I'm going to be able to do your breakfast this morning.'

'Don't worry,' he says. 'Let me get you something.'

'No, no, dear . . .' she protests. But he insists, cutting bread and toasting it over the range, making tea – though this time Mrs P is too weary to issue orders. He watches her nibble at the toast, feeding a good deal of it to Scooter, in between prolonged bouts of coughing.

'Shall I call a doctor?' he suggests. 'You look very pale.' Her breathing is laboured, too, needing to suck in air between tiny sips of tea.

'I'll be fine,' she wheezes. 'I get like this for a few days every year, with the damp, and this blasted weather doesn't help. I'll be right as rain tomorrow. My neighbour, Mrs Spriggs, will call in later.'

'Well, if you're sure,' Harri says. He takes Scooter into the back yard for much-needed relief, refreshes the teapot, shovels some coal into the range and – seeing wisps seeping under the back door – rolls up a small rug and wedges it against the gap. His landlady smiles weakly in thanks before another round of hacking, Scooter wide-eyed at her side.

'I'll be back later to check on you,' Harri promises.

Beyond the front door is a freezing, alternate world. A thick static vapour clashes with Harri's face as he steps into a grey-green abyss, as if he's been submerged in murky pondwater and only just able to see his feet, or the hand that automatically stretches out. This is Sherlock Holmes on a grand scale. He gasps at the sight, which sets off his own bout of coughing, as it catches in his throat and burns with a vile taste of sulphur. Pulling the scarf tight against his mouth, he shuffles to the end of the path and then inches his way along the road, forced to place one hand on successive garden fences as an anchor, then plunged into a brief panic when wood or brick gives way to an open gate or what must be an entrance to an alleyway. Woah! He rears up suddenly, coming face to face with another startled soul, just inches away. 'Sorry! Sorry,' Harri blurts to the body swathed in layers – a woman, he thinks – as they effect a comical dance, both reluctant to give up their precious lifeline.

How on earth is anyone or anything going to function in this? Or be found when they're so intent on hiding? Thankfully, that's no longer his problem.

The end of the road is only detected by a faint, muffled hum of traffic and the smudge of car headlights moving at a snail's pace, people represented by muted hacking in the near distance. Harri has never been so glad to see the yellow beacon of a British café, its rectangular glow shining out.

'Shut the door! Shut the door!' the owner cries as he enters, desperate to keep out the filthy fog invader. Inside, several tables are occupied, customers hunkered down in their thick overcoats and nursing hot drinks. The steam inside comes from the geyser up at the counter and is mercifully white, with no odour save for the coffee it brews. As Harri sits, the door opens again and the outline of Dexie ghosts in, though he'd be hard pressed to recognise her anywhere else, under a beret, two scarves and a thick short coat.

'I know, I know, I said this would be gone,' she says defensively, unwinding a length of wool from her face.

'Remind me never to rely on you for a weather forecast.'

She grins in return and signals to the waitress.

'You seem remarkably cheery,' Harri says, 'given that we've woken up to a scene from a horror film where a monster from the murky depths could rear up at any time.'

'That's because I'm not on a shift, having to help *everyone* across the road, instead of just children and old ladies.'

'Breakfast?' he suggests. 'In lieu of the lunch I was supposed to buy you in Oxford.'

'Yes, please, I'm starving. Our cook didn't make it into the section house, and there was only dry bread. Pretty stale, too.'

Ordering two full English with extra toast, they try to plan the day around the new encumbrance. 'The trains can't get in and out of London safely,' Dexie says. 'Though I heard on the radio that it's only affecting London.'

'How can that be?' To Harri, it feels as if the whole country must be plunged into this dystopian half-world. Right now, he can't imagine seeing blue sky ever again.

'Don't ask me the ins and outs of it, but some smart alec on the news said it's a freak weather front, where the cloud comes down and sits like a lid across London. That's how he explained it. There's no breeze, apparently, to blow it away. Meantime, millions of houses are burning coal to keep warm, and plenty of power stations like Battersea are constantly pumping out smoke, all of which gets trapped under this lid, because it's got nowhere else to go. Instead of simple fog, it's created this vile, smelly smog, apparently stretched across twenty miles.'

'So how long is this supposed to last?' Harri thinks of his short walk to the café, with not a breath of wind to shift the dense air.

Dexie shrugs. 'Usually, it lasts only a day or so,' she says. Then crinkles her mouth after a sip of coffee. 'Though . . .'

'Hmm?'

'I have to admit I've never known it this bad before.'

'Great,' Harri sighs. 'Well, I think there's little point in attempting to collect the car. But do you think we can make it to Scotland Yard on foot?'

'Oh yes,' she says confidently. 'I remembered to pack my homing device. We'll get there.'

'Then what?' he queries, feeling suddenly deflated. 'It seems a shame to waste your day off. A walk along the Thames might be a bit pointless, but how about a gallery, the National perhaps, and then lunch at the Café Royal?'

'You've just bought me breakfast,' she points out.

'And my gratitude knows no bounds when it comes to not having a bullet lodged in my neck.'

'That's a fair point,' she says. 'And I won't say no. I haven't been to the Café Royal since the war. I do remember they serve a very good martini.'

'Then we have a plan. A bit of culture, followed by martinis all round.'

Stocked up on eggs and coffee, Dexie pilots Harri slowly but with more confidence than most others shuffling their way through the mire, down Bloomsbury Street and along Charing Cross Road. There's little point taking the Tube, since the queues from several stations are stretched out onto the pavements, causing added chaos. The moving edifices of double-deckers, buttery lights aglow, are shunting forward only a yard or two at a time, and the orchestra of angry motorists on their horns has started up again. Finally, they reach New Scotland Yard, now dressed to cinematic effect in its Victorian fog finery.

'Here to see Superintendent Graham,' Harri says to the desk sergeant, pulling his shoulders back. Suddenly, he wants to be rid of this whole endeavour, and get on with his life. One that involves little excitement, and certainly no Russian spies in the perilous mix.

'He's expecting you, sir,' the desk man says.

'Is he?' As much as Harri is pleased not have to beg for an audience, he's startled – and slightly annoyed – at being so predictable.

'Fourth floor, sir, first on the lef—'

'Thank you, Sergeant, I know where it is.'

'It's entirely believable that Johnson has been in touch already,' Dexie says as they climb the stairs, reading him perfectly. 'They'll have guessed that we'd make our way here.'

'Hmm, suppose so.' And yet, since when did he become such an open book?

Graham's secretary is, of course, unsurprised to see Harri walk through the door and, accordingly, it's no shock – if very unwelcome – to note Johnson's form sat casually in front of the superintendent, the smoke of his cigarette adding to the general fug of haze in the office.

'Morning, Schroder.' Graham gets up, and seeing Dexie walk in behind, pulls up a third chair. 'I presume this is WPC Dexter?'

'Sir.' She nods.

'You got through this dratted fog,' he goes on. 'Quite apart from the effect on the city, it's very bad timing for us. Please, do sit down.'

'I only came to return my identity card and the money you gave,' Harri says sharply, pulling both from his suit pocket and laying them on the table. The offered chair remains empty.

'Well, let's not be hasty,' Graham tries to appease. 'I'm sure we can work this out.'

'I don't think so, sir.' Harri's tone is uncompromising. 'I'm all for a challenge, and perfectly willing to fight against fascism, but *not* when I have to fight both sides.' He throws a concerted look towards the other man, who sits motionless, staring at the floor. 'And Mr Johnson here knows exactly why I won't be continuing, quite apart from the fact that you can't actually see a thing outside, let alone search for a man who doesn't want to be found.'

He stands, feet astride, feeling better for having purged the weight of his frustration on someone other than a British spy. And yet, why does he get the feeling that this is not the release he'd been planning? Graham leans back in his large leather chair, as if signalling that, once again, he's giving way to Johnson.

It's then that the MI5 man finally moves, stubbing out his cigarette in the large ashtray on Graham's desk and rising, his face loaded. With ammunition, Harri detects.

'It does seem a little bit glib to use the phrase "turn a blind eye" on today of all days,' Johnson begins calmly. 'But it is the perfect description of past practices.' Now he looks at Harri directly, pupil to pupil, black to black. 'Yours, principally, Inspector Schroder, wouldn't you say?'

Oh, here we go. Harri prepares himself for the onslaught, having been subjected to a subtle yet insidious form of British blackmail before, from the armed forces hierarchy back in Hamburg: '*Do this, or we can't guarantee your promotion or the transfer you want.*' It's not the first time he's thought that Hitler's Nazis weren't alone in using dirty coercion to further their own ends.

Sensing Dexie shifting uncomfortably to his side, Harri opens with: 'Oh, and what particular misdemeanour were you thinking of? I'm fairly sure I have a whole range for you to choose from, those you've plucked from my very detailed file.' He aims a forced smile in Johnson's direction.

'There are several incidences of you turning that blind eye to black market trading back in Hamburg,' Johnson replies flatly.

Harri steps even closer, truly irritated now. 'Is that really the best you can manage? Come on, Johnson, I would have thought you might manufacture a bit of uncalled violence towards a prisoner, or my taking bribes from gangs of racketeers. Something a bit meatier.'

'You've been accused more than once of not arresting perpetrators of under-the-counter trading in the years after the war,' Johnson prattles on. 'More than once. Do you want me to quote the dates?'

'No, I don't!' Harri almost explodes. 'And do you know why, Mr MI5 Man? Because I can recall with absolute clarity when and why I broke the law that I am supposed to fastidiously uphold, day in, day out, in the shithole I call home.' Johnson flinches a little, looking as if he might regret putting a match to this particular fire. Graham says not a word to quell the outburst as Harri blazes on. 'I willingly became blind to a woman peddling on the street, to scrape just enough money to buy milk for her baby, and frequently to the children – probably younger than your own, if you have any – that are homeless and parentless, scrabbling on the ground for cigarette ends to make a pfennig that will see them buy a precious bread roll. A stale one at that. The man that owns the bar I frequent can only serve liquor bought on the black market, the same ex-soldier that has a gouged-out leg and four children to feed. And who happens to give this weary police officer much needed solace at the end of a very bad day. So, go ahead – fire me, or lock me up. I don't actually care.'

Breathless and strangely satisfied, Harri glares at Johnson.

'Bravo, Inspector Schroder,' he says with an unctuous air. 'I'm sure that we can all applaud your sacrifice—'

'It's not sacrifice!' Harri snaps back. 'It's called life, Johnson. And some people have a very poor one. Not that you would ever know.'

'Nevertheless, what you did remains a disciplinary offence,' Johnson goes on, regardless. 'At worst, sackable. Which is tricky for you, because I happen to think you do care about your job, very much so.'

Harri closes his mouth, trapping the angry words ready to spring forth. *Verdammt!* Johnson has read him perfectly.

He *does* care. 'Grumpy', 'curmudgeonly', 'dejected' – those are some of the words used to describe Harri Schroder over the years, but he gets results, in the right areas, he likes to think. The Kripo tolerate his unorthodox methods because of his success in taking major criminals off the street, gangsters and murderers included. Now, that same humane but unruly approach has come back to 'bite him on the arse', as his British squaddie friend Robbie Dawson was apt to say during his stint in Germany.

From the corner of his eye, Harri feels the heat of Dexie's glower, aimed at Johnson. 'How . . .?' she starts 'I'm really at a loss to understand how you can be so callous as to use blackmail on someone who is an ally in all of this?'

Graham shifts, as if to reprimand his junior officer, but thinks better of it.

It's Johnson who rounds on her with venom. 'It is you, Miss Dexter, who doesn't under—'

'Constable Dexter.'

'*Constable*. You can't possibly appreciate what's at stake here, for the British Government, and the pressure that's coming from above. We're walking on hot coals here, and without that identification we will get our feet well and truly burnt.' He scowls at them with intent. 'All of us.'

The silent stand-off lasts only a few seconds, until Harri decides he's had enough. Much more of this and Johnson will start accusing him of being a Nazi, and that he can really do without. 'All right, it's clear I'm not going to escape this easily,' he concedes bitterly. 'What do you propose we do to find Praxer? Please tell me you have a clever device that's able to see through walls, or else the dense cloud that's descended from God, because I can't see shit out there.'

Harri halts as he and Dexie arrive on the ground floor, a fresh filmic haze spread across the Yard's reception area, people squinting as they slip across the greasy floor tiles.

'Huh, that's put paid to our cocktail hour,' she says, though it's with more cheer than is warranted.

'Absolutely not!' Harri pronounces. 'I'm buying you that martini, if it's the last thing I do.'

She smiles. 'Nice idea, Harri, but do you think it's sensible?'

'Do you know, WPC Dexter, I'll say it once again – I really don't care. But I am certain it will improve the evening that's in store for us.'

Forced to acquiesce in the face of Johnson's leverage, the evening is set to be a challenge, not least because it involves two officers of the law posing as waiting staff in a high-end, high-stakes casino.

'I warn you now that I am probably the worst waiter in existence,' Harri had revealed upstairs. 'I got my first job in a bar when I was seventeen, for all of three days before being sacked for incompetence. The sheer amount of broken glasses cost twice my wages.'

Johnson brushed it off with a shrug. 'You'll do fine,' he said. 'We only need you in there long enough to get close to Praxer and make the identification. Since the fog came down, our sources tell us his aims for travelling outside the city have been shelved, at least until it clears. Unusually, he plans on visiting a friend's casino this evening, which will host only a select group of guests, including Praxer's wife.'

'And the Russians, are they on the guest list too?'

'No,' Johnson shot back. 'This intelligence is watertight.' He'd stopped briefly, as if considering his words carefully: 'I guarantee it.'

'But what happens if Praxer's wife recognises me, from the café yesterday?' Harri pitched.

'Then it's up to you to stay out of her eyeline,' Johnson said crossly. 'Hopefully, she won't have noticed you. Besides which, staff in those establishments are invisible to the wealthy people who patronise them.'

'Oh great,' Harri grumbled. 'A gun held to my head, and now I'm destined to be a leper to the great and the good.'

Johnson ignored this last remark and turned towards Dexie, his menace replaced with a firm, business-like expression. 'You'll be observing the wife, picking up any snippets you can from her conversations, though try not to hover too long and arouse suspicion.'

It was then that Harri had watched Dexie's mouth twist with anger again, as the stiff suit tried preaching surveillance techniques to a serving officer of the street. 'Teaching Grandma to suck eggs,' was another one of those phrases that came to mind.

'Insufferable fool,' he heard her mutter as they left Graham's office.

Through the windows of Scotland Yard, the weather front shows no signs of shifting – good news for Johnson's plan, but bad for the millions of ordinary folk across the city. They hear one constable report to the desk sergeant that the docks are at a standstill, with no shipping going in or out, and the foot patrols are at capacity, thieves are already taking advantage of the confusion to target empty houses, the old and the vulnerable.

'I can't face the Underground,' Dexie says, winding her scarf tightly to form a mask. 'It'll be chaos down there and quicker to walk to Regent Street. Agreed?'

'Agreed. Switch on that excellent radar, and I'll be your shadow.'

If it's at all possible, the smog outside has worsened. It's just past midday and the streetlights have been switched back on, creating a strange merge between day and night, while the phosphorous glow simply bounces back off the sickly, jaundiced vapour. Any hint of twinkly Christmas cheer has vanished, as the traffic gives off an invisible, impatient snarl, with a continuous background of emergency sirens sucked into the great, filthy vortex that is England's great capital. Hitting the freezing air, Harri feels as if he's as walked straight into a damp cobweb, pawing at the flesh above his scarf and sees his finger come away with grey, slimy film. And to think that only a week or so ago, he imagined missing the worst of the Hamburg winter.

They speak little on the walk over, he responding to Dexie's gesturing and short, muffled remarks through the wool of her scarf. 'This way,' he interprets, or 'left here'. By virtue of her innate sense of direction, they arrive in front of the still grand, though a little faded Café Royal.

'I bow to your skills as a walking compass, WPC Dexter,' Harri says, pulling down his scarf.

Drawing him to the side of the concierge, Dexie looks up into his face with a worried expression. 'What's wrong?' he says.

'The top of your face is grimy,' she says. 'Mine too, I don't doubt. Maybe we should sidle in to the bathrooms first and make ourselves presentable?'

‘Good idea.’

Arm in arm, they bluff it out past the concierge with large smiles as he’s distracted by guests appearing out of the gloom.

‘I feel like a naughty schoolchild,’ Dexie whispers when their feet hit the plush carpet and gentle chink-chink of London’s opulence. ‘And quite underdressed.’

‘That money in my pocket is as good as anyone else’s,’ Harri argues. ‘Meet you out here in five minutes, and we’ll sniff out the bar.’

In the bathroom, he draws a wet handkerchief across his nose and forehead, shocked at the grime lifted off, black as the inside of a car engine. What on earth can that be doing to the lungs of Londoners? His thoughts go back to Mrs P, slumped in front of the fire, and hopes the neighbour has arrived to check on her.

‘Ready?’ Dexie comes up behind him in the lobby. ‘I seem to have worked up a decent appetite on that walk over.’

‘Then I think we should go and watch the waiter intently as he serves our drinks, all in the interest of research, don’t you?’

The barman is slick and professional and the martini very good, as is the light lunch they order. From their corner table, they observe London’s monied classes gossip and laugh amid the mirrored gilt and chandeliers, with little thought, it seems, for the bedlam beyond the doors.

Dexie’s eye seems drawn to several couples taking to the small dancefloor as the piano player strikes up a tune. ‘Do you like to dance?’ Harri asks.

Her head whips around. ‘Me? Not often, my feet are best saved for the beat.’

'And here's me thinking there isn't much anything you can't do.'

'I'm sorry to disappoint you.' Her return look is strangely wistful. 'There are plenty of holes in my CV.'

'Actually, this is where I learnt to dance properly,' Harri goes on. 'In the main ballroom.'

'With your *wife*? Did you come here together?'

'No, sadly not,' he says, conscious of the faint waver in his voice. 'It was after . . . after the war. My good friend, Georgie, plied me with several drinks and dragged me onto the floor. It's one of her favourite places to dance, and we'd had a case in Hamburg where my lack of ballroom prowess was, let's say, noted. She vowed to teach me, and when she's in that mood, there's no objecting to Georgie.'

'I like the sound of her. Does that mean you trip across the floor like Fred Astaire nowadays?'

'Hardly. Though perhaps less like an oversized ogre with two left feet.' He swallows martini to mask a stab of feeling, back to a place he is generally reluctant to go, with Hella giggling at his poor attempt at dancing swing back in Hamburg. By contrast, his wife always moved with grace and rhythm, and he never minded when a much more able colleague from the station whisked her onto the dancefloor at the Alster Pavilion on the water's edge of the Elbe. He can picture her clearly, throwing her head back with pure abandon, twirling in time with the music. Oh, how he regrets not pushing that man aside and rising above that lack of confidence, so that he could have danced with his wife cheek to cheek, against the sweet fragrance of her skin. What he wouldn't give to be able to grasp at that opportunity again. And yet, what use are regrets? She's gone, and – the one thing he's learnt through the agony of grief – it's nothing but wasted effort.

'Harri?' Dexie is staring at him, gazing into his drink.

'Uh?' He raises himself, and then his cocktail. 'Here's to whatever tonight throws at us.'

'No guns, hopefully,' Dexie clinks hers against his and sips. 'Hmm, that is so nice.'

'Talking of which . . .' Harri puts down his glass in defiance. 'I've decided this is our last job for Johnson. Whatever else he has up his sleeve, I won't be beholden to his threats any more. It's a public place tonight, if a little exclusive, but we'll be in plain sight. I'll look Praxer straight in the eye, force some words out of him if I have to, and then we get out of there. We're done. Yes?'

She nods. 'Though . . .'

'Though what?'

She drains her glass. 'Nothing really, only I was quite enjoying being out of uniform, that's all. Especially in this weather.'

'Perhaps we'll go into hiding afterwards for a few days,' he suggests. 'From Johnson, Praxer and your boss. We'll say we got lost in the fog.'

'You're full of good ideas, aren't you?'

The National Gallery has disappeared from their planned itinerary in every way, as they weave around the statues on Trafalgar Square. Johnson has arranged for them to visit a small hotel nearby for a crash course in serving drinks, and when they cross the renowned piazza, the grand ivory portico of the gallery has vanished completely. Higher up, even Nelson and his own bird's eye view is veiled in the thick nimbus.

This time, Dexie is forced to pull Harri by the hand through the streams of people leaving work early on a Friday to beat the rush hour, though there's little hope of anyone moving at a pace. 'Every time we step out, it seems to get thicker,' he says, feeling his own chest tighten against the dense air.

'I heard someone say the radio is reporting worse to come,' Dexie tosses over her shoulder.

'Worse? How can it possibly get—Oi!' He's cut off by a heavy whump to his shoulder, a large man stumbling out of nowhere who's crippled by deep, viscous coughing, struggling to remain upright.

'Sorry, sorry,' the man splutters.

How bad does this have to get before the city stops entirely?

By the time they reach the hotel, Harri's mouth is dry, his tongue coated with a foul, stale film. Being considered as staff, they enter by the back door and quote the code Johnson has furnished: 'Simon sent us'. It's straight out of a bad spy novel, and Harri can't help wondering if Johnson has set out deliberately to make them feel foolish, or that it's truly part of the espionage world. Either way, it works, because they are shown into a private function room and, for the next hour or so, put through their paces in taking orders, the distinction between a dry and dirty martini (it's the level of vermouth and olive brine, apparently), plus how to pour and serve.

'And bow and scrape,' Harri grumbles in Dexie's ear.

'Shh!' she rebukes. 'I want to get this right, and get out of there in one piece.'

'Sorry.'

Finally, the hotelier dismisses them with a shrug, and a 'good luck' that Harri takes to be for his benefit. Despite his love of good food and drink and the intervening twenty years or so, it's obvious his skills as a waiter haven't improved.

'Listen, I'm exhausted,' Dexie says when they reach the vague area around Tottenham Court Road. 'I need a bath before we venture out tonight and at least half an hour where I'm horizontal.'

It's true. Quite apart from the black grease clinging to her cheeks, she looks weary of being the guide in criss-crossing the city virtually blindfolded. His guilt spikes at being so reliant. 'I'll find my way to Mrs P's,' he insists.

'Are you sure? Because I can . . .'

'No, really, you get off. I'll see you outside at Tottenham Court Road Tube at eight.'

'If you're sure.' She steps away, swallowed instantly by the grey and leaving his world feeling strangely empty, save for the stream of bodies tiptoeing their way to a home hearth and safety.

Harri leans against the damp, porous brickwork of a newsagent's and sniffs, out of habit principally. Once the bombs had stopped exploding in Hamburg and the air no longer saturated with cordite, it swiftly became his way of staking out the city and gauging its mood each morning. Mostly, the smell was bad – refuse, rats, human detritus, and the odd dead body found thawed under bricks as the winter snow receded – but it served to categorise between danger and peril, safety and sometimes pleasure.

Now, his nose is invaded by something toxic and putrid. He shivers under his coat, but feels grubby and sweat stained at the same time, hoping – rather selfishly – that Mrs P's boiler has been maintained by a constant shovelling of coal through the day. The mere thought of a six-inch bath of hot water seems like heaven right now.

* * *

Harri's own senses are tested to their limit and his eyes are stinging as he finally reaches Bayley Street, navigating largely by the neon lights of several cafés and a single launderette, counting the gateways to her door. But when he lets himself in, the hallway is in darkness again. Worse, so is the kitchen, when he's never glimpsed it without a glow of the fire or the small lamp that sits on the heavy wooden sideboard. He switches on the bulb, startled for a second by the vapour slithering like a slow-moving reptile about the unattended room, sucking out the oxygen and laying claim to any fresh air. *It's seizing everything*, he thinks, *down to the last particle*.

Harri retreats and listens in the cold void of the hallway. The other residents, he believes, are office workers and probably battling their way home right now. 'Mrs P,' he projects. 'Mrs Painter?' There's a weak cough behind a door that sits between the kitchen and the front parlour. 'Mrs P?' A second cough, then another. For a man who's battered his way through countless doors in criminal searches, Harri is hesitant on trying the handle behind the kitchen, feeling like a true invader. 'Where are you?'

'In here,' comes a feeble voice.

She's propped up in bed this time, with a blanket around her shoulders, in a bedroom little bigger than a decent-size cupboard. There's only one small window close to the ceiling, and the air, while stagnant, isn't fog-filled like the kitchen. 'Mrs Painter, how are you?'

'All right, dear.' Her voice is tiny and weak and comes from somewhere far away. Breaching the covers, Scooter's head emerges, a mournful look to his eyes.

'I hate to say it, Mrs P, but you don't sound it.' Harri has a sudden flash memory of being taken to see his grandmother when he was a child, in a similar bed-bound pose, long grey hair splayed around her shoulders. Only afterwards, when he was escorted to the funeral a short time later, did he understand that his beloved *Oma* had been in her death throes on that last visit. But Mrs P can't be dying, Harri argues to himself, because the felt petal hat is still fixed firmly in place. Even so, she doesn't look good: pale and wan, her bird-like ribcage giving off a fearsome rattle. 'Shall I call a doctor?'

'That's kind, Mr Schroder,' she says. 'But my neighbour has phoned for me, some hours ago. They'll be very busy, what with this weather. I'm sure someone will come soon enough.'

Maybe not, Harri thinks. He struggles to think what his mother would have done, or Hella during that awful time when Lily had croup as a baby. Steam, isn't that it? The irony is in creating more white mist, but steam is wet and opens up lung tissue, in contrast to this cloying vapour, which simply invades and clogs. And it's all they have to hand.

Once again, Harri banks up the fire in the kitchen range, brews tea (because doesn't tea solve everything in the British psyche?) and rummages to find a clean dish towel. He hasn't ever so much as shaken Mrs P's hand in their short history, so putting his long arm around her shoulders to help prop her up seems overly intimate, until she gives him a look of permission and understanding, and a 'thank you, dear', so reminiscent of his grandmother back when he was boy. While she hangs her head over the boiling water, shrouded in a towel to trap the steam, he makes her a dry cheese sandwich from what he can find in the larder.

'You can come again, Mr Schroder,' she says afterwards, with a welcome gleam in her eye, and voice that – Harri thinks – sounds less of a croak. 'I could get used to this pampering. Mr Painter used to bring me a cup of tea in bed every Sunday, God rest his soul.'

'Then that's what I shall do this very weekend,' Harri says. The smile he forces hides a niggling worry that there might not be a next Sunday for Mrs P if this weather doesn't let up. 'I do have to go out again this evening, and I'll be quite late. Will you be all right on your own?'

'Don't you worry, dear. I came through an entire house falling on top on me in the Blitz, so I'm sure a bit of fog won't see me off.' She reaches up and palms at her hat, as if it's some form of talisman, her defence against everything.

And I'll bet there wasn't a bomb powerful enough to drag that off your head. No wonder Hitler didn't have a hope of winning.

By the time Mrs P is dozing, and Harri feels able to leave her, there's little time for anything else. Without a fire, his room is freezing, white breath mixing with the yellow seepage from outside. On his bedroom wall, the small hot water geyser sputters into life, and while it's almost painful stripping down to his undervest for a wash, the leftover grey water says it was necessary. His cloth strips away the oily sheen from his face and hands especially, and the collar of his shirt is blackened, as if he's taken a nugget of coal from the kitchen scuttle and rubbed it directly on the white weave.

Does he feel refreshed enough to confront the evening ahead? Yes, and no. Just this morning, Harri had risen with a clearer head, in contrast to the fug beyond the window. At that point, his trip had been cut short by a combination of circumstance and Johnson's mendacity, but he still had several weeks of holiday to look forward to, starting with a day in one of his favourite cities, and in good company too. The rest – the return to Hamburg, his life unchanged – he would face later. Cross that bridge when he came to it, as the British are fond of saying.

Then Johnson had pulled blackmail from his bottomless

bag of dirty tricks, and set he and Dexie on another path. But Harri is freshly determined; this is the last drop of blood Johnson will squeeze from this particular stone. It ends tonight. As for tomorrow . . . the fog may lift, his life could change for the better. There's always hope. Or miracles.

Harri combs too much Brylcreem through his hair, and slicks it back, struggling to recognise the man in the mirror. Hopefully, Praxer will have the same difficulty. His aim is to get in and out without confrontation, or incurring the wrath of a man who has taken a very different path.

'Your martini, sir,' he parrots. 'Whisky or champagne?' Then sighs heavily. 'Jesus, Schroder, you're a joke.'

He checks on Mrs P just before leaving, a combined whinny of snores from Scooter mixing with the hiss of her chest, but he takes it as a reassuring sign of the breath within her. Leaving a note on the kitchen table for the other guests to look in on her, Harri feels his way down the path and along the road, noting that more than twenty-four hours of this filthy smog has made the pavements slippery underfoot. If it ices over, the hospitals will have the double jeopardy of broken ankles *and* rackety lungs to deal with.

The breakfast café at the end of the road is unlit, though the neon sign hanging in the window that says 'closed' acts as a necessary beacon, after which memory pilots him back to the Tube station through darkness and fog. Dexie is already there, stamping her feet against the cold and looking quite different. It takes several minutes before Harri pinpoints her hair as the reason, now pulled up off her neck and bundled under a woollen hat. Above her scarf, strands are falling on the nape of her pale skin, and he finds himself staring at it for no apparent reason.

'Did you get any rest?' she asks.

'A bit,' he lies, mainly because he's too tired to relay the entire saga of Mrs P. 'You?'

'I nabbed the bathroom and soaked for a good half an hour,' she says. 'It was bliss, until the water went cold and there wasn't any more. I wasn't too popular after that, so it was a relief to slink out.'

Slink. That seems the perfect description of their movements in the past couple of days. Harri thinks he would quite like to march across the capital, unabashed and unashamed, but, for now, slinking is required in the next few hours.

They wait for several minutes beside the station entrance, watching the eerie outline of buses and taxis inching their way forward, bumper to bumper, a gallery of vague faces peering through the condensation of the top deck windows, perhaps trying to weigh up the frustration of the bus's speed versus walking home blind.

'Do you think Johnson's man has got lost?' Dexie asks. 'More likely, he just can't see us in this. I'm sure we could walk to Mayfair more quickly than driving.'

'Probably,' Harri agrees, 'but judging by the state of my face earlier on, we might not be smart enough to grace the inside of a fashionable casino.'

'True,' she says. 'Though, I wish he would hurry up. My feet are like ice.' It's no wonder. In place of her brown brogues and tweed trousers, she has on a pair of black leather pumps over dark stockings, far more practical than the fashionable kitten heels he's glimpsed in various shop windows. She will, however, look like a waitress, albeit with frozen toes.

Finally, a car draws up and a man in a dark overcoat gets out and comes towards them, squinting in the gloom. He's almost face to face before he flashes some form of ID card, and although the action is too fast to absorb properly, Harri is satisfied this is Johnson's man. He wears an identical veil of arrogance, cut from the same security cloth.

'Mayfair?' he grunts. 'Casino?' When Harri nods, he instructs them to get in, and moves back behind the steering wheel without a word.

Dexie shivers in the back seat, while up front the driver keeps up a muttering commentary on the traffic chaos as they join the slow-moving convoy. There's no hurry, since high-class gamblers apparently don't start throwing their money around until at least ten. Hit by a sudden wave of fatigue, Harri rests his head back, feeling the unction of his hair on the worn leather, trying to work through their plan for the evening, if one actually exists. Johnson has some hand in trying to control the scene, as the club belongs to an acquaintance of Praxer's, where the staff are poorly paid and therefore open to a little extra in their pockets. Bribery, in plain English. As for the actors or the script, there's really no telling where it will go.

'And what if Praxer won't be drawn out, or leaves early?' Harri had quizzed Johnson earlier. 'Or he recognises me.'

'You're a detective, use your initiative,' he'd snapped back. 'We need that identification, and the sooner the better. You need to contact me the minute you have it. The very second, understand?'

'We're here.' The driver breaks through Harri's deliberations as he comes to a stop. 'This is where I've been told to leave you.'

Dexie sits forward, eyes shining, though in the gloom of the interior it's almost impossible to read her level of confidence. Or fear.

'Ready?' he says.

'As I'll ever be.'

Curtain up.

24

Role Play

5th December 1952

Dexie

In through the back entrance and a line of odorous bins, Mayfair is none too salubrious, much like the glitz of nightclubs around Leicester Square that Dexie has often viewed in the cold light of day: shabby and scruffy, and altogether less twinkly without the advantage of well-placed lighting. Down several steps and entering through a rickety back door, the basement kitchen also hides a multitude of these sins, and it's evident that it's not only the fog providing a veneer. A man in a grubby chef's apron herds them, snapping the door shut and grumbling about the climatic invader. Without need of an explanation, they are introduced to Charlie, the tall and gaunt head waiter who looks to be in his early thirties, and presumably the one whose palm has been well-greased by Johnson's lot. Cigarette in hand, he takes them past the tiny windowless staff room, where the air is fuggy, made thicker by a collection of men and women lounging and smoking. As nocturnal workers, and through the haze, their skin looks noticeably pallid. Languidly, one or two raise a hand when Charlie introduces 'Terry' and 'Betty'. She's no idea what Harri thinks about his given name, but who on earth came up with 'Betty'?

'We're not open yet, so I can take you upstairs and show you the layout,' Charlie says in his flat, East End accent, leading them up a set of well-trodden back steps.

Through a door at the top of a stairwell, they enter an entirely different domain. Mayfair houses are lofty enough, but it seems as if two large residences have been knocked through to create a sweeping rectangular room of high ceilings, with a reception facing the door, bathrooms and perhaps smaller private rooms to one side. Dexie's pumps sink into a deep-pile carpet of plush crimson, the décor above best described as opulent, in the way that bigger is better in some moneyed circles. The floor-to-ceiling windows are dressed in swathes of heavy purple velvet, closing off the world outside. Maybe because it's already a vacuum, there's only a faint seepage of smog. Were it not for a sickly smell of air freshener mixing with the sulphur, you could almost imagine the surrealism outside didn't exist.

Prudently, Dexie takes in the panorama. Bulbs in the chandeliers are not yet alight, so the dim view is from a selection of wall lamps dotted around the room, showing up Edwardian style sofas against each wall, with small side tables, leaving the floor free for the felted gaming tables, centred by a large roulette station, where a man in a waistcoat and bow tie is busy polishing the wooden wheel. 'Evenin',' he nods, only half looking up.

'So, rules for the casino,' Charlie begins his instruction. 'When they're at the tables, the punters will rarely signal for a drink with words' – his eyes roll in clear disdain – 'but simply move their fingers upwards.' He makes an all too brief flick of one digit, that's barely recognisable, except to the eagle eye. 'They expect you to be there in seconds, so keep your eyes peeled. If one says "my usual", don't question it, just indicate to the barman who they are – discreetly, mind – and he'll sort you out. The male waiters usually circulate the tables, while the girls take care of the ladies around the edge. Occasionally, wives or girlfriends play at the tables, but most tend to sit around, waiting for their other half to decide they've lost enough before they can go home.'

Dexie feels her hackles rise several inches, and Harri gives her a sideways look.

'Serve their drinks to the left, never to the right, and no glasses directly on the table, always use a coaster.' Charlie frowns at them, as if this is the most cardinal of sins they can commit. Dexie wonders how much he's been briefed as to their real identity or purpose – or the possible consequences. Not a great deal, from what he says next. 'Look I don't know who it is you're interested in, and I don't want to know, but there's a chance that your people might locate to a private room, for a more select game of cards. The ones with real money have that option. In that instance, I have to allocate a waiter to that room, and if you let me know, I'll move you in closer.' He holds his palms up in a need-to-know-nothing-else manner.

She watches Harri nod, his face betraying nothing else. What does she think of that prospect, being stuck in a room, likely with no windows and only one exit? Their safety for tonight is in the hands of someone they barely know, and whose other palm could well have been greased by a far richer adversary. It's not what anyone would relish, and yet how else can they get nose to nose with Praxer and escape what increasing feels like a rat-trap?

'Any questions?' Charlie says, when it's clear his briefing has ended.

A further grim prospect hits her, prompted by her experience of clubs on her patch, when she's been called in to play peacemaker or turf out a drunk. The hostesses, in their skimpy tops and tight skirts, sidle close to repellent men whose only attributes seem to be the money in their pocket. 'And am I expected to, you know, get up close and personal with the male guests?' Dexie asks, with a twist to her stomach.

Charlie shakes his head. 'No, there are strict rules here about guests engaging or touching, though they'll look you up and down plenty.' Unabashed, he does exactly that as he says it; she feels his eyes combing over her stockinged legs, up towards her midriff and over her breasts. She glares back in response. 'Don't forget, a lot of wives and mistresses are here in their finery, and so no flirting with their men,' Charlie instructs.

'I wasn't about to,' Dexie snaps.

'But you will be nice, *Betty*, won't you?' he presses. 'Smile. These people want to feel good, even when they're losing a lot of money.'

'More fool them.'

In the intervening half hour, both are issued with casino uniforms of black, Harri in trousers and waistcoat, and a crisp white shirt topped off with a bow tie, identical to Dexie, aside from her tight black skirt, which she tries pulling down to knee height. 'If my sergeant could see me in this!' she protests, and when Charlie casts a disappointed look at her flat pumps: 'I can't walk in heels, let alone serve drinks in them,' she adds. 'Besides, I'm too tall, and I'd look like a giraffe stumbling around.'

'Fair point,' he grunts. 'I could always put you in the bar area, away from the tables.'

'We stick together,' Harri cuts him off sharply. 'Eyes on each other at all times.'

'Whatever you say, mate.' Charlie sniffs. 'But if anything goes haywire, I deny everything, that's the deal. They don't pay me enough to get involved.'

There's a short staff briefing before the doors open at ten p.m., when the two take their places next to the bar with the other waiters, stiff and straight, as per Charlie's instructions. The first hour is slow, with a trickle of well-dressed lone men taking to the tables, the experienced waiters seeing to their requests.

'These are the hardened gamblers,' Charlie tells them in a whisper. 'They may look well-heeled, but a good half will be mortgaged up to the eyeballs and in hock to the casino. Their bar bill alone is more than I earn in a year.'

'So, when do the others come in?' Harri queries. In other words, when are they likely to spy their prey?

'Between eleven and midnight, once the club shows have finished,' Charlie says. 'Then it really livens up.'

They take it in turns serving a few guests with uncomplicated orders, Dexie highly amused to see Harri's look of triumph when he doesn't upend a cocktail over the already fairly drunk punter playing blackjack, and is slipped a tip for his efforts.

'See, you can do it.' Dexie sidles by on her way back to the bar, wearing an unmistakably sardonic smile. 'I foresee a whole new career before you, *Terry*.'

'And a man can quickly tire of a new friend, *Betty*,' he quips back.

They are silenced by a stern look from Charlie – house rules say no chit-chat between staff.

Dexie's back is aching and her feet sore as the clock crawls towards midnight; the beat is often draining, but it's far harder standing still and maintaining a set smile. She's focused on stifling a yawn when Harri moves in close and reaches for a glass behind the bar, shielding his face. 'I think we're on,' he says. 'The head barman has just sent down to the cellar for the best champagne, "for Mrs Remington". They must be arriving soon.'

She stiffens, suddenly wary and fully alert. The boredom of previous hours falls away, and Dexie is running with something quite new to her. In the dockyard, she and Harri had little time to prepare, the Russian and their guns coming out of nowhere, and her response necessarily rapid, with no time to think. Now, amid the soft, inoffensive tinkle of jazz, and the closeted feeling of this space, there is room to consider. Is it fear? No, she's tasted fear in the war, sometimes on the streets since, and this isn't the same ripple of terror. A form of trepidation, perhaps? With too much idle time to ponder, Dexie pinpoints what is making her scalp tingle and the stale casino air catch in her throat: the fact that this Praxer character may well meet his nemesis in Harri – the rattlesnake trapped in a cage of rats. Only which of them has the sharper eyesight and, if necessary, the bigger bite?

25

The Rat Trap

6th December 1952

Harri

A ripple of activity around the entrance signals the arrival of important guests, plus a look from Charlie to all of the surrounding waiters that needs no words. They all stand straight, pulling back shoulders. One tweaks at his bow tie, and – much like the unconscious mimicking of someone's yawn – Harri finds himself doing the same. Unwittingly, he draws in a breath, too. Is this truly the moment when he does come face to face with his old colleague, a man who at one time might have been something nearing a friend? Who grew to have the blood of millions on his hands?

It's a job, Schroder. You can't dwell on that. Do it, get out. Live your life.

They arrive in a small cluster, two women in glittery and expensive evening dress led towards the sofas, both chattering away to an evidently bored Mrs Remington. A heavy-set man with a cigar clamped between his teeth shows Remington to the roulette table, with a good deal of deference, clicking his fingers at a waiter, who appears neatly at his side.

Charlie sidles up beside Harri and bends discreetly to his ear. 'That's the owner, Julius Caine. Don't go anywhere near him, because he'll spot you a mile off as a fake. And these are very important guests, so keep sharp.'

Harri dips his head barely a millimetre; fine by him. It gives him permission to circulate and pick up snatches of Remington's conversation, to identify that tell-tale voice and fully observe his mannerisms. Anything to spark a memory from the past. So far, Remington in the flesh remains a total stranger, if a clearly rich and powerful one.

Charlie's take on this calibre of guest is both correct and convenient; the men neither look at nor acknowledge any of the waiting staff. Julius Caine barks his drinks order with his eyes directly on the gambling chips in front of them, while Remington is catered for without having to utter a word. To Harri's left, Dexie moves in towards the newly seated women, they too issuing orders for champagne with painted lips that barely move. In minutes, Dexie sets down glasses and pours the fizzing liquid, retreating just out of their eyeline. From the tilt of her head, he notes her intently absorbing everything within earshot.

To maintain his cover, Harri serves several other guests, the drunk man included, who seems to have taken a shine to him. 'Good man, good man,' he slurs, like some old army general, throwing around pound notes.

Moving to and fro, Harri's eyes skim over Remington, watching his hands, the back of his head and the line of his jaw. But this man is firmly shuttered. He smiles and laughs in all the right places at Caine's loud and ebullient conversation, but never raises his own voice. Crucially, he doesn't lay down a single gambling chip as the roulette wheel is sent spinning again and again. His eyes, by contrast, are fixed on the tiny ball as it bobbles each time. Never once does he look up and take in his surroundings or the company.

Why is he even here? Harri ponders. If he owns a rival casino, is it merely good relations to glad-hand the competition every so often, and ensure no one else is taking a larger piece of the punter's pie than is fair? Is there any 'fair' in gambling?

And still no 'tell' from Remington, no shunt or shift in Harri's memory. No Praxer coming into the light.

After twenty minutes or so, Mrs Remington tires of her champagne and female companions. All eyes switch to her, the male ones especially, as she uncrosses her long, stockinged legs, mutters her excuses and moves with elegance towards the roulette table. A chair is instantly provided next to her husband, and wordlessly he slides a stack of chips in front of her.

'Alicia, my darling, please afford me some luck at my own table,' Caine pleads loudly. 'I'm losing against my own house!'

'With pleasure,' she croons, sliding several chips on varying numbers. All on black, Harri notes with interest.

'No more bets,' the croupier calls, Harri's cue to circulate in clearing a dirty glass and skirting the table.

The first truly gleeful smile comes from Remington as the ball slots into one of his wife's numbers.

'Beginner's luck,' he says. 'Always the best type. Well done, darling.'

He puts a proprietorial arm around her bare shoulder. Harri can't be sure, but in that second is there the briefest of evasions, a shrinking from her husband's touch? It's so fleeting it barely registers.

Easier to register, in those few words, is Remington's accent. Upper class, but indeterminate of geography, in the same way people narrow their eyes at Harri's English inflection, trying to pinpoint quite where he comes from. At best, it's a tiny clue that Remington is affecting a persona, but nothing concrete. Johnson and half of London already knows of the fine upstanding businessman; it's the undercurrent they want.

Go on, give me something more.

Alicia Remington is on a winning streak, and with each triumph, she stands and claps her hands childishly, swallowing back mouthfuls of fresh champagne, so that Remington's hand creeping across her hip is soon much-needed physical support as she sways next to him.

'Alicia,' he mutters more than once. 'Don't you think it's time we went home?'

Riding a wave of success and alcohol, she' s having none of it. 'You're such a spoilsport, darling,' she whines. 'Just one more go.'

In turn, her victories are egged on by Julius Caine, who gets louder and more inebriated in support of her victories. 'Nonsense, Remington! Your wife's only getting started,' he blusters.

However much he loses tonight, Harri reasons this can only be good public relations for Caine – rich club members are looking on and watching the house lose, encouraged by turns to throw down their own money in hope that the luck will spread.

The saying has it right: it is 'a mug's game'.

★ ★ ★

With the clock approaching one, and the air blue with cigar smoke, Caine summons Charlie with a click of fingers, whispers in his ear and the small party begins moving from the table towards a closed door to one of the private rooms. In seconds, Harri is across the floor and at Charlie's side: 'We need to be in there.'

'Christ, no, these are Caine's guests, I can't—' But Harri's determined stare cuts him off. 'All right. It's your funeral,' Charlie accedes.

With weary expressions, the two other women traipse into the room, a smaller version of the lounge outside – windowless, with a neat ornate sofa, a low ceiling light hanging over a card table that seats at least eight, and a scaled down bar in the corner. Harri logs a single door in and out. As instructed by Charlie, Dexie joins Harri, where they take their places beside the bar, a knowing glance at each other. The door is shut and the air feels sealed. Tomb-like.

'Champagne and whisky,' Caine slurs loudly. 'Soda for Mr Remington.'

At this point, Harri suspects most of the guests would have trouble recognising their own mother, let alone an imposter with poor serving skills. All except Remington, who is stone-cold sober. Luckily, he still hasn't wasted a second's glance in Harri's direction.

A croupier is called for and the cards dealt for poker, a hand for Mrs Remington, though none for her husband. She squints at the numbers on her cards, wavering slightly. Harri reasons that Alicia Remington will soon be too drunk stay upright, meaning the couple will have to leave, the mission left unaccomplished.

Even in close proximity, Remington's character is constrained. What's more, time is running out.

'Anything?' Dexie whispers to Harri as she pours more champagne, her face turned away from the card table. 'Can you be at all sure?'

'Not yet. He's giving absolutely nothing away.'

'Perhaps we should turn up the dial?' she says, side-stepping away. 'Make some noise.'

'What do you mean?' he hisses. But she's already picked up a tray loaded with drinks. He's seen that particular expression before, on someone else – Georgie's look when she's been on mission. Dogged. And unstoppable. The closer Dexie marches towards Alicia Remington, the more Harri braces himself.

'Oh my God! I'm so sorry!' Dexie recoils suddenly, as her tray wobbles almost comically and topples towards the floor. Alicia Remington is yanked from her drunken stupor as the contents of three champagne glasses land squarely in the lap of her very costly dress.

'Stupid cow! How could you be so clumsy?' she spits at Dexie, leaping up with the shock, swaying so much that her husband pulls her down with one swipe of his hand, though his attention – and his ire – is focused on Dexie, who is blindly mopping with her cloth, a feigned look of horror across her features.

'I am so, so sorry,' Dexie prattles in a convincing fluster. 'I tripped on the carpet. Oh my God, what can I do?'

'You can get out,' Remington hisses through gritted teeth, a hand still on his wife, eyes ablaze. 'Go on, get out. OUT!'

The sleeping lion has been well and truly prodded, and the subsequent roar far louder than Harri would have anticipated. He judges it's his time to leap forward and dilute the situation. Grabbing a larger cloth from the bar, he's at the table in three strides, inches from the Remingtons, playing the peacekeeper.

'Go and get some water,' he snaps at Dexie, his face only inches from Remington, close enough to smell his expensive aftershave. 'I'm extremely sorry, sir, we will sort this immediately, and of course, cover the cost of any cleaning. Please do accept our apologies.'

But Remington doesn't seem of a mind to accept anything. His wife is whining loudly about her dress.

'Shut up, Alicia,' he swipes, as the room goes deathly quiet. Julius Caine is stock still in his seat, muzzled either by liquor, or Remington's fearsome reputation.

'Get that pathetic woman out of here, now,' Remington snarls, gesturing at Dexie, 'and then you will summon our car. Understand?' The vein at the side of his neck pulses under the ceiling light, and Harri notes one hand gripped around the table edge, knuckles turned white.

Does the same second play over and over, with the room frozen in time? Harri isn't sure. He only knows it's the exact point when the left side of Remington's jaw gives off the faintest twitch, and he swears he can actually hear the grinding of the man's teeth, molar upon molar, the rasp of enamel. The air feels as it did when the bombs rained down on Hamburg, stagnant before the chaos, and yet every atom dense with dread.

'DO YOU UNDERSTAND, MAN?' Remington's nostrils flare, as his voice goes not down, but up an octave, sending sparks flying inside Harri's brain. The memory that he must have somehow hidden deep within all the grief and the detritus of his life now erupts.

There you are, Helmut Praxer.

* * *

Police training school, northern Germany, 1933

Someone laughs, an uncontrolled release of mockery that mutes all voices and movement in the dormitory hut. It's high summer, temperatures are soaring, but inside the single-storey wooden building, the atmosphere plummets.

'What did you say?' Low and controlled, a voice breaks the icy silence.

'Nothing, n-nothing, I was . . .' The reply is pathetic in comparison, showing every weakness. 'I just thought it was . . . when you . . .'

'Funny? Is that what you think? That I'm funny*?' He's smiling, but it's borne not of wit or humour, only menace. He takes a step forward and the boy who laughed takes one backwards, shrinking. Alongside both figures, police recruit Harri Schroder is trying to decide which way to play the mediator this time, in order to save the boy's face, physically and metaphorically. At barely eighteen, his fellow recruit is not yet a man, and the result could be ugly in in every way.*

He steps into the space between the two, holding up his palms. 'Hey, he's just joking about, doesn't mean anything by it,' he entreats. 'Do you, Muller?

'No, no,' Muller stutters in his small voice. 'Nothing. I swear.'

'But he laughed, Schroder, I heard him, distinctly. Didn't you?' Helmut Praxer spins to face the ten or so other recruits planted like statues in the hut. 'Or am I suddenly going deaf?'

There's a shuffling of feet, an indistinct murmur that is neither yes or no. Schroder watches Praxer relish the abeyance of doing what bullies are apt to do: include everyone in the oily discomfort of their oppression. In their year's intake of just twenty, Praxer has honed his mastery of a subtle, sinister persecution over a few short months. He befriends each recruit, one by one, and then little by little, sets them against the others, so no one is left untouched or unscathed. Every last man standing is coated in guilt. One minute, Praxer is all smiles, jollying and offering up good odds for his betting schemes, the next demanding his money with his particular brand of veiled threat. As a group, they've only ever witnessed the self-styled leader throw one punch, but it was delivered with such force and venom that it broke the unfortunate boy's nose. Since then, the mere threat of his fury is enough to give him control. Like now.

Schroder is among the few who refuse to be drawn in, preferring to use indifference and a light touch of humour as their defence. More and more, though, he finds it harder to feign apathy. He reasons that if you can't fell them completely, bullies need smoothing down on occasion.

'Look, Praxer, he'll apologise. Won't you, Muller?' Schroder punts into the silence that's become a frisson of charged particles.

Muller nods mutely.

'For what?' Praxer sneers. 'Apologise for what?'

'For laughing,' Schroder says, confused.

'At what? What was he laughing at, precisely.' Praxer pushes at the crowd again. 'I want to hear him say it.'

Feet shift on the concrete floor. Everyone present knows the uncontrolled, high-pitch inflection to Praxer's voice is a sore subject, morphing to that of a young Fraulein when he gets agitated, a short and sharp note escaping spontaneously from his throat. It's a target for ridicule amid the group, but only ever out of Praxer's earshot. So, yes, everyone knows what he was laughing at. And that Praxer will demand his vengeance. Publicly.

Muller steps forward, head down. Even in the gloom of the hut, it's obvious he is trembling, like a man going to the gallows. 'I'm sorry if I was laughing at your . . . your voice, Praxer,' he says gravely. He flinches as his adversary steps ever closer and pulls up his chin with one finger, Praxer's thick red lips almost on Muller's mouth.

'Apology accepted,' he says, his voice so quiet that it's almost reasonable.

No one is quite sure what to do, wondering if a fist is about to follow the finger on Muller's flesh, ice and fire held aloft in the hut.

'Then, that's settled,' Schroder says, touching each man on the shoulder like a referee at a boxing match. 'We're all friends here, aren't we?'

The particles disperse. Everyone mutters a 'yes' in response, even if no one believes it. Muller peels away and walks from the hut, shoulders stooped, into a cluster of trees beyond.

He might as well have sacrificed several teeth or a nose that day to Praxer's fist, Harri later reflects, because that young boy lost far more in the exchange, his dignity and self-respect stolen.

He packs up and leaves training the next day, and no one hears from him again.

Praxer stares another half second, in the claustrophobic void of this now airless room. Behind him, Harri can sense that Dexie, despite being banished, hasn't made it out of the room. Even Praxer's wife has stopped babbling, rigid next to her husband. It's a room of statues.

Praxer stands slowly, the bulb highlighting a sheen on his skin. His facial surgery becomes quite apparent to Harri, the features appear stretched and distorted up close. It makes him look younger than his thirty-nine years, but also meaner. The rest comes from the foul mood which exudes outwards, as his eyes scrutinise what's in front of him.

They are now face to face, Praxer only millimetres shorter than Harri. The fiery light in his eyes goes up a notch.

'Well, well, well. If it isn't Harri Schroder,' he says in faultless public-school English. 'Fancy seeing you here.'

Bang to rights.

And no virtue in denial. 'Hello, Helmut, what an extraordinary coincidence.'

Praxer's lips brew a smile, translating to a full-bodied cackle, his head thrown back. Now, he is very much amused.

His laughter kick-starts the room, Julius Caine climbing out of his stupor and shouting for Charlie. Harri still has his eye on Praxer, and as the door flings open and bodies file in, he only half catches a concerted click of Praxer's fingers close to the table. Too late, he registers the directive: this is not the time for the pleasantries of champagne or cocktails. Clucking their complaints, the women are firmly herded from the room, Alicia and Dexie included, followed by two male guests at the poker table.

'Drinks and chips on the house,' Caine slurs as he ushers them towards the outside gaming tables.

Praxer steps backwards while three men, all tall, broad and decked out like nightclub bouncers, move in to create a corral of solid bulk around Harri. Their silent scowl needs no translation.

One dips his head towards Harri's ear, breath hot on his lobe. 'Go quietly?'

What else is there to but nod his acquiescence?

'Good,' Praxer says, still with a hint of amusement. 'Because I would so like to catch up with you, Schroder. I think it might be fun to talk about old times.'

Encircled by muscle, Harri is steered into the reception and towards the casino entrance, searching through the bodily gaps for Dexie. Despite the flash of temper, it's unclear if Praxer has made a connection between him and the bungling waitress. He tries to calculate: how many more hefty men in black are there? Enough to go after her? Despite the unsavoury prospect of a cosy reunion with Praxer, Harri's concern lies elsewhere. Where is she? Has Charlie got enough mettle in him to ghost her away?

The main door to the casino opens to a foul green swirl pushing its way in, as Harri is piloted face down towards the opening. He spots a pair of distinct black pumps to his left – standing alone. Thank God! His eyes snake upwards to the briefest of glimpses. Her face is flat, as a disinterested servant would be to an evening's events that don't concern her. It's behind her eyes that Harri catches Dexie's true alarm. She pulls front teeth over her bottom lip and bites down on the flesh – unease mixed with determination, he's guessing – and which only he can interpret as her silent message: *I will try. I will try my utmost.*

He blinks and purses his own lips together, projecting something back to her: *I know.*

'Move it,' one hulk grunts, giving him a shove into the sightless world beyond.

26

All at Sea

6th December 1952

Dexie

She doesn't wait for Charlie to find her. The second after Harri is ghosted away, Dexie pulls open the front door and runs out onto the steps, hurling herself into a wall of stinking cloud that might as well be a solid brick wall. There are muffled voices and the slam of a car door, the thrust of an exhaust and, very faintly, two red pinprick tail-lights disappearing into the distance. She scans left and right – the space is devoid of sound, but even if she could see a taxi and hail it, the driver would have neither hope nor will of trailing anything. In the middle of the road, she's left shivering in her skimpy skirt and blouse, cold seeping up through her thin-soled shoes, staring into a dense nothingness. Without her police uniform, she feels suddenly vulnerable, exposed, and – given what's just happened – sick to her stomach.

Driven by the freezing temperature and using the black iron railings as a guide, Dexie loops around to the back entrance and slips in. Amid the bustle of the kitchen and the frantic criss-crossing of staff, no one notices a woman grabbing her clothes and leaving by the same door.

Outside, she attempts to run, but the sodden air pushes into her lungs within seconds, giving rise to a bout of coughing that has her retching bile onto the pavement. Trying to take in air while repelling the toxic fog, she has time to calculate. Praxer knows, clearly.

He might not know precisely who is behind Harri's involvement, and it may take a 'chat' with his fellow German to extract the details of why, but he will discover there's a force determined to scupper his chances of signing that agreement. In the meantime, Praxer will go to ground. And with untold resources, he'll have plenty of bolt holes to choose from. What does that mean for Harri? A swift bullet in the back of the head, or is he now a hostage who's landed in the lap of the enemy? Dexie cannot – will not – contemplate the first. Working on the second assumption is all she has.

Damn it, woman, think! What can you do and who can you go to?

Unprepared to stand still, she walks as briskly as she dare, feeling her way along the iron railings to the street corner. The dim glow of a red phone box acts as a flare, and the address inside provides the bearing she needs. She's a mere ten-minute walk from West End Central – perhaps a little more in this weather, but if nothing else, there will be warmth, a cup of tea and a chance to set her head straight.

The truth is, there are no other options open, when the surrounding city is near paralysed, stuck firm in a putrid grey-green miasma that might as well be quicksand.

* * *

'Dexie! What in God's name are you doing here?' Sergeant Thomas has never been one to mince his words, but his tone tonight is one of surprise rather than challenge. Behind the front desk, his stance resembles the captain in the wheelhouse, wrestling for control while his vessel pitches violently in an ocean storm. And all behind a thick sea mist that pervades the ground floor of West End Central.

'I got caught out nearby, Sarge,' she lies. 'Thought I'd grab a cup of tea and see how things are here.'

'Haven't you been seconded elsewhere?' he asks, more curiosity than complaint. Dexie has always considered Sergeant Thomas one of the good 'uns, his language paternal rather than patronising. It doesn't change her current dilemma, but she is glad of a friendly face.

'I am, but this weather, you know . . . we've had to put things on hold,' she explains.

That's one way to describe it.

Sergeant Thomas leans his substantial girth over the counter and peers down at Dexie's inadequate footwear and thin stockings. His white eyebrows go up a notch. 'You look frozen. Go and get yourself a cuppa, warm up, and when you're done, bring me down one as well, there's a good girl? There are calls coming in thick and fast from the lads and lasses out there tonight. The thieves are taking every advantage, there's ambulances driving blind and needing our lot as a walking escort. It's bedlam.'

'Yes, Sarge.'

At gone two a.m., the canteen is virtually empty, since it's normally closed at this hour. But there's nothing ordinary about tonight, and extra bodies have been drafted in to cope with the demands of a city under siege, troops who will need something hot and filling when they eventually stagger back to base. Behind the teapot, Olive and her team of two kitchen hands are already cracking eggs and laying out rashers of bacon in Blitz-style readiness.

Dexie feels guilty then, taking her cup and a hastily made sandwich to a table, even when Olive insists she has something to eat.

'You need feeding up,' she fusses. 'Young girls are far too pale these days.'

Dexie can't begin to explain the reasons why colour has drained from her, all down to the fiasco of the past hour, but at the first bite, she appreciates Olive's care and wisdom. Gradually, blood starts moving through her veins again, her fingers flush to a near-pink, and there's feeling even as far as her toes. With sensation, however, comes a blunt insight into her predicament.

Ten minutes. She'll give herself ten minutes to think, to plan the next move, to work out some way of finding Harri, to right the wrong of her actions. Because the worst, most toxic element of the whole evening – the factor that creates fresh icicles inside her – is not nature's foul offering outside, but the bare-faced stupidity of a rash and naïve, wholly inexperienced constable: Dexter 722. The admission drills into her core.

How can I have been so foolish? So gung-ho as to play with the delicate balance of that room, tensions already heightened by too much alcohol and the adrenalin of gambling, waiting for a spark. And she'd provided it. Oh, hadn't she just! It merely goes to prove she is no detective, and not even close to owning the skills needed to be in CID.

'Deluded, Dexie, that's what you are,' she mumbles into her tea. 'And pitiful.'

The thought propels Harri to the forefront again. A pity-free zone, hadn't they agreed? And here she is, wallowing in it. It won't do, and won't get him back either. So, what next?

She's already peered into the CID office on her way to the canteen and it's empty of bodies. Inform Chief Inspector Banks in the morning? Superintendent Graham? But to what end? A physical search across the expanse of London is a mammoth undertaking in high summer, with long days and clear skies to help. Now that visibility is down to arm's length, it would be utterly pointless and a waste of manpower they don't have right now. If the spooks at MI5 – who already work in the shadows – have so far failed to track Praxer down, there's little chance the police will fare any better. As for Johnson, she has no faith in him caring, let alone taking action. At their brief meeting, she sensed he viewed Harri as cannon fodder for the whole operation. His focus now will be on the lost opportunity rather than the lost man.

In the last hour, her suspicions about men in charge have multiplied. Somewhere in her gut (though she's not inclined to trust in it wholly right now), Dexie feels that Harri's chances of survival are higher if this is kept under wraps. A need-to-know basis, in which the hunt is narrowed down and the whispers are less likely to reach Praxer or those friends of his in high places. She rubs at her eyes, sore and dry from the inside of the casino and the world outside, willing ideas into fruition.

Wolli!

It was the former Nazi-hunter's intelligence that pointed to Alicia Remington in the first place, and he seemed more empathetic to life in the field, even in their short meeting. The problem being, he'd scribbled his phone number down and given it to Harri, who pocketed it. But Dexie's nose also detected a certain loneliness in Wolli; from her time on the beat, she knows this makes him a creature of habit, hungry for his daily dose of contact, starting with breakfast at that café in Camden. She'll wager even these unsavoury conditions won't deter him from the morning ritual. And Harri's journalist friend, Georgie, will surely be able to put out some feelers? Both have to be worth a try. Anything is better than standing still, because when she does – like now – that's when her imagination runs wild, and her memory goes straight to the sight of that gun nestled into the back of Harri's neck. It may have been a different perpetrator at the docks, but one bullet triggers the same result as any other. A deadly one.

Pushing aside that groundswell of pity, she gulps down the remainder of her tea and picks herself up, ready to move forward.

27

Hotel Praxer

6th December 1952

Harri

Shoved into the back seat of a car, Harri sees from the snug inside that this is no Bentley, or chic limousine. It also smells of cheap cigarettes, the leather seats worn and patched in places. As he was bundled down the casino steps, he'd seen Praxer's form move towards a larger car parked in front, manhandling his inebriated wife into the back seat, almost as roughly as Harri being forced through the car door. Perhaps Praxer trusts the alcohol has numbed Alicia's senses in every way, and she'll remember very little in the cold light of day. Still, it didn't seem the way a man would treat a precious and beloved wife.

Harri has never been prone to claustrophobia, but in the cramped interior, hemmed in by the eerie sediment of fog and one hefty bouncer each side, his heart vaults from side to side, not helped by the prospect of his journey's end. One bouncer turns towards him, something soft and black in one hand. Harri stares back with a look of incredulity.

'Is that really necessary, in this?' he asks, gesturing at the stippled mix of nighttime navy and leaden fog nudged up against the car window.

'I think so,' the man grunts back, slipping a knitted hood over Harri's head. The car lurches away and then slows almost immediately, the driver's foot evidently stop-starting on the accelerator and shunting the passengers back and forward, pressing sour wool against Harri's nose and mouth. He concentrates on each breath, in, out, in, out, picturing himself as a set of bellows and attempting to banish the one vision he won't allow himself to think about yet: the picture of Dexie, watching him disappear into an abyss, and the unknown. More than the rank smell of someone else's fear steeped into the weave of the fabric, it creates a sickening roil to Harri's stomach, in how he would have felt if the tables were turned, the desolation and desperation combined. Blind, in a sooty labyrinth of a city.

There's one key advantage to Dexie being left out in the dark as the pursuer (and he has absolutely no doubt that she will pursue, given the last look they exchanged): she knows London inside out. What's that phrase he often quotes to his detective team back home, when they're all in need of a pep talk? *In the country of the blind, the one-eyed man is king.* Little did the great H G Wells know, but the author has it right even today. Dexie possesses the gift of insight, plus her innate sensors to call on.

The drive is short, that much Harri can tell, perhaps only half an hour, and they can't have covered many miles, because the muffled sound of sirens in the distance – ambulances and police – has been with them most of the way. He senses when they pull up off-road; all sounds of life are stifled by the fog, but for the crunch of gravel under the car tyres. His feet hit the stones as he is dragged unceremoniously from the car, sucking in air through the holy weave of the hood, foul on his tongue. His sense of smell, once ravaged by the trauma of war, has returned by degrees over the years, but there are no clues in this fetid cloud. Nor in the acoustics – the experience of living in bombed out Hamburg has nurtured certain senses in Harri, among them 'hearing' the space around him. It's proved invaluable when tracking the ingenious hideaways of racketeers, dangerous street gangs or a villain about to pounce. Once again, this quirk of English weather robs it all. With a vast sky and an entire galaxy above, he's in a tight vacuum.

There's a muted exchange, followed by Praxer's crisp tone out of the blackness. 'In the basement. I'll deal with him in the morning.'

'All right, boss.' The same gruff voice herds him onto smooth concrete underfoot, paving stones perhaps? They go left, ten or so strides along the side of a building, then right through a doorway, a clip of tiles beneath his shoes. It smells pleasantly of good food and baking. Is this the kitchen of a house belonging to Praxer, a dwelling? Maybe, but it's bound to be one of many. Five steps later, they are in a hallway, enclosed. A key is turned in a lock, the warmth around them sucked into a void as a blast of freezing air hits back.

'Down there,' the voice commands, a big hand gripping at Harri's shoulder from above as he's forced to feel each steep stair with his foot in the descent. He counts twelve. A shallow basement. And if the world outside counts as cold, this is several degrees lower. He shivers, from his prospects and the temperature, in nothing but his shirtsleeves and waistcoat.

At last, the hood is removed, a single dim bulb switched

on in its place. The big man, one of the bouncers from the casino, disappears and returns a minute later with a bucket, a jug of water and a half loaf of dry bread.

'Prisoner rations?' Harri scoffs, with a resigned smile. He has no weapon left, aside from wit.

If he had any, Bouncer Boy has lost his sense of humour this far into the night. 'Think yourself lucky to get that,' he grunts back. 'Sleep well, *Herr* Schroder.'

His broad form disappears up the stairs and the lock clicks behind him, but he does at least leave the light on. Harri blinks, adjusting his eyes to the sickly hue cast by the bulb. The space is almost empty, aside from a wooden pallet box, a few shelves and two thin blankets hooked on a rusty nail. It appears he's not the first guest to patronise Hotel Praxer. Quick scrutiny of the floor reveals no blood, but Harri notes the room is untouched by haze; no seepage from outside signals no windows or gaps. He wonders at the reserves of air, and how long one man can survive down here without a fresh supply of oxygen, whether if he falls asleep, he'll actually wake up. Maybe there's never a need to spill blood. Despite the unknown agenda for tomorrow and the anxiety that engenders, his energy is rapidly waning. After the long day trudging in air like quicksand, plus the evening's events, he needs to sleep, if only to have enough fight to match Praxer with words. Because if he remembers anything about his former police comrade, it's that Praxer fights a verbal duel with a rapier tongue. After which point, one of his lackeys might wield a more solid weapon.

28

Allies

6th December 1952

Dexie

Her eyes feel gritty and raw when she wakes, jolted into consciousness by the shrill bell of her alarm clock. Dexie lies in the darkness for a minute, her senses deadened by thick curtains and the cotton wool of the world. All but her nostrils, unfortunately. The noxious vapour has managed to wheedle its way in and under the window frame, when in summer it fails to admit any breeze or air.

Just gone seven. She remembers nothing after falling into bed at four a.m, having taken Sergeant Thomas his cup of tea from the station canteen, then – in a brief quiet period – watched him wilting across his desk as he drank. In a role reversal they will likely never speak of again, she commanded her superior to take a break, while she fielded the phone calls coming from police boxes across the patch. The break-ins being called in were two-fold: to report opportunist burglars who slid back into the fog with ease, and from the constables needing to breach the front door of the elderly and alone, those requesting ambulances that took hours to make it through. At other times, there was no need, the vulnerable having already succumbed to the airless invader.

It's now a killer fog – officially – with the hospital wards and emergency departments full to the brim with bronchial cases, the already coal-smudged lungs of Londoners surrendering to this new foe. If this goes on for much longer, the undertakers will be snowed under too.

Dexie hauls herself from bed and washes away last night's black coating from her face, grateful that one of the cooks has made it in on foot to the section house, bringing as much fresh bread as she can carry. Dexie is inclined to kiss her, and in fact does, planting one on the woman's cheek, so thankful for something inside her mouth that doesn't taste bitter. It's a brief respite as she chews on bread and jam, washed down with decent tea. Like the station canteen, the space is almost empty, and Dexie is flooded with guilt yet again, since her WPC colleagues will either be out battling the elements, or in bed after a long night. Twittering away in the corner, BBC News focuses on the traffic chaos, trains cancelled and flights grounded, plus all London football fixtures cancelled, since neither spectators nor players have any hope of seeing the pitch. No reports, however, of those suffocated by their own city's air, the numbers of sick or dying. Residents have been warned to stay at home, to hunker down and wait for the all-clear, though the weathermen have no idea when that might be. This great citadel – survivor of countless wars, pestilence, fire and the Fuhrer – has been petrified by nature. It might even be funny if it wasn't so tragic.

Dexie is bone tired, but three hours' sleep will have to

do, she tells herself, since it's probably more than Harri has managed. If he's still alive. Only that sliver of hope will drive her actions today; the signing is a mere three days away, but that remains Johnson's problem now. Her sole responsibility is to find Harri.

Before leaving, Dexie calls her mother's house from the payphone in the draughty hallway, unfazed when she hears it ring out. Instead, she dials the nurse's station at Bart's general medical ward, and learns from the receptionist that yes, Nurse Chadwick has taken a double shift.

'Yes? Who's speaking?' her mother's officious work voice comes over the line, the one that scolds patients when they've hopped out of bed for a sneaky smoke in the corridor.

'It's me, Mum – Dex . . . er, Helen.'

'What? Is everything all right? Where are you?' The matronly manner gives way to her familiar maternal angst.

'I'm fine, I'm at the section house.' Dexie shuffles her feet, scuffing one part of the lie.

'Oh, thank God,' Violet Chadwick says. 'And have you been out in this awful filth?'

'Yes, but I'm in one piece, I promise.' It's not quite the same as 'fine', she reasons. 'I'm just ringing to see if you're OK.'

'Me? Yes, of course. I stayed on for an extra shift at the hospital, and grabbed a couple of hours' sleep at the nursing home rather than fight this fog. And Lord knows, they need all hands on deck.'

'Is it as bad as they say on the radio, with so many people falling ill?'

Never one for dramatics, the sigh from Dexie's mother is nonetheless long and heavy down the line. 'Worse,' she reports. 'We're full on the ward, and the emergency department is ringing every ten minutes demanding more beds. Right now, we're cleaning out a storeroom to make into a small ward. I've never seen anything like this – people are dying, my love, and from the *weather*.'

'But are you all right?' Dexie presses. 'Never mind caring for others, you need to look after yourself.'

'Since when did you become Nurse Dexter?' the voice comes back crisply. 'Of course I'm all right, I'm safe here in the hospital. It's you that needs to be careful, out on that beat. Make sure you wear those masks they're issuing to the force.'

'I will,' Dexie pledges, with another guilty scuff of her shoe. 'Just get enough rest, Mum.'

'You too. Keep safe, darling.'

Dexie replaces the receiver, leaning her tired forehead against the noticeboard. As if there wasn't enough tug-of-war going on in her head, now she's added lying to her mother, and the guilt of it, at the age of thirty-three. On the plus side, her mother is in the best place, sheltered from the lurking, omniscient killer in the capital.

Killer. It jolts her tired brain back to the most pressing problem, the one that demands she confront one – or several – would-be predators head on.

Beyond the section house door, the fog has percolated to a stony grey, daylight just penetrating enough to make out the flag stones underfoot. Vehicle headlights blend into the murk, and it's even harder to spot them mounting the pavements and coming at you. The air echoes with unseen squeaks of surprise and profuse apologies as pedestrians collide with each other in avoiding danger. On foot, wearing her sturdiest walking shoes and with a thick scarf pulled tight up to her eyes, Dexie's innate compass is put to full use. Because it's Saturday, she's hopeful of finding Georgie at home in Islington, thankful for that large birch tree standing as a convenient landmark in front of the house.

The door opens a mere crack, and with a look of surprise. 'Can I help you?'

'Mrs Spender, erm Miss Young – Georgie?'

'Yes?' The face twists in confusion.

'I've come about Harri. He – I – we need your help.'

In the kitchen, with the children dispatched to play in their bedrooms, Georgie offers tea and an ear. 'Seriously, is he in real danger?'

Knowing what she does of Georgie, Dexie sees no reason to sugarcoat the truth. 'We have to assume so. Praxer didn't have his private army around him for nothing, and from what Harri says, this man is very unpredictable.'

'He said as much to me, though he didn't let on how dangerous it was.' Chin on her hands, Georgie wears her concern openly. 'And you feel it's best not to go to the police, to Scotland Yard?'

Slowly, Dexie shakes her head. 'I hate to say it, but I'm beginning to doubt the integrity of everyone involved, of maybe a leak on the inside. I have faith in my own station colleagues, but the CID office will be overrun today. Some of the deaths called in last night were tagged as suspicious, in the midst of everything else. There's not a single detective they'd be able to spare for a man who's simply gone missing.'

Dexie pauses, glancing at this woman whom Harri so clearly loves and admires, and whose angst is written all over her face. 'Georgie, do you think I'm doing the right thing, in not trusting others?' With fatigue and anxiety, her confidence has taken another tumble.

Georgie seems to rearrange her worrisome features, working her mouth into a weak smile. 'I think it's *your* instinct you should trust, as Harri's friend. And if that's what it's telling you, then it's more than likely right.'

'Thanks, I needed to hear that.' Right now, Dexie needs it more than breath itself.

'I'll do everything I can from this end,' Georgie says, rising from the table. 'Max is out on an early job, but I can ask a neighbour to watch the children and head into the *News Chronicle* offices, and then *The Times*. I've got some contacts there, who can talk to the business section for me. In the meantime, I'll call the crime desks, see if there are any whispers about Remington's dealings, any addresses or under-the-radar warehouses.'

Dexie shrugs, her face grave. 'Or news of a man's body turning up.'

'Yes, that too.'

'Listen, I'd better go. I've got one more avenue to try. After that, I'm at a dead end.'

She gets up from the table, reflecting on her poor choice of words.

They agree a three-way contact system – Dexie checking in on Georgie's home number at regular intervals, plus any messages to be left at West End Central and the section house.

'I'm convinced that if anyone can talk their way out of this, it's Harri,' Georgie says at the door. She pushes out another smile to paste over the unease.

'More than anything, I really hope you're right about that.'

29

Breakfast with the Enemy

6th December 1952

Harri

He's not quite sure which aches more – his back or the head that feels as if it's gone several rounds with a keg of German beer. The strongest variety. Harri stretches by degrees and pushes himself up to sitting from the cold concrete floor, bone and muscle creaking as he does so. When he rubs at his stubbled face, there's a firm imprint from the blanket that was wrapped around him and pushed into his cheek in the hope of forming it into a pillow. From the searing pain in his neck, it failed miserably.

'Fresh as a daisy, Schroder,' he grouses into the same sallow light. What time is it? How much sleep has he had? Some, judging by the unsavoury dreams of guns and death that riddled his mind as he came to every so often. Then there was Mrs P, who coloured his thoughts as he drifted off. He hoped then, as he does now, that the other lodgers will have checked on her, and she hasn't needed one of those ambulances struggling up the blind alleyways that London's famous streets have now become.

Reluctantly, Harri uses the bucket, its stale odour sucking up what's left of the usable oxygen in the room, then swills his mouth with water from the jug and gulps down some more, even though it leaves a bitter taste. It must be morning, he reasons, because there are footsteps across the floor above, and noises from the kitchen they entered last night. He forces himself to stretch fully, even when it hurts, bending his limbs so that if there is any chance of running in any direction, his body might not fail him in the crucial moment. Then, he waits. This proves to be the hardest part, because his conscious mind churns endlessly on the prospect of what he might face up above. How will Praxer view this meddling into his affairs? More than a mere inconvenience, that's for sure. Harri also knows their one-time comradeship and shared homeland are likely to have little bearing on today's outcome, since Praxer was always volatile, his behaviour often reckless and cruel. A loose cannon, you might say. Whether he's a former friend or current foe, there's no telling how he'll react to Harri's untimely presence.

Untold minutes go by before the lock turns, and Bouncer Boy – looking a damn sight better slept than Harri – descends the stairs. He laughs openly. 'Bad night, Mr Schroder? What a shame.'

'I realise beauty sleep is a must for men like you,' Harri quips back, 'but the handsome devils like myself can get away with it.'

Bouncer smiles, evidently amused. 'You look and smell like shit, if you don't mind me saying, but then so would I if I'd slept in this privy.'

'I might not recommend it to anyone as a five-star establishment.'

'You might not get to recommend anything, Mr Schroder.'

He beckons Harri up the stairs and into the hallway, darkened not by the décor, but the flat, leaden fuzz butting up against every visible window. All the interior lamps are on, creating an eerie mismatch between Harri's head – which insists it's daytime – and the half-light that surely indicates they're heading into dusk. An enticing smell of bacon wafting from the kitchen settles the issue: morning it is. In the austere dining room, two places are set at one end of a sizable mahogany table. Sweeping the room, he sees Praxer already seated at the head, dressed and groomed for the day.

'Ah.' He looks up from a copy of the *Daily Telegraph* as the two men enter. 'Harri. Do come in, please sit down.' Praxer beckons with a long, slim finger to the place beside him, paying no mind to his prisoner's dishevelled state, as if he's had nothing whatsoever to do with it. 'Thank you, Joseph, you can go now. Mrs Dane will see to you in the kitchen.'

'Yes, sir.'

Harri sits. Separating the pains coursing through his body, he realises the stab in his stomach is hunger, and if this is to be the last meal of a condemned man, he might as well enjoy it. Plus, the chair looks far more comfortable than the rickety pallet down below.

'Tea, or coffee?' Praxer asks, then with a conspiratorial smile: 'Don't tell my wife, but I've taught Mrs Dane to make coffee the German way, good and strong.' He says it as if they are two boys in the kindergarten back home, never mind captive and gaoler. Fuddled by lack of sleep, Harri is evermore bemused. Suddenly he doesn't trust his own memory, or anything else careering around his aching head.

Has he got it spectacularly wrong, and this is not Praxer before him, but a strange and innocent James Remington playing a bizarre power game?

'Yes, coffee then,' Harri says.

As the thick liquid pours, he takes the opportunity for further scrutiny of the industrial magnate to his right. Where the casino lighting showed up evidence of skin that has seen a surgeon's knife, here it's more flattering; if you didn't know where to look, you might not see the joins, the parts where one identity was unpicked and another sewn back in place. His shaven cheeks are smooth, jawline sharp, and his eyes more almond-shaped, in contrast to the hooded look of Praxer the police recruit. This man appears altogether more chiselled and handsome in the traditional sense than the man Harri knew almost twenty years ago. But what of his core?

Praxer sits back and sips. 'So, Harri, how do we solve this conundrum?'

'Conundrum?' *Act dumb, Schroder. Let him think he's got the better of you.* Playing for time is, after all, human nature when you're facing a firing squad.

'Oh, Harri,' he sighs, and suddenly the veneer melts away. Praxer himself peels off the mask, revealing that self-satisfied, faux friendly expression of decades before. 'There's no one to defend here but yourself. No peace-making role for you, not like in the old days.'

He's not denying their former association, and that's a worry. A big one.

'So, what then?' Harri asks, as calmly as he's able. 'You kill me. Dump my body in the Thames, only for me to float up as the fog clears, no wallet or identity card, perplexing the police. It's all very cinematic.'

'Ha!' Praxer throws his head back with laughter. 'Trust

you to think like that, Schroder. You always were a bit odd.'

Better odd than a Nazi. 'And yet, somehow, I don't imagine you're going to open the door and watch me disappear into the distance.'

'No, perhaps not,' Praxer says matter-of-factly. 'That is too much of a risk at this precise moment. But, you know, we have history, don't we, Harri, you and I? Once, I thought we might be good friends. Until . . .'

'The Fuhrer became your best pal.'

'I prefer to think that we went in different directions. Or rather you stood still and became a plodding policeman. And that's a shame, because I think you would have done well in the Reich. Heydrich and Himmler were always looking for good officers they could rely on.'

'Turn, you mean?' Harri punts. 'To be their little bully boys.'

'I grant you, those two weren't always terribly subtle about it.'

Behind this jolly banter, Harri begins to feel nauseous at Praxer's use of humour to hide his own involvement in such heinous crimes. 'From what I hear, you weren't necessarily subtle in your aims, Helmut,' he says. 'Invisible maybe. But very determined to do the Fuhrer's work.'

The door opens and a woman enters, bearing plates of a typically English breakfast, setting one down in front of each man. 'Thank you, Mrs Dane,' Praxer says politely, his Janus persona switching effortlessly. 'Looks delicious.' He forks hungrily at a fried egg as she leaves, chewing with enthusiasm. 'Mmm, *spiegelei*, my favourite.'

Harri doesn't know whether to laugh, cry or eat, such is the bizarre nature of this encounter. Self-preservation makes him picks up his own fork and go through the motions, though he has to agree with Praxer – Mrs Dane cooks a good egg, an admission that provokes another pinch to his stomach in the form of Mrs P.

'You haven't said what you're going to do,' Harri presses, halfway to clearing his plate.

'Do? I'm going to sit tight until this bloody English weather lifts, and then I'm going sign my agreement.' Praxer glances up briefly from his own food. 'Which I know you're aware of, so don't bother denying it.'

'And me?' Harri makes a point of raising his fork aloft and holding the enemy's eye. 'I think I'm entitled to know my fate, even if it's a courtesy between former comrades, don't you?'

Praxer smiles. 'Well, you're not actually, given that I hold all the cards, but because I'm a gentleman . . .'

'A very English gentleman.'

'Quite,' Praxer goes on, not rising to Harri's sarcastic riposte. 'I will tell you. Once the agreement is signed, you can go.'

For a second, Harri is struck dumb. It's not the answer he expected. 'Just walk out of here?'

Praxer chews thoughtfully on a slice of bacon. 'Yes. Why not?'

'Because of what I know. Of your past.'

'Which – if you could ever prove it – will be totally irrelevant once the ink is dry on that document.'

Harri watches the façade cracking by degrees. Praxer is holding his reasonable self together, but that smug curl to one side his mouth has broken through more than once. He just can't help being a self-satisfied bastard.

'Irrelevant how?' Harri pushes.

'Because of all the very important people involved. Surely, you can't imagine they care about much besides the enormous amounts of money they stand to make? If you do, you're more of an idealist than I imagined.'

'What about the British press?' Harri tries again. 'If they got hold of the story: British Government colluding with a former financier of the Holocaust . . . well, it would create an almighty backlash.'

Praxer doesn't baulk at the utterance of 'Holocaust', merely sets his knife and fork together. 'An accusation like that wouldn't have a chance,' he says with confidence. 'My friends in the British Government value their reputations too much to let it get out. They have a large influence over the press, and so it will never make it across a reporter's desk, let alone to any front page.'

Harri just stops himself from slumping backwards into the chair. Some things never change: Praxer has all the answers, masterminding so that everyone is beholden to him. Back in the day, almost every police recruit was in hock to his gambling racket, and it would have been a steady promotion to pulling purse strings for the Reich. Here and now, the stakes are substantially higher, but the outcome is the same: power. He holds it, and isn't about to let it go.

The exceptionally strong coffee has reawakened something in Harri but it still takes a moment to recall what day it is, given the blur of the last twelve hours. 'So, that's three days from now, the signing?'

'Correct.'

'And in the meantime, I'm to reside in the comfort of the basement suite? I don't mean to be rude, Helmut, but you'll never make it as a hotelier.'

Praxer laughs again, a full-bodied crow, eyes glinting with enjoyment against the flat light of the room. 'You know, Harri, despite you being far too worthy for my tastes, I can't help liking you. You always did amuse me.'

'I'm flattered.' He's not, but it seems the right thing to say.

'You should be. I don't warm to many people.'

That's an understatement, to which millions of your victims would attest to, Harri reasons. *If only they could.*

'So, do I get to climb out of the basement?' Harri isn't sure of his motives in pushing for it, or his possibility of escape beyond last night's cell, but he might – just might – emerge to spend his last days, or the rest of his life, without debilitating backache.

Praxer sniffs, and folds his napkin with precision, laying it neatly on the table. 'I'm sure we can sort something out.' His diverted expression drops like a stone. Grave and uncompromising, paring back the layers so that Harri identifies him more and more with each passing minute. 'Be wary, though – don't mistake my generosity for weakness. This business deal is worth more than any friendship, old or new, and I'm not a man affected by sentiment.'

Harri nods. 'Believe me, I would quite like to see my old crew back in Hamburg.'

Praxer looks at him quizzically. Harri wonders if he's trying to imagine what it's like to have friends, people who like you for what you are, rather than what trinkets you have, or the power you wield. Or perhaps he's assessing if his gamble, of keeping an old comrade alive, is worth the risk? In the next breath, the smooth guise of his second face is back in place, giving nothing away.

It creases as the door the dining room opens, disturbing the threads of smog that have crept in uninvited. 'Darling!' Praxer says with surprise. 'I thought you would sleep in a little.'

In her oyster-white silken robe, Alicia Remington wafts in like a tendril of mist, starts a little at the sight of Harri, but steps towards and nudges up against her husband's seated body. His arm goes out instantly to draw her in, while she pecks his oiled hair briefly and wriggles from his grasp, sitting in the chair opposite. Face on, she's far from the groomed woman who emerged from Sable Hair and Beauty; last night's eyeliner is smudged, her cheeks creased from sleep, lipstick faded and her hair pulled back in a cloth band. Unsurprisingly, she looks hungover, a redness in the whites of her eyes, and a greyness in her general pallor, matching the blank vista through the window.

'You didn't tell me we had guests,' she murmurs, squinting at Harri as she says it, though there's no hint of recognition, in picking out the waiter in the casino.

'An old friend,' Praxer says, with a smile, pouring her coffee. 'But you won't be seeing much of him. Harri here will be holed up in his room, with a book to write, won't you?'

'Yes, lots of things to mull over,' Harri says.

She flicks her eyes away with disinterest, then grimaces noticeably as she puts the coffee cup to her lips, shouting through the closed door to the kitchen. 'Mrs Dane! Mrs Dane! Can we have some proper coffee in here?'

Like a spoilt child, Harri observes. There's the briefest of flashes on her husband's face, but this one isn't difficult to read. Embarrassment. Praxer might well love his wife, but that doesn't stop him being irritated by her.

'Well, I'd better get my head down and work on that book,' Harri says, rising from his chair. In all honesty, he's bored by this faux geniality, when – through bitter experience – he knows exactly what lies beneath.

Praxer is up and at the door to the kitchen in seconds. He utters a few words to Joseph, who reappears to escort Harri away. Alicia Remington bats not an eyelid, at the stranger or the sentinel. Is this what she's used to? Blinkering herself to what's right in front of her? A strange, dishevelled man appearing and then vanishing.

'Sleep well, Harri, when you do get some rest,' Praxer says as a parting gesture, as if he really means it.

'I will, like a baby,' Harri replies.

If Praxer gets to lie, then so does he.

Bouncer Boy Joseph leads him back through the kitchen and towards the cellar entrance, a mild panic washing across Harri's face as the man-mountain places a hand on the doorknob, then turns and smirks. It seems that Praxer's self-satisfaction has spread to his employees, and Joseph is still enjoying his little joke. He moves into a mahogany-lined hallway and up the wide stairway to the first floor, where daylight is struggling to reach the upper levels.

'In here.' Disapproval and disdain are written all over the bodyguard's face as he opens a door to what must be a guest bedroom, giving a quick shove to Harri's shoulder in re-establishing who's boss.

'Don't think this is any picnic,' Joseph grunts. 'I'll be around all the time, and there's a man below the window, should you even attempt to get that far. But if were you, I'd just sit tight.' He pulls back the jacket of his suit, just enough to show the butt of a revolver nestled in his snug waistband.

'I wouldn't dream of it.' Harri smiles. 'Though I might dream of something else, since that bed does look very comfortable.'

With a parting scowl, Joseph closes the door and turns the key. The air is less stale than the basement, and without the cold dampness, but even with carpet underfoot it could hardly be called cosy. Harri is left staring at three decorated walls – and a set of solid bars over the windows, painted white in keeping with the frames. What kind of house is this, and does this room count as a first-class cell?

He sinks into the bed with a sense of frustration and relief combined, staring at the ceiling rose around the light fitting and calculating his options. At this precise moment, they number a big fat zero. If reluctant butler Joseph is to be his only contact over the next three days, there is no chance of escape. With the house shrouded in the fog, he guesses this bolthole is within London – he recalls the weathermen quoting a twenty-mile radius – so perhaps they're in a suburb of some kind? Somewhere fairly well-to-do, given the sweep of the gravel driveway. But north, south, east or west? His compass has been dulled by Mother Nature's cruel timing.

Harri turns instead to the consequences. If he's fed and watered for three days, until after the signing of this illustrious pact between powerful men (who are certain to become warmongers all over again), then what? Praxer's bonhomie this morning, his play at nostalgia, strikes Harri as just that – a game. The Janus face no longer hides the menace that's just skin deep, and Harri could so easily be a pawn in the game plan. He's no expert at chess, but even Inspektor Schroder knows they are throwaway pieces. Expendable.

There's a small sink in the corner, laid out with soap, a comb and a towel. Harri strips down to his trousers and begins washing away the grime and the memory of last night, shocked again at the leaden look of the rinse water, and wondering if it's caused by smog or filth from the cellar floor. Once it's gone, and his hair combed, he certainly looks more presentable. But for what? Who spruces themselves up to sit in a cell?

Lack of sleep from the night before, and the muffled

silence outside, causes his eyelids to droop as he lies on the soft mattress. Lingering thoughts, as he drifts, are of Dexie. Where is she, and what is she doing? Part of him hopes she's true to her silent promise, to find and liberate him from the unknown of Praxer's intent. The other, much larger slice of his thinking wants the smog to paralyse her movements, enough that she can't come looking. He wants her far away from Joseph and his ready revolver, or Praxer and his capricious rage.

Harri's own quiet wrath is contained, but only just, because there's nowhere for his anger to go. He could rattle the steel painted bars, but to what purpose? He's incapacitated and weakened, having allowed himself to be drawn into this situation. By what? A touch of flattery on Johnson's part, and self-conceit that he can actually right the wrongs of an entire war.

Schroder, you're such a damned idiot.

30

Eliza

6th Dec 1952

Dexie

The clock ticks towards ten thirty, though Dexie is loath to order anything else, after sinking two cups of the sludgy brown excuse for tea and cursing into the dregs. Her predictions about loneliness and human nature are clearly way off the mark, since the Camden café hosts only a smattering of customers.

Even the waitress is non-committal. 'Wolli? Oh, he's usually in by now. It's this weather. He might come in for lunch, I s'pose.'

Lunch? Time is ticking, each second of which could prove crucial to Harri, every minute marked by a further torque in her gut. *Oh Wolli, where are you?*

She'll give it another ten minutes, then make her way to Scotland Yard and somehow blag her way into the Records Office, to crawl over the files again and isolate any venues that belong to Remington Industries. Unless Georgie comes up with any fresh information, it's all that's left in Dexie's arsenal. Itching with frustration, she leafs through the morning's edition of the *Daily Express* left on the table, shocked that the only mention of London's devastation refers to traffic and crime, the tragedy of a lone woman battered by an opportunistic thief. There's no mention of sickness and deaths, the hospitals full, or police and ambulance services stretched to breaking point. Beyond this oppressive swathe, Britain's citizens are ignorant of what's fast becoming a tragedy in their own capital city. It's as if there's some conspiracy perpetrated by the government and the press, to keep the lid on the story, while the meteorological cap seals ever tighter. More and more, the place she calls home is beginning to feel like a prison.

Stop it, Dex! She rebukes herself for creating intrigue where there might not be any, an unhealthy consequence of dealing with Praxer, and Johnson, too.

'Hello, Wolli love, you're popular today – someone over there has been asking for you.' Dexie's head whips up as the shrill tone of the waitress breaks through, a finger pointed in her direction. Never has she been so pleased to see an older man limping towards her table, even if his face shows little delight. Instead, the Pole exudes a poor combination of being irked and hungover.

He sits heavily, positioning his leg and taking off his cap. 'Didn't think I'd see you again so soon. Where's your friend?'

'That's exactly why I'm here.'

Presumably cooking grease acts as a kind of fuel, or antidote to alcohol, because Wolli needs tea and a large plate of his 'usual' before he can speak. 'So, Praxer has your man?'

'Yes.'

'That's not good.'

Dexie pushes down a large swell of frustration. 'I do know that, Wolli. What I need is some help in where he might have been taken. I take it you are paid by Johnson and his outfit?'

'Peanuts,' he grunts, chewing on fried bread noisily.

His nonchalance is beginning to grate, and she resorts to her WPC persona – not the friendly female officer, but the one in uniform, her voice firm and uncompromising. 'Whether it's peanuts or not, I need your help. Harri needs it more than ever, and if you are serious about cutting out this . . . this canker of Nazism, you would help me.'

The knife clatters above the hum of the café as he slams it on the table with force. 'Listen, lady, I have spent years fighting those bastards, and a good portion of me' – he gestures to his damaged limb – 'so don't you dare question my efforts. Or my sacrifice.'

Her talk has certainly stirred him, but has she tipped him over the edge? 'I'm not questioning, Wolli,' Dexie goes on, adjusting her tone. 'I'm just worried. Very worried. And I've come to you because you are the only one who can help. Who might know something. Anything. Please.' Deference gradually gives way to pleading, but right now she doesn't care. And it's telling that he doesn't once suggest going to Johnson for help.

'Hmm.' Wolli chews some more. A second cup of sludge seems to bridge the fissure between them. His face softens, the bloodshot eyes just a bit brighter. 'Well, you're wrong about me,' he says. 'There's one other who knows more about Praxer than I do.'

Dexie's heart leaps and crashes against her gullet. 'Who? Are they in London?'

'Lucky for you, she is.'

'She?'

He nods. 'Eliza. I worked with her in Germany and Poland, during the war and after. Let's say she's got history with Praxer.'

'Which is?'

'That's for her to reveal if she chooses. The best I can do is contact her.'

'Can you do that? Right now?'

He sighs, heaves himself up with his stick and turns towards the back of the café and the phone on the counter. 'It'll cost you a jam roly-poly and custard.'

'Done,' she says. It's not time for elevenses, but who is she to question such a paltry fee?

Within several minutes, he slides back into his seat, wincing from the pain of movement.

'Well?' Dexie is conscious of her neck at full stretch, her voice high with expectation. Desperation, too.

'You're in luck. She's at home, and in a fairly good mood by the sounds of it. My advice would be to take advantage of that.' He eyes the yellowy-green soup beyond the café's plate glass window. 'Luck must really be with you because she lives not far from here.' He fishes in his pocket for a scrap of paper, finds an old shop receipt and, with a shaky hand, scribbles an address on the back.

'Thanks, Wolli,' Dexie says on getting up. 'I mean it. This might save Harri.'

'Well, if it does, just promise me you'll bring down Praxer. I can die a happy man then.'

'We'll do our best,' she says, albeit with a sharp twinge of guilt; her only motive at this point is getting Harri out alive. Praxer comes secondary to that.

'Be careful,' he says, tucking into his pudding as Dexie buttons her coat.

'I will. I know Praxer is . . .'

'Of Eliza, I mean,' he says. His pupils are black and small. Serious.

'Oh?'

'She . . . like so many of us . . . is damaged. Zealous. It makes her reckless, at times. That's all I'm saying. Watch your back.'

'Look after yourself, too, Wolli.'

'Always.' He waves with his spoon and goes back to his roly-poly as Dexie turns, pays the bill for his banquet and steps through the door, re-entering the nether world of Victorian London. As of now, this stupefying fog seems to be the least of her problems.

31

Tea and Sympathy

6th December 1952

Harri

A knock at the door stirs him from a type of waking dream, lulled by an intermittent clatter and coughing from the room underneath, Mrs Dane going about her business amid her smog-filled kitchen. Once or twice, he drifts into thinking it's Mrs P, and is almost driven to push himself off the bed and check on how she is. It's not so much the rap that pulls from this reverie, but that someone knocks at all. Prisoners aren't generally afforded such manners. Harri imagines it must be Joseph, squeezing every last drop of schoolboy glee from his little joke. He turns over on the bed, bent on proper sleep and robbing his gaoler of any satisfaction.

The key turns in the lock, though it's tentative. That does garner his attention, enough to lift one eyelid. The door opens several inches, a face filling the crack, and it's not a punch-drunk pugilist that peeks in.

'Erm, I brought you some tea, and cake.' Alicia Remington

eases in with a small tray, a smile on her lips. 'I hope I'm not disturbing you.'

Harri sits up and notes she looks much less hungover, dark hair styled and sprayed into place, her face freshly made-up. Only the fatigue in her eyes can't be painted over. 'No, you're not,' he says. 'I'm surprised, that's all. But pleasantly.'

She sets the tray on the bedside table next to him, and retreats to a stool in front of a sparse dressing table, crossing her long stockinged legs and resting her chin on one heel of her hand. Measuring him up.

'Er, would you like some tea?' he half-stammers. If she's intent on sending him off kilter, she's succeeded. By this display of compassion, but also by her continued presence.

'No, thank you. I've had so much tea I'm in danger of listing to one side.' She looks beyond the window – and the bars – and pushes out a lengthy sigh. 'This blasted weather. You just can't move anywhere.'

'No,' Harri agrees, stunned at her blissful naivety. Surely, if she unlocked his door, she must realise he's here against his will? And yet, she's treating him as a house guest at a large country gathering. He scrutinises as she stares through the window. What does she know and, more to the point, how good an actress is Alicia Remington? She's bored, plain and simple, come to prod at the sad old zoo bear in his cage, just to while away time.

'Do you like England?' she says. It's not Praxer's style of interrogation, but her direct question demands an answer.

'I do. Present weather excepted, of course.' *Current predicament, too.*

'I hear people saying it's all part and parcel of our wonderful country,' she complains. 'A little bit romantic, but to me it's simply filthy and disgusting.'

'Quite apart from people possibly losing their lives,' Harri adds.

'Hmm.' Again, she seems to have sidestepped the tragedy affecting those outside her world, and skated over his sarcasm. 'It's just going on too long now. My husband says we might be here for a few days.'

My husband. Harri wonders what she calls him, face to face – James or Helmut. And is she really Frau Praxer, with a well-applied veneer of Mrs Remington, a type of particularly robust varnish? 'We're waiting for wind,' he says.

'Excuse me?'

'The weathermen say we need a good breeze to shift this "lid" that's sitting over the city. A stiff breeze, as you English put it.' The way she whips her head upwards is telling. Perhaps she doesn't consider herself as British? Maybe that's why she's here now, come to view 'the German', as a potential ally. And perhaps he can gain something from that. Since there's nothing else to do, Harri thinks he might as well try.

'Well, I wish it would hurry up,' she says petulantly. 'I have all sorts of appointments.'

'Actually, I do too.'

'Oh?' Now her interest is garnered. 'Is it your wife or girlfriend back home, who's waiting to be taken out, wined and dined?'

'Exactly,' he lies. 'It's her birthday in two days, and I won't be very popular if I don't make it back.'

'No, I dare say you won't.' Her mouth turns down; this predicament seems to bother her far more than any impending execution in this unassuming suburb, or an entire city cloaked in deadly smog.

'Can't you make it back to Mayfair, even in this weather?' Harri chances. 'To your home?'

She pouts with displeasure. 'He says not, that we have to stay here. But it's *so* dull.'

'There's always the wireless, or a good book to read.'

'I thought that was your department,' she comes back, with a sly smile. 'Aren't you supposed to be writing one?'

Not once does she cast around for a typewriter or a notebook; not as naïve as she makes out, he thinks, with this disinterested wife persona. Evidently, she is enjoying this little game of tit-for-tat, a balm for her boredom.

'Sadly, I seem to have hit a dry patch,' he says. 'Though I could do with a book to read.'

Her sculpted eyebrows arch.

'Truly,' he adds. 'I need a boost for my imagination. Or a muse.'

'Any particular type?'

'Book or muse?'

She laughs. 'Something from the bookcase.'

'Well, if you're not willing to be my muse, I'll take a good crime novel,' he says, his words dense with irony. 'I like a bit of peril.'

'So I've heard, Herr Schroder.'

'As does your husband.'

With consummate skill, she ignores this last remark, filling the pause with a slow blink of her kohl-lined eyes that acts as snub, the type the upper classes do so well, honed over years of superiority. But her willing ignorance speaks volumes: Alicia Remington knows all too well about the Helmut Praxer that was. Even if she pretends otherwise, she sees it all, squirrelled away in her head alongside party invites and the best couturiers. The woman before him acts like a debutante and diva in unison, but she is more than that. She is complicit.

Plus, she's bored again. Of Harri this time. Moving to

the door, she opens it without a word, closes and locks it behind her. Five minutes later, the key inserts, turns and Alicia appears, proffering a hardback. 'Agatha Christie good enough for you?'

'Yes. And very British,' he says. 'Thank you.'

She takes one last look through the window, as if the shroud might have lifted in the last few minutes, huffs and slips back through the door. The lock clicks. Unconsciously, Harri waits for the inevitable scraping of the key being removed. Only there's nothing, except the faint shimmy of skirt against stockings as Mrs Remington walks across the landing. Unlike Joseph, she can't be used to the duties of a gatekeeper.

For a brief second, he considers the possibility that she's been purposely neglectful for her own amusement. But it doesn't stop him from kneeling, his eye to the keyhole, glad not to see anything but grey metal plugging the space. It's the oldest trick in the book – in fact, he might well have read it in the pages of the great Ms Christie. A search of the dressing table gives up nothing he needs, neither card nor paper, or a small thin implement. With an apology to the celebrated writer, he tears several pages from the novel, then begins stripping the pliable resin teeth from the comb on the sink, though they take some effort to snap. Finally, he has what he needs.

Hoping Joseph's heavy presence is not nearby, Harri slides the pages under the door, and prods gingerly at the key in the lock – too forceful and it will overshoot the paper, too little and it might fall sideways. Donk! He releases one lungful of air and pulls in another. Face squashed into the carpeted floor, he squints underneath, spying the key sitting on the paper, then draws the tiny page edge towards himself.

Careful, Schroder. Do not over-egg this omelette.

At the tiniest of clunks, his heart sinks. Clearly, this cunning scheme is better suited to one of Agatha Christie's draughty country mansions with polished wooden flooring, but unworkable in a modern home with thick pile carpet. The narrow stream of light under the door is just that – too thin for the chunky, old-fashioned key, now butted up against the wooden door. In hindsight, it was always too good to be true, a trick best suited to fiction.

Resigned, Harri draws the paper inwards and re-inserts the torn pages between the covers, sits back and opens the book at page one.

32

The Huntress

6th December 1952

Dexie

On a normal day, it would be a short journey to the address she's been given, but after several wrong turns and a calamitous fall off a kerb while coughing into her scarf, Dexie is running sweat under her coat, her skin freezing and clammy in tandem. Desperation oozes from every pore, and she's limping slightly, while time ticks away.

The building is easy to find, just off the pavement on Clarence Way, its six red-brick storeys looming as she gets closer, one of those post-war new builds that have sprung up across London, filling the toothy gaps left by the bombing. On the third floor, she finds number ten and raps four times.

A woman's voice comes through the wood. 'Yes?' Instantly suspicious.

Dexie leans in. 'Wolli sent me. He phoned you.'

'Name?'

'Dexie.'

There's the click of several successive bolts, and finally a face – or a portion of one. One eyeball swivels, combing every inch of the dark hallway. 'Anyone with you?'

'No, just me.'

'Got anything for me?'

Dexie holds up three packs of Player's that Wolli instructed her to buy – satisfying both password and addiction combined. The door opens just enough for her to slide in, and is re-locked with haste. It doesn't help that the flat feels instantly claustrophobic, and yet chilly at the same time. Modern post-war construction doesn't necessarily mean good quality, the miasma of outside sneaking in through the thin window frames to meet the equally static air. A sallow, yellow haze floats at head height, not helped when the woman paws eagerly at the cigarette packets and lights one, drawing hard on the tobacco.

The inner mist creates the sort of monochrome haze Dexie has seen many a time in films, the beauty of Greta Garbo or Sophia Loren pushing through a veil of romanticism. And this woman – Eliza – is beautiful. Or was, as she takes a step forward, her tall, angular body drawn into focus, and her face, too; Dexie sees the hardships that Wolli alluded to, etched on skin that's cracked, cheeks that are gaunt instead of smooth and envied. Her reddish hair has been hastily pinned, without much care for the outside world, and her silk dressing gown is soiled and darned in places.

'So?' Eliza says. 'Wolli tells me you need information.'

'I do. For a very good friend, who's in real danger.'

'What makes you so sure I have what you need?' she scoffs into the cigarette, reflecting disdain back on herself: look at me, how do you think *I* can help?

'Helmut Praxer.'

The cigarette is held partway to Eliza's mouth, half-forgotten at the utterance of his name. 'Shit.'

She smokes another while Dexie explains, coming clean about the proposed mission, their infiltration of the casino and Harri being snatched by Praxer's cronies. Why shouldn't she tell all? Johnson lied to both her and Harri, and so his organisation is undeserving of any protection. Eliza's reaction is anything but shock. She nods at intervals, but says nothing.

'Do you think you can help?' Dexie entreats when she's finished. 'Wolli says you know Praxer better than most.'

'I suppose I do,' Eliza drawls. Like Wolli, it's a mix of Eastern European and London dialect, with a flavour of French, too. 'Among other members of the Reich, I've been tracking him for years.'

'You're a Nazi hunter?'

Eliza laughs it off. 'You British! You love to pigeonhole people, label them and put them in a box.'

'Sorry, it's just . . .' Dexie glances at her watch. Almost midday, and they're sitting around making small talk. She needs something concrete to act upon, but Eliza seems unruffled and unwilling to be rushed.

'Did you know about the signing of this agreement being moved forward?' Dexie pushes, in a bid to hammer home the urgency. 'We have just three days.'

That's the spark to the fuse, judging by the way Eliza's head snaps upwards, alarm across her features. 'When was it changed?'

'Only recently, as far as I can tell.'

'Damn it!' The nostrils on her thin nose flare. Eliza re-fastens the belt on her dressing gown, its glossy length billowing as she sails towards a door off the living room, gesturing for Dexie to follow. 'I thought we had more time.'

Nazi hunter is more accurate than even Dexie imagined. There's one desk and a single chair in the small room, but the rest has been given over to several filing cabinets, boxes and large envelopes stacked high with names and dates marked into the sides. Pinned on the wall is a rogues' gallery of men in the sleek uniforms of the German army and the Waffen SS, self-satisfied smiles aimed at the camera lens.

Eliza delves into corner and heaves up a large cardboard box, landing it on the desk with a thud. 'This,' she says, 'is the celebrated Mr Remington, and his filthy Nazi past.'

'What are we looking for?' Dexie asks as they spread the contents over the living room floor, pushing aside the dirty cups and plates.

'I compiled a list of some properties he's used over the years, places that have been mentioned in company reports.'

'Business addresses?' Dexie queries. 'Harri and I already found some listed.'

Eyes down, scanning fast, Eliza shakes her head. 'Not all of them. Some were residential, and I checked up on a couple of the local ones, but they seemed to be empty. I'm wondering if those are a better possibility as a hideout.' She reaches for another cigarette in frustration. 'Christ, where is that bit of paper? I know I had it here somewhere.'

They sort methodically and silently. In among the piles of loose notes are several photographs that draw Dexie's attention. She picks up one, a formal black-and-white portrait of the type the Reich loved to take of their senior ranks: the more favoured the officer the better the quality of picture. This one is a studio shot on thick, photographic card, the subject in crisp, dark SS attire, similar to those pinned on the wall. Eliza glances up briefly. 'That's the only one of him in uniform I've ever been able to find,' she says. 'He was very careful even then to avoid being pictured.'

'This is Praxer?' Dexie is aghast. The man staring back at her is nothing like the Remington at the casino, flesh that is fuller and with pasty folds to his neck, no doubt due to the infamous good living of senior Reich officials. The Praxer who took Harri is thinner, with sharper features and a chiselled jaw, eyes of a different shape. She thinks he must have requested 'more handsome' on his wish list to the plastic surgeon.

Underneath is another photograph, reproduced on thinner paper, a formal group shot of dark-suited police recruits, with one individual circled in red pen. It's Praxer of old, if slightly leaner than his well-fed, fattened Führer days. Dexie pulls the picture closer, scanning the men for one in particular, and settling on a figure in the back row. A thinner face, for certain, perhaps a little less grizzled and with shorn hair, but the distinct lips and eyes tell her it's Harri. There's a mischievous tilt to his mouth. It reminds her of the training school pictures of Thomas, tucked away in a box at her mother's house. She gets them out from time to time, on the days when loneliness hangs heavy, looking into her husband's youthful face and pondering on what he was thinking, about how his life would turn out, long or short, happy or sad? He was blissfully naïve back then. They both were. Staring at the photo in her hand, she wonders the same about Harri. On the back it's dated 1934. What could Harri know then about the years to come, the gain of his wife and family, and the devastating loss, the entire world torn into shreds? Today's most pressing question hits home: is his life destined to be cut short, like Thomas'?

'Got it!' Eliza's voice is sharp and triumphant. 'I knew it was here.'

They sit side by side on the rug, Eliza pointing to each address in turn. 'This one is a flat in a busy block, so I think it's unlikely he'd use it as a hideout,' she reasons, 'and there's a mews house in Kensington, very central and nice and quiet, but it's tiny. They'll need bodyguards, and it would be too cramped, especially if the Princess Alicia is with them.' The twist of her features tells Dexie exactly what Eliza thinks of Mrs Remington. Her long finger goes to a third scribble. 'I went to this one, and it's definitely a possibility, in a suburb, so it would take time to drive in this weather, but not hours. A good-size but a relatively ordinary house, the type you might expect a manager of his to own. Detached with a large garden, and . . .' She closes her eyes in sifting her memory. 'Yes, I'm sure I remember noting an entrance to a basement, where they might have delivered coal. When I peered in the ground floor window it was furnished, but looked empty, if you know what I mean. Unlived in.'

'What does your gut tell you?' Dexie asks. It's ridiculous to imagine Harri's life balances on instinct, but it's all they have at this stage. And didn't Georgie – a surviving war reporter – attest to its value?

'I think it's a better bet than a warehouse,' Eliza argues. 'In recent months, Praxer has kept Alicia in his orbit, either through devotion, or he doesn't trust her to keep their secret close enough into her chest – too much title-tattle over cocktails. If he is this near to signing the agreement, she'll be with him. And believe me, the princess would not put up with roughing it in a warehouse.'

Dexie thinks hard; it will take time to travel to this house, wasted hours if it remains empty. Is there any way they can shore up their guess?

Georgie. She jumps up. 'Can I use your phone, Eliza?'

The man at the other end of Georgie's home number

reports she's gone to Fleet Street, with no messages left, and it takes another two calls to locate her in *The Times* business section. 'Any news?' Georgie's concern rebounds across the phone line.

'Not yet,' Dexie says. 'But we have an address that might be a possibility. Do you have anything to hand, like a rundown of staff homes or residential properties, something we can check it against?'

'Hang on.' There's a muffled conversation, and a shuffling of paper in the background. 'The business reporter has a list from Companies House of all the Remington assets. There's quite a few, and some could be residential, judging by the addresses. Have you got one in mind?'

The seconds feel like hours to Dexie as Georgie goes down a list, looking for a Trinity Lodge, in West Ealing. 'No. No. No . . .' she murmurs over the crackle of the phone line, from what seems a million miles away. A page flips. 'No No . . . hmm . . . no.'

Dexie is only half conscious of holding her breath. *Please let there be a yes.*

'Ah, here it is,' Georgie says at last.

A heavy lungful of air pushes into the receiver.

'According to this, it belongs to a Ralph Bertram, managing director . . .' Georgie explains. 'Wait a minute, Dexie . . .' Georgie's words becomes faint, as a voice in the background cuts into the conversation. 'What's that you say?' There's another muted exchange, and then she's back on the line. 'The correspondent here is sure that no such man exists. He's been looking into the company's books, and there's some suspicion of fraud, using fake employees as tax fronts.'

'That must be our target then,' Dexie says, nodding furiously at Eliza, who disappears into another room.

'A target for what?' Georgie's sudden alarm is loud and clear. 'What are you planning to do? Should I ring the police?'

Dexie hesitates. Yes, or no? She *is* the police, but what if it's a false alarm, amid current debacle outside, or that the heavy-handed sounds of the Met approaching prompts Praxer's men to take action? She knows from experience that desperate men do desperate things.

'No,' she says firmly. 'I'll sort the help myself. I know who to call.'

'Well, I'm sure I don't need to tell you to be careful,' Georgie adds. 'But do it anyway. Please. For both of you.'

'I will, I promise.' Dexie puts down the receiver, knowing she can speak for herself on that score. Though, perhaps, not for others. Not for Eliza, who has returned to the living room, fully dressed and tucking something into the waistband of her flannel trousers. Something bulky and heavy, with metal that shines out through the gauzy haze between them.

The thin eyebrows rise at Dexie's expression.

'I have a feeling we might need it,' she says drily.

33

Journey into the Unknown

6th December 1952

Dexie

The minute they step outside, Eliza is bent double by a prolonged coughing fit. 'Christ,' she splutters, pulling herself up finally. 'I didn't realise it was this bad. I haven't been beyond the front door in days.' She blinks into the milky nothingness.

'How far is this place?' Dexie asks.

'There's a bus. That's how I got there the first time. About thirty minutes, on a normal day.'

'There'll be no buses that far out now, even those in the city centre are at a snail's pace.'

Eliza casts around again. 'Then we're going to need a car.'

Behind the steering wheel, Dexie's discomfort is two-fold: driving into an abyss is one thing, but doing it in a stolen car adds a whole new dimension of unease. And criminality. Off the beat, out of uniform and plunged into this shadowy world, it's difficult to think of herself as an officer of the law. WPC Dexter: accessory to theft. That won't go down well on her personnel record, less so in court, and she doesn't want to think about Sergeant Thomas's view on it.

Eliza, on the hand, had been entirely blasé about picking the lock of a nearby Ford Anglia and hot wiring the ignition with ease. For a brief second, they'd considered collecting the Austin from outside Bethnal Green station where it's been sitting for two days, but that's on the other side of London, stealing more time they don't have. Thieving the nearest available vehicle seemed a more practical option, 'and besides, who will even notice the car being "borrowed" in this weather?' Eliza had argued, settling herself into the passenger seat. 'Praxer is on the move so often these days, we can't be sure what he will do. More than once I thought I'd caught up with him, only to be too late, sometimes by a matter of minutes.'

Dexie was forced to agree, her thoughts centred on Harri's limited life span; if he's ghosted to another location it will almost certainly mean failure on her part. Too little, too late. They have to get moving, and she's in no position to object, not with that gun fixed in Eliza's waistband and her eyes like gimlets, boring into the windscreen.

The journey is bumper to bumper at first, but the traffic soon peters out as they head further into the suburbs to the west of the centre. Gathering any sort of speed proves impossible, Dexie's foot hovering impatiently over the accelerator as she negotiates the stop-start traffic, plus the abandoned vehicles parked precariously along the roadside.

Eliza is silently staring at an old bronze compass she's produced, save for the odd 'watch out!' and 'it's left here', and with her nose almost touching the glass, so concentrated she doesn't even reach for a cigarette. Dexie is equally focused, but their progress is laboured and she twitches inside with curiosity.

'What's your issue with Praxer?' she asks at last. Dares to probe, if Wolli is right.

The head of red hair whips around. Eliza's look is so hardened, so full of bitterness, that Dexie almost loses control of the wheel. 'Is it not enough that he's a Nazi, and a murdering bastard?'

'Well, yes,' Dexie concedes. 'Only, I sense this is more . . . that it's personal for you. Your fervour, and everything back at the flat. Am I wrong?'

Eliza shoots back in her seat, as if the question is a weapon that's punched a hole in her stomach. 'Is that what Wolli told you?'

'No, he didn't say anything, only that I needed to find out for myself.' Dexie swallows. 'But given what might happen, and that you are happy enough to carry a weapon that I assume you know how to use, I feel I deserve some explanation.'

Their headlights nose between what's become drifting seams of fog, the car lurching forward in the few lighter patches. Eliza's silence crowds into the space between them. 'You're right,' she says at last. 'Praxer is one of many men I've been trying to hunt down, but he is, and always has been, the top of my list.'

'Oh?'

'Wolli and I worked together during the war, and then afterwards.'

'Polish resistance?'

'Yes. Both my parents were in the camps, and died there quite early in the war. I spent some time undercover in '43, courting top Nazis.' She scoffs again at her present self. 'Back in the days when I could ably attract a man's gaze. I don't mind admitting I bedded them for intelligence, and sick as that made me, I think it saved lives. A drop in the ocean, mind, to all those that were lost.'

Dexie's stomach pitches in sympathy, and then admiration. Her own time in the ARP pales in comparison. 'Was one of those men Praxer, that you courted?'

'Yes, and no,' Eliza says flatly. 'I got him as far as the bed and stripped him of that vile SS regalia, but with an entire bottle of brandy inside him, he couldn't perform. Not that he would let anything slip, nothing of value to the resistance, anyway. And yet, drunk as he was, he could quote the numbers before he passed out – of how many "units" could be dispatched in one go, babbling at how he'd calculated the transport and the gas needed, so he could "streamline the business", something the Fuhrer viewed as an absolute triumph, apparently.' She coughs up the words, as if heaving up a particularly foul poison.

'Weren't you tempted to kill him there and then?' It's out of Dexie's mouth before she has time to streamline her own thoughts.

'Yes, of course!' Eliza's head pivots again, irritation apparent. 'Equally, I was under strict orders – I had several officers in play at once, and the intelligence as a whole was too valuable. If I'd have taken a knife to Praxer, I wouldn't have lasted a day, along with several other women in our group.'

For a minute, there's nothing but the drone of the engine between them.

'You're wondering if I regret not killing him?' Eliza murmurs.

'Hmm.'

'Yes. Absolutely. If I'd known what he would go on to do, in the war and afterwards, I wouldn't have hesitated for a second. And gladly died for it.'

'And now?' Dexie questions. As a protector of this country's laws, is she actively driving someone towards murder? Or are they intent on apprehending a perpetrator of kidnap? The abduction not of a stranger, but someone she knows, and that – even in a short time – cannot bear to think as being harmed, let alone . . .

'Let's just see what we find, shall we?' Eliza's voice is forthright. 'Right now, I just want to look Praxer in the eye and watch him squirm.'

This time, her gaunt features turn defiantly towards the bleak world beyond the windscreen, a definitive full stop to their conversation.

34

Collateral

6th December 1952

Harri

He might have dozed again, though it's difficult to tell with the flat grey void in the window, no sign where the sun is, or if it's out there at all. Only Harri's stomach tells him time has moved on, with a pinch against his innards. He could do with another visit from Alicia Remington, more for the food she might bring rather than her self-serving chit-chat.

He gets up and stretches, moving to the window out of sheer habit and is hit with a sense of familiarity, in doing the same each morning in his Hamburg flat. That vista of concrete grey has become strangely comforting over the years, unlike the deathly sediment before him now, which seems hunkered low and determined. He peers through the iron bars into the filthy air, hoping something might have shifted in the time he's been asleep. Anything.

Spoke too soon, Schroder! Something *is* changing. Directly below his window, Harri just makes out the squat and solid black shape of a van, with movement of bodies around it. Squinting hard, he picks out Joseph's bulky outline, his voice directing what looks to be a large cylinder manoeuvred into the van's back doors.

'Make sure there's plenty of rope too,' Joseph's voice barks, as the other bodies work industriously.

'Yes, boss.'

Harri's mind calculates as his empty stomach plummets. Van. Rope. And a length of carpet perhaps? He adds the filthy flow of the Thames to the equation and comes up with a scenario he doesn't want to visualise, but which slams at his eyes, in glorious technicolour. 'You out and out idiot, Schroder,' he says aloud this time.

Of course, he never dreamed Praxer would let him go scot-free, but for one gullible moment, Harri thought his former comrade might keep him alive a little longer, like a cat that paws at a live mouse, simply for its own amusement. He had hoped for more time to think, act, or else find a weak point – a spark of humanity – in one of his gaolers, though he can't imagine who. Mrs Dane perhaps? Just enough leverage to talk his way out of certain death.

How could he be so stupid? Praxer has been relentless in his cruelty for years, so why would he stop now? Harri Schroder is no former friend of Helmut Praxer. He's collateral, plain and simple, and now rapidly evolving to dead weight.

Harri peers again at the industry below the window, just as Joseph's gruff tone drifts up: 'We leave in half an hour, all right, lads? The boss wants this sorted quickly.'

As if he has eyes in the back of his head, the big man turns his wide shoulders and – even through the gloom – Harri swears the face is directed up at him. It's impossible to see it clearly through the grey-green vapour, but every part of him imagines a smile creeping onto Joseph's lips, causing his insides to lurch again. This time, it's not through hunger.

35

Stand Off

6th December 1952

Dexie

The milometer says they've travelled a paltry eight miles, though the journey feels like an odyssey, Dexie's eyes perpetually wide and weary from the strain of dodging kerbs, lampposts and pedestrians. At several points, Eliza has needed to get out and peer closely at the street signs, before they finally reached the placard that says they are entering the borough of Ealing. Twice, they saw an ambulance crawl by, with a police escort walking in front, a lighted flare in the constable's hands. Twice, both women shrank back into the seats, as the officer stared in their direction, possibly more with surprise that they've ventured out at all.

'We're in the right area,' Eliza assures at last, checking a printed copy of the *A–Z* found in the car. It's a saving grace, since this is way off Dexie's patch and might as well be the Sahara in a sandstorm.

Several turns later, Eliza's focus switches from the map

to the street in sight. 'Drive slowly past this gatepost,' she instructs. 'I think we've just gone by the house.'

Dexie rolls to a gentle stop in a residential road where nothing and no one is moving, everyone hunkered down behind their solid front doors in shielding from the insidious killer outside.

On foot, they peer almost nose to nose at the painted house sign confirming it is Trinity Lodge. Inching through the open gate, Dexie strains to make out a large double-fronted brick house, with steps up to a front porch and mock Tudor décor around the window frames. Just the sort of comfortable home a bank manager might well entertain in, near enough for driving to the local golf course when the weather allows, and to his wife's bridge club. But is it also the hideaway of a former Nazi and now kidnapper?

'Have we got a plan?' Dexie whispers. Stunned by making it this far, she's now running with nerves at what will ensue. And nowhere to call for back-up. For the first time, it dawns that they are utterly alone – one unarmed constable, and one potential vigilante with a loaded gun. She rues the fact that her desperation to find Harri has overruled any common sense.

'We play lost and dumb,' Eliza says with the confidence of one who is practised in deceit. 'We've driven the car into a kerb, got a flat tyre and need to make a phone call. That should get us inside, OK?'

Dexie nods, banking on Praxer being the sort of man not to open the door to his own house, suddenly face-to-face with the clumsy waitress. 'And then what?'

This prompts nothing but an irritated look from Eliza.

There is a large sedan car and a black van parked in the driveway, and a glow from the bottom bay windows, where the curtains are drawn. Rather than shielding any wrongdoing, it's probably more of an attempt to repel the sulphury vapours, but a convenience for trespassers like them.

'Back door.' Eliza gestures, a patent wheeze in her voice after only several minutes' exposure.

Side-stepping the gravel where possible, they round the side of the house and listen for a moment outside what appears to be the kitchen, hearing alternate coughing and humming behind the half-glazed door. Dexie just catches Eliza patting at the bulge under her coat before she raps on the wood. There's a startled cry from inside and a dark shape moving behind the frosted glass, before a face appears in a gap of mere inches.

'Oh!' An older woman peers out, her mouth puckered with alarm. 'Er, can I help? Goodness, are you out selling something in this weather?' With one eye, her gaze sweeps left to right, beyond Eliza, to Dexie and the blank space either side.

'No, we're not selling anything,' Eliza says, in a beseeching, British tone that she pulls out from somewhere deep inside, a world away from the determined, bitter growl Dexie has grown used to. 'My cousin and I, we're driving to visit our grandmother, to check she's all right in this awful weather, but we've gone and hit a kerb. We've got a flat tyre, and I was wondering, do you have a telephone?'

'Erm, yes,' the woman says.

'Oh, thank goodness! Would we be able to use it, to ring a garage?' Eliza presses. 'We'll reimburse the cost, of course.'

Despite a look of sympathy on her face, the woman hesitates. 'Hmm, just a moment.'

It's when she shuts the door that Dexie is certain they have the right house. Why else wouldn't you invite two women in, out of the freezing cold? Without sight or much obvious sound, there's also a presence here Dexie can't quite explain. That it's lived in, and yet not someone's home. She's seen and felt the same before, assisting with a couple of police raids on high-end brothels – well-furnished homes that appear like innocent dwellings, but feel so impersonal once you're inside. A halfway house. From the outside, this is no classy bordello, but there's definitely some form of ill-repute surrounding it.

The door opens again, a few inches at first, and then fully. 'The phone is in the hallway, but you'll have to be quick and quiet,' the woman says, ushering them in at speed into the kitchen, fanning back the fog that attempts to follow. 'The owners are entertaining in the living room, and I can't disturb them.'

Dexie's conviction increases. Who on earth entertains amid the worst fog for years, that's now a city-wide disaster?

'Thank you so much, you're an absolute life saver,' Eliza gushes effusively, then aims a backward glance at Dexie. Her brow furrowed, she affirms with the tiniest of nods: they've narrowed it down well. This is the place.

'Through here.' The woman walks them into a hallway of dark wood, with a large set of stairs in the centre, but enough room for a small sofa next to a telephone table. 'Like I say, try not to be too long. Come into the kitchen when you're finished, and I'll put the kettle on while you wait for the mechanic. You must be frozen.'

Eliza makes a play of picking up the receiver as the kitchen door closes, though her attention is now on the space beyond and the murmur of conversation from the living room. She shrugs and holds up three fingers. Three voices?

Four, maybe? Dexie mouths silently back. It's been and gone in a heartbeat, but the glint that she sees in the other woman's eye – of excitement perhaps? – only increases her anxiety.

Clearly unfazed, Eliza pulls out a silver pistol from her back pocket that's smaller and lighter than the revolver already in her waistband. Slowly and quietly, she ratchets back the safety catch and holds it out, the metal shiny in the dim light of the hallway. With a resigned sigh, Dexie takes it.

She's never fired a weapon in her life, and doesn't intend to start now, but – she reasons – it might provide some extra persuasion, should they need it.

Eliza nods and reaches past the flap of her coat, hoisting the revolver up confidently as she flings open the living room door. Four faces whip towards the intruders in utter astonishment.

'What the—?' Praxer is the first to react angrily, though he doesn't rise up from his seat on the sofa. It's a big bear of a man who rushes forward, stopped in his tracks when Eliza swings out an arm, pointing her weapon assertively.

'Not another step,' she says, back to her Polish drawl, coated in bitterness. 'In fact, take two steps backwards. Now.'

The big man hesitates, perhaps deciding if he can rush and overpower her, and then catching the sheen of Dexie's pistol bringing up the rear. His hands go up, a quick glance backwards at Praxer and wife on the sofa, another man in an easy chair to left.

'Gun on the floor,' Eliza barks. 'Carefully.'

'OK.' Butt first, the big man slides a revolver from his waistband, bends his bulk towards the floor, and drops it with a clunk on the parquet wood. At a glance from Eliza, he kicks it softly away from him.

A grey-suited man in the easy chair is frozen, but gasps sharply when Eliza turns the revolver on him. The stuffy air catches in his throat and he begins coughing, unable to stop.

'For God's sake, someone give him water,' Eliza commands impatiently.

Alicia Remington shuffles in her seat and offers up a glass of clear liquid, which has some effect.

Then it's Praxer's turn to move. 'Who the fuck are you and what do you want?' He stands slowly, pulling up to full height, menace resonating from every inch of his body.

Dexie senses Eliza's body stiffen, her trigger finger twitching and her breath in short, sharp bursts. Clearly, she's waited years for this. To look him in the eye, point a weapon right between the two pupils and snuff out the arrogance that lays behind.

Christ, Eliza, not now! Dexie screams inside her own head. *We have a purpose here!* Wolli warned her, didn't he? That Eliza was – is – reckless. What's more, the resistance woman has never even met Harri, so why would she fight for his survival over her life's purpose?

'You have someone we want,' Eliza says firmly, to Dexie's utter surprise. 'Give him to us, and we'll go. Simple as that.'

Praxer jaw thrusts forward. 'And who would that be? We're just here enjoying a drink with our friend.' He gestures at the grey suit, now desperately trying to suppress a further bout of spluttering.

'Don't play games, Helmut. You might lie with ease to these people, but not me.'

Praxer stiffens visibly, in direct reference to his old identity. He manages a step forward as his eyes narrow to a slit, combing over Eliza. Deep behind his cold glare, he looks to be scouring his memory for signs of her.

'Darling?' Alicia Remington's voice rises up from the sofa, curious but strangely calm. She appears composed, far more than an average spouse when faced with two armed strangers bursting into a living room. Dexie watches her closely: the society darling has seen this before. Be it protection or aggression, it's a way of life behind her gilded facade. But the fact that a woman such as Eliza knows her husband of old – that does seem to irk Alicia Remington, and her face signals she wants to know how. Or at least for him to deny it publicly.

'Why don't you explain?' She nudges at her husband. 'Surely, this is a case of mistaken identity?'

'A mistake, Helmut, twice in quick succession?' Dexie

pipes up from behind. She can't help the jibe, and it forces Praxer's eyes to swing her way.

'Ah, the clumsy waitress,' he sneers. 'Sadly, we have no champagne for you to spill.'

'But we will need the waiter,' she shoots back. 'That's all we've come for.'

'He's not here,' the big man in the suit cuts in.

'You took him,' Dexie says. 'So, where is he?' *Please don't say he's dead.*

'Why would we hold him here?' the big man argues.

'For the same reason that everyone else is holed up behind closed doors,' Eliza argues firmly. 'This bloody weather. Because it's a nightmare moving around and you need to keep him close.'

With his years of experience at deception, Praxer's face is static. It's the big man who gives it away with a tiny tic, one eye flicked involuntarily at the ceiling.

'Check upstairs,' Eliza snaps at Dexie, her focus and her gun trained firmly on Praxer. 'Shoot the lock on any door if you have to.'

Reluctantly, Dexie backs towards the hallway, wary of finding another bodyguard on the landing above. Will she be forced to put a bullet in someone's leg, if only to disable them?

'Wait.' Praxer halts her progress, then turns to the big man. 'Joseph, give her the key. There's no need for violence here, we can sort this reasonably.'

'Can we?' Eliza questions. Her gaze hasn't left him for a second.

'Yes, I believe we can,' Praxer retorts, his eyes flickering, as if he is totting up the odds of facing one gun instead of two. 'Joseph?'

Covered by Dexie's pointed pistol, the big man reaches into his pocket and pulls out a key, handing it over with a silent scowl. She grabs it and is up the stairs in seconds, both arms outstretched on the gun as it leads into the unknown. 'Harri? Harri, where are you?' Her breath is fast, the words pushed with force, then listening out for any response. Have they sent her up here so they can corner Eliza alone, and he's already lying dead?

'*Dex?* Dexie?' The voice from behind a white-painted door is shocked and urgent, but familiar.

Fumbling in the lock, she can barely believe it's him, not until he's there in front of her, looking more captive than pristine waiter. Harri is, however, alive and seemingly unharmed, his pale features wracked with obvious relief.

'Jesus, Dexie! How on earth?'

'No time to explain,' she says, 'we need to get back downstairs.'

Below, the room remains static, like players on a giant board game. Eliza's arm trembles only slightly, extended and tense. Stalemate.

'I found him,' Dexie whispers, coming up from behind. 'We can go now.'

Eliza doesn't move. In complete contrast to Dexie's audible panting, her breath appears to have slowed to almost nothing.

'Come on, time to go,' Dexie urges. 'We have what we came for.'

'Do we?' The gun twitches. Dexie sees a single line of perspiration trickle behind her ear. This is exactly what Wolli warned about, and what she gambled with – Eliza's volatile nature against Harri's life.

'I'm here,' Harri hisses from the doorway, another nudge to their departure. 'Unharmed. Let's go.'

'I want one more thing from Herr Praxer,' Eliza says. 'Just one.'

'Which is?' Praxer's voice is calm and cold. Tiring of this stand-off, too, by the sounds of his tone.

'An admission.'

'Of? What is it that I'm supposed to have done, to upset you so much, Miss . . . I don't even know who you are.'

'Eleanor. Freiburg.' The name – doubtless one of her many identities – is clipped. Out of the blue, Eliza's voice morphs into a silken, sultry murmur, the syrup of pillow talk heavy with a Teutonic accent. 'Oh, Helmut,' she mocks him mercilessly, 'Helmut, you are so clever, so much more than all those other officers. Show me, darling, how clever you are, won't you?'

It's the same script she must have trotted out time and again when she cornered him in a bedroom, as bile bubbled in her throat, sick to her stomach. Almost ten years on, her hatred has not diminished.

Across the room, Dexie sees Praxer's jaw begin to grind, while behind him, Alicia Remington has the look of a woman on the verge of a cat fight.

Eliza, however, is entirely focused on her former Nazi of the bedchamber. 'Recognise me now, Helmut?' she says, the flint edge back in her voice. 'From all those fabulous Reich parties in Berlin. And then afterwards, in private.'

Behind him, Alicia twitches again, her face turned to granite, though her disgust seems to be aimed not at her husband, but on these two women who threaten her comfortable existence, the life she has built from a brand of selective naivety. Interlopers who dare to breach *her* house. *Her* bubble.

For one, brief second, Praxer looks as if he might do it. Concede, and even make some attempt at an apology, however false and pathetic. But then his face flattens. Still unreadable, but the hate is gone.

'Remington?' the man in the grey suit speaks for the first time, suddenly assertive. Concerned and suspicious, too. 'What is this? Who are these people?'

'It's nothing, George,' Praxer snaps. 'These *ladies*' – Dexie feels a spike of irritation in her gut as Eliza tenses even more beside her – 'have confused me with someone else and jumped to all sorts of conclusions. It is as Alicia says – a case of mistaken identity.'

George staggers upright from the soft armchair, his large girth suddenly apparent. 'But they can't get away with barging in here like this, pointing guns at us. You need to call the police, sure—'

'Shut up, George.' Praxer's lips move in isolation, eyes fixed ahead, the sheen on his skin immovable. 'I will deal with this. Please sit down.'

'Well, er . . .' But sit he does, suddenly cowed and dumbstruck.

Praxer's next words are aimed directly at Eliza. 'I am sorry. Is that what you need, Miss . . . what was it? Freiburg?'

There is a distinct crackle in the room. Dexie senses Harri can feel it too, hovering behind her in the doorway. This should be the end, the point at which she, Harri and Eliza beat a retreat, feeling their way to the car and lurching away under a milky cloak of near safety. Instead, Dexie braces herself for the fallout, the response to Praxer's words that are totally devoid of intent or feeling. Or meaning. Worse, they are dripping with hidden contempt.

'Not good enough,' Eliza says flatly.

'Oh, pardon me, should I ramp up my acting skills?' Praxer's face is suddenly more animated by a smirk. 'Would you like a touch of Humphrey Bogart, or that new, good-looking chap, Marlon Brando?'

'At least they might feign some penitence, or shame,'

Eliza seethes. From alongside, Dexie watches her shoulders tense again, as the voice spirals downwards. 'You might at least *pretend* to be sorry for killing millions, for the blood that's on your hands, for those women and children you sent to their deaths, with your fucking calculations.'

'Now, come on, young lady,' George splutters from his seat.

'I said SHUT UP, George!' Praxer screams, that distinct shrill breaking through, shattering the tension of the room. 'I am in charge here, and I call the shots. You hear me? ME. And no one else.'

Even before he says it, Dexie knows it's the tipping point. The hates exudes from across Eliza's body, her gun arm outstretched, trembling with fury and exertion, so that Dexie only sees the spasm of her finger at the last second. Too late. The sound is deafening but oddly contained in the room.

From the other side of the room, Alicia Remington is ahead of the game. 'NO!' she screams, leaping up and shoving her husband sideways in one lightning move, an act which leaves her – for a mere blink of an eye – in the space he occupied. And in line with the bullet from Eliza's gun.

Like a faulty film reel, everything stops. For another half second, they all stare at Mrs Remington, a red welt blooming against the silk of her dress, right where her questionable heart once beat. Instantly, Praxer is beside her, scooping up her limp body.

'JOSEPH!' he screams, his face a vengeful mask. But the big man doesn't need any instruction, because he's already lunging towards Eliza, sweeping up his weapon from near her feet, and has aimed. This time the shots ricochet around the room: one, two, three. The space beside Dexie is suddenly empty, the long, lean body crumpled. Through the clamour raging in her ears, she hears a single sound ooze into the room, almost a puff of vapour to join the indoor smog. She's heard it before, on the beat, in the back of an ambulance once – the death breath. Life extinguished.

'Dexie, NOW!' Harri snaps her back to the present, yanking forcefully on her arm and backwards towards the door, her feet slipping on the polished wood as the pistol drops from her hand. Almost spilling over, she somehow scrabbles to her feet and makes it to the front door that Harri has opened wide, plunging into the foul toxin crowding in to meet them. Ahead of her, Harri leaps into the dense cloud, as if it's a portal to another world, like Narnia, but what the hell is on the other side? Except there's nowhere else to go, with rapid footsteps chasing into the hallway, followed by Praxer's venomous screech. 'Don't just stand there, Joseph! Kill those bastards!'

Harri is there. Harri is on the other side of the smoky portal, snatching at her hand and dragging her past the black van and down the stony path.

One shot rings out from behind, glances off the metal and sends gravel spraying upwards. A second goes into the hedge inches away.

'Fuck!' the big man's frustrated shout is somewhere in the opaque hinterland.

'Please tell me you have a car,' Harri says, close into her ear.

His urgent breath against her skin sends another jolt through her.

'To your left,' she says. Now he hangs on to her coat sleeve as they run blind into the eerie silence of the street, almost crashing into the Anglia at full pelt. Wordlessly, they pile into the car as Dexie fumbles for the ignition, only slamming the doors shut when the engine fires and she pulls away in one seamless movement and a strained squeal of the engine.

'Anything behind?' Her nose is above the steering wheel as she forges ahead in the middle of the road, to avoid the cars parked on either side, and praying there'll be nothing else to dodge.

'I can't see anything,' Harri pants beside her.

'That's good.'

'No, I mean *nothing*,' he qualifies. 'They could be ten feet behind us for all I know.'

'Then stick your head out of the window and listen.'

'And get it shot off? I thought you were trying to save me.'

'I was, and did. But if they can't see you, then they can't shoot at you.'

He does, for a brief second, pulling back in and coughing out the noxious air that's rushed in to fill the tiny space.

'I can't hear anything,' Harri reports. 'No engine behind us.'

'Maybe they won't try to follow us in this,' Dexie says. Right now, her brain won't tolerate any complex thinking, not when it's crowded with the image of Eliza slipping to the floor as easily as shedding that silk dressing gown of hers. The sound and vision – the slump onto the expensive rug – dominates her mind. It horrifies her. Eyes glued to the road, she only has thoughts of escape, but in a minute corner of Dexie's reason, she knows it's not right.

Eliza is dead. They are hurtling into nothingness, towards the unknown.

Will anything ever feel right again?

36

A Woman in Need

6th December 1952

Harri

He's brimming with questions, not least where the hell they are, but Harri senses conversation is best left for later, perhaps when the woman next to him has stopped pulsing with electricity, though in the circumstances that might be some time. What's fortunate is that she seems to be funnelling everything into getting them as far away from that house as possible, her radar activated again.

What did just happen in that seemingly innocuous suburban house? Later, he might have to painstakingly piece it together with Dexie, but for now the immediate reality is that two women are dead. Alicia Remington is one of them – her glassy-eyed expression left that in no doubt – shot by an unknown woman who appeared to be seeking vengeance on Praxer. He may have dodged the bullet, but that red-haired woman took something precious from a fervent Nazi, robbed it from under his nose. Not just his wife, but his pride, too.

Knowing what Harri does of Praxer, the new and the old versions, they can expect retribution. A fresh reckoning will rain down on his head, and Dexie's. Which means they'd be as well to shelter from the storm that will already be gathering pace.

She doesn't speak again until they are heading east and begin to encounter more traffic, those big red dinosaur buses appearing suddenly, a sure sign they are nearing the city centre again.

'Where to now?' she says, eyes fixed straight ahead, a slight tremor in her words.

'My place,' Harri says.

Her head spins towards him. 'Is that wise?'

'Probably not, but I'm guessing – hoping – that Praxer's army won't be able to move any faster than us, and it might take him some time to re-group.'

'What are we going for? Because if you're simply picking up socks and the like, it's not worth the risk.'

With an odd type of delayed hysteria, he almost laughs, then thinks better of it. 'It's not that,' he says firmly. 'There's someone I need to check on.'

If he's totally honest, his landlady hasn't been at the forefront of his mind the entire time, and not since two people lost their lives in front of him less than an hour ago. Mrs P has, however, hovered on the periphery, as he floated in and out of sleep. Throughout Harri's musings over his own demise, he hoped she wasn't close to meeting hers, given that she wasn't a picture of health at their last encounter. Now, with the continuance of this suffocating weather and a newfound freedom to move and think, he's genuinely worried. A childish whim in Harri Schroder says no one else should lose their life today.

By some miracle, they draw up in Bayley Street unscathed and in record time. Dexie cuts the engine and almost slumps at the wheel, exhaustion pasted over her normally bright features, combined with anguish as she turns to look at him.

Where to even begin? He resolves to start with most pressing statement. 'Thank you,' he says. 'For coming. I owe you my future, my lif—'

'But people lost their lives,' she cuts in, with frustration rather than any anger directed at him. She exhales an even deeper sadness. 'I don't . . . I mean, what kind of world is this?'

'A cruel one,' Harri says. 'Praxer's life is full of glitz and glamour, but underneath it his existence is hard. There's no soft underbelly, just granite and flint. He's dealt in death for years, seen plenty of it.' Harri pauses. 'Who was that woman, by the way?'

'An old colleague of Wolli's, Polish, from the resistance days. Her name was Eliza, that's the name she goes by, anyhow.' Her eyes go up to that safe place on the car's ceiling, and there's a tightness in her neck as she swallows. 'Wolli did warn me, Harri. He said she could be reckless in her pursuit of old Nazis. I was so desperate, though, and I had no leads other than . . .'

'And it was her choice to come, wasn't it?' he's quick to point out, to assuage the guilt he can feel seeping from her. 'I take it you didn't put that gun to her head and make her come?'

'No, but . . .'

'But nothing, Dex.' He pulls in a breath. The cloying smog has been replaced with the taste of death on his tongue. 'I have known women like Eliza before, through the war, and they don't enter into that life without accepting death is a real possibility. By the sounds of it, she played a dangerous game back then, and survived. Some can let it go, and others can't. It was her choice to pursue Praxer, her choice to aim the gun at him. I understand your sadness, but back there, in that moment, she had full control.'

'And Alicia Remington, was she simply a victim?'

'Of getting in the way perhaps,' he says, and then casts back to the odd conversation they'd had in the bedroom, her self-selected knowledge of the atrocities financing her glamourous parties and elegant lifestyle. 'She didn't deserve to die, but equally, she was no innocent.'

'I suppose.' Dexie looks to him, as the one who knows more about this shady world of high-end criminals. 'And the fallout? I mean, I should report it, let the police know, so they investigate it.'

'Investigate what?' Harri argues. 'Those bodies will be ghosted away by now. Eliza will very likely be in the Thames, and Alicia dispatched to an undertaker in the know. There won't be a shred of evidence.' He doesn't elaborate on Joseph's preparations already in place, nor that roll of carpet which will be put to use after all.

'And the gunshots?' Dexie queries. 'That's not the type of neighbourhood ever to have seen a gunfight.'

'Easily explained away by an innocent car backfiring. That's if the neighbours heard anything at all. And you can bet your life savings the reliable housekeeper is paid handsomely to see or hear nothing.'

'But Praxer?' The alarm written across her entire face signals she already has the measure of him. 'He's not going to let this go, is he?'

'No, I don't think so.' In fact, Harri is convinced he won't. Travelling back almost twenty years, he vividly recalls three or four, perhaps as many six, incidences where Praxer held a deep grudge, and the vengeance he then sought. Those events would be nothing more than irritations compared with the cold-blooded killing of his wife. Praxer's view on it? He'll reason that, were it not for Harri, Eliza would never have turned up with a gun. Or intent. Dexie, too, will be absorbed into the Nazi's warped equation. So yes, they both need to look over their shoulders from now on, and way past the gloom of the fog. The irony isn't lost on Harri as he reaches for the Anglia's door handle; having concluded the search and fulfilled Johnson's brief, events have taken a dramatic U-turn.

The hunters have become the hunted.

'Let's see how Mrs P is first and then re-think,' Harri says, easing himself stiffly from the car. 'At the very least, there might be a cup of tea.'

Inside, however, the kettle is stone cold, and the kitchen range just warm, as if the fire hasn't been stoked since he left . . . when was that? Only yesterday evening. There's no sign of Scooter either.

'Mrs Painter?' Harri voice buffers against the damp smog now given free rein in the kitchen. Is she even here, perhaps been taken to hospital?

'I'll get a fire going, and the kettle on,' Dexie says, while Harri steps back into the hallway.

'Mrs P?' He stands, ear to the broom cupboard she calls a bedroom, and waits a second before turning the handle, squinting into the dimness. 'Mrs P, are you there?'

The tiniest shift of the eiderdown says yes, followed by a slight whimper. Woman or dog? When he rushes over to reach her, she's unmoving and it's only Scooter's head that lifts, his eyes mournful and rheumy. In contrast, Mrs P's head lolls to one side off the pillow, eyes closed and her mouth ajar. 'Dexie! In here!' Harri shouts, and then when she arrives at the bedside: 'Let's shift her up, she can't breathe in this position.'

Raising Mrs P's featherweight form to half-sitting, a small moan comes from her parched, cracked lips. Scooter nuzzles his nose in close, determined not to leave her side. 'She's dry as a bone, I'll get some water,' Dexie says.

'Mrs Painter, wake up, wake up!' Harri feels his desperation translate to his hands, shaking her a little too roughly, if only to get some response. It's then that the felt petal hat falls from its human perch, and that tolls like the death knell to Harri. *She can't die, not here or now, not from a bloody fog!*

'Get her to sip this.' Dexie is quickly at his side with a glass of cloudy water. 'I found some honey to stir into it.'

The rattle of a small engine exudes from Mrs P's chest, with the effect of repelling the water as they hold it to her lips, bubbles forming on the liquid in trying to coax it down.

'Come on, Mrs P, just a sip,' Harri pleads into the top of her head. 'You need to drink something. Please.'

Finally, he senses air travelling through her tiny frame, which seems to have become even more skeletal in less than twenty-four hours. Fighting against the rasp, her breath is wisp-like, insipid when up against the smog clogging her lungs.

Dexie shakes her head. 'Harri, she needs a hospital, and now.'

'I know, but you've seen what it's like out there. Have we any hope of getting an ambulance?' This time, it's he who casts his eyes to the ceiling, seeking inspiration or respite. Something concrete. 'We'll have to take her.'

Unfazed, Dexie nods. 'I'll find a blanket to wrap her in and get the car ready. In the meantime, put this on or you'll freeze.' She unhooks a man's overcoat from the back of the door and pushes it towards Harri. He hesitates – it must have belonged to Mrs P's late husband, but it has fresh purpose now, his own coat left back at the casino.

Harri bends to lift the fragile body, catching the faint odour of lavender water on her neck, and a croak that sounds like 'Schrod . . . Scoot . . .'

'He's here, he's fine, Mrs P,' he reassures. 'But you need help and we'll get you some, I promise. Soon.'

As he says it, he wonders if 'soon' is soon enough? Will he be in time to stop another death in his orbit?

37

A New Teammate

6th December 1952

Dexie

Her head drops into the steering wheel with a thump. 'Come on, *come on!*' she pleads to the engine that has chosen now, of all times, to succumb to the fog. Can cars even do that? Whatever the cause, the sound of a consistent smoker's cough is wheezing from the metal, as if it's trying desperately to jolt itself into action. Like so much of London, the spark of life is scuppered by the pervading damp.

'Shit!' Dexie bangs at the wheel in frustration. 'Not now!'

Her head is under the bonnet and peering at the workings when Harri appears, inching his way down the path with the lean, limp form of his landlady draped across his arms. Inevitably, the scruffy terrier is at his heel.

'What the . . .? His face dips further, if that's even possible.

'I've no idea what's wrong,' she says apologetically. Looking resigned, Harri only asks how far the nearest hospital is. The issue of a stolen car stuck outside his address seems way down on the list of things to worry about. A small sprinkling of luck must be hovering nearby, because the jumble of aged building which make up University College Hospital is only streets away. 'Can you make it?' Dexie asks.

Even through the darkness of evening and the fog, his face already looks pained with the weight, and for a moment, she thinks he's contemplating throwing Mrs P over his shoulder, in a typical fireman's lift. More efficient, but much less dignified. Instead, he gives small nod of the head, almost in answer to himself, and says: 'I'm fine, I'll make it. But let's go as fast as we can.'

More than ever, Dexie works to engage her innate sense of direction in leading the way, holding a torch that she found in the car, swinging it from front to back as a beacon for Harri to follow. His heavy wheeze is evident as he struggles to keep up and filter his own breath against the dense demon spectre, Scooter almost glued to his feet. No amount of coaxing could persuade the dog to stay at the house, and they'd soon given up.

They weave through the streets, encountering very few people until the imposing buildings on either side feel taller, then follow the ambulances and the figures walking with flares to lead the sick onto the hospital site and into the bays choked with gurneys. Some patients lay inert under blankets, others left with just enough energy to hack out the invader in their lungs. One or two have been discreetly placed at the end of a corridor, the sheet pulled up over the entire body, already lost. Dexie looks left and right for the white coat of a doctor, but Harri staggers up to a uniformed nurse who emerges from the hospital's back door, her eyes narrowed against the sting of the air.

'Help, can you please help?' he pants, legs bending under him.

The nurse stares wide-eyed at a fairytale figure from a cliched B-movie emerging through the mist, complete with dog, then starts into action. 'Yes, yes, of course.' She turns to shout behind her. 'Porter! Over here, we need a trolley now.'

Within seconds, Harri is able to place Mrs P's stilled body onto the white sheets, lowering her with a softness and a reverence that belies the urgency of her condition, and pulling the blanket across to cover her bare knees. Dexie ties Scooter to a lamppost outside with a stray piece of string, and as the trolley is whipped inside, they both follow in its wake, leaving behind the dog's high-pitched whimpering.

'She's been poorly since the fog hit,' Harri rushes to tell the attending staff, between heaving in breath himself. 'I found her like this today.'

'And how long ago was that?' a doctor demands as hospital staff crowd the bed, surrounded by thin curtains.

'Um, how long?' He's suddenly flustered with effort and concern. 'I don't . . .'

'Half an hour, maybe a bit longer,' Dexie fills in.

'Has she had anything?' the doctor questions. A black rubber mask is hooked over Mrs P's small face, followed by the reassuring hiss of an oxygen cylinder.

'Just some water with honey in it since yesterday. As far as we know.'

The doctor nods, his pale brow rippled and his mouth pursed, as he holds the chest piece of his stethoscope over the old woman's heart. He looks beyond exhausted. Much like her colleagues on the beat, he'll have been working solidly, with little respite; Dexie has to push back the guilt over not being out there and doing what her duty demands.

A nurse gently herds them out, claiming to need details. 'And so, she's your mother?' she queries at the nurses' desk.

'My landlady,' Harri reveals.

'And do you know of any relatives who live locally?'

'No, I've only lived there for a week or so.'

'Oh,' the nurse says, evidently surprised. 'Have you any information at all?'

He reels off the address and her surname, and that she's a widow. 'I think I remember seeing a letter addressed to a Mrs Ivy Painter. But that's it. I'm sorry.'

'Would you be able to find anything in the house?' the nurses presses. 'A ration book, or a bill, perhaps, that might have some further details on it, like her date of birth. Anything would be helpful.'

Harri and Dexie swap knowing looks. Going back to the digs was risky enough the first time, and utterly foolish to attempt it again. With Praxer's contacts, he'll locate the Bayley Street address in no time at all.

'I'm an off-duty policewoman,' Dexie pipes up. 'I'll get one of my station colleagues to go in and bring it to you.'

'What about a phone number, so we can contact you?' the nurse goes on with her list of questions. 'If she has no relatives . . .'

'Er, no, we'll call in,' Harri says abruptly. 'We're both on the job, and don't know where we'll be, not with this damned weather. It's a bugger, isn't it?' Dexie sees the effort as he wills a smile across his pained features. 'She will be all right, won't she?' he entreats.

The nurse nods briskly, without guarantees. 'We'll look after her, I promise. But please, do send in any details. And keep in touch, just in case.'

'We will,' Dexie reassures.

★ ★ ★

In the loading bay outside, Harri slumps against a damp wall, streaked with the grime of the past days. He pulls up an anxious Scooter into his arms and pushes his distress into the rough white fur. '*Scheisse*! What a mess,' he sighs. Then, to the dog's soft whine: 'It's all right, boy.'

Dexie stands silently. There's nothing she can say that's neither a lie nor useless in the situation. Pretending Mrs Painter will be fine is plainly wrong, because she doesn't know, not when her own mother says a simple fog has turned into a malevolent killer. And insisting they aren't both in danger, when they are relying on this fog to act like a solid shield, is blatantly untrue.

'Listen, Harri, Mrs P is in the best place,' she says instead. 'And we shouldn't be here. We need to find somewhere safe. Out of sight.'

He scoffs a laugh, gesturing to the world beyond. 'That's a joke.' Another sigh. 'But you're right, of course. The question is, where?'

'I'd suggest my section house, but if you're caught by the housekeeper in the women's corridor, you might consider Praxer as the more merciful. She's a dragon at the best of times and rumour has it she's got a custom-made truncheon to see off unwanted guests.'

'It's late and too dark to go searching for help in this. A hotel is our only option,' Harri proposes. 'Just for tonight.'

She has to agree. At this point, safety and anonymity trump any vanity, or a shadow over her reputation. Dexie simply wants a solid door between her and the outside world. Praxer, principally. A comfortable bed wouldn't go amiss either. 'And the dog?'

Harri's look is uncompromising. 'I promised her,' he shrugs. 'Besides, you said yourself, we can't risk going back to Bayley Street, and we can't abandon him. Do you know of somewhere around here that's small and discreet, and where we can smuggle in a small dog?'

'Luckily for you I do, but only on a professional basis. Which means it won't be the Ritz, and you might have to put up with a working tom in the room next door.'

'I believe the saying is that beggars can't be choosers?'

'It is, and no, we can't.' Still, Harri hesitates, and Dexie has to touch on his arm, as if to draw him away and say: *Let them do their job, trust them with Mrs P.* 'Come on, let's find a place to lie low, and lay our weary heads.'

'If only every woman of my acquaintance was as romantic as you, Helen Dexter.'

38
Lying Low

7th December 1952

Harri

He wakes as the light is coming up, though still dim through the thin, inadequate curtains. The lid has not lifted yet, one of the world's great capitals still paralysed. It takes Harri several seconds to realise he's lying flat, head on a pillow and, when he turns his head, sees Dexie's form, her back to him and still asleep, judging by her measured breathing. Scooter lies between them both, his tiny ribcage rising and falling.

Casting back, he walks himself through the events of last night: him unable to stifle a groan as he tried to get comfortable in the badly upholstered armchair, his neck still aching from the glorious basement floor of Hotel Praxer, and then Dexie whispering in the darkness: 'For goodness' sake, Harri, come on to the bed.'

Despite his joke the night before, there was nothing romantic in her proposition, merely a practical way of getting any sleep. The fact that they are both fully dressed with a small canine between them testifies to it. He also remembers that she needn't have whispered at all, since the couple next door were going at it hammer and tongs until past midnight, the squeaky bedframe under great strain on the other side of a paper thin wall. They'd both laughed about it, before falling silent with sheer exhaustion. The odour of their dinner prior to that lingers even now, the newspaper wrappings crumpled in the bin. They'd dropped into a fish and chip shop on the way, thinking that any hotel offering a cheap room and a good deal of anonymity would not have 'dining facilities', and that Helmut Praxer – certainly in his guise as James Remington – would not be seen dead in such an establishment, ordering cod and chips. Still, sitting side by side in the dreary, squalid room, Scooter wolfing down his share, it had been a feast fit for a king, the ginger beer a match for best *bierkeller* offering back home.

But that was yesterday. They'd survived the night, and today is another dawn. Harri yawns and wonders what in hell this day will bring. He eases himself off the bed gently and heads to the bathroom – they'd paid extra for what the grubby receptionist had grandly labelled an 'en suite', but is little more than a cupboard with a toilet and sink. The small hand towel is so threadbare he can see his own reflection when he holds it up against the tarnished mirror. Better than nothing, though. He's certainly looked better, the last two nights of fitful sleep etching history across his face. He needs a razor badly. A bath, too. What he wouldn't give right now to be in his tiny attic room at Mrs P's, shivering in front of his own sink and battling with the hot water geyser. Like so much in his life, Harri realises yet again that you don't miss what you really value until it's gone.

* * *

Dexie is awake when he re-enters the room, propped up against the wall that no longer quakes with seedy sexual encounter, scratching at Scooter's furry belly.

'Morning,' he says. 'Did you sleep at all?' *Well* seems overly optimistic.

'Um, I think I did.' She blinks in her recollection. 'Scooter kept me warm. You?'

'Yes, once I was on the bed, so thanks.'

She laughs. 'Gallantry and chastity are both overrated when you just need some decent shut-eye.'

'You weren't worried about your reputation being besmirched by spending the night with a strange man?'

She laughs again, truly amused. 'In this place? You have to be kidding. Besides, you're not strange. A bit odd at times, but I know that's just you.'

'Thanks.' A spring squeaks in complaint as he sits on the bed. He pulls a hand through his hair that badly needs a comb. His contrition needs no teasing out. 'Oh, Dexie, I'm so sorry.'

'For what?'

'Dragging you into this whole damned mess. For making you a fugitive in your own country. It's not what I intended, I promise. I got sucked in, thinking it would be a cut and dry case. It was entirely naïve of me.'

She shuffles herself upright. 'Well, don't be sorry,' she says firmly. 'Like I said before, it was my choice, and I stand by it. As for Eliza . . . I'll have to face my own demons over that in time, but having known her even for a few short hours, I feel sure she wouldn't want us to pull you out of Praxer's grip, only for him to triumph.'

He turns fully and looks into her weary but determined face. 'I really did opt for the right wingman, didn't I?'

'Wing-woman. And don't forget, you still have to explain

that to my sergeant once we get ourselves out of this mire. You really will need a suit of armour for that.'

Being Dexie, she comes up with a practical plan. Anticipating that the hotel will be almost empty – evenings and the night hours being its busy periods – she hires two relatively clean towels from reception, while Harri chances a flying visit to a newsagent several doors down that seems to stock everything behind the counter, though given the neighbourhood and its line of similar hostelries, it's no surprise. He buys a razor, soap, shampoo and a comb, plus a length of washing rope to fashion a makeshift lead for Scooter. They take it in turns to visit the communal bathroom that's seen better days, but the water is hot, and even without clean clothes, a bath and a shave is a revelation. Harri feels like a new man and his reflection confirms the improvement. Watching Dexie brush out her wet hair and stripped of her make-up, he thinks she looks more alive than he's seen before. From somewhere deep within, the word 'beautiful' pops up and, despite his best efforts, it will not be quashed.

Not now, Schroder. Too complicated by far. As if being the object of a manhunt with a dog in tow isn't tricky enough.

Before leaving, they plan a route avoiding the most obvious of locations that Praxer might search, while trying to garner vital information from Dexie's sources. Georgie has already been reassured, Harri sidling into a phone box the night before and ringing the house in Islington, to a resounding 'thank God!' from her.

'For pity's sake, Harri, try not to end up in the morgue, either of you,' she'd slightly lectured, although it was out of genuine concern.

He'd declined her offer of safe harbour for both of them, horrified at the thought of leading Praxer anywhere near her or the children, even if parking Scooter in Islington would have solved a major issue. It's just too risky. 'We'll be in touch,' he promised.

Once again, Wolli must be their first port of call; painful as it will be to reveal, he needs to know of Eliza's fate. And much as it irritates Harri, they should also get word to Johnson about Praxer's true identity, though he wonders what good it will do now. With two days until the signing, Praxer is bound to go further into hiding, leaving Joseph and his pals to go on safari for him and Dexie.

Outside, nothing has lifted. In fact, the air seems even thicker since his jaunt to the newsagent, and with fewer people about on a Sunday. Church bells clang tunelessly in the distance, sounding more like a warning of doomsday in the leaden expanse rather than any call to comfort. Harri slides into the nearest phone box as they leave the hotel, Dexie squeezing in alongside, Scooter at their feet. First, he dials the hospital number, but after being put through to various wards and departments, can't gain any news of Mrs P in the chaos. He's about to ask for a connection to the morgue, but thinks better of it. If she's there, he can't do anything about it, and blissful ignorance is better right now. He prefers to imagine Mrs Ivy Painter as still of this world.

They shuffle around to exchange places, enabling Dexie to dial the front desk at West End Central and asking them to dispatch a constable in search of Mrs P's details, fabricating a convincing story that the landlady is a close friend of her mother's. Her next call is to the local CID office, as Harri leans in close to hear the response.

'Louisa?' she asks when a woman's voice answers the phone. 'It's Dexie.' *The filing clerk*, she mouths to Harri.

'Dexie! Well, there's a surprise, I thought you were on secondment. What can I do for you?'

'Just checking in.' She adopts a forced, casual tone. 'I wondered if there were any reports overnight of suspicious deaths over the wire?'

'City or country?'

'London – Greater London,' Dexie qualifies.

'Is that for your investigation?' Despite speaking to a colleague, Louisa's voice hints at suspicion.

'Yes. We need to follow something up.'

'Anything in particular?' Louisa probes.

'Women, specifically.'

There's a pause and the flick of paper at the other end. 'I'm sure we had a couple of reports for the beat crews to check out. Wait a minute . . . yes, a patrol has gone out to one.'

Dexie's face floods with alarm. 'Any details yet?'

'A woman found on an abandoned bomb site,' Louisa reports. 'She may have simply collapsed in the fog, but we have to be sure.'

'How old?' Crowding the receiver, he's aware of Dexie counting the empty seconds too.

'Nothing exact, but her age is estimated at over sixty. And another pensioner found dead at home – sadly, that's not unusual in the last few days, but she had some sort of odd breathing apparatus nearby. We're looking into that. Nothing else suspicious. Is that what you wanted?'

Dexie deflates alongside. 'Yes, thanks Louisa. I'll see you soon, we'll catch up for a drink sometime, shall we?'

'Yes, when this ruddy fog goes, though I can't imagine when that will be. I think it's taken up residence.'

'I can't decide if that's a good or a bad thing,' Dexie says, as they hit the freezing air again, her voice muffled by a scarf tight over her mouth. 'Though I suppose it's no surprise that Praxer will have made everything disappear. That seems to be his expertise.'

'True,' Harri agrees. 'I'm afraid to say it, but I'm sure poor Eliza will long gone by now.' His stomach lurches at the thought of her body undergoing a gruesome and sad end, after her sacrifices during the war. Alicia Remington will be afforded a secret but decent burial, he imagines, and though she was clearly complicit in Praxer's success, no one deserves to be snuffed out like that. The more this goes on, the more of a filthy mess it becomes. 'I think the best thing we can do now is contact Johnson and then keep our heads down. Survival is now the prime objective. *Our* survival.'

'Agreed.' He feels her shiver noticeably inside her coat and ups the pace as they forge forward into the abyss of another day.

Oddly for a Sunday morning, Wolli's favoured café is open and busy, given it's the type of place where plenty of customers have a dog as their sole companion. With a tinge of sadness, Harri muses that loneliness doesn't take the weekend off for a good deal of people, in a city of over eight million. He spies Wolli in the corner, head dipped close into a Sunday paper and his maroon cap uppermost. The Pole is either dozing or reading intently, because they're sat opposite before his head snaps up.

'Christ! Are you trying to give me a heart attack?' He looks irritated at the intrusion, and Harri wonders if it's the effects of a heavy night before, hence the smell of strong coffee wafting from a cup by his side. 'So, you found him then?' he grunts, gesturing at Harri, and then Scooter, who nuzzles himself into Wolli's damaged leg. 'What's with the dog?'

'Nothing to do with Praxer,' Dexie says. 'He belongs to someone else.'

'Eliza came up trumps, did she?' Wolli swigs at his cup. 'I told you she's good.'

Dexie shifts awkwardly. 'Yes, Wolli, she did, but . . .'

He's not so hungover that he doesn't grasp something is awry. 'What happened?' His unshaven face is unexpectedly stricken, for a man who must have witnessed so much carnage and cruelty in his life.

They all lean in, aware of the small gaps between tables. 'We did manage to track Praxer,' Dexie begins, 'and it was, well I suppose it was going OK, if not exactly to plan. We'd almost made it, but then . . .'

'Eliza took things into her own hands.' Wolli makes an all too accurate guess, shaking his head.

'Yes, she did,' Dexie adds. 'It was what you said – she couldn't just leave it. She had a gun trained on him and wouldn't . . .'

Without any need for coffee, Wolli is now wide awake. 'Christ, she shot him?' he hisses into the sugar-crusted tabletop. For a fleeting second, his expression is actually hopeful – pleased, even – until he looks again at their faces. 'But she didn't kill him?'

'No.' Harri swallows, wishing in that moment he was back in Hamburg, in one of those cafés serving brandy at all hours of the day. In a pint glass, preferably. 'She did, however, kill Praxer's wife, before one of his men shot Eliza dead.'

'Fuck.' In five seconds, Wolli's flinty eyes go through a myriad of emotions: obvious distress over his former comrade, plus confusion and angst, rounding off with a palpable fear. He's silent through it all.

'Wolli?' Harri prods at his shock. 'Wolli, we have to ask for your help again.'

'Haven't I've done enough?' the Polish man spits back. 'And I definitely think *you've* done plenty in creating this almighty mess. Do you realise how vulnerable the whole ex-resistance network will be now? Praxer's men will shake the tree and see who falls, and then they'll force the rest out. With menaces.'

Equally, Harri is in no mood to brook refusal, not when their survival depends on it. 'Look, we didn't ask for this job, and we were press-ganged into it,' he rails, matching Wolli's stare and the sizzle of tension across the table. 'We need a safe house, somewhere for us to sit tight until Johnson can get us far enough away.'

'And what if I say no, and wash my hands of it?' Suddenly, every inch of the older man looks old, tired and beaten.

'We can't do anything, except go to Johnson direct,' Harri says plainly, glancing at Dexie for confirmation. 'But we don't trust him in the way we trust you, and I don't think it's in your nature to let people down. I imagine that you didn't do it all the way through the war, and since, or you wouldn't be here now.'

'You're a damned Kraut,' Wolli says, though it's more as a fact, as if he can't quite muster any hatred towards Harri.

'True. I also happen to be an anti-Nazi who would love to see Praxer face justice, and my partner here is British. And I take you to be human. Is that enough reason for you?'

Wolli's sigh is deep enough to send precious sugar crystals across the table. 'Wait here,' he huffs, then pauses. 'If I'm not back in fifteen minutes, go.'

'Go where?' Dexie asks.

'Anywhere, and fast,' Wolli says, nodding to the filth beyond the window. 'Disappear.'

It's an anxious time they spend waiting, watching the doorbell jangle with customers in and out, none with Wolli's distinct limp. Though neither Harri nor Dexie have an appetite, they order tea and toast when the waitress eyes them beadily, and feed it to Scooter, who is more than happy to oblige.

'So, what if he does come up with a safe place?' Dexie asks. 'How long do we stay, and what on earth do we do with Scooter?'

'I simply don't know how long,' Harri freely admits. 'Johnson got us into this, and so he can damn well get us out, and safely. As for Scooter, I think he might be an asset right now, since we'll have good reason to be on the streets walking about. Mrs P insists he's a good guard dog, who only barks at strangers, or if he feels threatened.'

Dexie looks less than convinced, but any argument is curtailed by the timely reappearance of Wolli. His face is grave and damp from the walk, but it doesn't reflect defeat.

'So?' Harri leans in again as the Pole eases himself down in the chair opposite.

'The word is out.' He signs to the waitress for tea.

'The word being?' Harri feels the strain in his neck travelling down to his chest.

'You must have done a great job of pissing Praxer off, because there's a price on your heads.'

'*Scheisse*!' Now Harri feels a powerful punch to his stomach. 'How much?'

'Enough to inspire heroics in some, though it does seem as if Praxer is keeping his hunting posse to a minimum, perhaps because he's lying low himself.'

'Which makes that safe house a priority,' Harri pushes. There's now a prize fight playing out in his gut.

'We have a place,' Wolli reports. 'It's not ideal, especially in this bloody weather, but it's all we have at short notice, and you'll have to get yourselves there.'

'Where is it?' Dexie asks.

'A barge moored on the Isle of Dogs.'

'And what happens if Praxer does locate us there?' she challenges. 'The Isle is like a limb sitting on the Thames, we'll be exposed, with nowhere to go.'

'Then you'll have to start rowing, won't you?' Wolli bites back. 'I'm not a damned travel agent.'

'It's fine,' Harri tries to appease. 'Thank you, Wolli. Will Johnson make contact?'

'Yes, later today, one of his men says. So, stay put, and no roaming around. The docks are at a standstill because of the fog, and so there'll only be a few people about, watchmen and the like. Don't go attracting attention.'

'We won't,' Dexie says, 'but what do we do about food, and some fuel for a fire? We'll freeze on a boat overnight without heat.'

'There's a woman nearby who "does" for us, discreetly. By the time you get there, she'll have left food and wood, enough for a couple of days.' He draws a rudimentary map on a napkin, and writes the name *Seahorse* next to it. 'She's a bit tired, but a sturdy vessel. I've spent a few nights on her myself.'

'Thanks,' Dexie says, as they go to leave. 'And I'm sorry about Eliza, I really am. She was a brave woman, I could tell that as soon as I met her.'

Unusually, emotion washes across Wolli's face and his mouth crimps. 'Too brave,' he says, setting his lips firmly together and mumbling into his newspaper. 'If you do one thing for her, just get that bastard. I don't care how you do it, but bring that man down.'

39

A Haven

7th December 1952

Dexie

Scooter strains on his makeshift lead as they navigate their way south towards the Thames, his nose hoovering the pavement, the damp no doubt throwing up a cornucopia of delights to his canine sense of smell. As if by instinct, Dexie notes that Harri has nudged closer, their shoulders touching, so that the trio move as a tight unit; even in this claustrophobic ocean, it makes her feel less exposed.

'What do you think about Scooter now?' she dares to question.

His head whips around, the fresh smell of Pears soap on his skin trouncing the air's sickly sulphur. 'What do you mean?'

'Wolli's advice, about keeping our heads down on the boat. Surely that's going to be harder with a dog?' She watches his nostrils flare, reason sparring with the emotions in his head, his hand tightens on the rope-lead. She's touched a nerve, clearly.

'Where do you propose we put him?' Harri challenges. 'There's no telling how long Mrs P will be in hospital, or even if . . .' He stops himself. 'The lodgers back in Bayley Street didn't exactly keep an eye on their own landlady, so who knows what will happen to a dog. Everyone we know and love is at risk if we go anywhere near them.'

Reluctantly, she has to concede he's right.

'And I promised her,' he adds.

Which is exactly the reason she'll lose this argument: the loyalty and reparation she senses in him, in every action. To do right. Dexie doesn't know the precise details of Harri's life before, during or after the war, only that he's paying a heavy personal price. And it's a cost that only ever seems to rise. 'OK,' she says.

'OK?'

'Yes, if that's how it has to be.'

'Thanks, Dex. I promise we'll keep him under wraps. From what I've seen, he's a quiet dog inside the house, and well behaved.'

She laughs. 'Let's face it, we need all the eyes and ears we can get.'

They walk south towards the Thames, after deciding that buses and Tubes with a dog in tow would attract too much attention. Amid little conversation, scarves wrapped tight over their mouths, Scooter scouts in front like a true hound. On occasion, Harri can't seem to help hacking into the thick wool, his eyes scanning each time for any undue attention. Fortunately, the weather means his noise is merely absorbed into the surrounding soundtrack, sporadic coughing acting like a warning klaxon as figures emerge from nowhere. Scooter is already proving his worth as he pilots them around any approaching feet.

By the time they reach the Lyons on the Strand, the swill of anxiety in Dexie's stomach has turned to hunger, and she stands outside while Harri goes in for sandwiches, an extra one for Scooter. They stop briefly nearby, sitting on a bench at the river wall and in front of the wide edifice of the Savoy, the impromptu lunch washed down with weak tea from a stall, helping to smooth the thickness in their throats. The air is no clearer down by the water, and only a slapping noise from below confirms the river is flowing. Scooter jumps up and nestles in between them, enjoying a brief snooze, while Dexie considers it the oddest picnic she's ever had.

'When this is all over, Johnson will treat us to dinner there,' Harri says, gesturing behind to a ghostly shadow of the grand hotel.

'Uh, really? I'm not sure I'd relish dinner with Johnson.'

'Not *with*,' Harri insists. 'Courtesy of, and Her Majesty's Treasury. I think they owe us that. Many courses and a bottle of champagne.'

'They do, and I look forward to it, but if it's all right with you, I prefer to work on our future for now.' She pushes herself off the cold bench, wriggles her toes into life and give thanks all over again that she's not wearing those dreadful beat shoes.

'Understood. So shall we forge onwards to our own luxury hotel?' Harri suggests.

'I think that tea really has gone to his head, don't you, Scoot?' she says, picking up the lead, acutely aware she's now reduced to conversing with a dog for assurance.

It's a longer route, but for safety's sake, they hug the river edge as a guide, meandering east past the magnificent but now invisible Tower Bridge, through Wapping and Limehouse. Twice, Dexie slows up at the sight of a small crowd gathered around some poor soul who has collapsed on the pavement, concerned voices calling for an ambulance and 'is she still breathing?'

'Come on,' Harri urges. 'You can't do anything, and we have to keep moving.'

Finally, the river path bends south into the teardrop of land that makes up the 'isle'. The scenery is shrouded but it's obvious in the houses and the people sidling by that this is far poorer than the West End streets Dexie treads every day. Men in tattered boots and threadbare jackets stoop as they pass, a Woodbine hanging from their lips. One woman with darkened lips shuffles slowly past, a gaggle of children hanging onto her skirt, none with the luxury of a thick winter coat, and those with smaller feet clop along in shoes several sizes too big. Their unified coughing sounds deep and ingrained, and must have lodged in their lungs way before this snap fog took hold. Gradually, rows of houses peter out and give way to warehouses, similar to where she and Harri first encountered Praxer – and the Russians. Are they still out there, stalking Praxer, hovering in this filthy grey world?

Cold, fear and fog breach the fibres of Dexie's coat, rippling into her body. *Safe haven, Dex*, she has to remind herself every few minutes. *We just sit it out. This mire cannot go on forever.*

Rationally, she knows there are millions of people spread across Greater London. In the Met they often struggle to find one runaway in the tiny square mile of Soho's streets, so what chance does Praxer have in this vast swathe of toxic cloud? That's her positive side. The negative portion in her insists the big man with a gun – the weapon that ended Eliza's life – is only two steps behind.

* * *

With faces necessarily swaddled, she and Harri work with an impromptu language of wide eyes, the arch of an eyebrow and the half-crease of a forehead in navigating the streets that turn to cobbled pathways, the clang of masts, boats nudging against the quayside and the faint swish of the Thames tide as a vital marker. Using Wolli's map, they locate the rough area of a man-made inlet, but fatigue, frustration and a lack of visibility force them to stop and ask a watchman for the exact whereabouts of the *Seahorse*. He looks them up and down with suspicion, as if he's calculating exactly why a couple with a dog are out here, in *this*. What are they escaping from? Or to? His lascivious grin suggests something unsavoury rather than illegal.

The old boy's directions are correct, though, and they find the *Seahorse* just before Dexie's feet part company with the rest of her body. Wolli was right: she's no pretty canal boat with flowerpots adorning her roof and twee curtains at the windows. In fact, there are few portals in the side of this sturdy, scruffy working barge, and the entrance is marked only by a flimsy gangplank at one end. Scooter tests the integrity of the wood and leads them on.

'Well, it's not freezing,' Harri announces as he finds the poorly hidden key and locates a paraffin lamp in the darkness of the interior.

If she could locate Wolli's woman who 'does', Dexie would shower her with thanks. A fire has been lit in a small wood burner, helping to mask the damp odour of vacancy, even when the fog hasn't penetrated the interior. Beside the tiny sink is a collection of fresh bread, margarine, eggs and bacon, proving that someone in Wolli's orbit holds sway over an extra ration book. There's also tea, milk and a small jar of Nescafe, and right in that moment, Dexie thinks she might not move out of this place for weeks. Scooter curls up on a small rug in front of the fire, his very presence making it instantly homely.

Harri is already at the far end of the barge's modest living quarter, beyond a small door. 'There's a sleeping area,' he calls, before his head emerges. 'You take the bed and I'll make do out here.' It's a stretch to say the bench seats lining each side of the barge wall constitute a sofa, but they are fairly soft, detachable and not filthy. With a pile of only slightly musty blankets, Dexie thinks they'll survive the weather at least. The rest is anyone's guess.

Harri sparks up the tiny, two ring gas stove, checks the water supply and puts the kettle on to boil.

'You seem to know what you're doing,' Dexie remarks.

'Me? Oh, yes, I suppose. A friend of mine owned a canal boat, and Hella and I borrowed it for a couple of holidays.' His pause in the dimness marks something, perhaps a memory flying in and hitting him right between the eyes, before his head snaps up. 'She did the navigating, or the driving, or whatever it is you do with boats, and I was the maintenance man.'

'Driving?' Dexie's laughter rings around the tiny space. 'Please tell me you never considered joining the navy.'

His wide smile glows white in the shadows. 'Lucky for the entire seafaring nation, I didn't.'

'Then let's hope we don't have to set sail in this beast to escape Praxer.'

'If we do, let me state it plainly – you are driving.'

Darkness is already descending by the time they settle in front of the fire in the late afternoon. Dexie pulls down the seat cushions and makes a nest on the floor with the blankets, as Harri cooks up the bacon and lowers himself with a tray of sandwiches and coffee. Scooter stirs from his deep sleep and crawls in beside them, while a small wireless to the side is tuned in low to the Home Service.

'Great picnic,' she says, a blanket around her shoulders, and toes that are warm enough to finally slip off her shoes. Despite being holed up in a run-down barge and on the run from a malicious Nazi in a weather vacuum, Dexie feels strangely relaxed. The dirty oppression of the clammy world outside has formed into a soft shell.

'Do you know, I actually prefer this kind of cosy arrangement to an outdoor summer's day,' Harri says, pinching off a nib of bacon for Scooter. 'Since we have so much experience, we Germans do winter quite well.'

'Present weather excepted, of course.'

'You're right on that score – wading through pea soup is not ideal, though it is working to our benefit right now. I'd say we're far more versatile than Praxer, what with all his good living as a rich businessman.'

'Just by roughing it, you mean?' she punts.

'Roughing it! I'll have you know, *madam*, this is pure opulence compared to some hovels I've seen in Hamburg.'

'Sorry, sir. Didn't mean to offe—'

Rat-tat-tat!

They both freeze, not only at the loud incursion on the window, but Scooter's sudden low whine of warning.

'Could that be Johnson?' Dexie whispers with alarm.

'Maybe. I'm fairly sure Praxer wouldn't bother knocking.' Harri pulls himself up smartly and peers through the makeshift curtains across the port window. 'Christ, it's that old bloke, the one who gave us directions.'

'What on earth can he want?' Her next thought steers towards danger: who's paid him to play the innocent caller? Are Praxer's men lying in wait behind?

The glow of paraffin lamps means there's no pretending

they aren't inside. Gingerly, Harri opens the door a few inches, just enough for Dexie to hear the exchange as she keeps hold of Scooter and quietens his throaty snarl.

'Thought you might need someone to fetch you milk in the morning?' the old man begins, with his raspy smoker's wheeze. 'So, you two lovebirds don't have to go out in this filthy weather. For a price, mind.'

'That's kind of you,' Harri says in a faux friendly voice. 'Some milk, and a pack of cigarettes would be good. Don't come by too early, though, eh?'

There's a bawdy edge to the man's cackle. 'I'll need some money up front,' he says, his presence lingering. Dexie's lungs are held in suspense, pressing Scooter into her chest.

'Of course.' Harri fishes in his trouser pocket for coins and hands them through the door. 'Keep whatever change you have.'

'Much obliged,' he croaks, his limping gait heard on the small landing stage and receding across the tiny gangplank.

'What was that was all about?' Dexie asks as Harri sits back down. 'Is he genuine – I mean, genuinely needy?'

'He certainly looked it, poor chap, though I don't think we'll see our milk or cigarettes. I'm fairly sure I was simply buying his silence.'

'We don't even smoke,' she points out.

'I know, but I thought it made us seem more like a couple looking for some privacy, and needing his discretion because of that.'

'Yes, I noticed you didn't object to him calling us "lovebirds".'

'Better that than the truth,' Harri says plainly.

When Johnson's knock does come, it doesn't startle in quite the same way, though they douse the lamp and Harri checks through the window again. The MI5 man lowers his head and crowds into the small space, peering at the surroundings with scorn and shivering under his heavy overcoat. 'Bloody hell, Wolli really does pick them, doesn't he?'

'Yes, he does,' Dexie pipes up defensively, her irritation spiked in his presence. 'And thank goodness we did have Wolli to rely on.'

Johnson ignores her inference, and sits at the bench seat, his leather gloved hands resting on his knees. 'I haven't got long, and we need to get this mess sorted.'

'This *mess*, as you casually term it, is our lives,' Harri starts. 'Under threat.'

'Which is exactly why you are here,' Johnson comes back, in the same elusory tone as their last meeting. *Not my fault, nothing to do with me.*

'It is. And I note we are not in a nice comfortable safe house in some anonymous suburb,' Harri goes again, 'but out on a limb, quite literally. Is that intentional, in case anything goes wrong – easy deniability on your part?' His face is a resolute stare that Johnson cannot ignore.

'Of course not!' Johnson insists. 'It's what the service could provide at short notice. And the safest, in the circumstances.'

Harri shakes his head in disbelief, but appears to let it go – for now. 'So, what is the news, or the word out there? Is Praxer intentionally looking for us, or have you got some idea where he is, so that you can bring him in?'

Again, Johnson brushes off the evident sarcasm, pulling at one finger of his glove. Nervously, it seems. 'His men are looking for you, with vigour I might add, after the debacle in Ealing, but no, we don't know Praxer's whereabouts right now. He will have gone underground completely.'

Dexie's palms go out in disbelief. 'How can that be?' she hisses. 'It was us that trailed Praxer's wife to the docks, and then *I* tracked him down with help of one person very much under the radar. And yet your entire organisation can't put two and two together. He's making a mockery of you. Meanwhile, we're stuck here like sitting ducks.'

Johnson flashes annoyance as he bristles. 'I really don't think you understand quite how delicate this situation—'

'That's all very well,' Harri cuts in, 'but we need to know what kind of surveillance you've got on *us*, in case Praxer decides to pay a house call.'

'You're safe here,' Johnson says, with confidence this time, though there are no details.

'I wish I could believe that,' Dexie says. 'This curtain of fog is by no means foolproof, and I'm guessing Praxer's grief is playing second best to his fury, and a need for revenge.'

Johnson pulls at his gloves again, picking at an invisible thread.

'So?' Harri presses. 'How long do we need to stay here, and when can you move us, well away from Praxer's wrath?'

'It depends on this weather entirely,' Johnson says. 'The trains out of London are at a standstill, and there are no flights. Driving is suicide, but I am working on a place within London.' He pauses, his face suddenly severe. 'First, I need to hear it from you, Schroder, and not second hand. Is the man who purports to be James Remington really the Helmut Praxer from your past?'

'Yes, there's no doubt in my mind, and not least because he recognised me. The way he spoke of old times together, too. It's Praxer all right.' Like Dexie, Harri looks perplexed at Johnson's question. Hasn't it already been established by everything that's gone before – the kidnap, and the shootings? Why is Johnson being so circumspect?

'Quite,' is all he will say. 'Good.'

But what's good about any of this? Dexie seethes silently, while Scooter's ear twitches in solidarity.

'And yet, is his identity of any use if you can't find Praxer before the signing, which is . . .?' Harri presses again.

'The day after tomorrow,' Johnson provides. 'Yes, time is running out for us. For this country, too.'

'Well, before you think otherwise, our job is done,' Harri insists. 'We delivered on our promise, and now we need to be allowed to walk away, legs and body intact.'

'Understood.' Johnson gets up. 'Stay here for tonight, and we'll review transport in the morning. I'll send word.'

Still, Dexie doesn't feel inclined to offer her gratitude. Awkwardly, they see him out of the boat, the faint outline of a second body on the quay, ready to whisk him away. Didn't he say driving was suicide?

'Do you think people like Johnson get specialist training in avoiding any straight question?' Harri says when they are alone again.

'Expert training,' she agrees. 'I wonder if he's married? I pity his poor wife if he is. You'd have to work at wheedling out any emotion, good or bad.'

40

Confessions

7th December 1952

Harri

'It is a bit like camping, isn't it?' Dexie says, when they're side by side in the nest again, the fire is stoked and more tea brewed.

'And when was the last time you slept in a tent?' Harri asks. 'I remember it as very wet and cold, and having damp socks throughout every trip.'

'Oh, that doesn't sound good. What made you keep doing it?'

'Parents and necessity,' he sighs. 'It's an unwritten German law – you *will* spend time in the great outdoors. And enjoy it.'

'That makes me glad to be British, and quite thankful for my annual week's holiday in Torquay as a child. A fairly run-down guest house, but it did have the virtue of a roof and walls.'

'Such luxury!' he cries. 'The question is: were you happy?'

Her pause is long enough that she covers it with a sip

of tea, and when Harri glances sideways, there's a stirring behind her eyes. Cushioned by the fog outside, only Scooter's gentle snoring penetrates the silence. 'Dex, did I say something wrong?'

'No . . . no.' Her words seem to travel from far away. 'I don't quite know where it came from, but what you said, it made me think about happiness, that's all.'

'I didn't mean to prod at anything, before your husband's death and . . .'

'You didn't,' she says. Sips again.

Harri scratches at Scooter's ears to fill the void, convinced this dog has now more than earned his keep.

Dexie turns just enough that he sees the glassy sheen in her eyes. 'Now, I should be the one saying sorry,' she says, brushing a thumb across her cheek as a teardrop tumbles. 'Daft woman.'

Harri transfers a hand from Scooter to hers, and squeezes down. 'It's been a tough few days,' he says. 'We're both exhausted.'

Dexie sniffs. 'It's not that. It's just – and now you're going to think I'm completely mad – but I actually feel quite safe here, right in this moment. And happy. And that's not something I've felt for a long time. Not both at the same time anyway.'

He doesn't prod or press, though he does sense the hurt radiating from within. Years of policing, and a near decade of his own pain, has taught Harri Schroder that confessions flow when the floodgates are opened voluntarily. And, in this case, Dexie is no exception.

In a low voice, she explains that Thomas Dexter had been a good man when they first met – friendly, reliable and kind; 'A credit to the force', his superiors extolled time and again. It was after they married that the traditional Tom changed to a different man entirely, becoming demanding and argumentative. Then, aggressive.

'I put it down to the job,' she says. 'I hoped it would get better after the war, but it only got worse when the men started coming back, injured or broken. He hid it well at the time, but I think Tom felt very guilty for staying behind and not fighting. Time and again when we were out, strangers would ask where he'd served, and the shame he felt grew to a rage, until nothing I said or did seemed to help.' She circles the rim of her mug with a finger.

'And he took it out on you?' Harri asks. Softly, because he senses her flow of hurt falter. Blocked by guilt. Again, he's known and seen it before, in victims mostly, but in friends too. Not forgetting his own substantial pot of remorse.

She wipes another tear. 'Yes, sometimes.' Pause. 'Actually, quite often.'

'Physically?

There's a slight wince. 'In every way.'

Scooter whimpers with a doggy dream and both reach out a hand to stroke at his furry torso. Finally, she turns fully and holds Harri's gaze.

'I've never told a soul before,' she says.

'Not even your mother?' He's both aghast and angry, but saddened too. At her isolation. The loneliness of an acidic secret.

'She wouldn't have understood,' Dexie says. 'She idolised Thomas, thought he was the perfect son-in-law – you know, man of the family after my father died. I was afraid that she wouldn't believe me, or for her to think I was an overdramatic, ungrateful wife. And I began to believe it too, that it was all my fault. My friends constantly told me I was the luckiest woman on earth, to be married with such a shortage of men. And there I was, miserable.'

'What about when he died?'

Dexie pushes out a breath more dense than anything beyond the tiny windows. 'I was devastated at such a horrible end for him, of course I was, but also . . . oh Christ . . . relieved, for myself. Isn't that awful? I felt I could live again. And then guilty, of course, that I was freed, and in not missing that version of Tom.'

'The guilt is a monster, isn't it?' Harri says into his lap.

She nods and smiles in sympathy. 'Yes, it is. A devil that visits night after night, day after day.'

'But you still joined the police, you moved on?'

'I felt some good had to come out of it, and Thomas – while a poor husband – had been a good officer. I couldn't take that away from him. And I like my job, on some days I love it. But I haven't had that feeling of contentment in a long time, and just then, in a flash moment, it hit me, sitting here on the floor of a scruffy old boat on the Thames. Hence the tears, and the confession. I'm sorry you had to be on the end of it, Harri.'

'There you go again, apologising for how you feel over what someone else did to you, which he had no right to do. You said yourself – we don't need to say sorry. We're here together, for better or for worse.'

She laughs out loud. 'There's really no need for marriage proposals.'

'You know what I mean, Dex. We're a team, with no pity and no excuses. And I'm sorry you had a marriage like that, because that should never happen between a man and a woman. Ever.'

Scooter rolls over, stretches his body and falls back into a blissful slumber.

'How is it that you see people like that, Harri?' she asks quizzically. 'Women. How have you dodged the caveman thinking of people like Harmer back in CID, or Thomas, or most of the London Met?'

He shakes his head. 'Um, I've never really considered it, but I suppose it came from my parents, my mother mainly. She was very clever and well read, but also quite a traditional German woman in some senses, in that she believed in the home and the family. Except that my father never took it for granted, and she wouldn't have let him anyway.'

'How do you mean?'

'Well, when she put food on the table, or made sure we had clean clothes as children, it was a valuable contribution to the family. I never saw it as anything other than half of the equation, and nor did my father. They worked as a unit all their married lives.'

'Ah, so that's why you turned out to be an angel in disguise.' This time she squeezes his rough hand.

'Me? Oh, I'm no angel, I assure you.' He ruffles Scooter's fur again, to cover a fiery, flash memory of his own. Maybe it is a day for confessions, to match Dexie's raw honesty?

'While we're here, laying bare, there is something I want to say,' Harri begins. 'Things you should know about me.'

He could easily tell her of the enduring guilt he feels over Hella and Lily, his lack of attention to his wife and child as the bombing raids in '43 annihilated Hamburg, his focus on work as chaos reigned across the city, and how Hella's fear turned fatal when the bombers threatened again and she sought sanctuary from the flames in a cupboard, only for the choking smoke to do its worst. Mother and child snuffed out. That particular chunk of shame sits at Harri Schroder's core nowadays, carefully wrapped. More relevant to the here and now is an ember of remorse that has smouldered for years, deeply buried until reignited by his reunion with an old comrade just days ago. Since then, it's been gaining heat under his skin. Uncomfortably so.

'It concerns Praxer,' he says, cautiously, because while he knows candour is the right path, that Dexie deserves to know of his capabilities, it still chills him to the core. The depths to which any man can sink.

'Yes?'

'That night at the casino, he alluded to us being friends, and I've played that down, to Johnson especially.'

'Ye . . . es?' He hears her curiosity aroused. Suspicion too.

'We were friends, at the very beginning,' Harri explains, his eyes boring into Scooter as an excuse not to have to face Dexie. 'Looking back, I was quite shy going into police training, just nineteen, and it was my first time away from home.' He swallows, feeling the grate of his Adam's apple. 'I'm not trying to excuse myself, just telling you how it was back then.'

'Go on.'

'Much like now, Praxer had an abundance of confidence from the outset. For some reason he took a shine to me on our first day, taking me under his wing, so to speak. He was self-assured and a bit brash, but not nasty or cruel, and I'll admit I was flattered. It wasn't just me, there was a group of about five or six of us who spent our time off together. Over the first few months, though, I noticed how Helmut would pit one lad against another. It was innocent at first, encouraging little competitions, where they would have to arm wrestle or run against each other. It meant, of course, that one was always better, or in favour. It was silly boys' stuff that gradually became more serious. The stakes became higher and higher, and then it began to go beyond into humiliation. He particularly liked to see men draw blood.'

'How did you feel about it?' Dexie asks.

'Awkward, but not self-assured enough to say anything. Certainly not brave enough. Later, I realised I could play peacemaker by using humour, but not then. Anyway, there was one in our group called Otto, who was very intelligent, but not particularly well-built or sporty, and inevitably he lost out on all these macho games of Praxer's.' The thick slick of remorse wells up inside. Twenty years on, Otto Rigert isn't a name that pops into Harri's consciousness very often. But when it does, a dense, nauseating feeling snakes through his organs and arteries, the boy's face crowding his vision. That frightened face.

'One day, we'd been given the afternoon off and spent it drinking by the riverside. Praxer was in a particularly tetchy mood, since one of the training officers had called him out in front of the class – taken him down a peg or two, you might say. He kept quiet but he was seething, I could tell. True to form, he initiated one of these games where we had to swing across the expanse of the river on a rope tied to a tree. All of us were too drunk to do it safely, but of course, also too pissed to realise that. And the rope snapped, with Otto hanging on, and he fell in. We all thought this was very funny, until I realised that Otto was distressed and in trouble, shouting that he couldn't swim. Helmut brushed it off, mocking him. "What sort of a German man can't swim?" he sneered. He kept telling Otto to get a grip and pull himself out. I could see he was in real trouble, but there was a malevolent look from Praxer that said: "No, don't help. Make him do it himself." In my stupid, inebriated state, I accepted that.'

Harri puts his head in both hands, the emotion threatening to spill. He can hear Otto's distinct boyish laugh in happier times, then his howls of distress that were drowned out by

Praxer's low sneer to 'leave him' and the rush of river flow. The water that became his grave.

'And?' Dexie says it in a way she already knows the outcome.

'Otto died,' Harri says, so quietly that even the dulled silence inside the *Seahorse* swallows it. 'At some point, he must have taken in a lungful of water, and then the river took him. In an instant, we'd sobered up, but by the time we caught up and fished him out, he was gone. That poor, intelligent, wonderful boy, who would have been ten times the police officer I've ever been.'

'You don't know that,' Dexie says.

'No, maybe I don't. But the point is, he never got the chance to prove it, because of me.'

'And others,' she argues. 'There were other people who could have saved him.'

'But it should have been me, Dex! I saw it first, I recognised his cry for help, and I should have been the one to ignore Praxer and dive in, to have stopped his cruelty.'

He watches her nose twitch, as she looks to the low ceiling of the boat, deliberating. 'Yes, there's no denying you might have saved Otto. But do you think that would have stopped Praxer and his brutality?' she reasons. 'It seems to me you're harbouring guilt not over one man, but the millions Praxer killed afterwards. Harri, it's a fact that in this world there are some very nasty people. Every working day I see the difference between villains and ordinary folk who make a choice about which side of the law they are on. A level above them are the Hitlers and the Praxers of this world, and we may never know what causes them to be so vicious. We can only do what we can to limit their effect over others.'

'But I didn't, that's the point!'

'And it wouldn't have changed Praxer joining the Nazi party, or doing what he did afterwards, that's *my* point.'

As he listens to Dexie, Harri's thinking poses a sudden question: how is it that he's been placed in the orbit of such sensible, reasoned women? His mother's influence was a birthright, but then there was Hella, Paula, Georgie, and now this wise WPC. Clearly, he's like a moth to a flame when it comes to such women. And that it's no bad thing.

'You're right – again,' he says. 'But it also makes me think we should be doing more than sitting here, hiding. We had a chance to stop him, and we didn't. That signing is less than forty-eight hours away.'

'Harri, we both risked our lives trying. Eliza lost hers. There are others out there with more resources, and the fire power to do it. Johnson for one. Not that he would ever get his hands dirty.'

He feels drained by the confession. These days, Otto drops sporadically into his consciousness, but the last time he spoke of it in detail was to Hella, and so it's been deeply buried for more than a decade. Digging up a guilty secret is eviscerating, and yet cathartic. So yes, he understands what Dexie means; sitting here, with her and Scooter, there is a sense of contentment, despite what he's just admitted. Inside a glorified tin bath, their little trio feels safe. Utterly bizarre, but true.

The moment is disturbed when she gets up to fiddle with the radio dial, hoofing out a breath – of effort or relief he can't tell. 'Now that we've revealed all, perhaps we should listen to something a bit more uplifting on the wireless,' she suggests. 'What do you think?'

'Good idea,' Harri agrees, as she twiddles to find the BBC light programme.

Yes, it's all very strange.

41

Contentment

8th December 1952

Dexie

She wakes in what feels like the early hours, though it's too dark to see her own watch, black as pitch. And freezing. Despite being fully dressed, Dexie is bone-cold and curled in a foetal position under two meagre blankets, hearing the barge crank around her and the gentle slap of water against the hull. The single round window is shut fast. It's proven efficient at keeping the fog at bay, but the tiny room now feels stuffy and oppressive, and she coughs several times at sucking in the cold, tainted air.

Shivering to incite some warmth, she blinks several times to centre herself. What day is it? Past midnight, surely, so Monday? The past days slot themselves into some vague extraordinary order, the last of which is Harri's revelation about his past with Praxer. He'd called the would-be Nazi a friend at one point, and for some reason that disturbs her more than his guilty confession over the poor drowned boy, which, in turn, spikes remorse in her. Dexie is apt to believe that everyone, even those who appear heinous, possess some redeeming features, though she's inclined to remove Hitler from that equation. Praxer can certainly turn on the charm, and may once have been genuinely amiable, before the evil took root.

The bigger question: does the revelation make her think any less of Harri – has he gone from angel to devil in in her estimation? She searches deep inside, but finds no contempt for his actions. Undeniably, he was remiss and flawed, but doesn't everyone harbour those failings in life, the conduct of a younger self making you squirm in hindsight? *We're all human*, she concludes, *though most of us are not malevolent.*

Awake and beyond chilled, she can't drift off again, needing something to warm the blood in her veins. Both blankets around her shoulders, she tiptoes into the darkness of the main galley, fumbling blindly towards the small gas ring. She can just make out the sleeping shapes of Harri and Scooter in front of the now dormant wood stove. He'd offered Scooter as a 'sleeping companion and breathing hot water bottle' before they settled for the night, but the wise old terrier was reluctant to leave the residual warmth of the fire. As she contemplates lighting the paraffin lamp or making tea blindly (and dangerously), there's movement from the floor.

'Can't you sleep?' Harri's voice comes out of the dark.

'No, sorry, I didn't mean to wake you. I'm cold, that's all. Freezing, in fact. I need some tea.'

Pause.

'Why don't you bring your blankets down here? We can share the fabric and the body heat, and Scooter.'

Another pause. Why not? They've already spent the night in a hotel bed, in what constituted a brothel, so how much worse can it look? And frankly, who to?

'I promise, I haven't taken a stitch of clothing off,' Harri encourages. 'It's too damned cold.'

'Then it's too good an offer to resist.'

She joins him on the makeshift bed of cushions, pooling their blankets. Dexie shivers as she worms herself in and Scooter moulds himself between the two like mercury. 'God, you're like ice!' Harri says, when her hand scrapes against his. Instinctively, perhaps, he grabs at it and begins rubbing at her skin, to inject some little heat from his own flesh. 'Come here.'

He draws her body into his, an arm around her shoulders, so that her head rests on the layers of clothes on his chest. Automatically, Dexie finds herself yielding to his shape with no other motive than sharing the radiating heat. Once she's there, in the crook of his arm and against the rise of his ribcage, there is an instant swell of comfort. It satisfies a craving she's worked hard to keep under wraps, both at work and in private. Right then, she thinks not so much of Thomas, but of being close to *someone*, and how nice that feels. Despite years of telling herself otherwise, it's clear to Dexie that she does miss it.

A slightly moist little nose nuzzles at her free hand from under the blanket, and there it is again, popping up unexpectedly. Contentment.

42
Exposure

8th December 1952

Harri

He comes to gradually, one eye open first on the sandy head of hair that's directly in front of his vision, the sensation of it almost touching his nose and just brushing his lips. What dim light there is creeps into the cabin, and with faint noises of activity beyond, Harri takes it to be morning. Another day in the land of the blind.

With his immediate memory still hazy, he gingerly stretches each finger to detect where his hands lie, one couched over the figure in front of him, the other caught underneath his own body, as they lie spooned together. In his much younger days (and a chequered love life that preceded Hella), the same scenario would have been accompanied by a hangover of gargantuan proportions, plus the mystery of how he came to be in someone's bed. And whose bed it was. Now, there's no headache, although his mouth feels like the bottom of a birdcage. But he has slept, and so, he thinks, has Dexie, after they shifted and nestled to feed warmth into each other. If they were stranded in the Antarctic, it would be deemed pure survival, but as his recall begins to clear, he thinks of it as pleasant. The closeness, the feeling of a woman's body next to his, even out of necessity. It's undoubtedly what made him fall into a deep and satisfied sleep. In the end, there could have been an armada outside and he wouldn't have noticed.

Dexie stirs and he feels her limbs stiffen as she comes to, and perhaps to the same realisation. 'Hmm.'

Thankfully, it seems to him more of a statement than a groan. Or regret.

'Are you awake, Harri?' she says softly.

'Yes, just. Did you sleep?'

'I must have, after I warmed up, thanks to you.' A small body wriggles to the top of the blankets, with a small, needy whine. 'Yes, and you too, Scoot.'

'He must be desperate to go out and relieve himself,' Harri says. 'If I take him, will you get the kettle on?'

'Deal,' she yawns. 'Though I'm so cosy now, I could stay here forever.'

'I wish we'd booked room service,' he says, hoisting himself up. 'Though I imagine that might have been pushing Wolli a step too far, and I'm not hopeful about our local chap. Come on, Scoot, time to brave the world.'

Out on the concrete verge beyond the gangplank, it's no surprise to find to the world unchanged. This fog is bedded in; after only four days, this already feels like a new way of life, existence in a muddy void. The only difference is a breath of wind felt against his cheek, teasing at the ribbons of vapour and sending them licking at their own tails. But that lid over the capital remains fixed in place and there's no sound of any industry on the dockside, only a faint noise on the periphery. Against the silence, Harri's head turns from side to side, listening intently for anyone close by. After the cocoon of the barge, this feels like acute exposure.

'Hurry up, Scooter,' he urges. 'It's freezing out here.'

Dexie is pouring from the pot as they go back in, handing him a steaming cup.

'Wonderful,' he sighs.

'On the subject of tea, we must have used quite a lot of water, because it's getting low. The milk, too. Do you think we should chance going to find some more?'

Harri deliberates into his cup. The more hours they spend undetected, the more he feels Praxer can't possibly root them out under this heavy shroud. But it's a foolish man who becomes overconfident.

'Let's leave it as late as we can,' he suggests. 'You never know, Johnson may send word he's found another place for us. We'll just be frugal with the water and milk.'

'All right. The good news is that we have plenty of bacon and eggs left.'

There's just enough wood to get the burner going again, leaving all three to camp out in front of the fire with a set of playing cards and a couple of cheap detective novels to pass the time. By three p.m., and after eking out the supplies, there's still no sign of Johnson or a messenger, so Harri reluctantly suggests they go 'foraging'.

'If we can find a phone box, we can try to gauge the situation.'

'Together?' Dexie suggests. 'As much as I don't want to risk anything, I really do need to stretch my legs.' With his usual acute timing, Scooter does just that, accompanied by a loud whinny. 'Him, too, by the sounds of it.'

On the quay, the temperature seems to have climbed a notch, but it's still bitterly cold; the toxic mass stings at Harri's throat, if not the ice burn of previous days. As per usual, the radio forecasts had been guarded about any promise of real improvement. Despite their arrival being only yesterday, he's disorientated as they hit the solid base beyond the gangplank. Which way did they come from? He sees Dexie casting about with the same bewilderment that sudden displacement brings. There's nothing within sight to use as a beacon, those markers you tie yourself to as a grounding for everyday life. He recalls the same sensation from the war, emerging from a basement shelter one morning after a heavy raid to find the Hamburg street gone. Not even in ruins, with the remnants of buildings sticking up like a bad set of teeth. It was simply absent, wiped from his consciousness, causing his head to physically spin, like a bad case of vertigo.

Instinctively, it's Scooter who paves the way again, nose to the floor as he steers them along the water's edge and back to what feels like civilisation, since guesswork is all they have. Dexie is quiet, her eyes swinging from one side to the other, and occasionally looking backwards, as they step in the dog's wake. After only ten minutes, they arrive at a small cluster of shops alongside a row of brick houses – a grocer, butcher and a bottle shop, with a few souls milling about. The old man is one of them, his head snapping up in surprise as they approach, ash from his permanent cigarette spraying the ground.

'Guv'nor,' he starts, 'I was just coming to bring your milk and the like. Any minute now.'

'It's fine,' Harri says, keen to avoid any kind of fuss. 'We'll sort ourselves in the shop. But you can tell me where the nearest phone box is?'

'Pub on the corner has one, but won't be open 'til later.

Near teatime.' He looks like he knows the opening hours off by heart.

'Thanks.'

In the tiny shop that doubles as a bakery, they find the essentials for another night on the *Seahorse*, plus a can of dog food for Scooter. Harri spies the front-page headline for the day's *London Evening Standard*, extolling the route for the Queen's upcoming coronation, and the *Daily Express*, which professes 'London at a Standstill' in bold, black lettering, with stories of babies being born in ambulances, and a bride forced to take the Tube to her own wedding. What about the destruction, and the Mrs Ps of this world? The toll on human life? How can that be so unimportant?

Scooter guides them back to the boat, conveniently via the harbour standpipe, where Harri tops up the water. In the tiny galley kitchen, Dexie tackles the raggedy-looking vegetables they've bought. 'I hope you like your carrots mangled,' she says, wielding a knife that barely warrants the description of a blade.

'Chopped, mangled, shredded – any which way is fine by me. But preferably cooked.' He finds these homely sounds comforting, but as the weak seepage of sun goes down on another day, Harri feels the play of domesticity replaced by a stirring in his nerves. Either Praxer is truly blindsided by grief over Alicia, or he really doesn't know where they are. A history going back two decades, plus a fresh wave of paranoia, is not enough to convince him of either. He feels a renewed urge to contact either Wolli or Johnson, the phone numbers of both secreted in his shoe for safekeeping. This time, he suggests going alone, with Scooter to lead the way. 'It's dark and now I know where to go, I'll be back in no time. I promise to bring back some brandy, too.'

'A perfect dessert,' Dexie agrees.

The pub is already open at five thirty, attracting a good deal more people than he's seen before, who, it seems, have braved the weather for company and a pint. In the corner, through the blue haze of cigarette smoke blending with the insidious pea-green, the old man is propping up the bar, focused on his glass. Chatter about this 'ruddy fog' seems to have diminished, as if it really is the new normal.

To Harri's great annoyance, there's no answer on Johnson's so-called 'emergency' line, and he slams down the receiver, only to pick it up again and dial Wolli's number. With the pubs now open, what are the chances of him being at his flat or boarding house, or wherever it is the Polish man lays his ageing head? And yet, it's the only option.

After several rings, and a yelling from the archetypal landlady to rival any foghorn, Wolli's voice is heard over the crackles. Amazingly, he sounds sober. 'Where are you?' he barks.

'We're at the boat, and pretty much stranded,' Harri says. 'No word from Johnson since yesterday. He says sit tight until he moves us, but we can't stay here, forever. We're running out of wood, and it's bloody freezing.'

'Never mind that,' Wolli says, obvious alarm travelling down the line now. 'I take it you haven't got the message?'

'*What* message?' Harri is straining to hear over the background noise of the pub, where the Blitz-style atmosphere has led to someone striking chords on an ancient piano.

'You need to get out!' Wolli is almost shouting now. 'Somehow Praxer knows. Don't ask me how, but he does, and the word is that he's fucking livid. With you, and with that woman. He blames you, so wherever you are now, don't go back to that boat . . .'

Wolli's next words are lost as Harri slams the receiver

into the cradle and bangs through the pub door at speed, hitting the hostile outside. 'Come on, Scoot, don't fail me now.'

The dog must catch the panic in his voice, because he's instantly straining on the lead in the direction of the *Seahorse*. Harri is pulled over the rough ground, his feet snagging on the mooring lines and stumbling over unseen chains, dodging poles that loom out of nowhere. His shoulder hits at one solid edifice and he cries out in pain and shock, almost tipping towards the water's edge that comes up at him in a flash. Nothing, however, stops Scooter's flight along the quay, until he slows and begins sniffing the air. Lord knows what he can smell through the acrid sulphur that's now days old, but Harri puts his trust in the canine's nose until, out of the gloom, tiny slivers of yellowy light become visible.

They stop and assess, listening for footsteps or the heavy breath of an unwelcome presence. Anything out of the ordinary. Harri even closes his eyes for a second to focus his hearing. There is nothing but the feeling – a good feeling – of familiarity surrounding the *Seahorse*, of that sense when he would arrive home from work in Hamburg and linger at the door of his apartment for a moment, listening to Hella singing to the wireless as she prepared their evening meal. That familiarity he misses so keenly.

Only Scooter's low growl cuts through the perfect scene in his head.

'What is it, boy?' he whispers. The ears flatten, the tiny black nose goes down near the gangplank, yanking on the lead to prevent Harri stepping onto the flimsy wood. '*Scheisse*,' he breathes.

Something isn't right.

43

Guests on Board

8th December 1952

Dexie

She's thinking of her mother as she stirs the small pot of soup, wondering – and worrying – about conditions at the hospital, and whether the staff have managed any respite from what must be endless demands of the sagging, sick capital. Dexie vows to make it up to her when this is all over, perhaps a few days on the coast for mother and daughter, in a nice hotel as a special treat. Her current break from the beat could hardly be called a holiday, though in some ways it's been pleasa—

The spoon stills in the swirl of liquid, her hand frozen, while the rest of her body follows suit. Is that . . .? She listens out, unconsciously attuned to Harri's gait, plus Scooter's tic-tac of claws on wood, ready to breathe again. Only the sound doesn't come. In its place, there's an almighty thump as the door is pushed through with force, and the big man – the one she knows as Eliza's killer – crowds in the doorway, followed by another, equally bulky form. Both sets of eyes take a mere second to comb the interior, peering beyond the statue of Dexie. Searching for one other, clearly.

She says and does nothing, because where is there to go? Her mother's wise words rush in: 'Save your breath to cool your porridge, my girl.' Good, maternal advice in the circumstances. *Think, don't act, Dex. Preserve your energy.*

'He's not here, boss,' the big man says after checking the tiny room at the rear.

'Then we'll just have to wait, won't we?' Praxer's slim frame emerges from behind the meat muscle, his face paler than she remembers. Pinched with grief? But not so distraught over his wife that he can't go hunting the day before a vital business venture. He wants Harri badly, she reasons. Craving vengeance.

'Where is he?' Big Man demands.

'Who?'

An impatient roll of the eyes. 'Your German detective.'

'He left,' she says flatly. 'Earlier today.'

Praxer scoffs, in the superior way he's no doubt mastered over the years. 'Oh, I don't think so, Miss . . .?'

'Nobody. I'm a nobody.'

'You may well be a nobody, Miss No-Name, but as far as I can tell, you are the one who brought that *person* into my house, the same woman who went on to shoot my wife. By my reckoning, you owe me a debt. A substantial one.'

'What could I possibly give you, a man who wants for nothing?' Every effort goes in calming her voice; from Harri she knows Praxer feeds off weakness, seeks to crush anyone who shows it, and God knows, he despises her enough already. Even with her police training in self-defence, she's no match for the bulk of the Big Man and his sidekick.

'Harri Schroder,' Praxer replies, not an ounce of emotion

in his voice. 'Give me Schroder and you can go. If he's the same gallant fool he always was, he won't have left you in the lurch. I know that for a fact. And certainly not here.' His nostrils flare with disdain at the cramped surroundings and, presumably, at the company he's forced to keep. 'So, if you won't point us in the right direction, we'll just have to sit it out.'

'You might as well take a seat, because you're in for a long wait,' she lies, then prays Harri will have sensed the signs or a change in atmosphere through the fug. *Something*. And that he will not walk that plank.

44
Running Blind

8th December 1952

Harri

His watch says the wait so far has gone beyond thirty minutes, though with each sixty seconds that pass, Harri's mind see-saws between a foolish but brave ambush, or total inaction, in trying to fathom which option will cause the least harm to Dexie. His own fate he's resigned to being in Praxer's hands; it's taken twenty years, but sudden clarity makes him think it was always going to end in a stand-off.

Squatting close to one end of the boat and with Scooter sat between his knees, Harri hears the slight but distinct roll of the hull and a vague outline of the barge's shift, knowing that Dexie's weight alone couldn't cause that movement. She has company. And while there's no guessing as to who it might be, he's surprised at how quiet the occupants are, with no raised voices or signs of struggle. What is going on in there?

The cold and a numbness in both feet forces him to stand, wincing at the pain of his toes coming to life, just as an indescribably large rat shoots past, its long tail snaking by. With his protective streak – and being a dog – Scooter can't help but react. Harri gasps in surprise and seizes the dog by the waist before he can go haring after the rodent, causing the scarf around his mouth to loosen. The fetid air rushes to the back of his throat, and he half chokes, a hand slammed across his mouth to stifle the sound. For a second, he thinks he's quashed it, only for the legacy of his damaged lungs to resurface. From the bottom of his ribcage, something brews – the feeling from back in the sanatorium, miniscule at first, yet destined to spill into a noisy hacking, unable to stop himself retching up the toxins that had taken hold. *Why now?*

Harri smothers the cough with combined will and the wool of his scarf as best he can, stepping away from the *Seahorse* and bending double, Scooter at his heels. It's enough to disturb the air around him, but will the sound travel in this?

He wipes his streaming eyes as the coughing finally abates, drawing in much needed oxygen, and a vile stench, through his nose. He tiptoes back to the boat.

Scooter's stance warns of a change, a slight tremble to his otherwise rigid body. Whoever has just emerged from barge door is not on Scooter's list of favoured people. It's no surprise because, backlit by the glow from inside, Harri sees the unmistakable broad shoulders of Joseph.

'Anything?' a voice probes from inside the cabin. Sharp, demanding and well-to-do. Harri is taken aback; he felt certain Praxer would seek revenge, but not here in person. Instead, he pictured them squaring up across an isolated warehouse, Praxer keen to witness the kill after Joseph had already primed and basted the meat. The bodyguard's outline ducks back inside the cabin, replaced momentarily by another enormous shadow in the dim light of the door.

So that's at least two to contend with, and maybe three –

Praxer always did surround himself with an army of acolytes – leaving Harri to debate the options. A firefight inside the boat would be bloody, and a certain end for Dexie, with a hail of bullets ricocheting off the metal. Besides, he has no weapon, meaning it would be tantamount to suicide. He must draw them out, away from her. Towards him, and then do what so much of his life has been about already – play it by the ear, as the English put it. Run. Hope. Pray a little. One of those options might work.

'Right, Scoot, you're on,' he whispers, untying the lead and steering him towards the gangplank after Joseph has gone back inside. 'Let loose, boy. Where's Dexie?' he goads the dog into his soft ear. 'Where is she? Find her, *go on*.'

A piercing volley of barks resounds in the still air, forcing the door to open again. 'What the fu—?' Joseph cries as Scooter darts back to Harri and together they run the length of the boat on the quay, whipping past Joseph's blindspot as bait, then crouching out of sight again.

'Oi, Benjy, move it!' the big man cries. 'There's someone out here.' Footsteps of the two rattle across the plank and onto terra firma. 'You go left, I'll take right,' Joseph instructs. 'Pound to a penny, it's Schroder. But be careful, he's a slippery bastard.'

The second man grunts as they both move off, Harri crouched behind a barrel, one hand on Scooter's tiny rack of ribs, quivering with anticipation. He may be Mrs P's 'baby' but he's a working dog now, a hunter by heritage. Harri thinks rapidly: is there another body left inside with Praxer, or would his supreme arrogance lead him to think he could handle Dexie if it came to a tussle? And does he have a gun? Within Inspektor Schroder's Kripo world, high-end criminals tend not to carry weapons, using menace and coercion instead. In Praxer's case, why change the habits of a lifetime?

Arming himself with a heavy metal crank from the quay,

he steals onto the deck and listens intently at the closed door. Mutterings only. Knowing Dexie, she'll be trying to calm the situation, no friendly chit-chat, but equally nothing to rile him further. Time is her best ally. She'll be seeking to lull him into a false sense of security, though with an ardent Nazi that may be an uphill task.

Hoping that Joseph and his pal are busy chasing shadows, Harri turns the door handle and enters, Scooter sliding in beside him. Good fortune puts Dexie nearest to him, sitting stiffly opposite Praxer, who is propped uncomfortably on the side seating in his heavy overcoat. Harri sees the slightest flash of alarm in his eyes at the sight of an old friend turned foe. The unease increases when Praxer spies the iron bar, then – like a veteran chameleon – his face settles on smug.

'You came back,' he says, flicking from Harri to Dexie. 'For her. You always were an incurable pushover for a woman in need, Schroder, and nothing has changed. Duty, is it, this time? Or something more?'

'Helmut.' Harri nods. 'Nice of you to stop by.'

'Oh, you know, time on my hands,' comes the seething reply. 'Now that I have no woman in my life to engage with. Unlike you, it seems. A cosy little love nest you have here.'

For a brief second, Harri thinks of offering up sympathy over Alicia, but bites his tongue; it won't go down well, not in Praxer's current mood. 'Lovely as this is, we have to go,' he says instead, seeing Dexie already slipping on her coat.

'Good luck then,' Praxer says calmly. 'There are men across this dock, so unless you fancy a quick dip – and I don't recommend the filthy chill of the Thames – you won't get far. I'll see you later, no doubt, for a more detailed *chat*. I planned on asking you if I should re-evaluate my options, having received a very favourable offer from my new friends, the Russians. I'm up against a deadline, but no matter, it can wait until later.'

His supreme confidence is absolute – and unnerving. He doesn't appear to be bluffing.

'Even so, I think we'll take our chances,' Harri manages. 'Dex?'

'Ready.' Her expression is steadfast, and there's no fear in her voice.

They slip out, their four-legged pilot back on the lead and forging ahead, just reaching the quay as gruff voices are heard, though it's impossible to tell how close – two, ten or twenty feet away. Instinctively, and in silence, Scooter cuts through the abyss in the opposite direction, nose to the floor, while Harri grabs at Dexie's hand, all three moving as a chain.

'To the pub, where there's plenty of people?' Dexie whispers as they stumble blindly, too fast for this sightless world, but not speedy enough for Harri's rising paranoia and heartrate.

'Yes, there's a phone, too. At the very least, Wolli might get help on the way, if he hasn't already.'

Praxer wasn't bluffing about his army of men. The alarm goes up around them, a series of unseen shouts that seem to encircle like an amphitheatre, and Harri begins to understand how those gladiators must have felt when the hungry lions were let loose in the colosseums of ancient Rome, forever at the mercy of a divine ruler. The Emperor Praxer. That's enough to make anyone shiver.

At last, the glow of the pub lights dawns up ahead, and for once, Scooter needs holding back. 'Hey, stop here, boy,' Harri coaxes. It's either silent, or the banging in his ears is shrouding the previous hubbub of noise. 'Dex, can you hear anything?' he asks.

She stops to tune in. 'Not really, though not sure what I'm listening for. And in this, would we hear it anyway?'

'Maybe not.' The din of that sing-song piano might well

be veiled by the cotton-wool world outside. Even so, he approaches with caution, peering through the saloon door. Reassuringly, there are people propping up the bar, but there's no music. A thin thread of suspicion continues to tug at Harri's senses, but he works to shake it off – there is nowhere else to summon help. It's when they enter and the door swings shut behind that Harri knows he should have trusted his instinct; the atmosphere is charged, a wary suspense and a lack of clinking glasses. It's as if the drinkers are going through the motions of a daily routine. Worse, they studiously avoid looking at the strangers who have appeared in their midst. Bribed or threatened to do so, it doesn't matter, only that some element has asserted its authority.

The Emperor Praxer.

'Let's go.' The words leach from between Harri's set lips. 'Now.'

Dexie doesn't flinch, except to turn on her heel smoothly.

At the last second, they lunge for the door, only to hear the scrape of a chair on the bare boards, and a 'That's them!' from one of the drinkers.

The sting of smoke from the pub is nothing as it gives way to the chill vapour of the outside, Harri dodging blindly to the right and away from the pub's glow, his fingers clutched around Dexie's coat, a clatter of footsteps behind that slow up and shuffle in confusion as their quarry melts instantly into the dense mist. 'Shit!' he hears in frustration, perhaps only feet away.

Something in Harri says they should keep to the water's edge, though he doesn't know why. If the Thames is anything like the River Elbe, as a means of escape it's tantamount to self-destruction, from the freezing depths and festering sewage. And yet, despite Praxer's own warning, it still represents openness, away from the claustrophobia of buildings and warehouses, where dark corners point to a dead end in more ways than one. Footsteps clips past on the cobbles and he yanks Dexie down behind a pile of fish pallets.

'I think we should follow the quay edge upwards, towards Limehouse,' he whispers, close into her cheek.

She nods. 'Take Scooter off the lead – we don't want him pulling us into hazards. If we get separated, he'll find one of us.'

'Good idea.' Harri slips the rope off with some reluctance, stroking at the dog's ear in apology. This is life and death – his and Dexie's – and no time to be sentimental about a dog, despite the simper that comes from him. 'It's all right, Scoot, you'll find your way.'

The four small legs easily keep up with their faltering pace, picking their way around the hazards of wooden poles and metal cleats along the edge, hopping over mooring lines. The progress is steady but slow and, more importantly, away from the threat. Every minute or so, they stop to catch a breath and listen, like a crewman on a submarine combing the deep seas for enemy sonar. When there's none, they press on.

The ghostly beacon of torchlight appears from nowhere, the orb increasing in size, muffled conversation and an unsuspecting couple suddenly on them, all four faces swaddled, scarf to scarf.

Harri grabs at Dexie's hand and feigns surprise. 'Oh, sorry, sorry,' he blusters. 'This damn fog, it's awful isn't it?'

'Dreadful,' the man concurs. 'Be careful, won't you? It's quite slippery up ahead.'

'We'll try, thank you,' Dexie says, then when they've disappeared: 'Do you think that means we're near the top of the isle? I've got no idea how far we've come.'

The pucker of her forehead tells him she feels out of her

depth, so used to having functioning sensors. Like so much around them, WPC Dexter looks to be adrift.

'We just have to keep going,' is all the comfort he can offer. 'We will get there.'

Another five minutes of hugging the water's edge for guidance, and Harri does sense a change. The air is equally dense, but there's less evidence of port industry – ropes are sporadically abandoned on the side and the moorings spaced out. Scooter's white form is barely visible a step ahead, but he stops and sniffs, his snout swaying left then right. Surely, they must be off the isle soon, Harri thinks, safer in the sprawl of London? Even Praxer hasn't got an army big enough to track them under this vast green shroud.

Several more steps and the terrier is suddenly rigid. His paws retreat, before the white of his teeth radiates through the gloom, followed by a menacing snarl.

'Quiet, boy,' Harri hisses.

'He's warning us,' Dexie whispers. 'There must be something up ahead. Let's veer right and loop around.' Spinning on her heel ninety degrees, she forges forward, and in one blink of an eye, Harri loses sight of her. A second later, there's the sound of contact, of flesh on something solid. Her cry is swallowed by the fog, and it's as if she's simply vanished.

'Dex . . . *Dex*? Where are you?' Nothing. He stumbles, arms outstretched, flailing and panicked. More and more, this day is like the re-run of a frequent bad dream he's haunted by, the one that sees him running through mud, or quicksand, never getting anywhere in trying to reach his wife and child. Two steps forward, and two back. Sinking.

'She's here,' a voice comes back. The stone-like monument of Joseph emerges, his sickening grin coming into focus. 'Hello again, Herr Schroder.'

45

Rough Justice?

8th December 1952

Dexie

His huge knuckles push into her collar as she's shuffled forward by the scruff of her neck, like a poorly strung marionette. Squirming does no good, given the small but hard shape pressed into her back is very likely the gun that did for poor Eliza. 'Move!' he grunts with venom.

She doesn't so much think, as react on pure impulse. 'Scoot! Scoot!' Dexie shouts, as Harri's alarmed face comes into view. She feels the tension in the big man's grip tighten; he must imagine she's warning Harri to flee. He throws her forcefully towards the cobbles and lunges for Harri, not noticing a white missile coming from the side, teeth bared. Rabid. No sweet lap dog here.

'Shit! What—?' The big man swipes furiously at the beast that's got a firm grip on his trouser leg. Scooter reacts viciously, the sound of a dog twice his size, his back legs dancing to dodge the huge human hand swatting at the air.

Dexie picks herself up and yanks at Harri's sleeve, pushing hard on her leg muscles to pull him away from the circling squall of man and dog.

Christ – which way? Her sense of direction has been entirely scrambled, and it's only instinct that pushes her onwards, Harri's urgent breath behind her as they slip and slide over the cobbles, trusting chance not to trip them up. Much like her ARP days, sometimes you have to just rely on the world not falling on top of you.

Not today. She's floored again by something rather than someone, her foot catching on a rope or a metal hook and her face slamming onto the hard grime. She lets fly with a cry she can't stifle.

'Dex!' Harri is on her in seconds, pulling her upright and coming in close. 'Your face, are you hurt?'

She paws at her cheek and the slick liquid that comes away on her hand as a dark green. 'It's a scratch,' she pants, testing her ankle and wincing, but it feels more of a sprain than a fracture when she pushes her sole to the ground. 'I'm all right.'

They break left, piloted by desperation, and don't stop until they reach the quayside. There, a high-pitched yelp pierces through the blanket of fog.

'Scooter,' Dexie murmurs. There's no telling what that man mountain might do to a dog if he's prepared to shoot a woman in cold blood.

'He'll be OK.' Harri tries to offer reassurance, though it's not convincing. 'We have to go.'

And go they do – right into the hands of an equally large comrade stationed on the water's edge. Plus two more, standing on each side of Praxer.

'I felt sure we'd meet again, Harri. And your good lady. Dex, isn't it?'

'Dexie,' she corrects, through gritted teeth. *Might as well die with an identity.* The thought flashes briefly, enough to spike a burn in her stomach.

'You're just in time to join us,' Praxer says, with self-satisfied smirk. Dexie looks over the edge of the wharf, at the bow of a motorised dinghy just visible below, though it's far less solid than the one used for his smart getaway after the Russian encounter. She calculates space for only six or so passengers. Damn it. Little room for manoeuvre.

'In,' one of the heavies instructs. She looks to Harri, whose eyes signal compliance, because as she steps down onto the wooden slats, it's clear that, yet again, there is nowhere else to go. The alternative is diving into the uninviting drink, the waterline then liberally sprayed with bullets from the big man, who appears out of the gloom, and in a foul temper.

'Sodding mutt,' he curses with a face like thunder. Blood glistens on his hand, and Dexie is sick at the thought: is it human or canine? *Oh, Scoot.*

'Joseph, radio ahead and make sure they're ready,' Praxer barks, in complete control. That is, until he steps down onto the boat, very gingerly and without his characteristic self-assurance. Leaning heavily on Joseph's arm as the vessel wavers, he descends and promptly sits to one side, his face tight with unease.

A fresh thought hits Dexie: *he doesn't like water.*

She glances at Harri, one eyebrow raised, receiving a rapid blink in response. With the boat's pilot, plus Praxer, two other heavies and two captives, the small craft sinks lower into the waterline. Dexie can't help but feel that once the bulk of Joseph comes aboard, they'll be almost eye to eye with the brown sludge of Thames soup.

Fate has other ideas. Silently, and with the stealth of a real missile this time, something white comes haring out of the gloom and runs full pelt at Joseph's legs while he's untying the rope tether. From the rear of the boat, Dexie glimpses the big man's knees buckle, and a brief but farcical windmilling of his arms as he pitches forward into the Thames. A resounding splosh rocks the already overloaded boat.

Praxer's high-pitch squeal of rage spews into the air. 'Fucking hell! Can't you lot—'

There's no concern in his voice for Joseph, whose heavy form can be heard flailing, and crying for help, pulled under by his sodden overcoat. The other men lurch to one side, peering to where green fog meets brown water – 'Where is he? Joseph!' – causing the craft to tilt.

'Keep still, you idiots, or we'll all be over!' Praxer screams.

Dexie shoots a wordless, loaded look at Harri. *Now*. In tandem, they lunge to the other side of the craft, shifting their weight left to right, left to right, as if they're on a fairground swing and inciting it to go higher or faster, relishing the thrill. Caught by surprise, the men inside the boat stumble and fall, as Joseph thrashes noisily and Scooter is barking his loudest from the water's edge, creating a cacophony not even the fog can mask. The boat pitches dangerously as Harri and Dexie rock to increase the listing, and its occupants are flung from side to side. Praxer clutches helplessly at the wooden surround, a look of true panic on his face.

'Do something!' he screeches, his voice beyond that distinct pitch of his.

One of the men struggles upright and lurches towards Dexie, just as she and Harri hurl their combined weight to the listed side. The bodyguard's flailing arm catches one of his comrades off-guard and they topple into the water with a splash.

'Hang on!' Harri cries. The boat tips almost ninety degrees, slapping fiercely against the tideline, sucking in water as it rights itself at the last instant. The third man jumps, sending another plume of silty water into the air. Harri and Dexie grip onto the seating and somehow shunt their weight to the opposite edge, the dinghy gradually righting itself on the surface. Dexie opens her eyes to feel the boat lighter, Harri squashed into her stinging cheek, both steeped in inches of freezing water.

'Have they . . .?

'Think so,' he says, clambering up and pulling frantically at the starter of the outboard motor, which has been flooded in the drowning. It's clear all three men have made it to the quay, scooping up Joseph as they clamber onto the concrete. Harri's efforts to re-ignite the engine spiral with desperation; soaking or not, the big man won't hesitate to scatter bullets into the darkness any second now. Yet, it's his booming voice that penetrates. 'Where's the boss? Where is he?' he roars, all focus on Praxer's whereabouts.

A strangulated cry from somewhere near the boat provides the answer. 'I can't swi . . . help, *helfen* . . . I ca . . .' Praxer's high tone of distress is diluted by the water that Dexie can almost feel slipping into his lungs, a just visible hand outstretched towards the boat, but too far for those on the quayside to see. Only Harri and Dexie are within reach.

The Nazi man – a killer of thousands, if not millions – is drowning, before their very eyes. Sweet judgement or rough justice?

46

The Choice

8th December 1952

Harri

He hesitates. Who wouldn't? It should be Otto's face that his memory throws up, thrashing against the current and begging for help. Oddly it isn't. As Praxer struggles to stay afloat, swallowing and spitting filthy water, what Harri sees in the smog-bound, silted river is the faces of so many he's met since the war's end: sons and daughters who will never meet their parents, widows, refugees whose families were victims of the camps, those who were sent to their deaths at the stroke of Praxer's pen. Thousands of them, millions maybe. So much sorrow and hate in those expressions, plus a need for revenge or closure. And he could give it to them, right now. Just by doing nothing.

There are those who want the revered James Remington to live, for financial gain, but as for Helmut Praxer – what has he given to world, aside from abject sorrow? Like Hitler, he's not only a scourge on the German nation, but on humanity as a whole.

Tell me why I should save him?

Harri looks at Dexie. For guidance? For that motivation to act, to save a life that can be spared? To remind him to be human?

For days now, they've communicated via a strange form of sign language in this mire – only a look, a frown or a half-word needed. Now, her startled eyes meet his. *It's your decision*, she's almost shouting, in complete silence: *You have to choose, Harri Schroder.*

His mind calculates at the speed of light: with Praxer dead, it would all be over, his men would flee without their emperor to command. The signing would be void, and the Russians would retreat, leaving the world safer, according to Johnson. Harri could go home to Hamburg, and before that to Oxford, perhaps with Dexie if she doesn't hate him, or to the seaside with Georgie and the children if they ever get to see the sun again. To live once more. And hasn't he already confessed that he's no angel, laying bare his faults?

Scheisse!

In one move, he tosses off his overcoat and grabs at a sodden rope at the bottom of the boat. Instinctively, Dexie takes the other end and winds it around her waist. 'I've got you,' she says.

He's over the side and slipping into the water in the next second, guided only by the gargling noise made by Praxer. Harri was always a strong swimmer but even his stroke is curbed by the icy temperature. Where the hell is he? Praxer's panic has taken him further from the boat and Harri can only follow the sound making its way through the dense swathe. His mouth meets a vile froth, water churned by Praxer's terror.

'Grab onto me!' Harri manages, the cold already robbing his breath.

'Help! Help!' Praxer pleads. 'I'm . . .' and then he's half under again.

'Grab onto me! Helmut, calm down! I'm right here.'

But there's only fingers clawing at him, unable to grasp. Harri pushes out his free hand, groping at the water again and again, an unctuous slime crossing his palm, but nothing tangible. 'Praxer! Helmut!'

The panic in his ears is deafening. His own, or the dying breaths of a desperate, drowning man? He can't tell, only that another image flashes across his eyes: the strangulating cries of those in the camp chambers, the spew of what promised to be cleansing water, but was in fact the mist of death.

Swiftly, everything fades. No panic, no gargle. No thrash or struggle. Then a mouthful of something so foul it makes Harri retch. He swallows, mouth and nose flooded, and retches again, everything closing over him, slipping and then plunging into a total, icy, filthy blindness. Black as hell.

And then nothing.

47

Submerged

8th December 1952

Dexie

Scooter is still barking frantically, with the shouts of men alongside, but she hears only silence – a great, blanketing void of splashing, flailing or panic, or anything that constitutes life still lived. The ghostly vapour coils above the water, teasing and mocking; she can't define the tangible world from this sham of reality, where it begins or ends.

'HARRI!' Dexie screams into her own silence. 'HARREEE!'

She pulls on the rope around her waist, only for it to come up empty in her hand. *No, no, NO.* Yanking at one oar wedged under the bench seat, she tries to shunt the boat forward with an uncoordinated frantic paddling, shouting his name over and over, while inside her head it beats with a rhythm of 'please, please, please'.

She stops, begs the water to still, and listens. 'QUIET!

SHUT UP!' she screams to the others, and even Scooter quits his incessant barking.

Nothing.

No.

Dexie squints hard, leaning so far over the boat edge she can smell the noxious effluent of London and Londoners. Is that . . . a bubble? Oxygen? Life? Or the end of it, a signal from the depths wending its way to the surface?

Another gurgle pops on the water. 'HARRI!'

The coils of fog parts like a wave as something breaches the surface, something dark, and still she can't discern Harri from Praxer, one who should live against one who doesn't deserve to.

Coughing, spluttering, a desperate search for breath, a pale face, and then weakly: 'Dex.'

It takes every ounce of her strength to pull Harri up and over the lip of the boat, his body a dead weight with exhaustion. Numbed, his system assumes control, shivering violently back into existence, while Dexie rubs furiously at his limbs, laying his overcoat on top, and adding her own to his layers.

'Sit up, Harri! Come on, you need to sit up!' she barks, becoming the fearsome WPC Dexter of the Met out of necessity. He's lolling, only kept conscious by his stomach ejecting the vile Thames water in fits and starts. 'Keep awake, Harri, keep with me,' she badgers.

The boat has drifted from the concrete edge, but they are somehow pulled back to the wharf, though Dexie doesn't have the space to fathom by whom, only conscious of one thing: he's alive.

As they draw nearer, she's aware of a second form of chaos on the quay – vague movement and the sounds of many more bodies than the small cluster of Praxer's men they left behind. There's shouting, and a good deal of what Sergeant Thomas refers to as 'argy-bargy', then a sound she recognises in an instant: police-issue boots on cobbles.

'What's going on?' Harri wheezes under her.

'Police, I think,' Dexie says. 'Maybe Wolli or Johnson, I don't know. It's help anyway. Our side, thankfully.'

She slumps backwards, holding Harri while he retches up more river water, while a tangle of thoughts shoots like arrows through the mist and into her brain. Yes, it's Wolli who likely called in help, maybe via Johnson. But the question that flashed through her mind only briefly in the midst of running for their lives, now lands with clarity: who tipped off Praxer about their refuge in the *Seahorse*? Who – in this dark, unseeing mass of millions – knew?

Wolli knew their exact whereabouts, though Harri's intuition for weeding out duplicity didn't seem spiked with the veteran Nazi hunter. Similarly, she'd considered Wolli grumpy and scornful, but true to his cause. What's more, Eliza trusted him.

That leaves Johnson. The lingering mistrust for the MI5 man multiplies in Dexie, though her thinking is muddied by the continued shuddering of Harri's body, ice still in his veins. She can't think straight, enough to condemn or acquit in this moment.

'Dex?' Harri croaks.

'Yes, what is it?'

'If Johnson is here, don't say anything, will you?'

'No, but why?' Is Harri harbouring the same suspicions?

'We need to talk first,' he mumbles, before his head lolls with fatigue.

'OK, but you're not in a fit state to do anything right now. For heaven's sake, lie back and let us look after you.'

'Yes, ma'am.'

* * *

At the wharf's edge, Dexie gives way to uniformed constables who drag Harri upright and virtually pull him onto land. They have a nest of blankets ready, and help him strip off sodden clothes, until he's swaddled in dry cloth. Dexie follows suit, a young constable shielding her as she sheds her wet outer layers, though frankly at that point she couldn't care less who sees her underwear. She drops to sit beside Harri and rub more heat into him, while someone runs to the pub for a bottle of brandy. With the liquor burning and warming their insides, there's a sudden whip of wind that feels so alien, followed by a faint patter, closer and more rapid, until a white furry body leaps on them both, with a volley of barks and a frantic wag of his tail.

'Scooter!' Dexie cries. 'Oh, little man, I thought we'd lost you.' Together, they comb over his body, relieved to find no blood, and that he seems no worse for wear after his double encounter with Joseph.

'You're far too nimble to get into real trouble, aren't you, boy?' Harri sinks his face into the fur, and it's clear that Scooter's presence is the best tonic right now.

The happy reunion is tempered by a human clip this time, and the appearance of a distinct pair of brogues. 'How are you both?' Johnson's face does show a level of concern as he looks down on them.

'Alive,' Harri mutters.

'Just,' Dexie adds bluntly. 'He needs to go to hospital – God only knows what poison he's ingested.'

'I'm fine, Dex, I don't need a hospital, only a long bath and some sleep.'

Johnson's feet shift. 'We do need to talk, urgently.'

'Well, *not now*,' Dexie insists, fixing him with one of her particular glares.

'First thing tomorrow, then,' Johnson shoots back. 'For the time being, there's a hotel not far from here, where you can clean up and rest. We'll bring you both some fresh clothes.'

'Only if they allow dogs,' Harri presses.

Johnson huffs, his patience evidently tested. 'All right, I'll clear it. And I'll see you in the morning. Then we'll talk.'

'One more thing,' Harri says as Johnson turns to go.

'What now?'

'We need your officers to make two calls for us, right away. Or neither us will be going to any hotel.'

'Go on.'

'Both to hospitals – there are people we need to know are safe.'

Johnson's heavy steps return five minutes later, his face above them veiled by the mist.

'Well?' Harri asks anxiously.

48

'I Tried'

8th December 1952

Dexie

Part of her would rather be at her mother's place, or even the familiarity of the section house, but there's no denying the plumbing system in this hotel is far superior to either. There's even the luxury of bubble bath, the foam covering the bruises beginning bloom across Dexie's aching limbs, the fallout from being tossed across the boat. Her raw cheek smarts, but she is blissfully warm under the water, wondering how Harri is faring in the room next door. She noted that his mood – his whole being, in fact – lifted noticeably once they received the news of Mrs P, in the hospital but very much alive, now on a ward and recovering. Then came word that her mother remains at Bart's – Nurse Chadwick is perfectly fine, apparently, and busy playing the eternal angel in a uniform.

Still, Dexie worries about Harri's state of mind. He barely said anything as they were ferried by police car to the hotel, in shock from the cold, she reasons. Maybe, too, the finality of it all. Plus, guilt and relief, all stirred up in a cauldron of emotions. Even without a personal connection to Praxer, she can't begin to unpick the events of the last few days, and actually doesn't want to, either. Not yet, and not alone.

Dry and clean, she lies on the bed, weary but not sleepy, then turns on the wireless, restless as the tinny twittering of the day's news needles at her brain. Finally, it seems the government have admitted this enduring scourge of weather has proved fatal, yet the figures seem paltry and far less than her mother implied. But it's now – officially – a killer fog. *And in so many ways.*

Too agitated to lie still, Dexie slips on a hotel dressing gown and tiptoes along the corridor.

'Harri?' She knocks twice on the door. There's the padding of feet and it opens, him dressed in oversized trousers and a type of fisherman's sweater. 'Where on earth did they go shopping for you, the Army and Navy Stores?'

He looks down at himself. 'Oh, yes, I suppose it's not very becoming. But it is warm, and clean. More importantly, it's dry and doesn't stink of fish. Come on in.'

She hesitates on the threshold. 'I only wanted to make sure you were all right.'

He grins. 'Are you worried about entering the hotel room of a single man in your robe?'

'No.' *Perhaps.*

'Because, you know, we have spent the night in a virtual brothel, and shared the floor of a boat. And I was just about to order some tea and dinner on room service, now that my stomach has purged itself of the Thames. Are you hungry?'

'Come to think of it, I am,' she says. 'Starving, in fact.'

The awkwardness falls away as she steps across the threshold, a déjà-vu moment with Scooter flat out on the bed and stirring in his doggy dream. Once the food arrives – an odd combination of soup, omelette and roast potatoes, given the kitchen is about to close – they sit side by side on the bed, the confines only slightly smaller than the dinghy, but a good deal more solid in its footing.

'It's like we're on a recurring picnic,' Harri says, offering titbits to Scooter, who opens one curious eye at the smell of food. 'Do you think the two of us will ever eat at a table together?'

'Absolutely,' she says. 'At the Savoy. I haven't forgotten your pledge.'

'Nor have I, as it happens.' He forks at a piece of potato, and stares at it. 'I did try, you know.'

'I know you did.'

His voice is smaller than she's heard before, laced with remorse. 'God only knows why, but I would have saved him, if I could. If he'd have let me.'

'You don't have to convince me, Harri. I was there. You had a choice, and you made it.'

He pushes away his plate with a sigh. 'But I did hesitate. You saw that, too. If I hadn't faltered, would he now be ali—'

'And you might not be human if you hadn't faltered,' she slices him off firmly. 'Harri, he was a monster, and that is not in question. If that boat had set off, I feel sure we would be dead by now, and I've no doubt he wouldn't have batted an eyelid at watching it. Praxer was all about survival, and the irony is that it led to his own demise. The world will not mourn him.'

'You're right,' he says. A faint smile irons out the worry lining his face. 'I really have made a habit of being in the company of very sensible women. How did that happen, to a man who has bodged his way through life?'

She giggles. 'Bodged?'

'Yes, bodged. I heard a builder say it once. It's the correct use, isn't it?'

'It is, but I think you're far from being a bodger, Harri Schroder.'

'Well, thank you, WPC Dexter, you can come again to my bedroom picnic. It's a very exclusive membership, mind.'

In the end, they do share a bed, but it's largely Scooter's fault, since he snuggles between them both, his back pressed against Dexie and his paws stretched into Harri. Trapped by a terrier, she rests her head back. The news on the wireless has given way to a musical programme, the soft notes floating over her. For the first time in days, there is no angst or threat underlying her contentment. Merely contentment.

Dexie wakes once in the night, Scooter having shifted and Harri rolled onto his side, both sound asleep. Right then, she could easily lift herself off the bed and return to her own room, to a bed much larger and more comfortable than her own back at the section house, enough to spread her limbs and luxuriate in crisp sheets for a few hours. Only she doesn't. The luxury is in the company, the soft whinny of Scooter's dreams and the solid presence of someone beside her, who happens to be very human, and very nice.

49

Lifted

9th December 1952

Harri

'Dex! Dexie!'

'What, what is it?' she mumbles sleepily.

He's reluctant to wake her, having lain there for an age, listening to her soft breathing and savouring each moment as the dawn came and smiling like an idiot to himself. But it's already gone eight, they have a meeting with Johnson, plus a decent hotel breakfast waiting downstairs. And then there's this. 'Look out the window,' he urges.

She rubs at her eyes, yawns and turns lazily towards the open curtains, her eyes focusing. He grins at her slight confusion and double take, followed by the realisation. 'Is that sunlight?'

It's like emerging from a subterranean bunker, or a prisoner released from solitary confinement. They stand and stare through the glass, blinking at the familiar view of London cloaked in its industrious grey, bathed in weak sun, but able to pick out buildings and the shunt of traffic on the Thames. The lid has finally lifted.

'It's so strange,' she murmurs. 'It's been . . . what, four or five days, and yet it seems like forever. I began to think that's how it would always be.'

'We can only hope it's an omen for things to come,' he says. 'A good one.' Harri draws a hand over his stubbled face. He's anxious to tie things up with Johnson, to finish it once and for all. 'Listen, I need a shave and a freshen up, and Scooter is probably keen for a quick walk outside to sort himself. Shall I see you downstairs in half an hour?'

'Perfect. Half an hour.'

Johnson is already seated in the opulent dining room when Harri arrives, followed by Dexie a few seconds later.

The service man looks very comfortable, as if he frequents this type of good hotel quite often. Plus, his mood looks somewhat lighter. 'Sleep well?' he says.

'Yes,' they chime, with a sideways glance.

'Excellent. So, you'll need a good breakfast.'

For what? Harri wonders. Johnson's tone leads him to think they won't be liberated from his grip just yet. 'What is the news after last night?' Harri asks, once they've ordered. 'Did you find him . . . his . . .?' There's a distinct pinch of guilt, but also a sickening realisation that he needs proof of it. For his own closure.

'Yes,' Johnson interjects. 'The divers were out last night to no avail, but now this weather has lifted, I got word this morning.'

'Have you seen it with your own eyes. It's him?'

Johnson shoots a puzzled look across the table, as if to say: how many recently drowned bodies do you think we'd find in the same location? 'Yes,' he says, lowering his voice. 'It's definitely Praxer.'

'And the others?' Dexie comes in. 'In the confusion last night, I couldn't tell how many you arrested. Was the one called Joseph among them?'

There's a sudden, distinct whine from under the tablecloth.

'He was.'

'Good,' Dexie says. 'He can be charged now. With murder. I'll testify to that in court, because . . .'

'We can't do that yet,' Johnson says, rather sheepishly in the face of Dexie's fervour.

She puts down her coffee cup with a resounding clunk on the table, a face brewing thunder. 'Why ever not?'

Johnson takes in a breath. Across the table, Harri watches him bracing for the backlash. 'There's something we need your help with. Both of you.' His palms go up in swift defence as a second cup slams down. 'I know, I know, but I promise, this is the last time we will ask. The last.'

'The very last – we have your word?' Harri presses, in a tone that can leave Johnson in no doubt of his irritation. 'The reliable word, the one you will keep? Because all *three* of us have somewhere else to be, and it is not here playing tea parties.'

'I promise.'

'You thought it was me, didn't you?' Johnson turns to face them both from the front seat of the car, the vehicle that is ploughing at speed through London's streets as if the last few days have never happened, an entirely clear sightline through the windscreen. Harri feels like a miner, emerging from weeks trapped underground in a deep and dangerous shaft.

'We thought what was you?' Harri asks. He knows perfectly well what Johnson means, but wants to draw him out. Toying with him, if he's honest.

'That I betrayed you to Praxer. Told him exactly where you'd be at the docks.'

Harri looks at Dexie, whose definitive answer is in her dark expression. 'It had crossed our minds,' he says, without committal. *And now, are you still bluffing?*

'But why would I?' Johnson pivots further in his seat, maybe to gauge their reactions, as if he really does care what they think of him.

Instantly, Dexie shifts forward in the back seat. 'You said yourself that Praxer has friends in high places, and who's to say you weren't one of them, orchestrating a double bluff? Don't forget, it was you who guided us to the casino, and we assume it was you who gave Wolli the OK to use the barge.' She holds his gaze, unwilling to let him escape from her accusation. 'You could have been on Praxer's payroll all the time, creating this fake effort to capture him, hoping it would fail at every turn, with us as the fall guys.'

'Fair point,' Johnson concedes. 'That's certainly an argument, only . . .'

'Only what?' Harri interrupts.

'It's not true,' he adds, resolutely. This time his gaze doesn't drop to the floor or shy away. 'But I agree that at times this wasn't the best executed of operations.'

'You can say that again.'

'Whatever your opinion, our objective, and my aim, was always to stop Praxer from signing that agreement.' Still, Johnson's features remain fixed.

'What about stopping him for good?' Dexie presses. 'Was his death something you put into the equation?'

Johnson shrugs. 'He is no loss to us,' he says. 'Or to the

world at large, I'm sure you'll agree, friend or no friend in the past.'

Harri feels Dexie' s hand squeeze down on his; it speaks volumes on their previous conversation, his regret and her subsequent assurances.

'It will probably never be made public, and you'll likely never see the benefits,' Johnson goes on, 'but let me assure you that this country is a safer place without that signed document, and the peril it would have created.'

'And the Russians?' Harri asks.

Johnson gives a mocking laugh. 'Huh, the spies on the ground, and those squirrelled away in the Soviet embassy, will never disappear, but they'll have moved onto another target by now. That's the Cold War for you.'

'So, what now?' Harri questions.

'We need further proof to wrap this up once and for all,' Johnson says. 'I'll brief you fully when we get there.'

Harri glances at Dexie and catches a wary look. Her face is guarded but not anxious, and it stills his own suspicions. Their trust in Johnson hangs in the balance, but his intent seems genuine now that the ticking time bomb has stopped. Besides, Harri is too weary to analyse it.

Scotland Yard looks more contemporary without its foggy Victorian coating, though still imposing. 'You can leave the dog in the car,' Johnson tries to instruct.

'He comes with us,' Harri says, without compromise.

The MI5 man nods. 'Fine. Are you both clear on what we're doing?'

'Let's just get this over with,' Harri says.

Up the stairs, the secretary is taken aback as the trio marches into the outer office, her eyes wide at Scooter's self-important patter of paws. 'Is he expecting you?'

'No,' Johnson says. 'But he will want to see us.'

'Well, all right, let me just check . . .' She's up and out of her chair, but Johnson is too swift. He forges through the door, Harri, Dexie and Scooter in his wake.

'Johnson!' Superintendent Graham tries hard to contain his shock, but it's there in the freeze of his lean face as he rises to offer a handshake, eyes following Scooter's claws clicking on the wood floor before the terrier seats himself in front of the fire. 'I'm surprised to see you here, that's all. I thought today was the big day, the signing?'

'It is.' Johnson lands himself heavily in one of the chairs facing Graham's desk, a dark look of displeasure in his creased brow.

'Am I to take it the operation was not a success?' The superintendent's eyebrows go up in alarm, then knit together. 'You . . .?'

'Yes, we failed,' Harri takes up the mantle. 'Our target was always one step ahead, had too many resources, and of course that bloody weather.'

'It was the worst possible timing,' Graham agrees. 'It's caused chaos for the Yard, and the Met as a whole. Terrible loss of life, too.'

'So, I hear,' Johnson says. 'Well, it's up to the politicians to work their magic now and save us from ourselves. We did all we could.'

'Anyway, I'm just here to return my card and the leftover expenses,' Harri pipes up, placing his police ID and a wad of cash on the desk. 'Also to say thank you for loaning the skills of WPC Dexter. Despite the outcome, she was invaluable as a detective.'

'Well done, Dexter.' Graham nods in deference. 'Though I expect you'll be glad to get back to the beat?'

'Not really, sir,' she says bluntly. 'I like being out of uniform.'

'Ah, well,' he stutters, 'we'll have to see what we can do.' His patience for small talk is clearly fading, as he begins to fiddle with his fountain pen again.

Johnson launches himself up and out of the chair. 'We'll leave you in peace, Superintendent. I expect you have a great deal to catch up on, after the last few days.'

'Yes, thank you, Johnson, there is something of an aftermath. But if you need anything else, please don't hesitate to call.'

Firm handshakes are exchanged over Graham's desk as they exit, a damning look from Scooter in being coaxed away from the fireplace. Beyond the door, they come to a halt.

'Can I help?' Graham's secretary says efficiently.

Johnson raises a finger to his lips and presses the intercom on the secretary's desk in time to hear the distinct click and whirr of a number being dialled from inside the office, followed by a lengthy pause.

Graham's voice comes over the crackling speaker, low and urgent into the handset.

'So, it's still on?' Pause. 'Are you sure? Yes, Johnson's just been in with those two clowns to close it down. I assume the Kraut will piss off back to Germany now, thank God. I assume, also, that my money will be ready, in full. And in cash.'

The muffled exchange is cut off by the loud trill of the secretary's phone next to Harri. It startles him, but Johnson is evidently not surprised. He grabs at the receiver on the second ring. 'Yes, good. Fine. You can stand him down now and do the necessary.'

Graham is still in the act of replacing his handset back

on its cradle, when Johnson launches himself back through Graham's door, followed by Harri and Dexie a second time. A look of guilt mingled with irritation flashes across his face, instantly recognisable to a Kripo man of twenty years.

Bang to rights.

'Good news, Graham?' Johnson can't help baiting. 'Have you been updated on the state of play?'

'What . . . no . . . I don't know what you're talking about,' the senior policeman stutters. He stands and pulls himself up to full height, clearly hoping to intimidate the MI5 man with rank, stature and pure bloody-mindedness. 'I was on a private call, if you must know and I don't appreciate—'

'Save it,' Johnson barks. 'Joseph is in our custody, and one of my men was right by his side when he took that call from you thirty seconds ago.'

'But . . .'

'Yes, he *was* in Praxer's office, in that precise moment, but now he'll be on his way to a jail cell,' Johnson explains. 'For a very long time.'

For a man who oversees thousands, with the safety of a city under his command, Harri thinks it takes an inordinate amount of time for the penny to drop with Graham. Once it does, he watches the realisation, then the machinations behind the superintendent's eyes. Will he come clean, or bluff it out? As one of Praxer's 'friends in high places' can he realistically wriggle out of this one?

'Praxer?' Graham asks, his voice stuck somewhere in his throat. 'I'm not sure what you're imply—'

'Save it, Superintendent. He's dead,' Johnson crows with satisfaction, casually lighting up a cigarette. 'So, not a failure, after all. I would show you the photographs but they are still being processed, and it's not a pretty sight.'

Graham flashes an enquiring look at Dexie, as if seeking

confirmation from a fellow officer; despite his treachery, he is asking for one last morsel of loyalty. When she nods, he drops heavily into his chair, his long lean body sagging inside the crisp uniform.

'I'll grant you, it was shrewd to remove yourself from your own office when I first met Schroder here,' Johnson goes on, his smug enjoyment all too evident. 'You made an excellent show of being discreet. How did you find out? A bug on the desk, a voice recorder, or another mole on the force, someone else on Praxer's payroll with good ears?'

Graham says nothing, staring into his lap with his pen untouched. Johnson seems unconcerned by the lack of answers, and Harri wonders if the officer will be put under intense pressure – the creative kind – by MI5 to reveal his collaborators. The senior man already looks broken by the revelation, and yet, does he deserve any sympathy? He took Praxer's money, and was on the way to betraying his country, if Johnson is to be believed.

Christ, is anyone telling the truth? Harri feels suddenly drained by this political maze. Outside, the skies are clear but in here it's still a moral fog. He's agitated, and rapidly running out of patience. 'Are we finished here?' he caps off Johnson's flow. 'You can stay, but Dexie and I have something important to do.'

'Yes,' Johnson concedes. 'You take the car. I'll be in touch, to sort out where we go from here.'

50

A Welcome Visitor

9th December 1952

Dexie

It's as if nothing untoward has happened; the traffic flows, as much as it ever does in London, and people march along the pavements, faces skewed by thought. Only once or twice, Dexie spies a pedestrian through the car window, looking skyward, perhaps to check if a sinister black cloud might visit again and wipe out everything they know and love. It's only when they arrive at the hospital that the repercussions of the last five days are apparent. She and Harri make their way to the upper floors, dodging porters who run back and forth at speed, transferring still very sick people on gurneys, as a continuous backdrop of coughing and hacking echoes down the long corridors. The vapour is gone but the sediment lingers.

'Keep still, Scoot!' Harri hisses inside his overcoat, rapidly collected from the Mayfair casino en route, along with his beloved trilby. He buttons it up to his neck, obscuring the dog's head under the thick wool; if you didn't already know him, he's simply a portly man, but to Dexie, he cuts a comical figure. 'Stop laughing,' he says. 'If you can think of a better way of smuggling him past the matron, then I'd like to hear it.'

'I can't,' she says. 'But it doesn't stop you looking like you ate a lot of pies.'

Harri hovers in the background, while Dexie takes the lead at the ward door. 'Bed three, but ten minutes only,' the nurse instructs, too distracted to look closely. 'She's still quite weak.'

Weak is not how Dexie would describe Mrs Painter. She's sitting up in bed, in a style of knitted bed jacket that possibly hails from the 1930s and almost certainly survived the Blitz. Compared to the limp body lain across Harri's arms in their dash to the hospital, the landlady is positively blooming. Her face lights up like Piccadilly Circus as they approach, primping the petal-style hat which is back in situ. All must be well with the world.

'Mr Schroder! How lovely to see you.' She's breathless and croaky, but the joy in her voice is evident. 'And you've brought a friend. So nice of you to come, dear.' Her tiny eyes sparkle in the once rounded face, thinner but animated.

'You have another visitor,' Harri says, pulling a flimsy fabric screen around the bed. He grins widely in producing Scooter from his confines of his coat, like a rabbit out of a hat.

Mrs P's face crimps with emotion, unable to hold back tears of relief.

'Oh, my darling boy, you're all right,' she sniffs, as her companion scrabbles to join her on the bed, nudging in tight and rubbing his face into her chest. Instantly, her face glows and even Scooter looks like he's smiling, the white tail beating like a military tattoo. 'Oh, Mr Schroder. They told me someone had brought me in, and I guessed it was you. And look at this! You cared for my wonderful boy, too. How can I ever thank you? I'll have to cook you one of my special breakfasts when I'm out of here. More than one, in fact.'

Harri demurrs weakly at such a pledge, and his features flood with pleasure at seeing this petite old woman alive and relatively well – his landlady, producer of the flaccid egg, but someone who he's come to value in such a short time. One thing is obvious to Dexie – he cares deeply.

Is that the moment when she sees Harri Schroder for the man he truly is, with utmost clarity? The past week has seen them face untold struggle, blind alleyways, danger and death. At every turn, he's been solid and supportive, though never overbearing. And yet when he tucks Scooter back under his coat and kisses Mrs P lightly on her forehead, promising to visit again, Dexie cannot help but feel a swelling in her throat at such tenderness. And that he's not afraid to show it.

She will miss Harri Schoder, the Kripo Inspektor, a good deal. She will miss her friend Harri even more.

Escaping the nurse sentinel without raising suspicion, Harri deposits Scooter on the ground outside the hospital.

'I really must buy the poor lad a proper lead, he can't be on a washing line forever,' he says, fiddling with the thin rope around his fingers.

It's obvious to Dexie that he's hesitating, playing for time before saying farewell. Once they debrief with Johnson, there's nothing else to do but to get back to normal life:

the section house, a light ragging from her desk sergeant, fetching tea and those bloody beat shoes.

'So, erm, I expect Johnson will want to meet tomorrow, or the day after,' Harri ventures. 'After that, our dinner at the Savoy? All manner of courses and cocktails. Maybe I'll even treat you to my dancing.'

'Courses and cocktails definitely, Herr Schroder. But the dancing will depend on how many martinis I have inside me.'

'A very wise move from an astute colleague,' he says.

They stand, pausing amid the hoots and toots of Bloomsbury. A bus grumbles by, coated in grime but nonetheless so vibrant and red in the city's newfound clarity. Is it her, or is the atmosphere between them suddenly dense again, with unease replacing that fickle climate?

Harri's feet shuffle. 'You take the car on,' he says.

'If you're sure?'

'Of course. Besides, Scooter needs a walk, and we'll try to find a pet shop on our way back to Mrs P's. I feel our remarkable guide dog deserves a bone, and then I'll get the place tidied and warmed up for when Mrs P comes home. She said the doctors may discharge her tomorrow or the day after. Though I might well sleep for the entire interim. You?'

'Sleep, definitely, but I'll go to my mother's, who must surely be taking a few days off by now.' Dexie swallows, her throat still tight with emotion. 'Time, I think, to appreciate what I have, right on my doorstep.'

He nods, with evident experience in such things. 'Well, give her my best, and I'll see you soon.'

'See you, Harri Schroder.'

He tips the trilby. 'WPC Dexter.'

* * *

Camden appears unchanged, though Dexie is reminded of her close proximity to Eliza's flat as she gets out of the car. She wonders what will happen to all the dead woman's things, all those files so painstakingly assembled, the years spent searching. Will Wolli see to them? For a man with little mobility, his influence stretches far and wide. She will insist that Johnson tracks down any living relatives, and that Eliza's sacrifice is recorded in black and white, something of her to live on.

For now, and with her mother's house in sight, Dexie's focus has to be on something else. Someone else. She lets herself into the hallway and immediately feels heat radiating from the kitchen, but no noise. Opening the door, she sees why; her mother, still in her starched uniform, is slumped on the chair beside the range and sighing rhythmically in a blissful sleep, a half-drunk cup of tea balanced on the arm. The teapot is on the table, knitted cosy in place. Home.

She tiptoes around and pours herself a cup, sitting and looking at her mother for a good while, the exhaustion that's etched into her face and the contortion of her limbs. They *will* spend more time together, Dexie vows. They'll go out and have fun, to the cinema or maybe to see a big band at the Hammersmith Palais. She recalls Mum and Dad dancing to music on the wireless in the kitchen just before the war, and they were good, her mother nimble on her feet. As a daughter, she'll make more effort. The two of them will live, rather than the life of widows.

'Oh, hello, love,' Mrs Chadwick stirs, blinking herself awake. 'How long have you been there?'

'Not long,' Dexie says. 'I didn't want to disturb you. Why don't I make us some breakfast – well, perhaps lunch now – and then you can go up to bed properly?'

'Will you, love? Oh, that would be so nice.'

Dexie moves towards the kettle, to warm the teapot. 'How many hours have you worked over the last few days?'

Mrs Chadwick sighs. 'Oh, I lost count. This is the first time I've been home since the fog came down. I kipped at the hospital and strip washed in the nurse's home.'

'And how was it?' Knowing the situation at West End Central, Dexie can guess the chaos, plus the need to decompress after a heavy shift.

Her mother's face grows dark in recollection. 'It was awful, Helen,' she says. 'They say on the news there might be hundreds dead by now, but I'll wager it's a lot more at the end of the day. It was as if people were drowning in air, instead of water. We didn't have enough oxygen or beds, sending men to be nursed on the maternity wards. There'll be people suffering for a long time to come.' She takes a sip of the old, cold tea, but doesn't wince. 'And how about you? Were you out in it, on shift?'

The truth is on her lips before Dexie swallows it back. There's enough for her mother to worry about, and it may come out in time. 'Yes, it was pretty chaotic,' she says. 'But you manage, don't you, with good people around you?'

'Yes, workmates get you through.' Her mother nods, stifling a yawn. 'Oh, how's that German friend of yours? I don't suppose he managed to get back home, what with no flights or trains out of London. Will he go back soon?'

'Soon,' Dexie says. There's a torque rising from somewhere in her gut and she pushes it back down, fussing with the teapot. 'So, how about some bacon?'

'Fried bread, too?'

'Why not, Mum? We deserve it.'

51

A Welcome Home

9th December 1952

Harri

He swears the hallway to Mrs P's is colder than outside, while the whole house has an air of desertion. Where on earth are the other lodgers? It's a weekday, so they're either at work, Harri imagines, or they decamped elsewhere when the fog came down, yet to return.

He deposits his hat on the stand in the hallway but retains the overcoat, at least until he's got the kitchen fire going. As he moves towards the kitchen door, there's a faint rustling from the other side. Perhaps one lodger is in, since Scooter doesn't seem alarmed, his tail wagging at being back home. Entering, the figure has his broad back to Harri, clad in an overcoat and bent over, rummaging, except it's not coals on the fire. Why would anyone be rifling through Mrs P's sideboard drawer?

Patently not a house guest. Harri grabs at the nearest

weapon to hand, which happens to be a wooden broom. Better than nothing.

'*Hey*, what the hell are you doing?' His own fierce bark causes Scooter to do the same – the sharp piercing yap of a terrier. The figure snaps up and spins, eyes ablaze in the darkness of the room, while Harri brandishes the sharper end of a cleaning implement.

'Jesus! Don't creep up on me like that? You trying to give me a heart attack again?'

'Me? Creep up?' Harri is incredulous. 'What on earth are *you* doing here?'

In their short acquaintance, Harri has seen Wolli in varying states – from irritated to exasperated, plus hungover – but never quite so shocked. He slumps on a chair, a hand on his chest, and Harri needs to make tea before he can collect himself. Once the pot is steeping, and Wolli has a cigarette in his shaky hand, Harri demands an explanation. The Pole draws hard on his Woodbine and considers.

'Ivy – Mrs P – and I go way back,' he says.

'Define "way back".' Harri has yet to be convinced Wolli's presence is entirely to the good, though it does explain why Scooter was so friendly when they first met in the café.

Again, Wolli deliberates, looks to be chewing over the options, perhaps how much to disclose. 'Before the war.'

'Did you know her husband?'

'Arthur? No, I only met him only once.'

'Then how do you know her and why are you here now, when she isn't?' Harri is beginning to feel irritated at Wolli's coyness. All he wants is to climb the stairs to his attic room with that whisky bottle, shiver himself to sleep under the blankets and wake up in a better frame of mind.

'Put it this way, there's more to Ivy Painter than her teapot and questionable cooking skills.'

Sleep and fatigue take a back seat as Wolli reveals an unseen side to Mrs P, a fluent German speaker (via a second cousin, apparently) who came to the attention of the SOE by pure chance. She spent her war years as a bombed-out housewife, but also as a shrewd listener, one who could wheedle out Fifth Columnists living in London in plain sight, those pro-Nazi sympathisers planting dangerous propaganda and whipping up support for Hitler.

'No one paid any mind to a chatty housewife who rattled on ten to the dozen,' Wolli says. 'And because they didn't consider her a threat, they tended to drop their guard. She was one of our best assets in teasing out information. I came by just to make sure there was nothing incriminating in her, let's say, archives while she's in hospital. Ivy's always been very careful, but you never know.'

'And is that why I was lodged here, so she could keep an eye on me?' There's anger and accusation in Harri's voice. Thick with hurt, too. Surely, not Mrs P?

'No!' Wolli assures. 'Ivy is long retired from that game. Nowadays, she is just as she appears, landlady of a guest house, who puts up those we need to billet for a while. Though I have to say her cooking hasn't improved. Sorry about that.'

'It's all right,' Harri says. 'I've become used to it, or fairly adept at avoiding it.'

'And a bit more than a guest, I hear,' Wolli adds. 'Seems we might be attending her funeral if it wasn't for you.'

Harri shrugs. 'She was ill and needed help. I couldn't just leave her.'

'Which is largely why you ended up in so much bother.'

'Not because of Mrs P!'

'No,' Wolli qualifies, 'but I don't doubt Johnson tapped into that side of you very well, a champion of the underdog. Praxer, too. Both yanked on your heartstrings, and one day that *will* get you killed, Herr Schroder.'

'Maybe,' Harri mutters. 'It sounds as if you don't like our illustrious MI5 man either.'

Wolli draws hard on his cigarette and tops up his teacup. 'We tolerate each other. Johnson is far less senior than he'd have you believe, but he does get things done. By hook or by crook.'

By hook or by crook. Sounds like my life to date.

'Do you trust him?' Harri punts. 'I'm not entirely sure he's giving us the whole picture even now.'

Wolli's hearty laugh brings on a coughing fit, which he stems by drawing in more smoke. 'Of course not – he's a bloody spy! Though I'm convinced he is our spy.'

'And you're not?' Harri retorts.

'I'm resistance, through and through,' Wolli corrects. 'There's a difference. And my war isn't over yet, not with men like Praxer still around.'

'You mean there's a lot more?' He feels naïve for asking it, but is curious to know.

'Put it this way, me and the leg can't afford to retire just yet.' Wolli pulls out a small hip flask from his coat pocket and tips a good measure into his teacup. 'But Praxer out of this world is a step forward, and for that we are extremely grateful. So, are you going to get that fire going or what? Because we have things to talk about.'

52

Just Dinner

12th December 1952

Dexie

She hasn't dressed up properly for some months now, the last time being a jazz night at the Locarno, and then she felt much less trepidation. The bulbs of a ballroom are dim, lively dancing masks the real you and the noise of the music helps to blur any intimacy. By contrast, the lighting in the Savoy dining room is bound to be subtle, Dexie thinks, but equally there is nowhere to hide. No uniform or warrant card, no heavy tweed or trilby of the plain clothes detective – in short, nothing to use as a shield. Not even the ominous clop of those dratted shoes. Tonight, she has to be herself.

'Is that even possible?' she ponders to the stranger in the mirror, the one whose hair has been styled and teased; despite all her protestations to Harri that it represents a whimsy and a waste of money, she had gone to the hairdresser out of desire rather than need. A desire for what? The fact that she's not certain only adds to her unease.

'Oh, Dex, get a grip,' she remonstrates with herself. 'It's just dinner. Food on a plate.'

Haven't they sat across a proper table many times already? Though it's largely been cafés where the food is fried and the tea comes from an endless tap. Tonight promises much more sophisticated cuisine, if the same Harri, and the same her. Essentially.

Yet this occasion already seems different: it's a celebration of their triumph (though when Eliza sneaks into her dreams it feels anything but), and a farewell too. Dexie sighs heavily, her breath prompting misty patches in the mirror as she goes to apply her lipstick. How does she feel about that?

She scowls at her own expression. 'Don't even go there,' she tells herself.

53

Our Dream Team

12th December 1952

Harri

'You look lovely.' Harri slips off the stool as Dexie walks into the Savoy bar, robbed of the air in his lungs for a second or so. She does – stunning in a sleek black cocktail dress, her hair pinned neatly off her neck, her make-up subtle but enough to amplify the sweep of her lips. He offers a hand, aware of the heat and moisture on his own palm, but when hers is warm to the touch, he draws it in. His closely shaven cheek meets with hers, and he places a short, neat kiss on her cheek. It feels right and proper. There's a light perfume on her neck, but it's still the same Dexie he nestled into on the *Seahorse*, that comforting scent of her rising above.

'You don't scrub up so bad yourself.' She smiles, making it suddenly easier.

There she is, the Dexie he feels he knows. 'Oh, this old thing.' He looks down at a new, navy suit, courtesy of another shopping trip with Georgie. 'Mrs P took one whiff of my others and confiscated them. At this very moment, I think she's going into a full-scale battle with her tin of Vim.'

They each slide onto a bar stool, two martinis appearing out of nowhere. She puts the glass to her lips and moues with pleasure. 'How is the indefatigable Mrs P?'

'Unrelenting,' he comes back. 'Of course, the doctor told her to take it easy at home, but that's a foreign language to her. I have instructed Scooter to pin her to the chair and demand to be fussed at every opportunity.'

'And the breakfasts?'

His face twists. 'Only one so far, thankfully. The rest I've engineered to cook myself and for her, as a "treat", but it really is survival on my part, bless her. Anyway, tonight is about very good food, and excellent cocktails. And us, the detective dream team.'

'I'll drink to that,' she says.

'This is beautiful,' she says as they are shown to their table at the hotel's infamous Grill. A soft, hushed purr of conversation drifts above the surrounding tables, from moneyed men and women with broad, white smiles and deep pockets. Dexie's eyes widen and sparkle, in awe and appreciation. But Harri has promised himself not to be overwhelmed or intimidated by the glint of chandeliers. The cash he has in his pocket is as good as any man's. He earned it. God knows, they both earned this. Over the past week, haven't they learnt the hard lesson that money doesn't always represent a moral solidity? Humility or humanity, either.

'Champagne?' he asks.

'Yes please, though I warn you, the bubbles do go straight to my head,' Dexie says.

'Then we'll drink it slowly. There are things to talk about.'

'Oh?'

But they get distracted by the menu of opulent choices, then food of their childhood – a common topic despite the miles of separation and the divide of culture. By the time they are spooning in a dessert of exquisite crème caramel, they've covered their school years and growing up as teenagers, the highs and lows of both. The war they skate over, and while Harri is thankful, he feels as if he could talk about it, even the worst times, with her. Right now, it feels as if he could tell her anything.

Dexie wriggles her nose as fresh champagne pops in her glass. 'So, what was it you wanted to talk about?'

'Oh, that? It can wait.' Harri's body is flush with alcohol and what he knows to be happiness, but suddenly he has cold feet. Why spoil the perfect evening?

'No, go on, I'm all ears,' she urges. 'You'll be leaving soon, and we might not get a chance.'

He takes in a breath, plus a mouthful of good wine. A large one. 'Well, that's it exactly.'

'What do you mean?'

'I might not be leaving, after all.'

'Really?'

Is she happy about that – or not? Is that crease to her eyebrows a disappointment, that this is not a timely farewell dinner?

'Wolli came to see me, with an offer,' he says.

'Go on.'

Verdammt! After seeming to read each other without a need for words, why is she suddenly so hard to gauge, her face so utterly blank? 'OK. Such is the gratitude of Her Majesty's government, or at least the secret part of it, I've been offered a lengthy sabbatical in England, on a detective team. Anywhere I choose, in fact.'

Now, she does smile, with what he hopes is genuine pleasure.

'That's great, Harri. You did say you've been looking for a fresh start.'

'Yes, I did. So, I've opted for Oxford.' He looks down and scrapes up the last of his crème caramel, though there's really little more than a smear on the plate. 'It's close enough to London, but also the countryside, and I don't think there can be too many murders among all those erudite students and dons. Some good detectives there, too, so I hear.'

'It sounds perfect, and you're obviously very fond of the city.' She scratches at her empty plate too, looks up with an expression of forced jollity. Despite his sudden inability to read her, that much he can tell. 'Then perhaps we'll get our day out in Oxford, after all?' she teases. 'You can show me around your new home, that quaint cottage with the roses around the door.'

The clamour in his ears is suddenly agonising, the chink of glasses a near din of Big Ben at midnight and a rushing of tidal water. *Damn it, say it man! Do it. Grab at life.*

'There's one other thing,' he ventures. 'Wolli and Johnson know of your equal hand in everything, and so the offer extends to you as well. A place on a detective squad, just as you wanted.'

She freezes, glass held aloft. 'Me? In Oxford, you mean?'

'No, no, anywhere you like. In London, if you want. Only . . .'

Should he go on? One half of him argues that it's been only ten days, a mere snippet of existence. The other half says it's time that can't be compared with anything ordinary, when trust forged itself so rapidly, the feeling of being entirely at ease with someone, even to laugh in the darkest moments. Does it matter whether it's ten days, ten weeks or ten months? He thinks of another saying: *when you know, you know*. Or is he simply making that one up, because he believes it – wants it – to be true?

'. . . Only I was wondering,' he ventures.

'Yes?' She's not smiling, but neither is she frowning.

'If you might come with me,' he blurts. 'If you want to, that is. Different stations, obviously, but the rest of the time, you and me. The two of us, you know . . . together.'

'The dream team?'

'*Our* dream team,' he dares.

There's a bright, fleeting smile of understanding, but which falls from her face all too soon. 'Harri, you know I can't give you . . .' Her words are slow and considered. 'The thing is, I would always want to work, and not do the housewife . . . I'm not looking for . . .'

'Me neither,' he's quick to say. 'I'm not searching for anything, Dex. Except you. Only you.'

Two seconds in silence, then five. Ten is unbearable.

Finally, her hand crawls across the white, pristine tablecloth and finds his. Her grasp on his fingers is warm, and her grip feels certain. 'Then yes, Harri Schroder.'

'Yes?' He sits back in shock. 'You mean it?'

She nods, the tiny bulb of a tear forming along the kohl-lined ridge of one sparkling eye. He pulls up her hand and puts her long fingers to his lips, already thinking of the kiss they may exchange later, in private. In full.

'I think we should celebrate with that dance,' she says. 'I can't possibly live my life with a man who won't take me for a twirl every so often.'

'You're prepared to risk it without another cocktail?'

'Right now, I think life is all about taking chances, Inspector Schroder, don't you? Being brave.' She smiles, broadly, and beautifully. 'Besides, thanks to my beloved beat shoes and the glorious Metropolitan Constabulary, I have developed toes of solid steel.'

'Then I am entirely in your capable hands, WPC Dexter.'

'It's Helen. Tonight, I am Helen.'

28 March 1953

Venice, Italy

Dear Georgie

I've always wanted to write to you from a far-flung place, given your track record of travel, and so here it is – not the other side of the world, I grant you, but a fantasy in my own mind. What a breathtaking city this is!

It was Dexie's idea to get married in Venice, one of her childhood dreams apparently, and although we had to placate her mother a little by promising the 'real' ceremony at a registry office in Camden, the event here was magical. A little bit strange, too, since we needed to coax the little old woman from a nearby trattoria to be our witness, our very own Italian Mrs P! She did, however, make us some arancini for an impromptu wedding breakfast, and it was – without exaggeration – food from the gods. Even as a good German boy, I may have found a substitute for my mother's homemade wurst.

And before you even ask – yes of course, we did

the gondola ride in celebration. It's a must for couples in love, slicing between the palazzos and under the Rialto bridge, with Dexie to share in the wonder. More than once, we pinched each other for our good fortune. Georgie, you know all too well that I thought – was convinced – I might never find this level of happiness again. And so . . . you know the rest, too. I am a man with a smile on my craggy old face.

We have four more days to drink in this incredible place, then it's back to Oxford and work. I've settled into my station, with a whole range of crimes to solve – believe me, Oxford isn't all dreaming spires and students from the pages of *Brideshead Revisited* (it's apparently a rite of passage to read Waugh's book before planning to live there). It is a challenge at times, but one which I'm relishing. My wife (yes, my wife!) is loving her work as Detective Constable Dexter – you of all people know the benefits of choosing your own name and identity – and I hear on the grapevine that she's blazing quite a trail in the division. Ha ha, they'll soon be calling me 'Mr Dexter', for which I won't mind one little bit, though Max and I might need to retire for a manly pint of ale very soon.

Speaking of which, I hope you, Max and the children can visit us in the summer, we've plenty of room in our cottage, plus, wait for it – a new addition to entertain Margot and Elias! He's a little miniature Schnauzer, a small canine legacy from the homeland, I like to think. I favoured Wolf as a name, but Dexie put her foot down because he's far too cute (he really is), and so he's Wilf. Mrs P and Scooter gave him full approval when they came to visit recently, and we adore him.

Sometimes, George, I sit out in my garden, next to the obligatory rose bushes, and I wonder how I ever got here? Hella and Lily will never leave me, but on occasion I have to hold my breath, in case the whole perfect vision just blows away, like a fragile dandelion clock on a breeze. Do you ever get that feeling when you gaze at your sleeping babies?

Hmm, I'm getting maudlin, and too wordy for a journalist even of your stature. Enough to say I had to write you this letter, because there's too much happiness to squeeze onto a postcard.

We're off now for an Italian aperitif, and to eat perfect pasta by the canal side, where I'll pull in my breath again so it all doesn't melt away too soon.

Ciao, from your beloved grumpy Inspektor, Harri.
X

Acknowledgements

Book on book, this section never gets any easier, simply because the further into their own mind a writer meanders, the more they need real life to fall back on when finally poking a head above the tenuous wall of words.

It's precisely why I need to dispense so many thanks: to my wonderful agent, Broo Doherty of DHH Literary Agency, for her continued wisdom and diplomacy when I get my knickers in a twist, and for a damned a good laugh. Also, to the marketing, editorial, PR and sales teams at Avon and HarperCollins worldwide, who put my books on shelves, both real and virtual, and then holler about them loudly on all manner of platforms. For this book, in particular, incoming editor Emma Grundy Haigh helped to shape and mould it, along with copy-editor Dushi Horti. I'm always so grateful to anyone who helps in the tangible production of my books, enabling each edition to make it into the world – production people, drivers, stackers and sellers. As ever, you are my champions.

I couldn't do this without a great circle of family and friends who continue to bolster me in every way: the maternity crew (gracious enough to let me feel I'm still one of them), the dog walkers and the coffee slurpers, and those with big shoulders for me to lean/cry on. In the writing world, there are so many constants: the 'Write Shower of Babes' of authors Sarah Steele, Mel Golding and Emma Flint, plus the vast swathe of talent we have in the Stroud Valleys and beyond. To fellow scribes LP Fergusson (Loraine), Lorna (Elle) Cook and Hannah Dolby, I say thanks for wonderful support from afar. I maintain that exchanging silly memes is a form of therapy and can be counted as work.

Readers – it goes without saying that no writer does this without people to put a hand in their pocket and stump up cash for the streams of consciousness that plop out of our heads, aided and abetted by the bloggers, bookworms and podcasters. You all get a medal in my mind.

Finally, gratitude to two of my biggest advocates: my mum, Stella, always the first to read and tell me whether my characters cut the mustard, and to my furry muse mutt, Basil. It's no coincidence that I've written a loyal canine into this book, because Bas is toiling with me in various cafés each and every day, keeping an eye on my coffee consumption and his own wage in biscuits. Thanks, Bas.

Germany, 1944. Anke Hoff is assigned as midwife to one of Hitler's inner circle. If she refuses, her family will die.

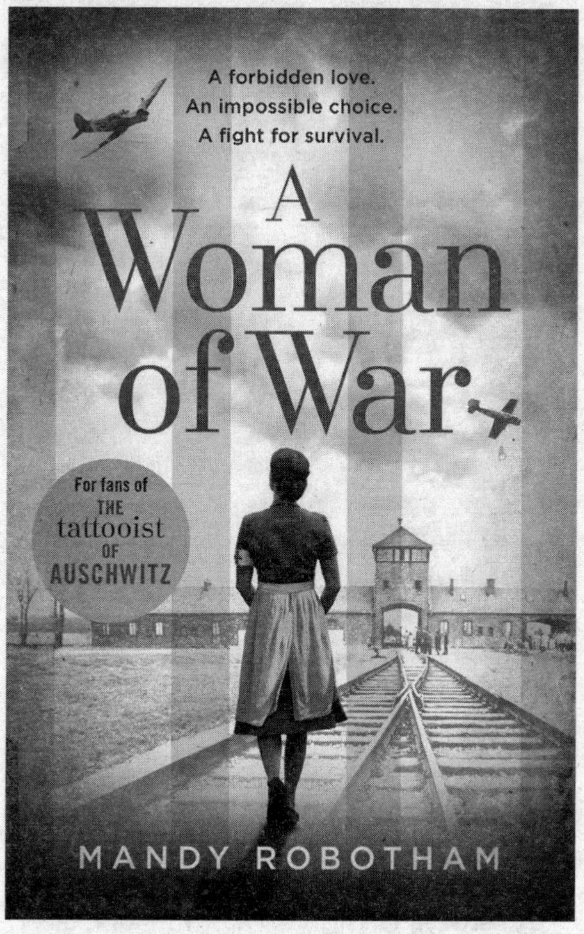

A forbidden love.
An impossible choice.
A fight for survival.
A Woman of War
For fans of THE tattooist OF AUSCHWITZ
MANDY ROBOTHAM

For readers of *The Tattooist of Auschwitz* comes a gritty tale of courage, betrayal and love in the most unlikely of places.

The world is at war, and Stella Jilani is leading a double life.

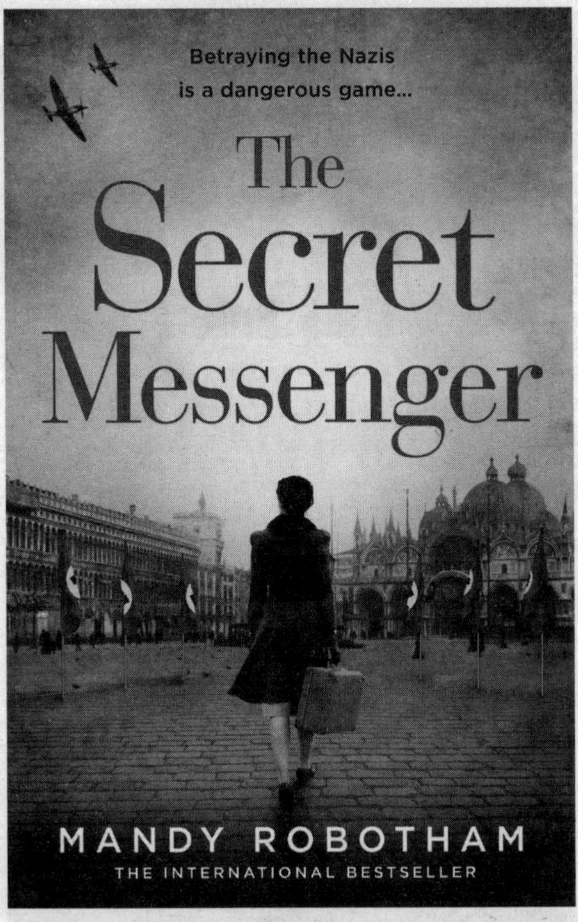
Betraying the Nazis
is a dangerous game...
The
Secret
Messenger
MANDY ROBOTHAM
THE INTERNATIONAL BESTSELLER

Set between German-occupied 1940s Venice and modern-day London, this is a fascinating tale of the bravery of everyday women in the darkest corners of WWII.

Norway, 1942. Rumi Orlstad is grieving the loss of her husband at the hands of Hitler. And now she will make them pay.

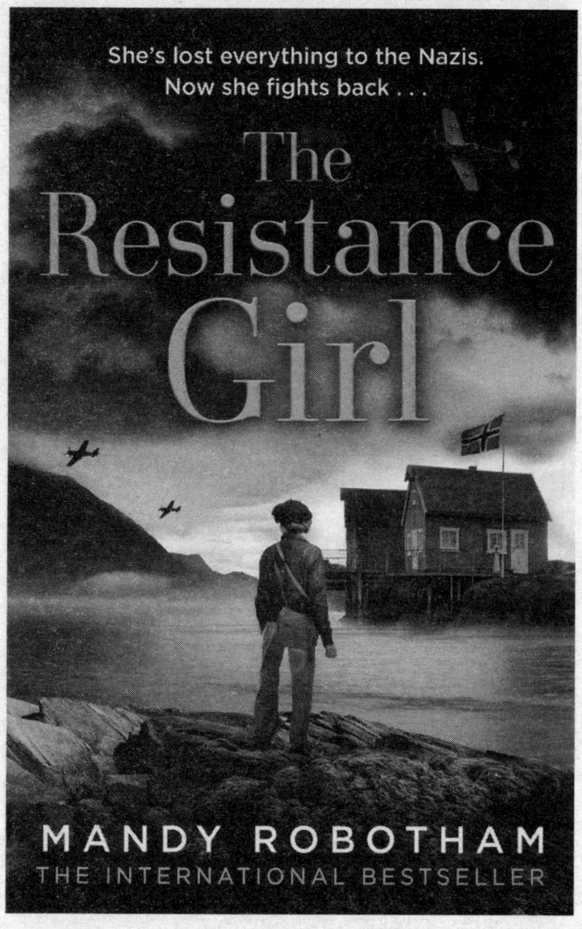

She's lost everything to the Nazis.
Now she fights back . . .
The Resistance Girl
MANDY ROBOTHAM
THE INTERNATIONAL BESTSELLER

A heartbreaking tale of the sacrifices ordinary people made to keep friends, family, strangers – and hope – alive.

A city divided.
Two sisters torn apart.
One impossible choice . . .

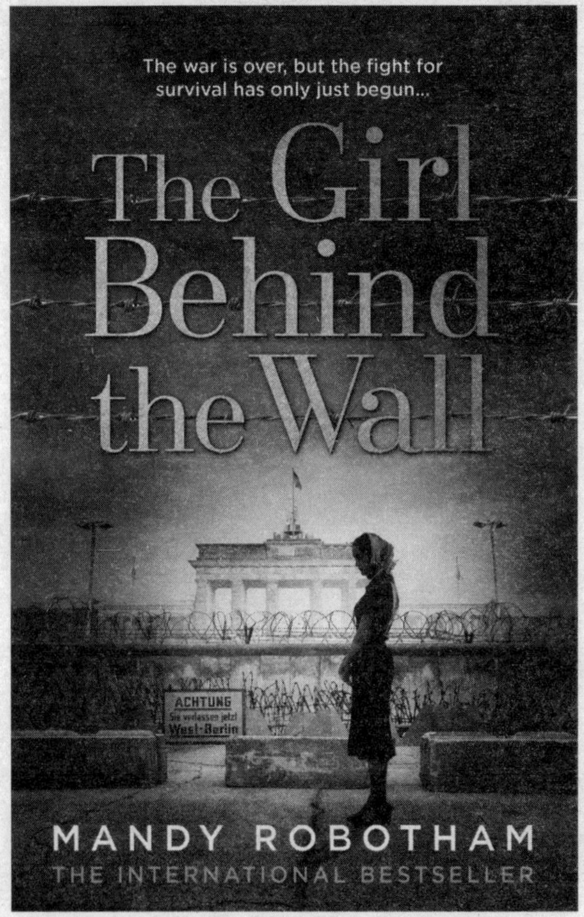

The war is over, but the fight for survival has only just begun...
The Girl Behind the Wall
ACHTUNG
West-Berlin
MANDY ROBOTHAM
THE INTERNATIONAL BESTSELLER

Set against the dawn of the cold war, this is a timely reminder that, even in the darkest of places, love will guide you home.

***Berlin, 1938*. It's the height of summer, and Germany is on the brink of war.**

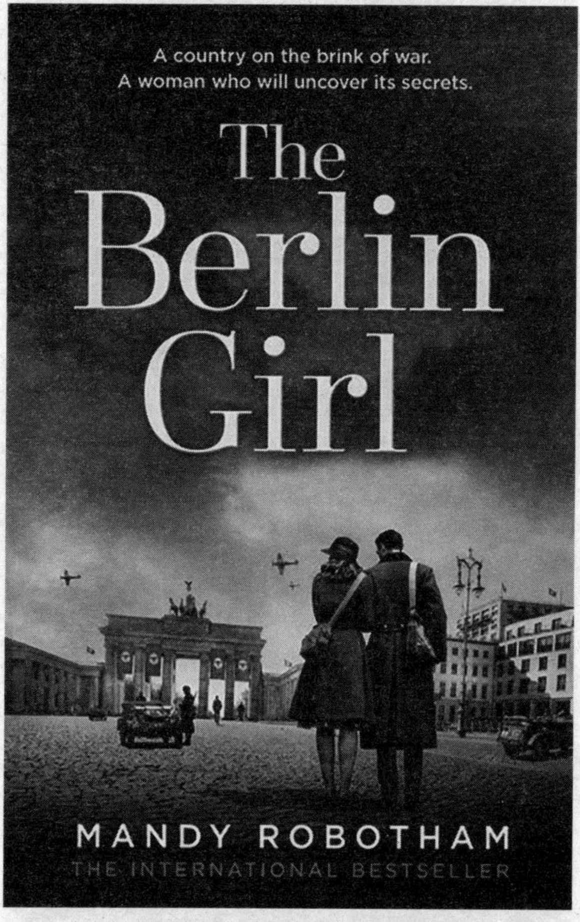
A country on the brink of war.
A woman who will uncover its secrets.
The Berlin Girl
MANDY ROBOTHAM
THE INTERNATIONAL BESTSELLER

From the internationally bestselling author comes the heart-wrenching story of a world about to be forever changed.

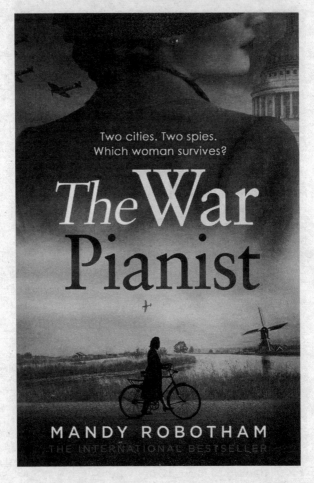

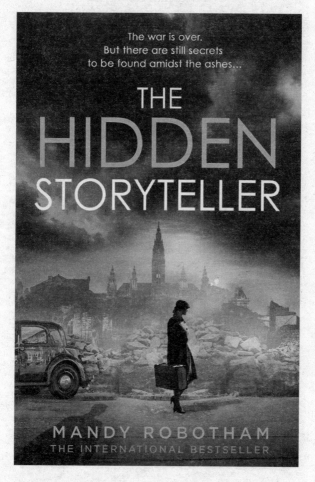